Twice WAKE ME

BOOK ONE

TRICE McINTYRE

Interior Formatting: Champagne Book Design
Cover Design: Murphy Rae
Editor: Joseph Editorial Services, LLC
Publisher: Nova Hearts, LLC

Trice McIntyre
Website: tricemcintyre.com

For my butterfly warrior, Christine Johnson,
my late grandmother,
and every soul out there whispering "I'm okay"
when you're anything but.

For the ones who smile through the storm,
quietly breaking while holding everyone else together.
For the backs that ache from carrying too much
grief, guilt, responsibility and still showing up.

For the ones afraid to try again,
because the last fall left scars you still hide.
And yet, here you are… trying anyway.

You remind me of butterflies
delicate, but not weak.
Marked by change, but still beautiful.
Soft wings, but hard-won flight.

This story is for you.
The ones who've lost, who've loved and found the beauty in love.

Let's get quiet for a moment.
Let's get lost in the pages…to feel the heat, the spice of it.
Let's find ourselves again, piece by piece,
in the beauty tucked between the lines.

Just Love,
Trice McIntyre

AUTHOR'S NOTE

Thank you for being a part of Cassidy & Kylo's journey through *Twice: Wake Me*. Their story isn't always easy, but it's beautiful and uniquely theirs to experience.

Parts of this book will touch on Lupus, an autoimmune disease that deeply impacted the life of my late grandmother, Christine Johnson. While this is a work of fiction, Lupus is very real. I not only witnessed its effects firsthand growing up, but I've also had the honor of speaking with incredible butterfly warriors, people who face this disease every day with strength, resilience, and an unshakable spirit. They inspired me to do more.

If some of the symptoms in this book feel real, it's because they are. I've seen them. I've lived beside them. I've listened to those willing to share their journeys. Lupus doesn't just affect the person diagnosed, it also weighs heavily on the families and loved ones who walk this path beside them.

Because of these conversations and my personal connection to this fight, a portion of the proceeds from every sale of this novel will be donated to the **Lupus Foundation of America.**

If you'd like to make a separate donation, here's how to help:

Lupus Foundation of America, Inc.
1-800-558-0121
www.lupus.org

If you or someone you know is struggling with the weight of it all, please remember you are not alone.
National Hotline for Mental Health Crises & Suicide Prevention (NAMI)
1-800-273-TALK (8255)

WAKE ME

CHAPTER 1

THE DAY I LOST EVERYTHING

Cassidy

"**K**EEP MOVING!" I SHOUT AT THE GRID LOCKED TRAFFIC ON I-85, my frustration boiling over as I glare at the unmoving cars ahead. Just fifteen minutes from home, but with traffic stretching for miles ahead of me, it feels like I'm a lifetime away. Normally, the extra time in the car to myself would be okay, but today is different.

Getting home is my only concern.

Taking the exit ramp, a sea of flashing red brake lights fills my view, and frustration grows with every precious second that ticks by. I silently wish there was another path through the interstate. But, bracing myself for the truth is all I have.

I may not make it.

No, don't think that. You'll make it. You have no choice.

The steering wheel becomes my refuge as my fingers dig into its surface, my stomach churning with a swarm of butterflies. "Please," I whisper, through the anxious breath lost somewhere within my tight chest.

If my track meet wasn't today, being stuck in miles of traffic with this relentless sun determined to blind me through my visor would not be happening. *Why did I even go?*

I shield my view from the sun's rays, making me blink rapidly until the haze fades into a side road. The emergency lane is empty.

Without a second thought, my small BMW becomes victim to the bumpy road as my heart pounds my chest harder than a bass drum. The sensation of my inner organs vibrating from the rough terrain threatening to rip my tires apart makes me queasy, but I ignore it.

Even the two-digit white speedometer numbers don't slow me as sixty-five changes to seventy. The police will have to pull me over today because this car is not stopping. I grip the steering wheel tighter, fighting against the nausea boiling in the pit of my stomach. With a surge of adrenaline, I hit eighty, hoping to pass the cars stuck on the interstate while in my own personal lane.

"Please let everything be okay," I whisper to myself as a buzzing noise in my backseat takes my attention.

Is that my phone?

I barely hear the vibrating noise over the blaring chorus of Katy Perry screaming for fireworks, like it's July fourth. I reach to turn off the music, only to realize that no incoming call is displaying on my dashboard. My Bluetooth isn't connecting. Suddenly, finding my phone becomes urgent. Stretching my arm around to the backseat, I feel along the floorboard for any sign of my lifeline. I'd received a call to get home as my meet was over and in my rush to start the car, I tossed my phone somewhere in the back seat. My sole thought was to get home.

Maneuvering the car while searching behind my seat, a flash of light catches my peripheral, snapping my attention back on the road.

Out of nowhere, a white pickup truck swerves into my lane, making me lose control. I jerk the wheel hard to the right to avoid the truck that's slowing in front of me, causing my rear end to spin out. Clutching the steering wheel tighter than before, and slamming the brakes, I try not to panic as Katy continues to scream like she's on fire.

Didn't I turn it off?

The truck suddenly veers back onto the highway, inches away from me, colliding with the old Dodge Ram. Control slips away as my BMW skids dangerously toward an abandoned car on the shoulder.

Where did that car come from?

"Please stop! Please!" I beg, pumping the brakes to the floor and praying for a miracle. An accident is the last thing needed right now. Luckily, I slightly miss the parked car by inches, crashing off the road as the muddy ditch and skinny pine trees consume my view.

The impact sends my chest crashing into the steering wheel, knocking the breath out of my lungs. Panic surges as my car slams into the ditch, abruptly coming to a halt. Outside, orange dust swirls my car, creating a suffocating cloud as Katy Perry's voice fades into silence. My fingers tremble like they're frostbitten as I struggle to catch my breath, checking to ensure my arms, legs, back and head are okay.

Looking at the cloudy dirt storm outside threatens to collapse my lungs of any remaining oxygen. Keeping the coughing at bay and calming my vibrating foot from trembling too hard against the gas pedal is not coming easy. As the nervous air caves my stomach in and out, I say a silent prayer of thanks that my car stopped.

How did that happen so fast? My attention drifted from the road for a second to find my...

My phone.

Why did I do that?

The horrifying thought of what could have happened has sweat trickling down the tunnel of my back. Amid the stress from my earlier track races, the anxiousness of the wreck and the chaos awaiting me at home all collide, threatening to take me. *Calm down.*

One thought at a time. One breath at a time, I remind myself, as my mom taught me.

Resting my pulsating head on the steering wheel, my mind drifts back to the disaster of my track meet from earlier today. It was the last meet of my senior year and college scouts lined the sidelines, pacing, eager to spot the next best recruit. The packed stands had crowds that could fill a football stadium, all drawn by my high school's reputation for producing top athletes. Friends and family cheered for their favorites, but no one was there for me, Reagan Cassidy Pittman, the girl with three D-1 track scholarships. It didn't matter, though… I came up dead last in all my races.

Dismissing that thought before fear and guilt take control, my mind slips back to my phone. Somehow, from the chaos of the accident, my phone landed on the passenger floorboard. I grab it, afraid of the life-changing news it may hold as the shattered screen takes my attention.

"Really!" *What else can happen today?* My frustration spills over.

I bend to massage my sore ankle, realizing my cleats and tape are still on. *How did I not notice?* I peel the tape off slowly, feeling it tug at my skin with each pull.

Leaning back, I rub my burning skin while watching the dust settle, almost enough to see traffic still congested in my rearview mirror. Dealing with any damage right now isn't an option; it needs to start. Whispering another silent prayer that it holds up long enough to get me home, I push the brake and clutch together, holding my breath. The engine sputters to life, and I can't help but shout, "Yes!"

Shifting into first, I ease off the clutch slowly, hoping to get enough traction to get out of the ditch. Nothing happens. All I hear is mud sloshing the car, splattering dirt across my rear window.

I try again, shifting into reverse, pressing the gas pedal almost to the floor. "Come on!" I beg, desperation creeping into my voice.

After what seemed like forever, my car lurched back and

moved. I exhale, relief flooding over me as it jerks from the ditch, nearly making me lose control again. I hit the brakes hard, shifting into first gear and steer back onto my personal emergency lane. The phone vibrates again, but my nerves won't allow me to check it. That will have to wait until later.

As I cruise steadily back in the lane, my heart settles, but then I spot the cause for the traffic congestion. An overturned van lies smashed beyond recognition, debris scattered across both south and north bound lanes with traffic halted for miles.

"Is that …" I begin, but stop the thought before it can fully take root. I try not to look, but the white plastic bags fluttering in the wind between the police and firefighters have my attention. "One, two, three body bags," I count, shaking my head in disbelief.

Looking for that phone was a mistake. That could have easily been me.

As I ease past the accident, the highway opens up from the heartbreaking scene, providing my escape. Mine and a few other cars linger in the emergency lane, making our way to freedom. I eye the congested pile in my rearview mirror, hitting ten to sixty in a heartbeat, burning at least a half tank of gas as if it were nothing.

After what seems an eternity, I pull into our twisted driveway, gripping the steering wheel more, praying no one is heading my way. Each familiar curve brings back memories of riding bikes, go karts and four-wheelers with my sisters. The memories rush through my mind as I think of all the fun we had and hoping this doesn't replace them. But as I emerge from the last curve, confusion washes over me at the sight of our house.

What's going on?

Why are they here?

My mind races with questions as I struggle to swallow the largest lump that's ever lodged in my throat, threatening to choke me. But, similar to everything else today, my throat refuses to cooperate. I can't swallow and I can't breathe. The closer I get to the house, the more my heartbeat races. The red and blue flashing lights behind my vision come back, demanding that I vomit to relieve myself of the nausea refusing to be denied any longer.

Heat washes over me like a wave, and my mouth runs dry. Not caring if my car rolls off the driveway, I barely shift into neutral before yanking up the emergency brakes and doubling over to vomit on the white driveway.

My grip on the door handle tightens, bruising my palm as dry heaves rack my body, leaving me weak from my throat fire. Wiping the sweat from my forehead with a trembling hand, I hesitantly raise my gaze to spot an ambulance backed up to the stairs. "Please, no… I can't… I can't do this!"

Somehow, I find the energy to sprint toward our front door, skipping every other step, oblivious to the scorching concrete beneath my bare feet as I burst inside. I don't need my keycard; the door is already unlocked. What I step into feels surreal… family, hospital staff and Dad's employees all turn to me, taking in my bare feet, track shorts and the remnants of vomit on my shirt, sorrow flooding them.

Not that look.

"No," I murmur. Taking a step back, my throbbing head rests in my palm as I struggle to catch my breath from my sprint, trying to evade the outstretched hands reaching for me.

"Reagan… Reagan."

I hear Miss Rita's voice drift through the surrounding chaos, but I can't process it, can't even respond with the buzzing noise taking over. All I can do is hope, but the weight of multiple gazes piercing me in our circular foyer, their expressions heavy with pity, is too much.

Why are so many people here?

Everything's happening so fast, whirlwinds of emotions leave me paralyzed, unsure of my next move.

How do I get to her?

I'm losing it.

I try to slow my racing thoughts, but the surrounding noise

grows louder, drowning out my attempts to think. My fingers tangle in my hair, pulling it away from my face as I search for my escape route.

My instincts kick in, guiding me through the crowd on my left as I take every other step, adrenaline propelling me forward toward her room. Normally, I wouldn't cling to the cold, iron-railing, curved staircase that my sisters used to slide on as kids, but my breath comes in ragged gasps, slowing me. As I make it to the top, my foot catches on the last step, and I stumble.

"Ow," I moan as I crash onto the floor, my knee slamming against the marble tiles. Stars dance in my vision as I try shaking off the dazed feeling settling over me. My gaze shifts to the space between the bottom of my sister's suite door and the floor as darkness looms inside. Then I scan the length of our hallway to the white double doors at the end. Light seeps from beneath, igniting a whirlwind of "what if's" in my mind.

Get it together.

The thumping of footsteps approaching from downstairs jerks me back, and I notice blood dripping onto the floor from my knee. *What else can go wrong today?* The last thing I want to do is explain an injury to the schools interested in me. I stretch my leg, feeling the sting of the scrape already bruising. Sluggishly, I push myself off the hard marble floor, away from all stares coming my way. I don't want their help; I am okay.

I limp toward her room, blood from my hands smearing onto my track shorts and the wall. Common sense slows me from putting too much weight on my injured knee, so I ease into a limp down the hallway, pushing through the pain.

Good, not too bad, I assure myself as I place more weight on it. I get to the curved white molding around my sister's door, where all the dates, ages and heights are. A tradition she never missed. My fingers rest on the year 2017, when everything was perfect, when we were all happy, and I wasn't drowning in worry.

But as I turn back to the double doors, I notice my bloody

handprints on the wall, reminiscent of the turkey hands my family used to make during Thanksgiving. A bittersweet smile tugs at my lips, but the thought of my dad discovering this mess gets my attention. Shaking off the memory, I focus on the double doors waiting at the end of the hallway. I limp past my sister's room, leaving more red turkey handprints along the way, blood trickling past my calf to the floor. I should stop and clean the mess resembling a Thanksgiving kindergarten project gone wrong, but I won't.

My heart pounds in my ears, drowning out the buzzing noise from earlier as the hallway stretches on, the double doors looming larger with each step. How can all this be happening at once?

Don't think bad.

I try tricking myself into thinking maybe everything is okay as a soft voice whispers, "Baby girl, come with me."

Come where?

Leaving is not an option. I ignore the gentle hand on my shoulder, overwhelmed by everything happening around me. The hands reaching out, the warm tears streaming down my cheeks and the pitying stares make me want to do one thing: scream. So, I do.

"No! Let me go!"

My world seems to freeze as my screams echo through the house, silencing everyone. Pitying stares fall on me as I yank my shoulder away, limping from my sister's room. Each step cuts through me with a mix of dread, fear, and pain, leading to more dry heaves. My emotions overtake me, leaving me no idea how to handle this trap. A familiar anger rises within me, with a desperate urge to lash out, to escape. I don't want my heart to harden, but battling against bitterness and anger feels like a losing fight. The cracks are forming, and the need to run overwhelms me.

I stand still, feeling someone close behind me, almost breathing within my shirt from behind, wanting to provide some sort of comfort. But they don't. Finally, I reach the edge of the white crown molding to the double doors.

I faintly touch the cold metal door handle, my deepest fears crushing into me with a force that leaves me breathless. I can't seem to catch the next inhale as panic settles in. Frozen, my hand rests on the door handle.

How many times had I held this cold metal wishing things were different? Hoping everything magically returns to normal.

Anxiety, which haunts my nights, keeps me from pushing the lever to open it. I can't. I won't face the answers waiting on the other side. The weight of the darkness creeps up my spine, forcing my breath to quicken, but somehow, I find the strength to push the door lever.

And there it is…my worst fear laid bare before me. My dad's gaze land in my hollow soul with an expression that will haunt me forever.

This cannot be happening… How?

I dig my nails into my palms, piercing my skin as shivers race up my arms. Hope drains from my dad, as I feel a piece of my heart slipping away. He seems to fade before me. He's getting smaller and smaller, as if being swallowed by the darkness closing in. My legs feel as if I've run a marathon, struggling to hold me upright as everything blurs around the edges.

Everything slows, no light, no hope… just me fading into a minuscule pinpoint of nothingness as I feel my glass become half empty.

"Why?" I whisper.

The word faintly escapes my lips as the darkness takes hold.

CHAPTER 2

ICE (CRYOTHERAPY DUNGEON)

Cassidy
Three Years Later

I T'S ME AND THE ORANGE TRACK OF HARRIS FIELD GETTING to know each other as I pound the pavement, one spike digging in after the next. This is my official introduction to the next four years and reintroduction to my first friend: the track field. Together we take on the torture of this sweet Southern hospitality with hundred-degree rays searing my skin, and sticky smothering humidity creating a suffocating layer. Whoever is holding the breeze hostage isn't letting anything escape the trees today. If I pass out, the prognosis would no doubt read severe dehydration accompanied with third-degree burns from the stings of pure fire hitting me.

I stop at the white cinder track curb that encircles the inner grass, taking a moment to stretch my legs. Ants scatter at my feet, possibly fleeing my odor. They seem unbothered, not touching my cleats, creating a path around my spikes as if to avoid my scent. I must smell bad to keep ants away. My attention drifts to the little insects as the familiar dampness of tears come freely. Running has always been my way to escape, but my thoughts still creep in, dragging me to a reality I can't escape. Three years have passed, but the pieces of me remain shattered.

I lick my lips, tasting the salt from my tears and quickly wipe them away, hoping no one is around to witness my daily crumble. But why would anyone be here, anyway?

Move-in day for incoming freshmen at North Carolina A &M is in full swing. Most students are probably trying to escape to their newfound freedom away from helicopter parents instead of being tormented by this fireball.

I wonder if my roommate made it.

Wiping the sweat from my forehead, I watch my tiny ant companions scatter further away from my stench, while my final tear drop provides them with a little salt water for the day.

Okay, get it together.

Maybe what I need on this first day at A&M is some ice to help with my knee and cool my armpits before they become a weapon of mass destruction.

I head toward the gray benches, in need of a power wash, and toss my backpack straps over my shoulders for the long walk to the gym.

Hopefully, my makeshift cryotherapy room is unoccupied. I noticed it during my tour of the sports facility. The large, oval tin tub with an ice machine loud enough to wake the dead is its only asset.

I already miss my cryotherapy chamber. My dad bought it for me years ago after reading it was the best thing for injuries. My mom almost fainted when he told her the cost. But after my quick recoveries, she stopped complaining. She even used it when her joints ached.

As I step into the dilapidated training room, a group of athletes leave their stench in my path. Our combined odors could suffocate anything living here.

"Hey beautiful," one calls out. I ignore him. He keeps walking, which is a relief. I am not interested. My mission is to soak, with no interruptions.

When I open the door to the training room, the musty odor of week-old socks and putrid smell of football equipment greets me with welcome arms. A sandblaster couldn't tackle the challenge of cleaning the musk ingrained in the walls at this point. The fumes hang in the air like dark clouds waiting to unleash chaos.

At least no one's here but me.

Perfect.

The foot fungus room, making my skin itch, has one piece of furniture clean enough to place my backpack. A wooden corner table, literally on its last legs with two missing legs, props in the corner. Someone should demolish this building and clean it from the foundation up.

I toss my bag on the table and walk to the oversized tin tub, spotting dirt in every corner. There's no way I'm getting into that without a gallon of bleach.

After a quick inspection, I fill the tub with lukewarm water, and toss in some lavender for my armpits, adding ice to make it colder. It takes maybe ten minutes to fill the tin can, which could have been here when my mom graduated from A&M.

Stripping down to my two-piece bikini, I ease into the water inch by inch. The initial shock of the ice water sends agony through me, but at least it smells fresh.

As I sink deeper, a shivering breath escapes past my teeth, chattering uncontrollably. I can't tell if the white cloud is condensation or my imagination fleeing my lips. But I force myself to relax, despite the cold surrounding me. Whoever came up with this form of muscle therapy obviously never tested it out.

"Torture," I whisper, enduring the remaining shock of ice around my arms and shoulders, wishing my brain would get the message to relax.

I reach for my eye mask and AirPods from the nearby table, wanting to drown out everything with music. Of all songs, "In the

Air Tonight" plays. Most young women my age have no clue who Phil Collins is, *but I do.* My mom's nurse used to mimic the drummers' beat all the time during her stretching routines.

The beat of the drums pulls my thoughts to her delicate fingers resting on her ivory comforter, the faint moans of her pain echoing in my ears night after night. Not once did she complain while awake, but her dreams betrayed her suffering. *My poor mom.* I sink deeper into the ice, thinking that if she could endure that pain, a little ice is nothing.

I let the water freeze my chin, spreading my thighs to allow the ice to soothe the ache in my knee. "Phil, please take away the pain from my heart and knee," I whisper. My voice trembles. Tears threaten to spill, and I imagine them freezing on contact with the icy air.

A few minutes in, I hear the door creak open, reminding me of a killer sneaking in for the attack in a horror movie.

Did I forget to lock it?

I hope that guy from earlier isn't back. No longer noticing the chill of the water, I sit up quickly, remove my mask and AirPods, and place them back on the side table.

Anxiety creeps in, tightening my chest. *How did I forget to lock the door?* To ensure my safety, I take a few seconds to steady myself and clear my vision. When it does, I'm met with the sight of the most sculpted chest I've ever seen. The definition is unreal, every ridge and line perfectly etched. Where is his shirt?

He gasps, startled. "My boy told me no one was in here. No sign on the door."

That slow, raspy voice caught me off guard. It hits in a way that makes my frozen brain falter even more. "Yes. Yes. I got in a few minutes ago," I say, my voice wavering. Maybe my brain is frozen.

I force my gaze upward, breaking from his chest to broad shoulders, then to his face. Eventually my eyes land on the most breathtaking hazel-brown eyes I've ever seen. *Did someone drip golden honey in them?* They're warm, piercing and distracting. "Whew...." Wait, *did I say that aloud?* God, I hope I didn't.

"I had... I had this scheduled. I'll be done in five minutes, and I'll go," I stammer, wondering why I'm acting so... *Where are my words?*

He approaches slowly, running his long finger along the rim of the tub. Did time stop?

What is wrong with me? *Pull it together.* "Did you hear me?" I raise my voice faintly to get his attention.

"Move over," he says, his calm words catching me off guard as he removes his sweatpants, not breaking his stare on me. My eyes betray me, darting to his hands, revealing a body that could easily pass for Wolverine, except for one area that appears larger than most.

What am I doing? *Stop looking.*

"It's good you set it up. You knew I was coming," he says, a slight smirk playing on his straight pearly whites.

"You cannot get in here!" I say, trying to regain control of the situation. "I have seven minutes left. Leave!"

"Move over," he orders, more authoritative, his focus still fixed on me.

I sit up straighter, water sloshing around me. "Did you not hear me? I have..."

But my words catch in my throat as he dips his massive foot into the tub. He winces, jerking it back slightly.

"Man, that's icicle!" he exclaims, shaking his head but not retreating.

I can't believe he's actually getting into my tub. "Do not get in here. I reserved this tub for myself. It's my time. Do you understand?" My forehead must be a roadmap of veins from the tension building.

"Relax," he says, his voice smooth, low and calm. "I won't bite... unless." His eyes slowly trace the line of my neck, lingering long enough for me to wonder if he can see my jugular pulsing beneath my skin.

He hesitates, staring at the ice cubes bobbing around his ridiculously muscular legs, not moving. *He's afraid of ice.*

"Scared of a little cold?" I ask, surprised by my sarcasm. *Where did that come from?*

Gripping the rim of the tub like it might save him, he closes his eyelids and begins easing down, mimicking my earlier movements. I watch as he stills himself against the icy challenge, his discomfort clear despite his effort to hide it. My legs pull closer to my chest instinctively.

He exhales hard, his brows furrowing as curiosity dances in his expression. "You're cold. Move closer."

I blink, unsure if I heard him right. "What did you say?" I heard him, but I want to see if he'll say it again.

He stares at me long, hard and unashamed before he answers. "You're cold. Move closer." His eyes travel deliberately downward to his thighs. He leans back, resting his muscular arms behind his head, like he owns the tub or the entire room. There's not a hint of weakness in him, only confidence radiating like a challenge I'm not sure I want to meet.

"No!" I reply, curling my knees tighter against my chest. The hum of the ice machine fills the silent air, a contrast to the heat simmering under his gaze.

"You'd like it," he says leisurely, his eyes lingering far too long on my chest.

"With the shrinkage, there's probably nothing to enjoy," I reply, wondering *where did that come from? Shrinkage?* What would I know about shrinkage? Only moments ago, I was mentally comparing his chest to a Marvel superhero.

He nods, unfazed by my comment, his gaze still fixed on the ice floating around me. "What's your name?" he asks, one eyebrow raised, his patience thinning.

"You're not getting my name."

"You're driving this campus crazy," he says, leaning forward, mapping every inch of me like he's committing it to memory. "How old are you?"

The barrage of questions is it. What makes him think he can ask me anything? I'm definitely convinced I should leave. He wants answers that a random is not getting. I've had enough.

But as I move to climb out, I remember I'm wearing a two-piece bikini. *Why did I think that was a good idea today?*

I glance at him, trying to gauge his next move. "I'm getting out. Turn around," I demand, hoping he will respect at least that boundary.

He sits up straighter, the corner of his lips curling, as if my discomfort brings him pleasure. "I'm good. Get out," he says, his voice dripping with challenge. His honey eyes burn into mine, daring me to move. "Get out, beautiful." Did his voice just drop an octave? Or is it my imagination?

"Fine. I will leave." Forget the two-piece. He's probably seen a million bodies, anyway.

I grip the edge of the tub and step out, aware of his gaze on me. The heat floods me as I feel completely exposed, his presence amplifying every second of embarrassment.

"Damn. You're inviting," he says, and I don't need to turn around to know he's sitting up, water splashing softly to get a better view. "You should stay longer and get comfortable," he suggests.

Snatching my towel from my bag, I dry off in record time, without uttering a word. He's making me far more uncomfortable than I want to admit. As I tie my sweats, I feel his gaze on me, heavy and unrelenting. My hands tremble as I shove my things into my backpack, fumbling more than usual. Why is this man, this stranger, making me so anxious?

"Hey beautiful," he says, his confidence filling the room, overpowering even the potent scent of bleach.

I don't respond, frozen, watching as he steps out of the tub with a deliberate slowness. Water droplets trail down his sculpted chest. My feet feel cemented to the floor, as though quicksand has swallowed me. *Move, Cassidy! Legs, please move.*

He approaches me cautiously, daring me to breathe, saying, "You were wrong." His voice is low, carrying a strange mixture of amusement and challenge.

My heart pounds in my chest as I force myself to step back toward the door, desperate to break free from the pull of his presence. "Wrong?" I whisper, my voice barely audible even to myself. *Why am I whispering?*

"There's no shrinkage," he says, his eyes drifting purposely downward to the front of his boxer briefs before coming back to mine. "Not after watching you."

His words and his suggestions hit like thunder. "You should stay longer and get comfortable."

My gaze wavers, catching the way he bites his lower lip, and I feel my resolve slipping.

Don't look down. Do not look down.

Instead, I open the door with shaky fingers, flicking off the light switch as I step into the hallway. The last thing I hear as I close the door behind me is his voice, calling after me with a loud, "Wait!"

But I don't wait, and I don't look back. I leave him behind, wet and dripping.

CHAPTER 3

NEW Q (ROOMMATE)

Cassidy

I RUSH BACK TO MY DORM, RELIEVED TO FIND IT EMPTY, FOR now. There's no sign of my roommate. Hopefully she'll show up soon because the silence feels like a blessing and a curse.

I want to unpack before she arrives, but I slide down against the old gray door, my back pressed to its icy surface. The memories of my dad, Miss Rita and my sisters leaving hours ago hit hard, bringing gut wrenching pain that makes nausea set in immediately. I'd held back the tears as long as I could, swallowing them down and holding my breath to keep them at bay.

I get up and walk over to my wrinkled linen curtains that my mom picked for this room. Her touch, her taste, her spirit is here, woven into every fold of fabric. Pulling back the curtains, I look out the window; the scene bringing everything rushing back, the moment my dad walked away, with my sisters huddled close to his side. He wore a hat pulled low, dark shades, blending in with the incoming first-year students and parents helping with move-in day. No one recognized him.

That moment should have been so different. I wanted both my mom and dad to be here, standing together. My tears fall freely now, raw and uncontrollable, spilling from a place so tender it physically hurts. I still can't understand why my mom had to go. Why her?

She was a fighter, battling lupus until it ravaged her body, leaving her unable to walk. Her beautiful hair fell out, with kidney disease chaining her to daily dialysis treatments that ended her life. In those last months, I dropped everything, except the track, to be with her, spending every moment I could soaking up her wisdom, her stories and laughter.

She died in my dad's arms while I was rushing home from my last track meet. My dad believed she was waiting for my last big moment, my high school graduation.

I miss her more than I can express. There's no one like her in the world. She could be direct when required, but she carried herself with a grace that left others in awe. My dad saw her as poised and elegant; we saw her as our endlessly patient mom to three different girls. She made our little family her entire world. Every game, every party, every tiny melt down, she was there steadily making everything okay. She shopped for three unique styles, handled each trivial meltdown with ease and kept us grounded.

She did it all. And now, without her, I feel lost. She should be here to make this space feel like home, decorate my room, and to reassure me with her warm, powerful hug that I've made the right decision to attend A&M.

Tears stream my face, the most I've cried since the funeral three years ago. Maybe the weight of being strong for my fifteen-year-old sisters, Nori and Lelah, is finally becoming too much. Or maybe my repeated reassurance to Miss Rita, our nanny… no our grandmother, by love, not blood… is no longer convincing.

Choosing A&M was a simple decision. It's my mom's alma mater, the place where her stories began, including Dad. It feels like the only place I should be. Plus, it keeps me close to home, close enough to be there for Nori, Lelah or even Miss Rita.

I stare out the window again, on my tiptoes, hoping to see my reason for a living walk past the tall magnolia trees lining the entrance, knowing they left hours ago. I try to control my emotions, but it's hard without them being near. My sobs build quickly, and I fight the urge to let them explode, inhaling, pressing my tongue against my palate to suppress the storm brewing inside.

So caught up in my spiral, I didn't notice someone else until it's too late. I'm not alone in our tiny dorm room anymore. Turning around, I'm surprised by the girl in front of me.

"So, you're the roommate?" she asks, dripping with sarcasm, scanning me from toe to head.

I blink, taking in her appearance. She's my height, with streaks of blonde in her crew cut and flawless makeup. I bet her driver's license photo could pass for a magazine cover shoot. She holds my gaze as if challenging me to a blinking contest. Her boyish vibe, mixed with her confident demeanor, makes her presence bold.

I opted not to meet my roommate beforehand. When my mom started at A&M, she didn't have a clue who her roommate would be until move-in day. So, I did the same, choosing to meet my roommate on day one rather than being paired with someone based on similar interests.

"So, you're Cassidy Pittman, track star who could have gone anywhere in the country but chose A&M because of this being her mom's alma mater."

My lips part as the salty taste of my tears lingers. "Yes, I'm Cassidy Pittman," I reply, as nonchalant as possible.

She laughs. "The internet has everything. Don't worry, lovely. Your secret's safe with me. I know who you are, and honestly, it doesn't matter," she shifts her weight to one hip, crossing her arms. "I'm Rathina Hargrove. But everyone calls me Raith, similar to the Rolls-Royce Wraith, minus the W. It rhymes with faith."

I stay silent, waiting, unsure how to respond.

She grins knowingly, continuing, "I decided not to meet you for this very moment. That look of, 'What the hell?' on your face is straight crazy," she laughs, maybe at my apparent confusion.

"So, what's up with all the tears?" she asks, scanning like she's trying to solve a problem. "This is college. We're about to have all the freedom in the world to do absolutely whatever we want."

I wipe my face quickly. "Only having a moment," I explain, turning toward my bed, unsure how to handle her presence. *This isn't what I expected.* "So, where are you from?" I ask, hoping to relax this a little.

"You seriously came to school without knowing who you'd be rooming with for the next year? At A&M, of all places?"

I guess she's going to ignore my question. *Fine, I'll play the game.* "Sometimes the unknown is better. Less judgment," I reply calmly.

She pauses, tilting her head slightly. I can see her weighing my words as her attention drifts to her side of the room. "Wise words," she mumbles, with a whatever tone.

"Raith! Raith!" a woman's voice calls from outside our dorm. "Why did you leave so fast? And why are we carrying all this stuff from the truck for you?" Moments later, five people pop in, each loaded with Raith's belongings. They might be her mom, dad and three brothers, but their mixed ethnicities make it hard to be sure.

The woman, I assume, is Raith's mom, her gaze lingering on my undoubtedly red, swollen eyes. "So, you are Cassidy?" she asks kindly.

I guess Raith shared my name with her mom. "Yes, I am," I reply, attempting to sound okay.

"I'm Raith's mom," she says warmly. I hesitate, stepping forward and extending my hand for a handshake but to my surprise, she pulls me into an embrace. Her hug, so firm, warm and comforting, reminds me of the kind my mom used to give. I melt into her arms, smiling inwardly, feeling oddly grateful. It's as if my mom sent this angel at the perfect time.

"Really, Ma? Let her go. Everyone's not a hugger," Raith interjects, rolling her eyes.

Raith's mom ignores her. She steps back, her piercing blue eyes filled with concern. "Are you okay?" she asks, gently.

"Yes, I'm okay," I lie, a tad embarrassed. She senses something is off. I drop my gaze, pretending to focus on my ragged fingernails and the delicate charm on my bracelet.

Raith's mom rests her hand gently on my shoulder. "Has your family left?" she asks tentatively. I recognize that hesitation; I've often heard that tone over the past three years.

"Yes, they left earlier." Her expression softens further, her lips tightening into a thin line. I can tell this woman has a gentle spirit.

Not sure what else to say, I turn away to face the bare, cinder block walls on my half of the room. The emptiness of the space mirrors the loneliness tightening in my chest. I should have hung something on the wall. That would help ease the suffocating pity drilling into me. Raith must have told her parents about my past.

"Oh, I wanted to meet them. Maybe later," Raith's mom says, breaking the silence.

"Yes, maybe," I respond quietly, my voice lacking the conviction I wish it had.

Just as I'm searching for a way to escape this moment, I feel tiny arms circle my waist. Surprised, I look down and see short, chubby fingers sticky with what looks like candy residue gripping me tightly. It's Raith's little brother, dressed adorably in a Spider Man costume with mismatched socks. It's as if this entire family can sense the emptiness I've been trying so hard to hide.

He looks at me with wide, sparkling eyes. "You're pretty. Can you be my girlfriend?" he asks, his little eyes filled with innocence and hope.

Interesting. I never thought my first girlfriend request would come from a six-year-old Spiderman. But who can say no to him? "This is the sweetest thing anyone has asked me."

"Yes, if it's okay," I glance at Raith, hoping she's cool with my response. She rolls her eyes and shrugs through a small smile.

"Yes! Yes!" he shouts, jumping up and down. "I will have the prettiest girl in the first grade!"

Raith groans. "What's going on? I told y'all not to say a word, and here we go. Mom, you're over here hugging her like she's your long-lost daughter, and now Spiderman here is planning a wedding!"

Her mom chuckles, ignoring Raith's outburst. "Please excuse Raith's manners. I'm Sockie, and this is my husband, Mr. Hargrove," she says, gesturing toward the tall, quiet man standing at the door. "Oh, and these are Raith's brothers, Amir, Harley and Tris."

Her family is strikingly diverse. Mr. Hargrove is tall and lean with a somber demeanor that seems to hold years of wisdom. The triplets, with their Asian background, are hitting their growth spurts at different points with their Starbucks tall, grande and venti heights. And Sockie, with her tall frame, long blonde hair and confident elegance, is definitely the alpha of this pack.

I wonder if she ever modeled?

"Nice to meet you all," I say, relaxing partially.

Just as quickly as they arrive with all Raith's things, she was escorting them out, not letting her mom unpack a single item. "Crew, let's go," Raith announces.

They hesitate, exchanging questioning glances, maybe realizing what's happening. With sadness etched on their faces, all three boys rush to Raith, wrapping themselves around her.

"Look, you guys stay in trouble. Take care of the crew. Finger paint the walls, break everything in sight and play video games all night," Raith teases, a mischievous grin spreading across her lips.

"For real?" my Spiderman asks, his tiny face lit wide with curiosity, reminding me of similar moments with my sisters.

Raith crouches down, ruffling all their straight black hair simultaneously as they turn to leave, pushing and shoving along the way. I bet there's never a dull moment in the Hargrove's home with those three.

Mr. Hargrove lingers behind, watching his daughter. After a moment, he reaches into his pocket and pulls out a wadded piece of paper, handing it to her. His gaze lingers, filled with unspoken questions, as if wondering *how they got to this moment so fast?* Then, with a deep exhale, the kind that carries the weight of eighteen years, he hugs her. A tear escapes his eye, but he wipes it away quickly. Without a word, he turns and walks away.

We all watch him leave. And it hits me. He hasn't said a word since he entered.

My dad's exit was different. I had to console my entire family. Both my sisters struggled with my decision to stay on campus. I could commute from home. It's only an hour and a half away, but I appreciated the distance campus life provided. I needed the space, independence and separation. It wasn't only about convenience; it was for *me*.

Raith's mom interrupts my thoughts. "Raith, he's trying his best to hold it in. Honestly, sweetheart, he's dreaded this day from the moment you bounced into his life."

"I know," Raith replies, looking withdrawn and uncertain how to handle the moment.

"Sweetheart, please call him. This will be difficult, and he needs to hear from you daily. Maybe even more. Remember, it was you and him first."

Raith fumbles with her phone as her mom steps closer for a hug. "I know," Raith murmurs, her discomfort palpable.

Sockie turns to me with a smile. "The boys, especially one, are already in awe of you. You two together might drive this campus a little crazy. Remember why you're here. Please be careful, Raith."

"Okay, Mom," Raith replies, with her "mom" sounding forced. *I wonder why.*

"Come here, sweetheart." Sockie pulls Raith into another

hug, but Raith appears uncomfortable in her mom's embrace. *Interesting.*

I turn away, giving them privacy as tears threaten to trace my cheeks. She has everything I want, a family that's present.

Why did this have to happen to my mom?

My life was good. Then lupus came out of nowhere, ripping the heart from our home.

Raith walks out with her family, leaving me alone in my thoughts.

I move to the window, standing where my dad stood earlier. Through the glass, I watch as the entire clan hugs Raith. The boys are each trying to get close to her, pulling and pushing for a hug. It's chaotic and sweet all at once.

Raith eventually sits on the stairs alone, watching them walk away. Her head lowers and I glimpse her wiping her face.

Wait, is she crying? Yeah, she's wiping something from her face. Interesting. Maybe she's not so tough after all. She rises sluggishly and heads back upstairs.

Raith silently walks back in. It sounds as if she's unpacking, but with my back turned, I can't be sure. I wish I had more patience for wanting to know things. According to my mom, I took after my dad. No patience and not willing to wait for answers. *Should I ask her? Or should I wait?* Maybe I should give it some time. Her family just left. But the curiosity building inside me is going to lead to sleepless nights.

With hesitation, I get up the nerve to ask, "I have a question." She turns to face me, wearing the same inquisitive expression from earlier.

I take in the clothes scattered on her bed, noticing how feminine they seem. "No idea how to ask…" my voice trails off as caution creeps in.

"Ask, Track Star," she replies, annoyance clear.

Here goes. "Do you prefer men or women?"

She pauses, her lips tightening slightly. Her reaction makes me regret my question. "You're straight to the point, aren't you, Track Star?" she says, quick but not unkind.

Maybe my timing was off. I wait for her next words, trying not to shrink from the intimidation she's throwing my way.

"Look," she finally says, "let's just say I am the Q in LGBTQIA+." Her words land firmly.

I recognize the lesbian, gay, bisexual and transgender of the acronym, but the Q I A and plus are unfamiliar. She's waiting for my reaction. I don't want to assume the wrong meaning. "What does that mean?" I ask carefully.

Her expression softens. "I call the Q questionable," she says, her stare serious and intense, which makes me more curious.

"So, you're telling me Q stands for questionable?" I repeat my words, wanting to understand.

She gets up from her bed, walking my way, taking a deep breath. "I'm telling you, I'm still exploring my sexuality and gender." She sounds winded, as if she explains this all the time.

"Oh," I say, my mind trying to process her words.

She waves her hand in the air, smiling. "Have you explored your sexuality?"

Her question catches me off guard. I started the conversation, so it's only fair I answer, but how do I even begin? Saying *I like boys* sounds childish and awkward. Moments like this remind me how out of touch I feel compared to others my age.

Before I can answer, she continues. "Lost for words, Track Star? Maybe I can introduce you to something new," she says, her attention shifting to my chest, her breathing intensifying as she steps closer, filling the air with her familiar male scent cologne.

I step up to the imaginary line in my mind, crossing it to affirm my sexuality. "I'm into men… only."

I watch her surprised expression fade into a half grin as she steps back, nodding. "This may work out," she says, sizing me up again, but with some apprehension. "For the record, I was testing your balls. But honestly, you're too pretty for my type. This much beauty in one room is going to be dangerous for this campus," she adds with a wink. "You know how to fight?"

The surprise in her voice is amusing. "You think clueless is my middle name? I hold a third-degree black belt in taekwondo and have security training. So, are we straight?" I pause, realizing what I just said. *Why did I say that?*

Raith stares at me, attempting to suppress a laugh at my obvious wrong choice of words. "Well, one of us is straight. Right?" I ask, wondering how I get myself in these scenarios with my untimely words.

She bursts into laughter, replying, "Yeah, we're straight, Track Star."

"I'm bad with comebacks, a horrible joke teller and my thoughts are slightly… different," I admit, wondering why my big reveal is so fast.

She chokes back her laughter, smiling. "Look, no need to explain. We'll figure all that out later."

Both of us laugh lightly as the mood changes and my stomach breaks the silence, growling loud, in our new space after our awkward intro. I ignore my embarrassment. "I think I'm hungry," I admit.

She smirks, gesturing at my stomach. "You think? What the hell was that? Did your stomach just talk to me, or is something trying to eat its way out of you?"

I laugh, feeling a spark of relief that maybe we'll work out as roommates.

"Let's go check out the scenery and find some food before that comes out," she says, pointing at my stomach. Glancing at her still packed side of the room, she adds, "I can unpack later."

I pause before leaving my new home as another tear threatens to fall. "Please," I whisper to myself as I close the door to my new home.

CHAPTER 4

WORD OF THE DAY: DAMN

Cassidy

MY FIRST MONTH WENT BY QUICKER THAN I EXPECTED, with Raith and me becoming quite the pair on campus. Most seem to try to figure out if we are a couple or not since we're always together. Honestly, I don't care what others think. Raith is becoming the friend that I've never had and that's not changing.

We've spent so many late nights talking until sunrise, without a care for our early classes. Somehow, we still make it to class because skipping is not an option for either of us.

Raith's upbringing is nothing like mine. She was adopted by her dad as a newborn after a football injury left him incapable of having children. Later, he married her mom, who ironically also couldn't have children. Together, they adopted three boys, triplets from South Korea. Through our late-night conversations, I learned finding her biological parents was her focus during high school, which made her mean and distant toward her adoptive parents. Eventually, she discovered her biological mom was Black and died from an overdose, leaving no trace of her father.

"Stop staring," Raith teases from across the room. "You're always in another world. Were you thinking of your mom?"

Over the past days, Raith has learned everything there is to know concerning me. It feels good to share my past with someone outside my family. I've broken down crying at least twice, while she sat quietly, offering nothing but her presence and comfort.

"Yeah, I was," I admit, hating to say it. I feel guilty that she's dealing with my sadness while she's so full of life.

Raith stretches against my bed, comfortably nestled into my at least ten pillows she's claimed as hers. "Do you know what dorm she stayed in when she was here?" she asks, tilting her head back to look at me.

I glance at her sprawled out form and can't help but smile. Raith says my bed is more comfortable than a hotel suite. Maybe I should spruce up her side of the room. That poor, lonely yellow pillow on her bed could use some company. A few extra cushions might get her to her side instead of mine.

"Track Star, did you hear me?" she probes, waiting for my response.

I open my hands, noticing half-moon indentions from my nails near my bracelet, not realizing I was digging into my skin. Leaning back in my desk chair, I take in the white walled room with its peeling paint, torn blinds and exposed piping. It's old and cramped and I'm sure my mom would've joked about adding some wallpaper or something.

Raith leans in, her face alight with intrigue. "No shit! She stayed in this dorm?"

I nod slowly. "How did you guess?"

"Your eyes give away everything," she replies, straightening her posture as if preparing for a formal interrogation. "What room number?"

I hesitate. She might think I'm insane once she hears this. Dropping my voice to a whisper, I say. "Three-three-three-four."

I can almost hear Raith's brain working in overdrive. "You're telling me you're in the exact room your mom lived in?"

"Yes," I confirm quietly.

"How the hell did you manage that?"

I shrug. "Well, the school wanted me for track, so they rolled out the red carpet to get me. I was surprised anyone wanted me after declining my D-1 scholarships three years ago, but A &M was still interested. So, I asked if her old room could be mine. Rockefeller is the oldest dormitory on campus, according to my dad. He wanted me in a newer freshman dorm, but A&M didn't require me to stay with the other freshman because I'm older, thanks to that three-year gap. So… here I am."

I pause, wiping my nose with tissue, replaced three times. "This room is the *real* reason I came to A&M," I admit, my voice barely a whisper. "It probably sounds crazy, but I needed to feel her presence again. The house was too overwhelming, everyone always asking if I was okay. I needed to be close to her, but away from everything else."

"Stop explaining," Raith interrupts, "I get it."

I'm always so caught up in my own feelings that I never stop to consider Raith losing her own mom. It may have been different, but she still lost her. I hug her tighter, reminding myself to be a better friend.

We release each other simultaneously. "Thanks for dealing with me. Babysitting your depressing roommate shouldn't be anyone's freshman highlight."

"Babysitting?" She scoffs. "I'm not babysitting you. You're my girl. I've never had any close friends before, but now I have you."

I lean in, holding her hands, promising, "You'll always have me."

"Good. I'm headed to the computer lab. These IT classes are already kicking my ass. You good?"

"Yeah," I say, nodding. "I'm going to the track to run some laps, then to hit the ice."

"Why you torture yourself with that ice crap?"

"My knee needs it," I reply, shrugging. "The season's coming, and the ice helps with inflammation."

"Look, at this rate, you're gonna freeze your v completely shut," she jokes, pinching the air as if sealing something off.

"Whatever," I roll my eyes, half-smiling. Never knowing what she'll say next. "I'll meet you at the café around five-thirty."

"Cool. Be careful," she says, slinging her bag over her shoulder.

"Back at you," I reply before heading out.

The track is about a mile south of campus. As I walk, I take in North Carolina's autumn beauty. The leaves have turned rustic oranges, browns, and yellows, scattered against a backdrop of fluffy white clouds. The humidity still clings to the air, threatening evening storms, making me pick up my pace.

Once at the track, I ease into a steady rhythm, losing myself in each footfall. The clatter of my spikes against the pavement calms me, allowing me to escape into the familiar pace of my run. If my legs would let me, I could do this for hours. Running is my absolute "go to," my calm in a world that never stops spinning.

As fall approaches and the evenings shorten, darkness creeps in sooner, forcing me to end my run earlier than I'd prefer. *I wish I had more time.*

After my lavender ice soak, I make it to the café to meet Raith without any interruptions. *I wonder who he is.* My thoughts drift back to the last time I was here, remembering the unwelcome visitor, bigfoot, as I call him. He seemed too old to be a student but had a youthful feel. *Why am I even thinking about him?* He was rude anyway.

Stepping into the cafeteria, the noise of chattering students, blaring music and the aroma of at least six different food stations greet me. Not being one for crowds, eating here is always a challenge. The first week, I tried eating in my room, but Raith wasn't having it. Maybe it's my age or her insistence on helping me integrate, but skipping the cafeteria isn't an option. Still, it's better now than how Dad described it in his day. We have a daily hibachi station and juice bar, quite the upgrade, according to Dad.

I hesitate at the entrance, torn between staying and leaving, when Raith pops up like a jack-in-the-box, waving me to the center of the chaos. *Why is she always in the thick of everything?*

Dinner companions, courtesy of Raith, are always a gamble. She rarely meets a stranger and can strike up a conversation with anyone, anywhere.

I approach her table carrying my salad, fruit, and vegetable juice. Glancing at Raith's plate, I nearly gag. She's piled two steaks, mac and cheese, cabbage, and cornbread high into one big mountain. She is so okay with her food touching and mixing into one giant mess.

She notices me shaking my head. "Yes, Track Star, the plan is to eat it all so just sit and watch."

"Who eats like that?" I say. "You have the appetite of a pregnant whale. You should have gained at least twenty pounds this week but somehow you managed to keep that brick house figure," I grin, trying to hold back my laughter and mild nausea at her overloaded plate.

Hearing Louy and Brian's contagious laughter makes everyone else join.

"Hi!" Louy's greeting comes out in a slow, high pitch, reminding me of a cat meowing for attention.

"What's up, you two?" I ask, eyeing them both. They come as a pair similar to me and Raith.

Brian's gaze lands on Raith's plate, causing his hand to hang in midair. "Watching Raith eat the entire cafeteria. Literally. This is her second plate."

"Doesn't surprise me," I say, taking in the chaotic, mountain-like heap of food. It looks like the Blue Ridge Mountains smothered in steak and mac and cheese.

"Look, I'm going into hibernation this weekend. That means bed rotting until three tomorrow," Raith says between bites, feigning seriousness. "So, Track Star, no lights, no noise, and no movement. I need all this beauty rest coming my way."

I nod in agreement, thinking, *why is she smacking loud enough to be heard across campus?* She eats and sleeps with the raw intensity of a wild animal, no shame and no hesitation.

"So, did you freeze it shut during your ice bath?" Raith teases, enjoying the attention she gets from bringing up my "v-jay."

"No, I wasn't there long. And my vagina is okay, thanks for asking." Both B and Louy burst into laughter.

"Look, stay out of that ice. It'll close you up...completely," Raith warns, pinching her fingers together to emphasize. "Google it. That shit's real."

Thankfully, Brian interjects taking my mind off the ridiculous notion of my v-jay actually closing. *Why do I even listen to Raith?* "Damn, another girl was kidnapped. She lives across from campus," he says, his voice growing cautiously serious, forehead creasing with worry.

"When?" I ask, suddenly alert.

Brian squints at his phone as if struggling to read the tiny print. "It's breaking news on the local channels. Not sure when it happened," he mutters, concern etching his voice.

This is the third girl reported missing in the past three months. It's hard not to worry. I hope they catch whoever's responsible before my dad decides to move in with me or drag me home.

Louy leans closer to Brian, practically climbing over my shoulder to the front entrance, almost falling out of his chair, shouting, "Damn, damn, damn!" His voice echoes through the cafeteria, turning heads our way. *Why are all my friends always so dramatic?*

"What is it?" Raith asks, turning toward the entrance, unfazed by the commotion.

"Oh, nothing's wrong, hunty! Everything's right with the world when eye candy steps on the scene." Louy points toward the entrance.

"Eye candy, Louy? Already tasted it?" I tease, intrigued by the new crush that has him so animated.

Following Louy's gaze, I'm struck speechless. Louy's eye candy scans the café, brow furrowed as if searching for someone, until his gaze locks onto mine. *Why did I look*, I scold myself as our eyes meet across the waves of student hair. It takes real effort to turn away quickly.

"Got damn! I could do some interesting things to that specimen. Starting by letting my clothes fall to the floor," Raith says, making me wonder if *damn* is the word for the day.

"You and me both," Louy chimes in, pounding Raith.

I zero in on my salad, eggs, cheese and croutons, wishing I could dissolve into ranch dressing and vanish. I hope he didn't notice me. *Why is he here? Maybe that wasn't even him.*

Raith, never one to miss a beat, notices my reaction. She taps the bony part of my shoulder as persistently as a nagging child. "Track Star, what is it?"

Why does she notice everything? "I met him a while back," I admit, not wanting to explain our awkward encounter in the ice bath a few weeks ago. "He has an extremely foul mouth."

"Friend, I'd let that mouth work absolute miracles on me," Brian interjects. "But you do know who he is, right?"

"Why would I know him?" I ask, my curiosity piqued. "Who is he?"

"That's Kylo Blade," Brian explains, leaning forward as if sharing a secret. "He's a professional soccer player with the US team. He played overseas and signed a mega contract a few years ago. He's got major endorsements from Adidas and Gatorade. He's basically the face of Adidas now. Surely, you've seen his commercials. He was recently in Milan for Gucci's exclusive fashion week back in July. With that face he could open any door and anybody," Brian finishes with a knowing smirk, trailing off following Louy's gaze.

"Never heard of him," I shrug, trying to sound indifferent. "I don't watch much TV."

Brian raises a doubtful eyebrow. "He graduated from A&M and donates a ton of money here every year. His main trainer's still on campus, so he's around in the off season."

"Wait, wait a minute," Raith's neck twists to a sharp 45-degree angle, eerily reminiscent of a possessed demon. "Did you say you were in the same room with that man?" She points in his direction.

"Stop pointing, Raith!" I hiss loud enough to draw a few looks our way. "Yes, I left so he could use the ice."

Raith squeezes my arm, eyes wide with disbelief. "My ultra mature, all too proper friend, if I'd been in the same room with that gift from the gods, my clothes would have disintegrated on the spot. I'd have christened him right there and then! Just thinking about it is making me hot! Damn it...fan me Louy, fan me!"

She commands as if expecting Louy to produce a fan out of thin air. Why is she so dramatic? And another "*damn*."

I watch as Louy fans Raith with a handful of napkins, turning this entire scene into something that could land them on stage. I'd rather crawl under the table and become permanently attached like the old chewing gum stuck beneath it.

Louy deliberately glances past my shoulder, again, sizing up the approaching footsteps I sense behind me. "Oh, hell. Mr. Handsome is headed our way."

CHAPTER 5

HONEY & ICE

Cassidy

"WHAT!" I EXCLAIM, MY HEART POUNDING. WHY IS HE coming over here?

"Yes, he's definitely headed this way," Brian confirms, flashing the widest smile, making me feel unsteady for some reason.

I turn around just as Mr. Honey Eyes approaches our table, commanding every pair of eyes in his path. He's with another guy, both of them big, athletic and definitely football or soccer players.

"Ice Girl, you left our tub way too soon," he says, focusing solely on me.

"That's not my name and it wasn't our tub. You got in without my permission," I reply, trying to sound firm, though my voice wavers.

"Wait, hold up, Kylo got in ice?" the other guy adds, amused. "This dude breaks down like a baby when a cold plunge is necessary." His friend laughs, and it's clear Kylo isn't pleased with the confession.

Kylo hits him on the shoulder. "Enough, Chris."

"I heard they had to push your ass in ice," Chris continues, enjoying himself.

Kylo glares, irritation clear in his tightened jaw. "Please excuse Kylo's bad manners. Christian Warren," he introduces himself, aiming his handshake at Raith, ignoring the rest of us.

Raith, however, is too busy devouring Kylo to acknowledge Christian. "Who is this?" She asks, voice steady, as if Kylo's the prize steak set before her. No apology, no courtesy…just raw curiosity.

If I could melt into the floor and become a piece of tile, I would. Why does she turn every situation into such a mess?

Raith finally acknowledges the rest of us. "I'm Raith. These are our friends, Brian and Louy."

Both Brian and Louy gaze at Kylo, practically begging for a nod or a smile. Why is everyone so fixated on him? And here I sit trying to disappear into my salad, wishing I'd never glanced up from my plate in the first place.

"Would you care to join us for dinner in this fine establishment of a cafeteria?" Raith asks in her fake European accent, enjoying her teasing.

My questioning glare goes unnoticed as Raith purposely avoids my stare. Why did she invite them to sit with us?

"Dinner in this establishment?" Kylo replies with a raspy, British accent as he takes his seat directly across from me. "Sounds tempting."

"I didn't get a name earlier in *our bath*," he states. "I'm Kylo… Blade."

I don't respond. My cheeks heat under Raith's piercing gaze burning a hole in my skull. "Cassidy," she prods, using my name which she rarely does. "Care to tell us how you met Mr. Blade?"

Silence descends on the table. Everyone's waiting except Kylo, who seems too caught up rearranging his dinner. My nerves tighten like a drawn bowstring.

"Raith, I did not share anything," I say at last. "He got in the ice after I was already using it. You know what?" I pause, feeling frustrated. "If you would excuse me, I'm heading back to our room. It was a pleasure meeting you," I say, shaking Christian's hand but avoiding Kylo's gaze. He gets no attention from me. "Raith, I'll see you later."

"Cassidy, you didn't eat anything. You want me to bring you something?" Raith asks, concern mixing with confusion.

"No, I have my juice," I reply, slipping into the crowd and out the cafeteria.

The cool evening air hits my face, a welcome antidote to the heat flushing through my body. That man has an effect on me. I can't explain it and my armpits are sticky, as if I've been running a marathon. How is that even possible?

"Cassidy?" a familiar voice breaks my thoughts. Walker steps out of the shadows. "What's going on?"

"I'm okay," I lie, but I can't shake the lingering agitation. Why am I fooling myself? I know the reason and it has everything to do with a voice not of this world.

"Cassidy," Walker repeats, his brows furrowing.

"Sorry," I force a small smile. Walker and I share every class; he's more stable than the chaos I just left. "Did you finish the Calculus assignment they posted on canvas yesterday?"

Walker's connect the dot freckle face contorts in confusion. With all those freckles, he looks younger than he is… eighteen, maybe nineteen at the most. "We had homework?"

"Uh, yeah. You're going to fail if you don't start paying attention."

"Yes, Mom, I hear you," he teases me mockingly. "I came to college to get away from that nagging. Where're you headed?"

I point toward Rockefeller Hall. It's easy to spot with our ancient air conditioner units dripping rusty streaks down the brick. "My dorm."

"You're not hanging out with that crazy roommate of yours tonight?" Walker asks, twirling a finger near his temple.

"No one calls her crazy but me," I say, surprised with how quickly I defended Raith.

"Okay, okay," Walker says, raising his hand in a mock arrest. "I get it," he steps back, still grinning. "I'll walk with you."

"No need, I got her." The deep raspy voice comes from behind me, carrying a hint of anger. How is it this is my third time hearing his voice, yet it already feels so familiar?

I turn to see Kylo Blade standing there, expression carved of stone, glaring at Walker as if daring him to protest.

"I'm okay. I don't need anyone walking me," I say firmly, trying to regain control. I refuse to let my irritation spill onto Walker, but I'm not exactly excited to see Blade either.

"Walker, I'll see you in class tomorrow. Text me if you need help with Calculus."

"Bet," Walker says, eyeing Blade warily before stepping away. He looks like he wants to say something else but leaves instead.

I get my speed walking into a full pace, determined to leave him. *Why is he here?* I left him in the cafeteria for a reason...actually several reasons.

"Slow down. I want to talk to you," he calls out.

Something about his voice pulls me in a way that's hard to explain. Frustration? Curiosity? I'm not sure but I stop abruptly, causing him to nearly stumble into me. I turn hesitantly, meeting his gaze. Are his eyes brown and green? Maybe they're green with a hint of hazel in the center. Such a unique mixture of light and dark. They should have their own category. Wait...I'm distracted again. Focus, Cassidy.

"About what?" I ask, my voice strained. "You've been rude since we first met, barging into my ice bath, making obnoxious comments and then sitting with us in the cafeteria like you owned the place. I don't need anyone walking me anywhere. Leave."

I spin on my heel and set off again, picking up speed.

"Damn girl, you walk fast. I'm sorry for earlier!" he shouts.

I pause, surprised. When I turn, he's closer than I expected, his expression uncertain. *Has he ever said sorry before?*

I tilt my head, fighting the strange warmth in my chest. "Now go," I say, resuming my pace.

"Did you hear me?" he calls, sounding more confused, maybe a little impatient.

"Yes, I heard you," I reply, not looking back. "Am I missing something?"

I reach the stairs of my old dorm building, the metal railing cool and steady beneath my grip. I risk a glance over my shoulder. He's still there, arms folded, one hand rubbing his chin, lips parted as if in mid-thought. *Why did I turn around?*

He approaches steadily, as though gauging if I'm planning to escape, his eyes fixed on me. "Give me a moment," he says, voice low.

"A moment for what?" I ask, tightening my hold on the railing. His scent drifts closer, something warm and woodsy that makes my heart speed. *He smells so good.* The air thickens with tension, and I can't help but wonder what is happening to me.

His gaze intensifies, curiosity heating the space between us as his eyes cover my face, lingering on my lips. "Sorry for earlier," he repeats, and for a moment, I feel myself caught in his aura, captivated by the allure of him, his…wait a minute. What am I thinking and why am I sweating again? What is wrong with me?

"Look," I say, sounding like Raith. "We've met maybe twice. We don't know each other and I don't expect to see you again. Apology accepted." Without waiting on a response, I head up the stairs, determined not to look back. Still, I can sense him in the same spot that I left him in practically drilling holes in me with those eyes. Those eyes, those eyes. Why do his eyes have to be so… find a word Cassidy.

Once upstairs, I rush to my window and hide behind one khaki curtain, peeking out to watch him leave. His broad shoulders and bow legs move with a confidence that makes the magnolia-line path look like a personal runway. If this soccer thing does not work out, he could easily model. My thoughts wonder and I shake my head. I need to stop.

The door slams, interrupting me out of my runway imagination. "Oh, Ice Girl, come here. We have to talk. What have you done to Mr. Kylo Blaaaaade?" She draws out his name, eyes gleaming with curiosity.

"What are you talking about? Ask what he did to me," I counter crossing my arms.

"Okay, spill it. Start from the beginning. Slower this time and don't leave out a single detail."

I sit on Raith's bed, clutching her one yellow pillow as though it were a protective shield. I tell her everything…how we met in the ice bath, how he barged in and how I left him downstairs.

Raith's mouth drops. "Wait a minute, you saw that man in nothing but boxer briefs?"

"Yes," I say, feeling the heat creep up my neck as I recall his sculpted form. "He's built like an ancient Greek sculpture. You know, like the Laocoon and His Sons statue in the Vatican Museum."

"A what?" Raith laughs, trying not to roll her eyes. "Girl, speak English. Greek sculpture or not, I'd call him a masterpiece. I don't know about your La-whatever statue, but he's got a voice like Armando Lowrey, Mike Lowrey's son in *Bad Boys*, and a face that leaves me speechless. *Fine* isn't enough. When you left, he looked lost like he wanted to follow you. Christian teased him and he got pissed off. He left his meal untouched and stormed out."

She stops, her already slanted gaze narrowing into a line, hinting at her curiosity, "Yeah, he was going after you, Ice Girl. He told Christian to shut the hell up and that he had to get something. I just saw him walking back. He looked at me and shook his head, then strutted his fine ass off campus with all eyes on him," she stops, nodding her head. "Yep, every eye was on him. What did you say to that gift?"

"Well, he apologized to me, for earlier. I accepted his apology and left."

Raith's glare makes it clear she sees me as the crazy one in this episode. "You left that specimen of a man downstairs after he came after you?"

"Yes, I did. He was rude when we first met. I forgot to mention I had a bikini on in the tub. So, he saw me. Like, *all* of me…."

"Damn, that's the problem. I know that body and those thighs are enough to make a gay man straight. You left that part out. That's the most important part."

I laugh mildly. "My body is not all that. Plus he's an athlete with all this stuff going for him. He can have whoever he wants."

Raith snorts. "Girl please. You got in his head, no doubt. Otherwise he would have stayed and finished his meal. He straight left without eating his chicken. He may have his picks, but you got in his head."

"I highly doubt that. He's just used to people worshipping him. I'm heading to shower. I have a community service project tomorrow morning," I say. "I'll let you bed rot until I'm back around four o'clock p.m. Are you sure you have enough food in your system for the night and day?"

"Whatever," Raith replies, rolling her eyes. "You could have had a whole lot in your system if you'd gotten comfortable on K Blade."

Well damn. She absolutely has no filters.

CHAPTER 6

SHOCK AFTER THE SERVE

Cassidy

I WAKE ODDLY EXHAUSTED FOR SOME REASON, BUT FULL OF excitement to get to my girl. I'm on my way to see my reason for smiling on so many bad days. I started volunteering at Smith Complex three years ago shortly after my mom's death, to help fill my void. That same decision, staying home instead of heading to college, frustrated my dad. Looking back, he was right, but I'll never tell him that. I should have started then but I couldn't leave my family. Four months before I was supposed to move into my dorm, my mom passed. The night it happened, I knew I wasn't going anywhere. My family needed me, and nothing would change my mind.

I sacrificed three D-1 track scholarships and countless opportunities to stay home and take care of everyone. I wouldn't change that for anything. Now, thanks to my dad's connections, I got a chance to come to A&M. It's not D-1, but it's exactly where I want to be. So, here I am...a twenty-one-year-old freshman with maybe one year of track eligibility left.

I step into Smith Complex, and before I can take it all in, I hear a familiar voice.

"Cassey!" Brooklyn shrieks, launching herself at me with the force of a tiny rocket. Her tennis racket clatters behind her as she wraps her arms around my waist, nearly knocking the wind out of me.

"Brooklyn!" I exclaim, warmth flooding my chest. I've been working with her for the past three years. During my mom's death, she was my unique little light that brought me joy every Tuesday and Thursday. She was my escape, my reason to smile amid the darkness. I spot Ellen Thomas, Brooklyn's mom, hurrying over, puffing with exertion.

"I've never seen her run that fast," Ellen says, breathless and misty-eyed with pride. "Cassidy. Sweetheart, it's so good to see you. Brooklyn has asked about you every single day."

We embrace tightly. Ellen has been my unofficial counselor these past three years, her quiet wisdom helping me so much.

"Ohhhh. I missed my girl," I say, running my fingers through her curly pigtails, remembering when they were shorter.

Ellen's voice softens, concern evident in her eyes. "I almost called, but I didn't want to bother you. My college years were amazing, and I want you to have that experience. You deserve that, sweet girl. How are you?"

Before I can answer, Brooklyn tugs at my hand. "Cassey, Cassey let's go!" She's already dragging me toward the tennis courts. I glance back at Ellen, unable to get my normal *I'm okay* out. Instead, I say, "I have my girl for three hours. Enjoy your day."

Before Ellen can respond, I reassure her, "I have your personal cell, work cell and 911 on speed dial."

"Bye Mom!" Brooklyn shouts, as I wink at Ellen.

As we stroll along the sidewalk, I watch Brooklyn's pigtails bounce with each step. Her pink tennis shoes scuff softly on the pavement, and I check her eyes to see if her little cute red glasses are correcting her strabismus.

Her left pupil still wanders a little in her glasses as she slides the frames to the tip of her nose, signaling a serious update coming. "I have a new friend, Cassey."

"Who?" I ask, my curiosity piqued as she nears the courts.

"Yep, he was here maybe three weeks ago. He comes to the courts every Tuesday. His name is Captain K!"

"Interesting name," I say, wondering who's this new friend that has her so excited.

"That's my nickname for him. He's big, really big! Ginormous like a superhero!" She stretches her tiny arms wide, demonstrating his size.

A sting of jealousy hits me. *Who has my ladybug's attention?*

We head inside, choosing a court away from the other kids until our doubles match starts. We practice forehands and backhands, rallying back and forth until we're out of breath and need a quick break. Brooklyn dives into her snack bag searching for something sweet. I normally buy her a couple of sweets to ensure she is overly sugared once home with her mom. Today's candy apple is sure to get us both hyper before our match.

"Cassey," her little voice is adorable.

"Yes, Ladybug?"

She adjusts her glasses, a sign that another serious question is coming. "Do you have a boyfriend?"

I arch an eyebrow, surprised at the turn in conversation. "No, Ladybug." *If you consider a first grade Spiderman, maybe I do.*

"Why not?" she presses, making me wonder where this is coming from.

"No time for a boyfriend," I say with a shrug. "Do you have one?"

"No, silly. I'm seven. But if I did have a boyfriend, it would definitely be Captain K." I can't help but wonder *who is this Captain K that has all of my Brooklyn's attention.?* I'll have to ask Ellen.

"Team twelve," a referee calls from the tall white chair overlooking our courts.

"Coming," I respond, grabbing a few wet wipes to clean us both from the sticky candy apple residue. "That's us, Ladybug. Let's go."

We make our way to the assigned court. Our opponents, a

middle-aged man and younger boy, size me and Ladybug up, gauging our skills. I pull Brooklyn aside for a pep talk. "You ready?"

"Yes, Cassey!" she beams with excitement as I pull her headband over her curls. She holds her tiny fist out for a bump, shouting, "Let's get it!"

We play three games, and win them all. Brooklyn's excitement is over the top, and I know the candy apple is kicking her into major overload. *Ellen's going to kill me for this.*

Good thing I brought bread from the cafeteria for us and the ducks. Hopefully, that will give us enough time for the sugar to wear off before Ellen picks her up. "Okay, Ladybug, our ducks are waiting," I say, gliding her to the pond.

Brooklyn walks faster than me, her slight limp doing nothing to slow her down. Her pigtails bounce like springs. Ellen told me there are more surgeries to help correct her limp. She's faced more hardship in seven years than most do in a lifetime.

Without warning, Brooklyn takes off running toward the bench near the pond. Dropping everything, I sprint after her, wondering how she got so far ahead.

"Brooklyn stop!" I shout, but she ignores me, racing toward someone sitting alone on the bench. "Brooklyn!" I scream again, watching helplessly as she launches herself into the arms of a startled stranger.

"Captain K! Captain K!" she screams, her excitement startling a flock of blackbirds from the nearby trees, sending them flapping skyward.

I slow to a halt, speechless. The man lifts his head just in time to catch her mid-leap. My chest tightens as I recognize him, his gaze locking onto mine, shock spreading across his face. *How is this possible?*

CHAPTER 7

SITTING IN THE TREE...KISSING

Cassidy

WHAT IS KYLO BLADE DOING HOLDING MY LADYBUG?
My mind overloads with questions, each one unanswered and I feel my anger rising fast.

Brooklyn squeals "Captain K! Captain K!" I swear if she yells
his name again I might take flight with the black birds that she
screamed away earlier.

"Brooklyn," he whispers, hesitating as she wraps her tiny arms
around him. "How'd you get here?" His eyes dart in my direction,
full of confusion and something else I can't place.

Even from where I'm standing, I see him trying to understand how I'm here. "Cassidy? Cassey?" he asks. "You're Brooklyn's
Cassey?"

He steps closer with the same *what in the world* expression I
possibly have on my face as I answer with a question of my own.
"And you're Brooklyn's Captain K?"

Time stalls, just like it did in that cryotherapy dungeon weeks
ago, both of us staring. I hear Brooklyn snickering, breaking the
silence. "Why are you two looking at each other with goofy eyes?"

Goofy eyes. *Wonderful.* Exactly what I need, getting caught by a seven-year-old staring at her superhero. "Ladybug, I met him at school."

She sets her hands on her tiny hips, glancing between us. "You did? How'd you do that?"

"Yeah, Cassey," he teases, using Brooklyn's nickname for me as if it's always been his. "How'd you do that?" His stare captures me again. I'm stuck, entranced by his eyes, his voice, his presence.

"I… I don't remember," I stammer, hoping to end her questions before they spiral out of control.

"Captain K," Brooklyn chimes in. "Cassey and I are going to feed the ducks. Please come with us. Please, please, please."

She's my ladybug, not his. But now he's here, holding her hand, and she's inviting him along. He looks at her small fingers tucked safely inside his much larger hand, then at me. "Please, please!" he says.

Before I can get a word in, Brooklyn screams, "Yes!" seemingly answering for me.

"I guess that's a yes," I say, reluctantly scooping up my bag from where I dropped it earlier. For a little girl with a limp, she's so fast and now he's coming along.

Forced to watch the two of them side by side, I see Brooklyn skipping to match his long strides. I can't help noticing how his t-shirt clings to his muscular arms and shorts hug his thighs. Even this simple outfit has him ready for a runway. *Why am I looking* and why am I glued to his bowed legs demanding all attention. I half expect that if he doesn't stop at the entrance of the pond, it may split similar to the Red Sea, allowing him to swagger on through. I tear my eyes away to find a spot to lie my blanket near the water's edge.

"Hurry, Cassey! The ducks are hungry!" Ladybug's enthusiastic scream convinces me that candy apples are off the treat list.

"Hold on," I say, digging into my backpack for the stale wheat bread I snagged from the cafeteria.

I hand out pieces carefully. For Kylo, I drop bread into his palm avoiding contact as ducks swarm around us, racing for their midday feast.

I love this. My mom used to bring my sisters and me here, along with Miss Rita. She believed in escaping life's hustle to reconnect with nature. Her words echo in my mind. *"Flowers are the stars of the earth."* She could lie for hours, gazing at clouds, listening to the leaves rustle, insisting the first Wonder of the World should have been the clouds. Even sick, she never felt sorry for herself. We buried ourselves in her light to avoid our pain. That was the main thing that kept us going, and I think she knew it. We didn't fall apart every second of the day after witnessing her spirit. She fought through unimaginable pain with a smile on her face. She did this every day to help us during the hardest moments in her life.

A tear escapes before I notice it. Suddenly, a finger traces an S shape down my cheek, wiping it away. I flinch, startled. I hadn't realized I was kneeling or that I'd dropped the bread. "You okay, Cassey?"

I smile at him calling me Cassey for the second time. Only Brooklyn calls me that. I hesitate. "Yes, I'm okay."

He exhales softly. "Beautiful," then turns his attention back to Brooklyn. *Is he calling me beautiful?* "I come here during the off season to clear my head," he explains. "That's how I met Brooklyn. Her mom was trying to teach her tennis, but she wanted Cassey… you. So, I helped. I've been here every Tuesday since. She's an angel. She and her mom are coming to our first home game when the season starts."

I'm too stunned to speak. He's so different now, nothing like the arrogant guy I'd met before. "What about you? How do you know Brooklyn?" he asks, settling back onto my blanket without an invitation, resting his arms behind his head. He stares up at the circling black birds, looking completely at ease.

I follow his gaze, hoping we're not in the line for a poop bomb above. "I've worked with Brooklyn for years," I say quietly. "School started in August and my classes don't allow me much time to see her. So, since Raith had no weekend plans, I called her mom yesterday to see if she would bring her today." My hands fidget, unsure what to do with themselves. *What is wrong with me?*

"Glad you made that call," he says, sounding as surprised by his words as I am.

"Not so close to the pond, Ladybug!" I call out, noticing her leaning toward the water's edge.

"Okay Cassey!" she hollers back, still feeding the ducks the last of the bread.

I rush over, scooping her into my arms, pulling her safely from the water and maybe Kylo's heat. We tumble onto the grass for our usual tickle session, fully aware he's watching us. Maybe he's a superhero with special powers because the heat from him is making me hotter by the second. *Get it together.*

"Cassidy there you are!" I hear Ellen's voice ring out. I look up spotting her in the distance, having to walk further than usual to find us. But how is it time for her to be here so fast?

"Mommy, make Cassey stop!" Brooklyn giggles, squirming as I tickle her even more.

"She's your official tickle monster, kiddo. Not stopping," Ellen teases. I finally ease up, helping Brooklyn brush off the leaves and pine straw clinging stubbornly to her clothes and hair. We always end up dirty after our tennis days.

As I steady Brooklyn, Kylo rises from the blanket. Ellen glances his way, and I can see her protective instincts kicking in. "Kylo. I didn't see you over there. What are you doing here?" *How could she miss him? He's huge.*

Ellen takes in the casualness of us, her piercing green eyes trying to piece together the scene…Kylo on my blanket, Brooklyn chattering away and me looking embarrassed. "Have you two met?"

"Yes," we answer in unison. *Please, no more questions.*

Ellen looks between us, as if realizing something we don't. Turning her attention back to Brooklyn, she says, "Okay, kiddo, let's go."

"No, Mom! Can I stay with Captain K and Cassey!" Brooklyn pleads, her eyes wide with hope.

"Every Saturday I'm not at a track meet, I am here with you," I try explaining, hoping this will help Ellen.

"So, next Saturday?" The pleading in her question almost breaks me.

I hug her tightly, inhaling her familiar scent of Downy Unstoppable beads in her clothes. "Yes. Next Saturday." I didn't realize how much I would miss Brooklyn and my family until now.

She releases me, skipping over to Kylo. "Captain K, can you come on Saturday instead of Tuesday?" she asks, making me wonder *how is she so close to him already?*

He replies, "I'll check my schedule. But, if I can't make it Saturday, I'll definitely be here Tuesday." He looks directly at me as if wanting to say more.

Ellen breaks in before Kylo can finish. "Let's go, kiddo."

I reach over, giving her a gentle pinch on the bridge of her nose and another hug. "I will miss you until next Saturday, Ladybug."

She spreads her arms wide in dramatic Brooklyn fashion, looking between me and Kylo. "Captain K, can you walk Cassey to her car? She's always alone and sad. Maybe she needs to smile more, but she needs protection."

So, I need protection from *her* superhero. I shake my head, trying to remember if I was this forward at her age.

"That mouth of hers is full of surprises. Brooklyn that's it, little motor mouth," Ellen says. I completely agree with the motor mouth part.

Before Ellen can pull her away, Kylo looks at Brooklyn and answers, "Yes, Brooklyn. I will take care of Cassey just for you." Was there an emphasis on his "care" or was it just my imagination? Maybe it's nothing or maybe it's just my temperature spiraling out of control again, making me hear things.

"Okay, good!" she screams, not giving me a chance to object as she skips hand in hand with Ellen, humming the song "Sitting

in a Tree." *I can't believe she did that. How does she know that song?*
She has to be seventy instead of seven.

I pick up my stuff and pack everything in my backpack to head
to the bus stop with one thing on my mind: getting away from him.
He's too close and beginning to make me sweat again. He has to
have better things to do than take "care" of me.

I walk past him, hoping he'll leave but luck's not on my side.
"Where's your car?" he asks.

I answer, not risking a glance back. "I took the bus from campus. So, I'll take it back." I pick up my pace to avoid him, but that
effort proves futile as he catches me in two strides.

"Wait, let me get you back. This area is bad... really bad. It's
not safe around here. Trust me. I'm headed to campus to meet
Christian. I can have you back in ten minutes instead of forty-five
on the bus," he stops walking, as if expecting me to do the same.
And I do because, for some reason, I get lost in those honey-brown
eyes, drawn in as if a bird diving in the ocean for its next meal. *Raith
would roll her eyes with that description.*

But he's right. This was my first time taking the bus and the
urine smell alone was enough to make me change my mind. Dad
would die if he knew I took it alone to this area. I normally drive
my car and call him once I arrive, but first-year students cannot
have cars on campus. He couldn't be a kidnapper, a famous soccer
player that plays tennis with Brooklyn. *Could he?* Before I realize
it, I hear myself agreeing, "Okay."

The surprise on his face is amusing. "Alright, my truck's over
here."

CHAPTER 8

SO...I'M BORING YOU?

Cassidy

WE WALK IN SILENCE TOWARD HIS TRUCK, AND I'M SUR-prised when he opens the passenger door for me. I didn't take him as the type to even acknowledge basic etiquette like opening a door. I climb in, struggling slightly to crawl into my seat. *Is this truck lifted?* Everything about him and his truck is oversized.

Once inside his black F-150 with tires larger than my entire car, we head to campus. I place my backpack on my thighs, need-ing something to occupy my hands from resting awkwardly in my lap. *Why am I so nervous and hot?* Maybe he notices as he sets his air conditioner at sixty-five. *Fifty-five would probably cool me.*

Even though his truck is huge, he fills the space with his frame, leaving little room to breathe. There's no way he could fold himself into the passenger seat of my convertible, he's too broad and long. I watch as he presses the metallic gas pedal, merging into traffic, handling the truck with a control that draws me in. His right arm is straight on the steering wheel, leaning toward the window with his hat backward, making it hard for me to focus on anything else.

What the heck is happening? If I cursed, I might say "hell" but I don't swear.

"Cassey, where are you from?" he asks, breaking the silence. His attempt at small talk is a relief from the questions swirling in my head.

I peel my gaze away, pretending to focus on the road ahead, before answering. "Born and raised an hour and a half away from here. You?"

"Near here. An hour drive in the other direction, in a small town called Anderson. I went to A&M five years ago for soccer."

I'm aware of his soccer background after listening to Brian brag. "Soccer?" I ask, genuinely curious. I don't see him as that type. His body's built more for the gridiron, resembling a football safety or wide receiver. He seems too imposing for the soccer field.

"Yeah. Not a sport most see me playing. I had a bet with my brother about soccer. If I made the soccer team and started the entire season, the car was mine," he pauses, looking past the red traffic light. "Moms worked hard for a beat up motor on wheels that made it to school and back before leaking half a quart of oil. It was supposed to be mine in two years once he left for school," he continues, his thumb tapping the steering wheel harder. "I made the team, got the car earlier and a little more."

His story feels incomplete, leaving me wanting more. "He is the reason for all of this?" I ask.

"Yeah, he gave me more than he'll ever understand," he responds, a slight crack in his voice. There's something he's holding back. It carries a sense of familiarity. It's the weight of loss.

He tightens his grip on the steering wheel, forcing his frustration into it, his arms flexing as he drives. His muscles are so well-defined. I have never called a man beautiful, but the baby face he should've outgrown is…find the word, Cassidy.

"What does Cassey do for fun?" he shifts the conversation, and the subject change is another welcome distraction, giving me something else to focus on besides his arms and my lost vocabulary.

That's a good question, something I never considered. Fun? Do I even have fun? It's been me, my family, track and Brooklyn for the past three years. Nothing else.

"Cassey?" Kylo interrupts my thoughts, asking again, "You know… hanging out, drinking, partying, vacationing?"

"Fun?" I repeat, stalling to come up with an answer that's not so boring. But why would boring be a concern? I answer honestly. "Pretty much whatever Raith wants to do. I don't party much. I'd rather be in the dorm. Raith on the other hand is the life of every party. She doesn't miss anything on campus and drags me around introducing me as her BH."

"BH?" he asks, raising an eyebrow.

The embarrassment of explaining Raith's nickname for me makes me hesitate, but I tell him anyway. "Boring Human." His slight chuckle shows off his side smile and a cute dimple.

"Yes, that's the affectionate acronym she calls me."

"And you let her get away with that?"

I shrug. "It doesn't bother me. Honestly, I'd rather be in my room with a book or doing nothing. According to her, I won't have anything to tell my grandkids."

"Raith will," he says, dryly. "Christian mentioned her a few times," he pauses, then asks, "What books do you read?"

This surprises me. "You sure you want to know?"

"I asked, didn't I?" he quirks a brow, seemingly amused.

"I recently finished reading *War and Peace* by Leo Tolstoy, *The Lord of the Rings* by JRR Tolkien, *Beloved*, by Toni Morrison and *I Know Why the Caged Birds Sing* by Maya Angelou," I stop, noticing he's, wait…is he yawning? "Am I boring you?"

He smiles. "I'm playing with you. Keep going."

He was actually yawning. This shouldn't shock me, considering everything else about him. Rude, disrespectful, arrogant, inconsiderate, and blunt are a few words that come to mind. "Keep going," he repeats, interrupting my list of adjectives for him.

I pause, unsure if I should continue.

"Tell me more."

I'm uncertain, but I continue. "My range of books is broad, but horror mixed with romance is my favorite."

"Horror and romance?" he ask, drumming the steering wheel again while waiting at the light. Does he have somewhere else to be?

"Yeah. My contrast. Both make it impossible to put the book down. A little mystery tied in with the two sometimes moves the story line to different perspectives, leading to some satisfying outcomes."

"Satisfying? How so?" He looks genuinely interested.

I didn't expect him to catch that. Even with his yawning, his listening skills are not bad. "They both take me away to places where my reality doesn't exist," I stop, realizing I've shared-too much.

Suddenly, he turns into a strip mall parking lot. "Where are you going?" I ask as he backs into two parking spaces far from the newer stores.

He puts the truck in park, leaning in just enough for me to catch another whiff of his intoxicating scent. "Relax. I'm not planning to kidnap you. Besides, you think Ellen would let Brooklyn talk you into getting in my truck if I wasn't good? Why do you need to go to a place where reality doesn't exist?"

I lean my head back against the headrest, trying to think of a way to end this conversation quickly. I can't think of anything to say, so I reply, "Venturing to different places through my books takes my mind off my reality."

He studies me, his gaze searching. "What's wrong with it?"

Does he catch everything? I lean my head back again, trying to figure out how to answer. Why would I share anything with him? We hardly know each other. "Nothing," I eventually answer.

"I don't give up easily…even with my reality," he says and the intensity firing is enough to confirm his statement. *What do I say after that?*

"You see that new ice cream cookie shop over there? You want to give it a try?" He points to the shop on the corner of the strip mall. "According to my trainer, sweets are a part of my daily nutrition."

Ice cream? The conversation whiplash leaves me dizzy. "Every day?" I ask.

"Sugar's my only vice. You okay with indulging?"

Was it my imagination, again, or did he put emphasis on the word *indulging*. "Is that the only bad thing?" I ask, hoping my cynicism is evident.

"You surprised?"

"Some athletes have a bit of a reputation for doing everything."

"That *some is not me*. Back in the day during my freshman year, getting bent was a daily with me and my roommates. I could have been an alcoholic back then. One weekend, we binged for twenty straight hours. The last thing I remember was finding my roommate trying to eat his shadow off the street outside the dorm. That stunned me into straight soberness. Bro' was trippin' so hard I had to fight him to keep from eating concrete. He left two teeth on the ground that night."

I can't help but laugh. "Did that really happen?"

"Hell yeah!" he says, then points to the ice cream shop. "You good?"

"Do they have pecan praline?" I ask, trying to focus on something normal.

"Pecan praline?" he repeats.

How does he make *pecan praline* sound so good? And why am I getting hot, again? *Focus, Cassidy.* "Yes. I could eat it every day if my abs could handle it."

"I'll keep that in mind," he replies, lowering his gaze to my stomach. "And that four pack with that two-piece bikini is on point."

His direct words should not surprise me after our ice tub introduction, but they still do. Even his honey's lingering around my stomach is bold. *What's wrong with him?* I reply, "Thank you, I think. Why are you parked so far away?"

"Cardio," he grins. "And no door dings on my truck," he moves to open his door, pausing. "You coming?"

"Could you just grab mine?"

The look of agitation creeping across his face is new. "Why?"

"You're a social media magnet and that type of attention is too much for me."

"You don't want to be seen with me?" His amused smile surfaces again, dimpling his cheek.

I meet his gaze. "I don't want TikTok videos and IG reels with Captain K. That's all."

He studies me long and hard. "I'll make it more private," he grabs the sunshade from behind the seat, placing it over the windshield, slams the door and walks inside without saying another word. *Why the mood swing? And why is my temperature through the roof again?*

I gauge when to peek behind the windshield with perfect timing, seeing him walk to the truck. Two girls take in every part of his Idris Elba like walk with no shame. He seems not to notice.

CHAPTER 9

LET ME TASTE...

Cassidy

H E GETS BACK INSIDE WITH ANOTHER DOOR SLAM AND yanks the ice cream cone in my direction a bit too quickly. The praline scoop slips, tumbling off the cone and landing cold against my thigh. A shock of frigid sweetness runs down my skin, just above where my shorts end.

"That's cold!" I squeal, frantically trying to wipe it with my hand.

"Hold on and sit back," he says, voice edged with impatience. He leans closer, filling my senses with the subtle warmth of his scent. Opening the glove compartment, he searches for something... napkins, I hope.

"I have wipes in my backpack," I start to say, but my words trail off when I catch him looking at my thigh, following the sticky path of melted praline. Why did I wear these shorts? They're exposing too much of my inner thigh.

He lifts his gaze, meeting my eyes, and for a moment, I forget to breathe. "Can I get it?" he whispers, his voice low, faint and almost unrecognizable.

Unable to reply, I'm stunned as his tongue slips between his parted lips. Before I can refuse or agree, he bends down and licks the ice cream from my thigh. His eyes stay locked on mine as he does it with unspoken questions lingering between us. He's careful, not letting his tongue graze my skin. His heavy breathing creates a freezing sensation, making me lift off the seat.

"Be still, beautiful," he says when I flinch. Then I feel it, his warm tongue chasing a stray drop of cream running between my thighs.

I wasn't ready for the sensation of his hot long tongue on my skin, licking back and forth, making me cross my legs from the intensity building within. "What are you doing?"

"Giving you something to tell your grandkids. Relax."

He finishes every drop, leaving no trace of ice cream. His slippery tongue glides up my leg, savoring me as his favorite treat, pulling soft whimpers from my throat. "Please," I whisper, unsure what I'm begging for…maybe to stop, maybe to continue. My thoughts dissolve into sensations. His hands grip both my legs firmly, and I feel him tasting, savoring my skin, heat and coolness colliding at every nerve ending. *How did he eat it that fast?*

He meets my gaze, again. "Please what, Cassey? These sexy ass thighs have been on my mind since you climbed in this truck." His confession knocks the air from my lungs as his rough, calloused hands grasp both my legs, licking them with the hunger of a man who hasn't eaten in days. "No napkins with you, beautiful." His breathing picks up and so does mine.

"Please," I trail off again, my body reacting on its own as I feel the tip of his tongue forming S shapes on the sensitive skin behind my knee. I realize my hands are in his hair urging him closer to my inner thigh. The dazed, unfamiliar sensation he's creating with his wet lips has me all over the place.

"I need to taste," he pleads with his tongue, craving nothing but the sugar he desires.

Again, before I can answer, I feel his teeth biting into my flesh, piercing deep into my skin as a mixture of pleasure and pain ignites my unknown desire. "Please," I beg again, unable to control the arch in my back and the yearning between my legs.

"Please...what?"

I stay silent, unsure what I want, as he unbuckles my safety belt, and adjusts my seat all in one move. "You've been on my mind since the ice. Let me see this," he confesses. "I need to see this body without these shorts." There's no arrogance now, just raw need and curiosity. His honey hazel eyes drop to my midsection, and I feel as if I'm under a warm spotlight, every sense magnified. He pulls my shorts away from my hips, exposing my thong.

Why am I not stopping him? Raith keeps telling me to live a little, that I'm too innocent for my age and need to have some fun or do something crazy. Well, here it is...sitting in a truck outside a strip mall with a guy I don't know. *This is definitely crazy.*

"Let me taste you," Kylo says, voice low and intense, drawing my gaze to him.

The thought to deny disappears. "Can anyone see us?"

"Hell no," he answers firmly. "I'd never let anyone see you. I'm going to eat you until your sweetness drips down my mouth. Forget the ice cream," he says, setting the cone on the floorboard.

Breathless from his words, I hear myself mumble a faint. "Okay."

This is so new. *What is he getting ready to do?* Kylo effortlessly shifts my body on the seat, pulling my shorts off with careful but certain hands. He pauses as if waiting for my objection as tension hangs in the air, thick with anticipation. I feel my heart racing at the uncertainty of it all.

The cool seat is a stark contrast to the heat I feel building between my thighs, sending shivers through me as I grapple with the conflicting sensations. Each moment stretches out, and I can't help but wonder how this will go. I feel so embarrassed by my nakedness in his truck as he positions my legs over his shoulders, exposing my thong to his face. I'm glad Raith convinced me to get a wax as his hot breath fans over me, causing me to shiver and inhale, tightening my core as he adjusts his body in the truck. *What is he going to do?* He spreads my thighs wider, lowering his head until the tip of his tongue touches the thin fabric of my thong around my delicate area.

"Ohhh," I lean back, biting my lip and grasping the seat. The sensation of his warm wet tongue moving on my thong back and forth has me arching my chest and holding my breath.

I press his muscular, hard shoulders downward, drawing him closer to the inside of my thighs. He's hardly touching me, and I find myself grinding against his face to lick my uncharted area. With one swift move, he tongues my thong away from my center, allowing him access to my wetness. The sensation of him blowing and kissing me is too much to handle as his tongue glides, leaving me on the verge of exploding from within. I claw at his hair, forcing him closer to me as he traces over my sensitive slit, flicking back and forth. I have never, ever felt so, so...

"Kylo!" I scream, with him sucking me urgently, sending waves of pleasure through me. And then he stops.

"Don't stop!" My own voice pleading, nearly desperate. Practically begging, I lean over, watching as he scoops a spoonful of ice cream from his cup, placing the sweetness on me. "So cold!" I shiver, drawing in my stomach, as I feel the ice cream dripping to my...

"Sweet," he whispers, ripping my thong into shreds, spreading my legs even wider, forcing me to turn away from his intensity. He licks the ice cream with a desperation of someone craving food for survival. The hot and cold combination of his tongue licking every inch has me all over the place, building pleasure that can't be put into words.

"It's too much!" I gasp, but he only tightens his grip, pressing my foot to the steering wheel forcing me to surrender fully. My body needs release, my movements no longer my own.

"Be still and let me get this praline," he murmurs, voice muffled against my skin.

I believe him now, he wasn't playing when he said he wanted to taste me. He's devouring me as if I were the last woman alive, his grip firm, refusing to let go. His nails pierce my skin, making me thirst for more with his strong mouth conquering my every thought, until exploding is my only wish.

"Kylo, please!" I moan and grind my hips more toward his mouth, feeling myself reaching beyond anything I understand.

"You smell so damn good," he growls, and just when I can't take anymore he stops. As if he knew what was coming. "Not yet," he says, taunting me gently.

"Please, Kylo. Please," I pant, hardly recognizing my voice. As I beg he slips his tongue inside me, darting in and around, stimulating me beyond any of my expectations. The sensation of his moist tongue inside makes me pull his head closer, not caring because this feeling is new, and I want more. He groans as he plunges inside me over and over again, the tip of his nose pressed against my clit, rubbing my soft bud while he enters me with his tongue repeatedly. *How is he able to do this and breathe at the same time?* I dig my nails into his back, possibly causing bruises. He's making me lose my mind as I reach a point of no understanding.

"Kylo!" The pleading escapes me, foreign and desperate, as he slips his tongue out and latches on me, sucking for dear life. I feel myself falling over the edge, sending my entire body into a high unlike anything in the world. The intensity of my climax makes me scream as if I'm having an out of body experience.

"Please don't stop!"

I cum so hard that the keys clatter from the vibration of the truck, my body unable to remain still.

"Kylo!" I surprise myself with my moans as he continues to drink me. Another climax rips through me, leaving me open, wet, and out of breath.

"Give me all of it," he moans with the sexiest request I've ever heard.

I lose control of my legs, my body and possibly my mind,

collapsing in his truck. Exhaling, I realize I've never felt anything this intense in my life and it's something I will never tell my grandkids.

He pushes his nose up against me, inhaling as if I am the last thing he will ever smell. "You smell so damn good, girl. I could lick this tight little body inside and out every day." His half closed, desire filled eyes study me, as if trying to figure out something deeper. "I want you," he confesses softly. "I need you." Almost pleading, he starts pulling at his shorts when out of nowhere a crashing sound escalates from the rear of the truck, triggering the alarm.

"Damn! What was that?" He turns, attempting to look through his tinted window. "Someone hit my truck!" he squints, trying to see out the dark glass, fumbling with the fob to stop the alarm. "What the hell?"

Both of us notice a girl inspecting the back end of his truck, the interruption bringing the moment front and center. Kylo looks at me, confusion crossing his handsome features…a look I was not expecting. *Regret.*

"Damn," he swears under his breath, but loud enough to be heard. The weight of his words hang in the air, amplifying the tension between us. "How'd this happen?" He fidgets with his keys, looking out the window at the woman who hit his truck, then adjusts his shorts. He gets out to talk to the girl, and they both survey their cars. Everything must be fine since the lady pulls off as he runs toward the ice cream shop.

What just happened? Did I really let him have oral sex with me in a parking lot? Was I possibly going to have sex with him if the girl hadn't hit his truck?

I sit up to find my torn thong, partially wet shorts and the wipes I was initially looking for in my bag caught in a whirlwind of emotions. I try cleaning myself of melted ice cream and the evidence of what we did.

He jumps back in the truck as I pull up my shorts, handing me a couple of napkins, with a *what have I done* expression. The air between us grows heavy with discomfort, partially since he hasn't said a word, while shame and guilt began to settle over me.

After a long pause, he starts the truck, avoiding my presence as he adjusts the air while driving back to campus in complete silence.

"That got out of control," he says, his voice low and uncertain. "I'll get you back to campus."

That's it. Is that all he has to say? I should have never let this happen. Why did I let him do this? I struggle to remain calm, but my anger rises.

Once back on campus, he pulls up to my dorm, and I reach for the door handle. I grab my backpack and open the door to leave. "Wait, why you getting out so fast?"

I snatch my leg away from his rough calloused hands, asking, "What is it?"

"Cassey, wait. I need to figure out...I mean," he stutters, words failing him.

The emotions that threatened to spill out the entire ride back to campus don't come because I make them stop. But *why am I feeling this way?* It doesn't make sense. I met him a few weeks ago... though it *seems much longer.*

I refuse to look back. He won't see me as a weak, inexperienced college girl who can't handle a little foreplay, even if that's exactly what I am. This was just a ride home, nothing more.

I jump out of his truck, hearing him calling behind me, "Cassey, wait..."

CHAPTER 10

INTRODUCING K BLADE

Kylo Blade

I SIT IN MY TRUCK, ENGINE RUNNING, NOT MOVING, WATCH-ing those legs disappear up the concrete sidewalk. I've seen plenty of women walk away before, some crying, cursing, scream-ing even running back... but I've never had one that didn't look back. Her ass isn't looking back and running sure as shit isn't hap-pening. She didn't look back in the ice, didn't look back at her dorm steps and now she's not looking back at my truck. Her defiance ig-nites something foreign inside me.

I bet those shorts are making that swishing noise similar to my aunt's church stockings, as her thighs hit that fabric over her bare ass. The image cuts through me, raising questions I never thought I'd ask.

Who is she?

Does she run track with those thighs?

How old is she?

And then the biggest question. *Why do I care?*

A woman's body has never left me second-guessing myself like this. I'm a grown ass man that can fly women in from different countries daily. But here I am, confused by a girl who just walked out of my truck without looking back, leaving me with her fading scent and the sweetness of her taste.

The "that" in my mind is unclear. The "that" is me slipping between those legs, which is rare. I don't go down on women. But with her, I did without hesitation, in a damn strip mall parking lot, sneaking around like a reckless teenager.

I continue thumping the steering wheel, realizing something. I want it again. Fuck, *I need to taste it again.*

But what's bothering me is how did this happen so fast? My self-control has always been my power. But something's different with her. The way she touched me, her nervous response and how she came so hard that it rocked my truck... shook my confidence. Normally I walk away unfazed. Now I'm questioning ... She's under my skin.

Seeing her at the park with Brooklyn caught me off guard, too. I thought my mind was playing tricks on me, but no, it was her. I recognized those thighs and pretty face living rent free in my mind for days. Her patience with Brooklyn was genuine and mature, making me question her age.

She feels young, untouched with the way she jumped with my licks on those thighs. I hope she's not under eighteen because jail isn't for me. But she's not a child; the way she handled that moment, her careful patience, suggests more experience, more steadiness than a teenager could have.

My mind races, telling me answers that isn't coming fast enough. I look back at her stomping the pavement with so much force it could crack the ground. She's mad as hell. *Intriguing.*

Her refusal to come into the ice cream shop because she doesn't want to be seen with me hit different. Even seeing her with that kid who had more freckles than skin pissed me off. I could have bust his forehead in if he hadn't left, but I know my agent would have an issue with that. *Where is this coming from?*

She's igniting something in me that isn't slowing. My attention drifts back to her thighs, the way they flex and move as she climbs the stairs two at a time, her focus locked ahead, still not looking back and unaware of my stare. I should get out of my truck and throw her over my shoulders to feel the sensation of those taut hamstrings against my skin once more.

I couldn't tear my gaze off those thighs popping with muscles when she walked toward me earlier, her five-six frame and nice ass commanding attention. She's not a part of the itty-bitty club; those full C's, maybe D's, peeked through her t-shirt asking for me. She's blessed with that body, no surgery, just good ass genes. I recognize the type 'cause she's soft in all the right places.

She's getting attention. That's for sure. She has that unapologetically bold, *unable to blink* type of beauty. The kind that makes grown ass men take notice. But the combination of her body and face is too much for these college boys. She's not meant for boys; she needs a real man. *She needs me.*

She hits the top step and finally looks back, not at me though. *Did I stop breathing?* This effect… is different. She twirls a loose strand of hair through her fingers, gripping the same stair rail that I backed her up against. Her gaze is distant as if she's trying to recall something. Then she pulls away, opening the dorm door, leaving me with a last glimpse of those calves made for four-inch heels.

Shit. I messed up.

I remain in the circular parking lot, reluctant to leave campus, trying to figure out my next move.

Damn what's her last name?

How did I not get that? Finding her is going to be hard unless I stalk. I hate to admit that I thought about it weeks ago when she left me in the ice hard as a rock.

But first, I need to handle a minor issue by the name of Sarah Sims. She's been around for years, with no real claim. A convenient arrangement is what she is.

My phone vibrates…Sarah. Speak of the devil.

"Sweetheart, where are you? I thought we were going to dinner today," she whines. I grit my teeth, focusing on the ice cream stain on my seat. If not for this heat, I might leave that stain as a reminder of the sweetness I tasted.

"No dinner," I say, cutting her off. She tries to smooth it over talking about agents and publicity, but I'm done. I don't need her PR stunts anymore. She's the one that needs me, not the other way around.

I'm pending a movie deal and a modeling contract with Gucci but I can get all that without her. She needs me. Plus, we were never together. "No dinner," I reply.

"Well, okay honey. But do not forget our outing next weekend. We have to go. This could be lucrative for the both of us long-term. Where are you, Kylo?" she pauses. I hang up, not answering her question. She knows not to question my whereabouts.

I met her at dinner during my second soccer season in Europe. I was with my agent, and she was with her parents. I knew what she was up to when she caught my eye during dinner, lifting her skirt and spreading those legs wide enough to be seen. She excused herself from her parents' table, walked over to mine and placed her thong on my salad plate. I took one look at my agent and told him to give me a minute. I followed her to the men's room and rubbed on that bare ass until she was begging for release. Damn restroom was shut down for a minute.

I was a young broke kid from North Carolina with new money. Sarah comes from old money. Her family took me in so fast I thought it was a joke. Yacht vacations in Belize, Cannes Film Festival, Formula One Monaco Grand Prix and the Cartier Queen's Cup were just a few of our vacations. We were everywhere, with photographers and paparazzi never missing a date. It made me wonder how they knew our locations. But photos meant exposure and connections, leading to more money for a broke kid from the south with new money. I was smart enough to get that.

Sarah told me more than once, hell daily, that marriage was next. Our lifestyle was a guarantee for the rest of our lives due to dear old Dad paying for everything. But marriage? Hell no.

I had sex with her once off the Sea Cliffs of Molokai, Hawaii with her head hanging over a 3000-foot drop over the Pacific Ocean. We were so high the cloud mist was the only thing keeping me cool. I hit it so hard I could have pushed her off the cliff into the Pacific Ocean. She didn't even look back to question her life in my hands or complain. She had marks and bruises on her back from the dirt. Damn, I can still hear the red dirt rubbing her bare skin raw as I pushed her beyond her limit.

I'm not a one-woman man. She accepted that a long time ago. She's used to it and never complains, which is why she's still here.

But something's different with me and it's not Sarah. It's the face of a goddess, with eyes seductive enough to make me explode in this truck, and heart-shaped lips I haven't even kissed yet. Brooklyn's Cassey and the Cassidy that I met weeks ago has me with questions. But Cass was who she was today, forcing me to bury my head between those thighs so I could taste. *How can anything be that sweet?* The strength in those hamstrings told me something. She wants this just as much as I do.

Christian has a cousin working in the registrar's office. I'll start there, searching for every Cassidy, Cassey and Cass. I look back at the dorm again, determination firing through my veins. "I'll find you, Cass," I whisper into the silence of my truck, my mind set on seeing those thighs again.

CHAPTER 11

ONE THOUSAND THIRD TIME

Cassidy

O VER THE NEXT FEW DAYS, KEEPING MY MIND OFF KYLO and his truck is not easy. *Why did I do that?* I've asked myself that question at least a thousand times.

How can a simple touch be so encompassing? Raith would laugh at my choice of words, calling it too mature, but I never knew anything could feel that way. The seat clawing, toe curling, head spinning scene has me embarrassed from my own response. He took control of me as if I already belonged to him, and somehow I went along with it.

He does not have my number, so expecting a call from him may not happen. Even though I was mad when I left him in the truck, a part of me secretly hopes he finds a way to reach me. I could ask Raith to track down Christian, but that question will never come. I can't believe I let him do that to me in his truck.

"Cassidy!" Raith's high pitch scream startles me out of my daydream.

"Yes, what is it?" I ask, trying to shake off my thoughts.

"You're always lost in that head of yours."

I sigh because she's right. "So, what's the game plan for the day? No bed rotting?"

"No, we're getting out. I feel that something's wrong with you."

Raith's ability to read others is downright strange. Maybe it's my imagination, but I swear she's a mind reader. I sit up on my bed. "What's the plan?" My body still feels drained from tennis practice, especially fighting flies while Brooklyn enjoyed her snow cone. I hate admitting to myself that I slowed my pace, half hoping Kylo would show up. But there was no sign of him.

"Cassidy!" Raith screams again.

I jump, surprised at how fast my thoughts went back to him. Trying to save face, I ask, "What?"

"Get out of your head, Cassidy," Raith replies, eyeing me suspiciously. "The fair is on the agenda today. I got tickets for Brian and Louy, too. So, we're all game. You in?"

"Sure," I say, hoping my enthusiasm sounds genuine.

"And to answer your earlier bed rotting question," Raith continues, flipping her hair. "Beauty rest is crucial for looking this good. Ten hours is a daily requirement," she strolls into the restroom, and I shake my head, wondering who can keep their eyelids closed for that long.

We get to the fair for a late lunch. Nothing compares to the aroma of corn dogs, popcorn and cotton candy, blending into that once-a-year smell. Usually, I wouldn't go near a fair food trailer without visible health codes displayed, but today I'm letting loose. A Krispy Kreme doughnut cheeseburger, cotton candy and lemonade are calling my name.

I sink my teeth into the burger, savoring the sweet glaze of the doughnut, the charcoal grill flavor of the hamburger and spicy sauce dripping down the wrapper. *This is so good.*

I take a deep sigh, savoring all the flavors until the silence captures my attention along with Raith's dumbfounded stare. "Cassidy, what's going on with you?" she asks, narrowing her eyes.

"Nothing. I'm simply trying not to be…" I trail off, suddenly short on words.

Brian interjects with a grin, "Mature… always by the book… on the straight and narrow… a little boring."

Raith chimes in, "Predictable… planning everything… mother of the group…"

"Okay, okay I get it," I say, lifting my hand in mock surrender. "I was born old, and I'm three years older than you all. Maybe I could relax a little. I guess I *can* be uptight."

"So, you are doing this by eating like the prized pig at this fair?" Raith laughs.

"Yes, I rarely eat more than 1,500 calories a day. I know this greasy, heart-attack-on-a-plate is at least three thousand calories, so, I'm living a little," I pop a fried butter stick into my mouth, trying not to think about my arteries.

"Cassidy, you have the body of an twenty-five year-old stripper, the face of Miss America, and the soul of an eighty-year-old grandmother." Everyone laughs at Raith. "Okay, Miss Loose and Free, you want this candy apple?"

I reach for the shiny red apple, similar to the one I bought Brooklyn. "Yes, pass that high fructose corn syrup over here."

"See what I mean?" Raith smirks. "Who else casually brings up *high-fructose* at the fair?"

"Whatever, pass it over." I can't figure out why I feel different today, but something tells me it has a lot to do with how wide my legs were in a Ford F-150 last week.

We're about to hop on our tenth ride for the day when Brian leans in, whispering, "Okay, don't look back, but I think this guy is following us."

Of course, Raith immediately turns around.

"Raith!" Brian hisses. "I said don't look back!"

"Dude, that scream whisper of yours is louder than a bullhorn. Where is he, B?" Raith asks.

"Beside the State Fair prized pig fence on the left. Let's stop up here at this turkey leg stand," Brian suggests, trying to sound casual.

"Oh, hell no," Raith declares, grabbing my arm. "We're going straight to the car. I'm not waiting for a creeper attack. Let's go, Cassidy," Raith demands.

"Really, Raith!" Louy's high pitch shriek in the background is enough to draw everyone's attention, including the creeper.

"Look, I don't do crazy," Raith mutters, her voice on the edge of panic. "Plus, I've had enough of this fair. We've been on almost every ride." Hearing the unfamiliar panic in Raith's voice has me on her heels as we push toward the exit.

A thick crowd gathers at the gates, giving me a chance to look back to see Brian's creeper. I glance through the crowds of fairgoers spotting a tall, skinny, spaced out guy staring directly at us. Chills creep up my spine. He doesn't move, even as people skirt around him. Something feels off, like he's not fully there.

Raith turns, pulling my arm. "Let's go, Cassidy. This guy is fucking weird."

She's right, but my curiosity flares. I peek between my curls one more time. He's still there, unchanged, giving me a silent, unsettling stare. The vibe is straight Michael Myers without the chef's knife. I decide not to look back again.

We ride back to campus in Brian's car, all of us checking mirrors and windows at every traffic light. Once at the dorm, Raith and I fumble to lock our door at the same time, both on edge. Finally safe inside, I try changing the subject.

"Raith, I forgot…there's a benefit gala at A&M tomorrow night. Are you still coming with me?"

"Do you even have to ask? Free food, top A&M donors, rich men and women all in one place…hell yeah. I'm in. And if I'm lucky, maybe someone will take me home for the evening," she adds with a wink. "And not this dorm, their home."

I roll my eyes at her.

"Look, all of us didn't grow up in your lifestyle, Miss Thing. But seriously, who will be there tomorrow?"

"Not sure," I reply, carefully measuring my words. "They're honoring my mom for her philanthropic contributions to A&M."

"Mrs. Pittman was truly amazing. I wish I could have met her."

"I wish you could have, too. She would've made sure you had your own bedroom at our place. I remember during the holidays we couldn't open a single Christmas gift until everyone at the shelter had theirs first. She died trying to help the world… and us."

I feel the familiar swell of tears and press my tongue hard against the roof of my mouth, clutching my bracelet to stave off the lump in my throat. I've got to control this.

Sensing I'm struggling, Raith heads to her closet. "Okay. Which one should I wear tomorrow?" she asks, changing the subject with perfect timing.

I appreciate the subject change. "Let me see what you got."

She tries on a sequined, silver, mini dress with a deep V-neck and pairs it with strappy silver sandals to complete the outfit.

"You're not going anywhere with me and Dad tomorrow in that dress," I say, half joking, half serious. "He'll take one look at you and have a heart attack."

"I told you I'm looking for money and food. If Mr. John Pittman's open to it, I can be a good step mommy," Raith teases.

"Stay away from my dad, Miss College Tuition Payoff," I warn playfully but firm. I might be joking, but the protective note in my voice doesn't go unnoticed.

"Track Star, I'm just saying, you never know," Raith smirks, putting the dress back in the closet. "Speaking of man, have you heard from K Blade?"

Just the mention of his name makes me hotter. *Why?* She will never know what happened in his truck. I'm too embarrassed to share that. "No, I haven't heard from him."

"Humph…I'm telling you, that beautiful beast is into you."

"Beautiful beast, Raith? Where do you come up with this stuff?" I roll my eyes.

"Look, that man is gorgeous, and I know he smells good and by the way he walks, I can tell he knows how to work some magic under the sheets."

She's definitely right about that…at least the magic part. The memory of the truck scene won't leave my dreams. "He probably has a girlfriend. A man like that isn't single," I say.

"He may have women, sure, but the way he looked at you in the cafeteria was nothing but lust."

"What do you mean?" I ask, curious.

"That man was looking straight crazy when you left. Then his expression changed to something more… animalistic."

"Animalistic?" I repeat, intrigued despite myself.

"Yes. That's the word for today. Animalistic. He bit his bottom lip so hard I thought I saw blood. And the way he was staring at you, lost in a daze, unable to pull away. Then he got up and left. He left his fried chicken on the table that I finished eating for him."

"Wait, Raith, you ate his left-over food?"

"Hell yeah, I did. But stay on subject. He left his food because of you. Have you ever seen a man leave his food on the table in the cafeteria? It's like those golden maple syrup eyes of his were staring right through you, trying to pull you back. Even Brian mentioned it after we left."

"Golden maple syrup eyes, Raith?" I repeat, trying not to laugh at her phrase similar to my honey hazel eyes.

"Cassidy, is that all you got from what I said? Yes, golden maple syrup eyes. Hell, they almost made me," she stops herself, grinning mischievously. "You know what I mean."

"Raith!"

"Look, that man wants you. We just need to make sure he realizes it."

"No, we don't need to make him do anything," I say firmly,

trying to sound confident. "I'm sure he's busy with practice, soccer, traveling and whatever else fills his schedule."

I attempt to believe my own words, but deep down, I'm fooling myself. The truth is, I want to see him again. I want to do more than see him. I want to trace my tongue along that bulging vein running the length of his muscular arm. *Where did that come from?* Something is seriously wrong with me.

"Okay, Ms. Prim," Raith says, steering the conversation in a safer direction. "What are you wearing tomorrow night?"

I pull out a white, strapless, Halston dress that hits above my knees.

"That's not what I was expecting, Ms. Prim. Please try that on," Raith insists.

I slip into the dress and my Tom Ford heels, walking the short path between our beds. Raith's rare silence gets my attention. "What is it? Is it okay?"

"Girl, someone's going to have a straight up orgasm just looking at you in that dress tomorrow."

"Orgasm, Raith?"

"Yeah, even the women will be on you in that dress. It's sexy, crisp and I'd call it animalistic if I post about it. I will amp up our makeup tomorrow night. For real, if you weren't my girl, I would hate you."

"Why?"

"Track Star, you're beautiful and smart with a body and you don't even realize it. Do you even recognize the effect you have when you enter a room? I see how everyone looks at us when we're out. They always take a second, sometimes third, look at you."

"You're exaggerating," I say, kneeling to remove my heels. These are the last pair my mom ever ordered for me. They are my special occasion shoes because they have to last forever.

Raith interrupts my thoughts. "We'll both work that party tomorrow night."

"That's not my plan, Raith," I add.

"I know. I know… That's why you're my girl," she says, softly. "You balance out my crazy. But fair warning, my goal tomorrow night is to land a full ride scholarship in the form of a rich man or woman."

She pauses, possibly noticing my mood change, as I place my heels back in my shoe bag and into the box. *That is the last pair of shoes my mom will ever buy me.*

"Someone will notice you tomorrow. Trust me," Raith says, her voice reflecting my mood.

I take off my dress, my mind bouncing from sadness to confusion, from my mom to Kylo. Even though my frustrations were running wild after our moment, episode, whatever it was in his truck, his attention is all I want. All of this feels so new. Only a few weeks have passed since those honey hazels stared into my soul with the confidence of a lion in heat. And here I am, asking myself the same question, for the one thousand third time: how did this happen?

CHAPTER 12

THAT WHITE DRESS

Kylo

I T TAKES ALL MY WILLPOWER NOT TO DRIVE AWAY FROM SARAH's house. I don't care about pending shit. Dealing with her petty, nagging ass needs to be over. This ends tonight.

My console signals an incoming call. The only *Miss Blade* in my world.

"Miss Blade. What's up?" I answer, forcing a lightness into my voice.

"That would be Mom to you," she replies with a laugh, her warmth breaking through my frustration. "Just checking in, my love. Haven't heard from you. You okay, son?"

I spoke with her two days ago, but she deserves more time. We lost my older brother years ago in a car accident. He was on his way to football practice when a truck t-boned him. He died before anyone could help.

Don't go there.

After that, I shut down everything good in my life and let the bad take over. It took effort, but Mom got me straight with some tough love. Hard to believe, but she can drop more F-bombs than

Jeezy in one breath, then whip up a home cooked meal in the same hour.

I love that woman. She's the main reason Kylo Blade exists today.

What she sacrificed for us back in the day still bothers me. For as long as I can remember, she worked two jobs, leaving my older brother, Tron, to take care of me. Those days were hard as hell. Making it home sometimes was a straight miracle. Our neighborhood was dangerous in the worst way, so sprinting home to dodge stray bullets became our norm. That's why soccer came naturally for me, running was survival.

We didn't have much growing up, but there was always food. Miss Blade made sure her two athletes had food on the table to keep us going on the field. But I always felt she didn't eat enough, or not at all. I never saw her eat. My Aunt Diane let it slip when I left for A&M that she would eat once a day. That kind of sacrifice, her going hungry so we could stay strong, made me kill on the soccer field for that win.

When I came into decent money, buying her a house was first. Even though she was set on working until her social security check kicked in, I managed to have both of her jobs "laid off." She still talks about how bad the economy was back then and how rough it was at her age to find another job. With some convincing and guidance from Christian's mom, she's now the world's worst traveling bridge player. She and Aunt Diane hit tournaments twice a month, mostly to lose, as she puts it.

I know the answer before I ask, but I ask anyway. "How'd the bridge tournament go?"

She inhales softly, "Well, your aunt and I came up short again this time. But we'll get them next weekend. We're heading to Charleston, South Carolina on Thursday."

While she's talking, I transfer two thousand into her account. "Call my travel agent for a room," I say.

"Sweetie, you don't have to do that," she protests, her voice gentle. "My social security and retirement take care of me just fine every month." When she calls me "*Sweetie*" it usually means she's trying to talk me out of something.

"Miss Blade," I start.

She cuts me off. "I don't need your money, Kylo."

I transfer the funds anyway. She's stubborn and should know by now listening is not one of my strong suits.

"Is the gala tonight at the school?" she asks, bringing my attention back to Sarah's condo.

"Yes, On my way there." I wait for the familiar pause in my head. Five, four, three, two...

"Are you taking Sarah?" she finally asks. Aunt Diane told me that Miss Blade secretly dislikes Sarah. Dislike is the strongest word she'd use. "Hate" isn't in her vocabulary.

"Yes," I admit, sighing softly. "I'm parked outside her condo now."

Another pause. I feel her thoughts turning behind the silence.

"Okay," she says at last. "Have a good evening and be careful." She always ends every conversation with "be careful" and the same three words that follow.

"Love you, son."

I grin into the phone, my frustration with the night easing a bit. "I love you, too, Miss Blade."

Aunt Diane says Miss Blade thinks Sarah is a money hungry, attention seeking, stepping stone. She's right about most of it, except the money part. Sarah's family has old money, enough to bank roll half the state if they choose to.

I climb out of my truck and head toward Sarah's three-story condo, the place she rents six months every year to stay close to me. Even when I'm overseas, she finds a way to track me. *Crazy ass.*

She opens the door wearing a skimpy red dress with lace cut-outs, telling me how the evening will end... on her balcony, or on her tiger print ottoman. One more night is happening because that's what I want.

"I recognize that look," she says, trailing her fingers down my chest and resting them against me. "And the answer is no, we have to go," she says, leaning in so her breath warms my jawline. "If you behave this evening, I'll bring you back here afterward and make sure you don't regret it."

I yank her closer, crushing my mouth against hers, forcing my tongue between her parted lips, tasting her surprise, trying to bruise her smart-ass mouth. She loops her arms around my neck, hooking one leg around my waist like a pole dancer, giving me all the access I need. I slap her thigh to raise her dress, slipping my fingers under it, pinching her nipple through the thin fabric. My other hand dips inside her thong, sliding between her thighs, making sure she's dripping wet and moaning before I pull away, leaving her gasping.

She needs a reminder of who's in control and her words mean nothing.

"Blade, come back. I want," she begs, voice desperate trailing off as I step out of the condo, leaving her screaming my name.

On my way to my truck, I realize something. Her ass is no longer a necessity. And I know why. The "something" is Cassey. Fucking Cass. She's been an unstoppable force grinding through my mind, haunting my nights. *How can anyone taste that sweet?*

My contact in the registrar's office still hasn't turned up anyone named Cassidy, Cass or Cassey at the school. But there's a short list of students with restricted records due to family confidentiality. I've been on campus so much this week that my old coach joked about me trying out for A&M's soccer team again.

I have to figure this out by tomorrow since I'm out of town for the next two weeks. Seeing her may not be enough. But, getting lost between those thighs will be my enough.

The slam of my truck door, and sound of gum popping pulls me to the present. Sarah sits there, her perfume lingering, legs parted enough to suggest what she wants.

"Where did you go? You were in a zone when I got in," she leans in, her pointed nails scraping my arm. "You okay?"

I stare at her confusion, not saying a word. Those blue eyes know nothing about that zone but my bed sheets do. Without answering, I dig into the glove compartment, grabbing wipes to scrub Sarah's scent off my hands.

We're early at the gala, only a handful of guests wandering through my alma mater's hall. Back in the day, A&M was the first school that gave me real attention with a soccer scholarship. A kid my size, from the wrong side of town, wasn't the usual soccer type. Our high school barely had a soccer coach. He doubled as the basketball coach, part-time football coach, athletic director and even drove the team bus. He probably mopped floors when the janitors didn't show up.

Starting at A&M, my soccer skills were basic at best. According to Coach, speed and mental toughness were all that got me there. Most of the players were here on student visas, unable to make their home country teams. I was the only stateside scholarship my freshman year, and that made me push harder.

I hated seeing those scholarships not going to kids who grew up like me. Determined to prove I *deserved* mine, I made the soccer field home, practicing until I hit a hundred shots each day. I worked so hard my toes would bleed every night. In the end, Coach Smith noticed the broke kid from the south who wouldn't quit and started working with me one-on-one. By my sophomore year, I knew this was my future. I fell in hard with the escape the kick gave me.

By my junior year, I studied other players, figuring out their weaknesses, playing both defense and offense, training my vision until I could read the field from every angle. Around the end of my junior year, professional teams began paying attention, but all the offers came from overseas.

My first big break was with the Reds Liverpool Football Club in England. I left my senior year with a promise to Miss Blade that I'd finish my degree. I played there for four years, returning home for a month during the off season and Christmas.

Being away so young was rough. Adapting to a new culture, figuring out foreign directions, adjusting to different foods, and learning to drive on the opposite side of the road were all hard for me. I hated it at times and missed my folks back home. That home sickness taught me one thing: family is more important than any dime.

My agent knew I wanted to be with the US team. I absorbed every technique I learned in Europe clubs and combined them with everything I knew from home, shaping myself into a complete player. My passing, ability to make split second decisions and on field vision set me apart. I played every style I could, to get attention to get home.

When the opportunity hit, the US League took notice, offering me a contract I couldn't refuse. I returned to the states a season ago to play with the US team.

My fame was instant, catching both my folks and me by surprise. Without Tron, it's me, Miss Blade, Aunt Diane, Uncle Joe and their daughters now. The man called my father left years ago, never looking back.

Adjusting to the spotlight hasn't been easy, especially after growing up surrounded by silence. I'm used to the quiet of nothing. But, thanks to my endorsements, most people recognize me wherever I go. Soccer might not be the biggest sport in the States, but my name and face, tied to the deals, have gained me recognition.

Scanning Kellogg Hall at A&M, I see nothing but money in the expensive decorations, flowers and servers. I hope they're using the donations right. Throwing funds at entertainment to impress the *who's who* is not my style. The mayor, a handful of top tier athletes, and other wealthy alumni with deep pockets, are mingling, enjoying the festivities and drinks while eyeing the women.

This lifestyle was new for me when I came into money. I didn't even have a suit growing up so having a closet full is still different. When we went to church, it was always in hand-me-down old clothes. Sarah was born into this world and knows how to play the game. Her family loves the spotlight, and she plays her role.

I'm already looking for the exit. Crowds don't bother me. No doubt, I can handle any room. But I hate the fakeness that comes with these events. I make my way to speak with a few retired and current players in attendance, while Sarah takes center stage, attempting to take the crowd with her presence. I guess the gala can officially begin now that she's here to work the room.

Finding a quiet corner away from autograph-seekers and starstruck fans, I scope out the scene. I don't mind autographs for kids, but the women, especially married ones, come with jealous husbands. Trust me, if I wanted wives, they'd be mine.

My gaze drifts toward the jazz band, then up the black circular staircase leading to the bar area. My attention lands on the most enticing, muscular legs ascending step by step, each movement synchronized with the bass guitar's rhythm. These aren't just any legs; they're the kind that make you want to leave heels on and spread wide. *Is she walking in slow motion?* I lean in to get a better look, but a taller gentleman blocks my view. Damn. Whoever she is, that's the kind of wife I'd take for the night from a jealous ass husband, no regrets.

"Women are definitely in the building tonight," Christian says. He appears at my side, scanning the crowd like a predator ready to attack.

"Yes, they are," I agree, trying one last time to catch another glimpse of those legs on the stairs, but she's gone now.

"I see Sarah's working the room," Christian nods toward her. We watch as she hugs a past NFL linebacker with a full-frontal embrace drawing attention. She's probably trying to arouse the poor man enough to leave him begging.

"This shit ends tonight."

Christian chuckles. "Good luck with that. It'll take a bulldozer to pry those claws off."

Sarah makes eye contact and signals me to come over. "You're being summoned," Christian says, amused.

I nod, accepting my fate for the moment.

Dapping Christian up, I ask, "Where you sitting?"

"Upstairs," he replies. "Can't afford the big baller seats like yourself in the front. I'll see you tomorrow."

"Alright, bet," Christian says.

"For sho'," I add, leaving me to deal with Sarah.

As she approaches, she loops her arms through mine, pressing her curves against my side. "What are you doing?" I ask.

"Claiming what belongs to me," she says, batting her long lashes, her voice dripping with more than just want.

"This is over." My voice is quiet but firm, always aware of the ears trying to catch a story.

She tightens her grip on my arm. "I understand, sweetie, but I still want you. I need you inside me. Let's go to the restroom and finish what you started at my apartment."

"No. We need to find our seats. After that I'm taking you home."

"Please do. My inner thigh is dripping." Her words do nothing to turn me on. I ignore her.

A waiter in a crisp tuxedo shirt and a full-length black apron leads us to the stage area. The centerpieces on the tables are draped with flowers taller than Sarah. As we approach our table, I notice we're seated with the top elites, as Christian mentioned. I paid a thousand dollars per seat. My accountant said it's a write off since the proceeds go toward scholarships for A&M. That's the only reason I'm here.

As we near the table, I spot John Pittman, the founder and owner of Pittman Enterprises, one of the top movie production companies, known for blockbuster hits grossing millions. *How the hell did I get this seat?* He stands as we approach.

"Kylo Blade, my man, please have a seat." Mr. Pittman pauses mid-sentence as his gaze drifts to Sarah. "Oh, and your lovely guest," he adds.

Before I can get a word in, Sarah steps forward, sliding into Mr. Pittman's arms. "Mr. Pittman. Sarah Sims," she announces. "The actress looking for a leading role in one of your upcoming block-buster films. Plus, I believe you know my dad."

Her third person introduction with that irritating voice makes me clench my jaw. She's overplaying her hand. I see it in her non-stop rambling. She's hiding something, pushing too hard. I should've left her ass at home.

"Is that right?" Mr. Pittman arches an eyebrow, a smile playing on his lips.

"Please excuse her, Mr. Pittman. She tends to sell herself wherever she goes." Pittman's eyes linger on Sarah's lace covered curves before shifting back to me. Even at his age, he still has that dog in him.

"Let's take our seats," he says, steering the conversation. "You two are seated next to my daughter. Here she is now," he says, looking over my shoulder.

I turn, curious, and there she is, the same white dress, those unforgettable legs ascending the circular staircase. She's descending the last few steps, hand lightly on the rail, her straight hair flowing over her chest, partially hiding her face. I can sense every man within sight watching her, and I don't have to look away to confirm it.

As she lifts her head her hair shifts aside, exposing the most exotic, striking canvas I've ever seen, staring straight at me.

Damn, it's Cassey.

CHAPTER 13

RED LIPSTICK ON A HEART

Kylo

THE SILENCE STRETCHES AS HER PRESENCE INVADES ME, A force I can't seem to understand. Her straight hair rests on her chest, a few strands slipping into her cleavage. The soft hue of her skin, at the tips of her breasts has my mouth moist. Her strapless white dress hugs every hourglass curve perfectly, making it seem almost wrong to let her wear it in public. Her makeup is natural because too much would take away from her essence. She doesn't need it, but the red lipstick on those heart-shaped lips, parted just enough to show a slight gap, makes me want to inhale her and suck her dry.

Those legs, disappearing into that white dress, land into Tom Ford sandals. Each step accentuating her sexy ankle encircling the signature gold padlock, unlocking something I can't name. I could drop to my knees to unlock whatever secrets she holds. *Did I think key to my heart?* I can't tear my eyes away from her, but the anger rising beneath the surface at everyone else's gaze is boiling. *What is that?* This girl, this woman, is beyond stunning, leaving me thirsty for words I don't have.

Everyone else fades, lost in her pull. As if on cue, the jazz band stops playing, stretching the hush even longer until an irritating voice cuts through my veins. "Hi, I'm Kylo's girlfriend, Sarah."

Cassey nods, pressing her red lips together, then recovers with a slight smile. Is that concern on her face? Her recovery is too quick… damn, quicker than I'd hoped.

"Please, forgive my boyfriend," Sarah interjects, her fingers brushing my tux, sparking anger beneath my collar. "He's acting so strange this evening. Are you getting sick, honey?"

"I'm good," I reply, keeping my focus fixed on Cassey's lips as I extend my hand. "Cassey, is it?" I ask, intentionally using Brooklyn's nickname, testing her reaction.

She meets my gaze, sizing me with an intensity that's not hers. There's a hint of arrogance or confidence I didn't expect.

"Nice to meet you," she says, her dark, seductive eyes twinkling with mischief as she emphasizes "*you*" ignoring Sarah. I wasn't expecting that reaction, but it does something to me. *Turns me on and heightens my attraction.*

"Everyone, please take your seats," she requests, leaving my hand hanging in midair, taking control of our awkward introduction.

Mr. Pittman and I both assist Cassey, as I let Sarah pull out her own chair. She knows she's not my girlfriend. Why did she say that shit, anyway? Her ass is taking an Uber home for sho'.

Mr. Pittman introduces the entire table since he's familiar with all the guests. During the first, second, and third course, his conversation revolves around soccer. How in the hell does he know so much about the game?

I keep glancing in Cassey's direction since she's between Mr. Pittman and me, and it's driving me insane. The sight of her skin against that white dress is a distraction not on tonight's menu. I try avoiding her out of respect for Mr. Pittman, but she's making it hard to think straight.

My mind begins to wonder. How old is she? She looks young. At twenty-six, there's no way Pittman would approve if she's eighteen. That would make me nearly eight years older, almost enough to make me feel like a creeper. *Damn.*

I use my napkin to wipe the perspiration from my forehead, even though the air isn't warm. My body temp is out the roof. It feels hot as hell. Her closeness is taking me out, and the bulge between my legs isn't helping me concentrate.

Finally, the program begins with the introduction of A&M's president. Hopefully, Mr. Pittman will shut up so I can stop getting distracted by Cassey. Something about what happened in my truck feels off. This girl is practically royalty, and I crossed that line with her in a strip mall parking lot. I'm starting to feel guilty about how I treated her in the locker room, too. She's silent, her luscious lips not letting out a single word to me or anyone at the table.

Mr. Pittman leans over, clasping Cassey's hands. *I recognize those hands and so does my hair.* Damn, I miss them. She knew my spot without being told. "Are you okay, my love?" he asks, softly.

She searches into her dad's firm gaze, maybe for understanding before answering, "Yes. A little tired."

"Blade," Mr. Pittman calls my name while still holding the hand that belongs in my hair. *What is wrong with me?*

Here we go again with the talking. "Yes, Mr. Pittman?"

"My daughter is an athlete. She had D-1 track scholarships waiting for her three years ago, but she turned them down. Everyone wanted her, but she ended up at A&M this past fall," he explains.

I notice a shift in his mood. Cassey looks up at her dad, reaching to gently cup his chin. "I would not have it any other way," she says, sincerity clear in her voice. Something I've never noticed in a woman before.

He leans into his daughter's hands, a tender smile on his face. "I know baby girl." Mr. Pittman is no doubt wrapped around his daughter's little finger. I get it. *I'm there with him.*

I glance at my program, uninterested in the gala, and remove Sarah's hand from my thigh. She knows not to say a word at this point until she is spoken to.

My mind zeros in on one thing: her age. Mr. Pittman said she took a three-year gap before starting at A&M. That means she has to be at least twenty-one or twenty-two.

The gala moderator calls Mr. Pittman to the stage for a special award. I glance at my program; he's receiving the Philanthropist of the Year award. As he makes his way up, he leans in to kiss her cheek. She stands, hugging him and wiping the corner of his eye. When she sits back down, I notice a tear rolling down her high cheekbones, her fingers holding a charm on her bracelet. *A purple and gold butterfly?*

If I could carry her out of this place and protect her from whatever pain that tear is about, I would. I need to talk to her. I have to explain this nonstop chatterbox sitting next to me.

The award is in memory of Cassey's mother, who passed away a couple of years ago. She was an A&M alumna who provided fifteen scholarships annually to underprivileged kids, over 400 kids impacted. Now Mr. Pittman continues those donations under his wife's foundation.

Damn, I am an ass and now understand what she meant by her "reality" in my truck.

I glance at Cassey as Mr. Pittman accepts the award, her tears soaking her pretty skin. Reaching into my tux jacket pocket, I offer her my handkerchief. She takes it, without looking at me or saying thank you, wiping away the pain while admiring her dad.

I feel her slipping from my reach. I've got to explain things… soon. As her dad approaches the table, Cassey stands and excuses herself.

Fuck it, I can't stay seated. I stand and follow her.

"Blade, where are you going?" Sarah asks, pleading for something that's never going to happen.

I stare at her briefly, wondering how to make her vanish into thin air. "I need to get something," I say, watching her sink back into her chair. She knows better than to come after me.

CHAPTER 14

NO AIR LEFT

Cassidy

THE WALLS SEEM TO CLOSE IN AROUND ME, SQUEEZING MY chest until my air passage shrinks to the size of a needle's eye. I need fresh cold air and fast. I rush toward the stairs leading to the infamous Grove Raith mentioned a few days ago. She's been here a couple of times, and I can only hope no one else is caught up there in the moment. Taking the third flight of concrete steps two at a time, I refuse to let my four-inch stilettos slow me down. I burst through the top door, relieved to find it unlocked.

Fresh, cool air hits my face, and I gasp trying to take a deep breath, but the panic hits full force. It tightens my chest, refusing to let it expand fully. I spread my arms wide, desperate to draw in more air as my body starts to overheat from the inside out.

It's not working. I need relief... something cold. *Calm down,* I tell myself, trying to regain control. But what's that noise? Are those my heels clicking or my heartbeat pounding in my ears? Am I moving too fast? I'm losing it. The only thing that will help is a sub-zero chill to cool my pouring sweat. I need something cold.

I can't breathe. My thoughts spiral as I drop to my knees on the cool concrete, desperate to calm my mind and stay ahead of my nerves. "Please let this be quick," I pray quietly. "Please…"

Then, I hear the door open behind me. I glance over my shoulder, half hoping to see Dad. I need him, but I don't want him to worry.

My vision blurs as strong arms lift my shoulders. I recognize that sweet woodsy scent, and undeniable sense of strength. I know exactly who it is, but I can't pull away. I'm too weak and struggling to breathe, almost fainting from the panic attack.

"Focus on my chest," Kylo says softly. "Feel the rise and fall of my breathing, and let your body do the same. I've got you. Just match my rhythm."

I want to tear myself away, rip his arm off for invading my space, but I'm too weak, too desperate for relief to fight him off. Instead, I sink back into him, focusing on the steady rise and fall of his hard chest against my back. His deep inhales and exhales send warm currents of air along my neck, stirring my hair with each breath.

"Breathe, beautiful," he murmurs, tightening his hold. Moving my arms is impossible. "Focus on my chest, I've got you."

Slowly, more air seeps into my lungs. This is working. He rests his hands gently on my stomach, and I lean forward, feeling his hot breath flow between my dress and back, soothing and grounding me.

"You're inhaling. I feel you," he whispers, voice full of encouragement. "Keep going, one breath at a time."

Gradually, my heartbeat slows to a normal rhythm and my breathing evens out. The crushing pressure in my chest eases. How does he know how to do this so well? I feel better, transitioning from panic attack temperature to my broken thermometer heat.

My senses return fully, and that's when I notice it, his erection pressing hard against me. A flush of heat that has nothing to do with panic courses through my body. Hesitantly, I turn, meeting his warm, honey hazels, and carefully pulling away from his bulge. He doesn't try to stop me.

"Thank you," I say softly, my voice trembling slightly. "Thank you for helping me."

"You're welcome," he replies, eyes steady on mine as though he's trying to unravel some secret. He reaches to tuck my hair behind my ear, his thumb brushing sweat from my forehead.

Self-conscious, I pull my hair back. "I must look awful."

He frowns, confusion taking over his features. "That's impossible," he whispers, sincerity running through his voice.

I swallow. "How did you learn that…that technique?" I ask, genuinely curious.

"Christian's sister used to have panic attacks," he explains. "We'd be at dinner, and she would have one. Christian always did this for her because he knew how scared she was. This was my first time trying it with anyone. When I saw you bent over, it damn near scared me to death, but I could tell something was off. Didn't know if it was going to work. But I had to try."

He lifts my chin, making me look at him. "Are you okay?"

His concern almost feels believable. Almost.

"Yes, I'm okay," I say, my voice quieter. "I haven't had one in three years." It came out of nowhere this time.

I glance at my manicure and the charm on my bracelet, wondering if I should join Raith more often for a mani and pedi. They look nice. Without another word, I turn toward the exit. There's no point staying here any longer.

My heels click loudly on the concrete as I walk away, making me question whether I need new ones. Suddenly, I feel him behind me. His strong hands wrap around my wrist, covering my bracelet, not letting go. I stare at his hand, careful not to meet his gaze, knowing exactly what will happen if I do.

"I appreciate the help," I say, my voice firm, "but you should get back to your person at the table. Do not ever touch me or make any contact with me again. Understand?" I yank my wrist from his hold, not waiting for an answer, and turn to leave.

He steps in front of the Grove's door, blocking my exit. Shock is written all over his face. *He didn't expect this reaction.* "Move, my dad maybe worried," I say, watching him step aside, bewildered. I refuse to be anyone's second choice. That will never happen.

He reaches for the door handle again, blocking my way out. "Wait… Give me a chance to explain. You have to get this."

"Get what?" I ask, keeping my voice low but tense. "That you had oral sex with me in your truck as a little side piece while your girl waited at home. My dad's probably looking for me. Move!" His hands fall from the door handle, confusion taking over. Maybe no woman has ever screamed at him before.

He raises both hands in the air, as if surrendering. "She's not my girl. This shit is only for PR…"

I place my index finger over his lips, to silence him, immediately regretting the contact with their softness. "Stop. This isn't my business. You don't owe me an explanation. We had a moment in your truck. Honestly, I never expected to see you again," I lie, trying to maintain control.

He takes my hand from his lips and presses it against his chest. *Why did he do that?* "Was it just a moment for you?" The overhead light reflects the golden sparks in his eyes, penetrating my soul. How does he pull me in so easily? *How?*

Without giving me a chance to respond, he closes the distance, invading my personal space, his aura telling me what he wants. "It wasn't just a moment for me. I've thought about what happened in the truck since that day. I looked for you on campus. I even had one of Christian's friends try to find you, since I didn't know your last name. I've been on campus so much that the soccer coach wants me back on his team," he pauses, as if weighing his next words. "I can't get you out of my mind. Sarah is not my girl. Tonight is a business arrangement. That's it."

I glance at his hand holding mine against his chest. "Why me,

Kylo? You've been rude, arrogant and now this. Am I supposed to ignore it all? To just forget everything that's happened?"

He seems uncertain, caught off guard by my question. "Forget some things but remember this."

He leans in, his lips brushing softly against mine with a tender urgency, as if asking silently for permission to get closer. His kiss is gentle, his mouth parting mine with a quiet longing, seeking forgiveness. His hands drift to my hips, pulling me nearer, his touch both careful and commanding.

My mind screams for logic, telling me to push him away, but with him so close, my brain refuses to listen. I place my hands on his chest, intending to create distance, yet his arms remain motionless. *Move hands… please…*my thoughts beg, but my body fails to obey.

CHAPTER 15

WHAT Y'ALL DOING?

Cassidy

INSTEAD, MY HANDS LOOP AROUND HIS NECK, FINGERS TAN-gling loosely in his hair, as I open my mouth, letting his tongue explore every corner of me. A hint of insecurity lingers, but I dive into the kiss just as hard as his lips claim mine. *Why?* The taste of him, the sensation of his tongue exploring, sends desire shooting through my body as the kiss deepens. A soft moan escapes him, as his hands caress me.

Without breaking our kiss, he lifts me, guiding me to the side of the building where a dim, flickering lamp casts just enough light. He presses me against him, never breaking the kiss, removing his jacket and placing it on a narrow ledge behind me. Now we're face-to-face, my body aligned with his tall frame.

"This white dress will never get dirty," he murmurs, his voice low. "I have plans for it… plans that involve tasting every part of you, inside and out."

His intense gaze forces me to look away. "Why would you say that?" I ask, barely a whisper.

"That's my plan," he replies, igniting something unknown. I

can't stop myself with this man. Feeling a surge of more confidence, I lean in, pulling him closer.

He sucks on my bottom lip, then trails his warm tongue near my neck, biting gently at first, then harder, testing my tolerance. The sensation is intoxicating and better than any runners high. His hands finds the zipper of my dress and I tense. He notices.

"Can I see you?" he whispers, eyes flicking downward. "It's been a distraction all evening."

His gaze sears into my chest, revealing what he wants to see.

"Stop with the frown lines," he murmurs softly, brushing a finger along my jaw. "You're thinking too hard. No one's up here. Let me…" His eyes drift down again, urging my dress with his stare. "Can I?"

I nod, unable to deny him. He unzips my dress, leaving my strapless, lacy, white bra on as the fabric drapes around my waist.

All of my insecurities resurface as I watch him take me in. "Damn," he whispers, his eyes filled with confusion and awe. "How can you be this beautiful?"

I try lowering my head again, but he holds me steady. This type of attention is new to me. No one has ever looked at me this way before.

He forms a gentle v beneath my chin, lifting it higher. "Don't ever shy away," he murmurs. "You're stunning, inside and out. You have no reason to ever lower your head."

His fingers leave my chin, gliding down the center of my chest until they reach the delicate lace of my bra. With ease, he unhooks it, and the cool night air grazes my now-exposed breasts. I shiver, his words and the temperature both sending chills through me.

"Damn you are intoxicating. Come here." His voice is low and charged. The night air and his words give me my zero chill, igniting a deeper desire for whatever he's offering. He runs his long fingers between the center of my cleavage, without touching my sensitive peaks, making lazy circles with his fingertip until he reaches my nipple. My grip on the window sill tightens; I want him, I need him. When he pinches my nipples gently, pleasure radiates through me, forcing a gasp to break from my lips. *Breathe Cassidy,* I remind myself.

"Most women pay for these, but you're natural," he says, twisting my peaks, making me lean into the roughness of his fingers, giving me a pleasure I've never experienced before. The sensation is mind blowing and the moans escaping me sound foreign.

"I need," I start, but the words fail me once again. Embarrassment has given way to a deep longing I can't even understand. I'm unsure what I want, but I think he knows… as his wet lips close over my nipple a surge of desire arches my back into him.

"This feels so good. Please don't ever stop," I beg, pressing my breast deeper into his warm wet mouth, a silent plea for attention I crave.

His lips move to my other breast, teasing my nipple with a rhythm that sends trembles of pleasure racing through me, making it harden more into a sensitive peak. My legs curl around his waist, pulling him closer as he lavishes both my breasts with hot attention, transforming them into hardened peaks of painful desire. Each pull and suck of his mouth ignites a burning hunger within, pushing me closer to the edge.

"Ahhhhh!" The surprise hits me as his teeth sink in, biting, radiating a burning heat. It feels as though my skin has been singed, leaving an angry mark that pulses with an insistent throb. I want his teeth to dig into until it satisfies the ache that's begging for attention. *What is wrong… with me?*

"Do it again," I whisper. "With your teeth!"

He looks at me in awe as his body radiates with something I can't identify. "You're a bad girl my sweet, Cass," he says, lifting my arms above my head. My hands rest on the cold window behind me, giving him complete access to my breasts. His curly hair consuming my view is all I see as he leans into me, licking my nipples, one long tongue stroke at a time, sucking and biting as if I'm the ice cream from the truck. The sensations are too much, pushing me to the edge. He presses my wrists against the grimy window, his fingers twisting around mine with a possessive grip, holding me captive in our moment. His other hand slips beneath the fabric up my dress, igniting a fire of anticipation that races through me. "I need another taste of you, sexy," he murmurs, his voice low and husky.

With a deft motion, he uses his hips to push my legs wide apart, creating an intoxicating sense of vulnerability. His hand slides between my thighs, his fingers teasingly creeping higher. Each caress sends a wave of desire through me, urging me to open more.

He stops everything, and I know why. "Open your eyes, Cass." I do, meeting his gaze. It's a blend of unspoken hunger and something else, like he wants to punish and devour me at the same time.

Raith dared me to go commando this evening, claiming I was too matronly to handle the "nice cool breeze" without a thong. I never would have considered it on my own, but now I'm glad I did, judging by the need simmering hunger in Kylo's honey hazels as he whispers, "No thong?"

Before I can even answer, my dress becomes a ring of fabric around my waist, exposing me to the cool air as his fingers explore my wetness. He circles my most sensitive spot, alternating between sucking and biting my breasts. The urgency takes me into a realm I've never known, faster and faster, he rubs his fingers, each movement stripping away any control I thought I had.

"I need this around me. You're so wet it's running down your thighs. Damn!" he growls, his voice thick with desire.

"Don't stop," I plead, the sensations striping away any control I had left. Clinging to his neck for dear life, I refuse to let him move an inch. The sensation builds at a dizzying pace, inside and out, until a raw, embarrassing scream escapes my lips. It's too much. I'm cumming so hard, the force sends tremors throughout my entire body. I collapse against his chest, unable to think or calm my breathing as my body shatters into a foreign place.

Resting on his shoulder, I struggle to catch my breath, my mind drifting into a blissful fog. I hope this is not why my mom loved the word bliss. That was… I can't quite find the words as I get lost into his broad, firm and protective chest. *I feel safe.* He gradually removes his hand from between my thighs, then brings his fingers to his sexy lips, sucking them clean. His eyes roll back as he savors my taste. "You smell so damn good," he whispers, voice low and satisfied.

"I can't believe you did that," I manage to say, still breathless.

"What part?" he asks.

"Sucking… your fingers with my…with me…with," I trail off, unable to form the words, still lost in the shock and pleasure of what just happened.

He presses his finger on my lips, silencing my stuttering. "Believe it. I plan to savor every inch of you." He leans in, licking both my nipples again, reigniting everything inside me. I pull him closer, craving more.

"Zipping this dress is not what I want," he murmurs. "But I need to get you back." His voice is low, conflicted. He's telling me what we both know, we can't stay hidden up here all night.

"What do you want, Kylo?" I ask, though his dazed eyes already hint at the answer.

"To run my tongue up those beautiful thighs, and let your wetness drip onto my face." His words hit me in a place already aching.

"Do whatever you want," I whisper, making sure he hears every word.

He steps back, resting his chin on his hand, eyes fixed on my breasts. "Cassey, we need to get you back. Pittman no doubt has a search team out for you by now."

He uses Brooklyn's nick name for me, likely to get my attention, but it has the opposite effect. There's one thing on my mind, and it's not my dad. "Do it," I demand, leaving no room for refusal. For the first time in a long time, I know exactly what I want.

He wastes no second, crushing his lips against mine with a force that steals my breath. In an heartbeat, I'm off the window sill, my back pressed against his solid chest. His rough hands exploring my breasts, fueled by a desperate hunger. I melt into him as he sweeps my hair aside, trailing hot kisses along my neck. "Hold the wall, Cass," he commands, his voice thick with lust.

"You need to go back but I can't stop," he says, his fingers trailing up my thigh, zeroing in on my wetness. "Damn, your ass is so fine."

I brace myself against the wall, heart hammering in my chest racing as his fingers slip inside, teasing me and driving me higher. "Don't stop, Kylo!" I cry out, each thrust of his finger sending pleasure crashing over me. I grind against him desperate for more, lost in sensation.

"Why are you so tight?" he whispers, more statement than question, and I understand the reason. But I don't care. I just need him. He leans closer, both hands working between my thighs, teasing and fingering my slickness, igniting a desire that makes me want to climb up his body, to get even closer to him, if that's even possible. The sound of my arousal fills the air, wet and urgent.

"You're so damn wet," he says, voice raged, as I hear the unmistakable sound of his zipper coming down, heightening my anticipation.

"Cassidy!"

Wait, am I hearing things? Did someone call my name? *Please let me be imagining this.*

"Cassidy!"

It's Raith, of all people, and Kylo's hands slip away.

He curses under his breath. "Who the fuck is that? Raith?"

I nod, yelling, "Raith is that you?"

"Yes!" she shouts back. "Where you at?"

"Just…hold on," I say, struggling to slow my mind and find my bra, all while feeling the guilt creeping up my spine from the truck.

Raith's timing couldn't be worse. Or maybe she just saved me from further embarrassment. My hands are shaking so badly that hooking my bra clasps feels impossible. I want this man more than anything, but reality slams into me and I remember who's waiting for him downstairs.

"Raith, give me a moment. I'm coming."

"Let me help," he mutters, snapping my bra into place. Then, almost under his breath, he adds. "I wish you were… cumming. This keeps happening." Frustration hangs thick as he plants a kiss on my forehead before turning me around to zip my dress. Flipping a bit of fabric inside, he looks as if searching for something, then squeezes the bridge of his nose, struggling to steady his breathing. Once I'm presentable, he re-buttons his shirt, hiding those muscles from my view.

"I wanted to stop you earlier," I manage, voice unsteady, "but I didn't have the willpower. Kylo, I'm not a side piece."

"No, you're not," he replies, lifting my fingers to his lips again, gently sucking their tips. It feels so good, but I force myself to focus.

"I will not be that woman," I say firmly. "Call her and end it."

He removes my hand apparently caught off guard with my request. "What did you say?" he asks.

"If you want anything…anything to do with me," I repeat, "you'll take out your phone, call the lady in red and make sure she knows it's over."

He holds my hand to his chest, studying me as if he's seeing me for the first time. "You're different," he says, but pulls out his phone.

"Cassidy!" Raith shouts again, her voice echoing from the exit door. How did I forget her that quick?

"I'm over here!" I scream, pretending to flatten the frizz in my hair and straighten my clothes, but seriously eavesdropping on the conversation.

"Sarah," he says into his phone, pausing. "It's over. No more PR arrangements. Christian or an Uber can take you home," he waits a moment, holding the phone away from his ear, allowing me to hear her irritating screams. How can anyone deal with her nail scratching chalkboard voice? Sitting at the table with her for an hour was more than enough.

He hangs up, turning that intense gaze on me. "She said I couldn't keep my eyes off you," he mutters, attention drifting to my chest. I knew he was watching. I could almost hear it. It was so deafening that it turned me on. I hate to admit it, but it made me want him even with Sarah hanging on to his last breath.

"Cassidy!" Raith's voice brings me back. "General Pittman is about to call security and maybe the FBI if you don't show up soon and I mean really soon," she calls, then notices Kylo. "Ohhhhh, I see why you are out here. Can't say that I blame you. What y'all doing?" Raith asks, mimicking Tiffany Haddish. They have to be related because she has the expression and neck rolling thing perfect.

Shyness flushes through me, leaving me slow to respond. "I just needed some fresh air," I say, leaving out the panic attack that led us here.

Raith waves a dismissive hand. "Look roomie, there's no time for an explanation. We gotta get you back downstairs, like, now."

"Okay," I manage, not wanting to leave as Kylo pulls me closer.

"Cass, give me your number. I'm not losing you again. Are y'all headed back to the dorm?" he asks, pulling out his phone.

"Yes, my dad's taking us back," I say softly.

His arms tighten around my waist before he releases me to add my number into his phone. "I'll come through at eleven. You good with that?"

"Yes," I reply too quickly. *Calm down.*

"Cassidy we've gotta go before Lieutenant Pittman busts through these doors. Trust me you don't want that," Raith warns, eyes fixed on my neck. "Damn Blade, what did you do to her?"

Confused, I follow her gaze. "What is it?"

"You have hickies everywhere." Heat crawls up my chest, realizing she'll want a replay later. I glance down at the top of my dress, spotting red bright bruises and bite marks forming around my chest.

Kylo's fingertips gently touch my neck, his expression shifts from surprise to concern. "Damn. My control is just off with you.

Does it hurt?" he asks, voice a mix of shock and worry as he inspects the marks on my neck and shoulders.

"Wait a minute. Did you say control?" Raith asks, eyeing Kylo like he's a buffet at Golden Corral. One of her favorite buffet spots.

I ignore her. She makes every situation crazier. "No, it doesn't hurt."

"Look, Cassidy wrap my sarong around you. That'll cover you up. Plus, I can show this booty off to Mr. Pittman." She's changed his title from General to Lieutenant to Mr. Pittman in ten seconds and is now offering her booty for display.

Kylo laughs. "You're on some crazy shit, for real."

"Exactly," I add, slipping Raith's sarong over my shoulders. Kylo's eyes drift down my body, freezing me in place. He stops where his fingers brought me to an orgasm moments earlier, paralyzing me to the floor. I couldn't move if I wanted to.

"We gotta go!" Raith urges, but we both ignore her.

"There's something different about you," he says, voice low and intent. "Be ready at eleven o'clock."

I nod, agreeing with whatever he's saying since I've lost the ability to form coherent words. He tugs me closer for a soft kiss, whispering against my lips, "See you at eleven. This is…" he trails off, locking eyes with me before turning toward the door.

CHAPTER 16

RUNNING TO REAGAN

Kylo

STEPPING BACK INSIDE THE NOW EMPTY GALA, I SEE IT'S over. A cleaning crew passes me with tired expressions, hating their jobs clattering plates loud enough to be mistaken for broken glass. I pass the waiters, hoping to go unnoticed. I'm not in the mood for small talk. As I approach the foyer, I spot a familiar group near our old table. Damn, Pittman's surrounded by a crowd of security. He stands with his arms crossed, exuding an air of calm, but I'd bet money he's looking for Cass.

"Kylo!"

That irritating voice makes me grit my teeth. Damn, I thought she was gone.

"I am not leaving this gala without you. We came here together, and you're taking me home. Trust me, a scene is the last thing you want or need. Take me home, Kylo."

Over Sarah's shoulder, I check Cass and Raith returning to talk with Mr. Pittman. Damn, that white dress is fucking everything on her. She locks eyes with me, silently urging me to leave Sarah standing here to catch that Uber. She's probably worried I'll end up at Sarah's for the night. Sarah's red dress makes her intentions clear, but I'm only interested in one thing now, and it's wearing white and probably wet.

Sarah follows my gaze. "That girl is practically royalty," she spits, "and more than likely a damn virgin. She won't understand your lifestyle…our lifestyle."

I walk away. She knows not to talk to me that way.

"Kylo!" she screams, her voice echoing too damn loud in this empty space. Has she lost her mind?

As I reach the gala doors, I feel the weight of curious eyes on us. "Stay the fuck away from me. We're done," I growl back, daring her to follow, not giving a damn how she gets home.

"You'll never get away from me, Kylo. Never!" she shrieks.

She's crazier than I thought.

I run to my truck, not from Sarah but to get back to Cass. I have to sort this out. Whatever is happening between us is different. I've never followed, engaged or even asked a woman anything. Do we talk? The thought of talking is foreign, but there's something pulling that I can't escape. I need to know more about her. Maybe calling would be safer, because every time we're near each other, I want to rip her clothes off to satisfy this insane thirst. I can't control it.

Exiting the gala, a flickering streetlight catches my eye, barely illuminating the parking lot and reflecting off my truck in bursts. Hundreds of bugs swarm around the dying light, the other lamp remains dark. *A&M should use the funds from tonight's gala to repair lights instead of blowing it on food.* It's too dark out here for anyone to wander alone.

I slow down… something feels wrong. Did I see someone move? The light dims and brightens again as I approach my truck, revealing a figure edging closer. Someone's there.

"Hey Blade!" a deep voice calls out, catching me off guard. A dude's face fades in and out beneath the failing light.

I stand still, tension building. "What's up?"

"How does Cassidy taste?" the figure hisses.

"What did you say, motherfucker?" His words are clear, but the anger building inside me makes it hard to stay calm. I round the front of the truck as he backs away. "Speak up, I don't think I heard you," I snarl.

"Oh, you'll hear me… and so will she." He bolts between the cars before I can reach him. His timing is perfect as the lights dim, leaving me in the dark, unable to chase his ass.

Who the hell was that, and how does he know Cass? Damn! No chance to grab him or get a good look at him in that damn hoodie. Fuck! *How does she taste?* Why would he ask that shit? What would he know about her? Rage explodes and I'm past the point of pissed. I want to lay hands on him for even mentioning her. I need to find him. Now. *Fuck!*

Headlights from a black SUV swing my attention back to the Kellogg Center's entrance. Cass appears with her dad and Raith, stepping into the safety of waiting security. *How is she that beautiful?* I watch them carefully, making sure she gets in the SUV without incident. One of the guards touches her back to guide her inside and I get pissed. *Get your fucking hands off her.* The door slams, and the Tahoe pulls away, speeding off. She's safe at least for now.

The urge to make sure she's straight takes over. *Why?* But something else is happening. Watching her get in that truck calms me in a way I can't explain. *How did that even happen?*

I reach my hotel, one I booked away from home, with nothing on my mind but the word. Taste. Who the hell was he, and why am I this protective already?

Maybe it started at the park…or even in the ice. The way she was with Brooklyn, that smile, those thighs and what we did tonight. I can't risk being alone with her in public again. Not because I don't want it, but because we'd go viral, quick.

But that damn white dress.

How can anyone make a dress look that good? Those curves hit every spot. I know she felt me during her panic attack earlier, being an *ass*. She was hardly breathing, and I was acting like a straight fifteen-year-old virgin. The thought of her without a thong has me rock hard. Why did she do that? She maybe a...nah, too early to tell. When I bit her neck, she wanted more. It had me sucking with the hunger of a damn vampire seeking blood, digging my teeth into her soft flesh, with an intensity that still has questions lingering. I couldn't stop and knew marks were going to be there. But I wanted them on her as proof that she's mine. No doubt she will be.

I lift my fingers, inhaling her scent on my skin, hoping she's not one of those who graduated from high school at the age of sixteen. *I'll find out her age tonight.*

Once inside the hotel I put on my shades, hoping to miss the paparazzi lurking around the lobby. I hate how forceful they can be, but I put up with them because of my agent. The media is okay, but the paparazzi is constant. This lifestyle comes with consequences, and the lack of privacy is a part of it.

I make it to the elevator unnoticed. As the doors close, I pull out my phone to Google John Pittman's daughter. There she is, all over the internet but not as Cassidy. She's Reagan Pittman.

No wonder I couldn't find "Cassidy" at school. She's been using an alias for privacy. That explains why she was cautious at the ice cream shop. Scrolling through a few family photos, I see mostly older pictures. Even as a kid, I can see the making of a stunning woman, but one stands out: her in a white bikini by a pool on her twentieth birthday. The caption reads "Reagan Pittman killing it per usual." That was last year. She's twenty-one now. *Good.* I hesitate to press the comments knowing they'll piss me off.

Her dad has probably had a hard time keeping us all away, which makes me question how I approach him. He caught my eye on her during dinner, saw me glancing at her a couple of times. He and I have crossed paths in a few private settings, but never acknowledged each other.

I change into sweats and a t-shirt, still unsure how the night will go. But there's one small matter I need to handle, that damn dress. I was able to get the name and size while zipping her. I text my assistant, telling her to order that Halston dress in a size four. I've got plans for that dress, and she'll definitely need another one when I'm finished.

When she told me to go ahead earlier, that hunger to get in that wetness left me with no self-control. I should have stopped myself, but I couldn't. I experienced the *pull*. I've seen it in movies, even heard about it from older friends with wives, but I never thought it was real.

Until tonight.

If her friend hadn't interrupted us, there's nothing on earth that could have kept me out of her. That *pull* was real beyond my control and kept me on her.

I'm so caught up in my thoughts I accidently take the main elevator instead of the back entrance. Part of the media's job description must be tracking every move, and they do it well. I'll need a different hotel next time I need space away from home.

Exiting the hotel, I spot at least six paparazzi camped outside.

"Kylo? How's the season going?"

"Blade? How does it feel to be the highest paid soccer athlete in the States?"

"Kylo? Any more endorsements coming?"

"Blade? Kylo?"

"Not today," I mutter, pushing through them. The bellman tosses me my keys. He knows the drill and I jet to my truck. I should've driven home instead of getting a hotel. But home was an hour away, and I wasn't up for the drive.

I pull out with two cars trailing me. "Damn it!" I slam the steering wheel. I'm not bringing this chaos to Cass. She told me she values her privacy, and I plan to protect that for as long as possible. I floor the gas, I need to lose them.

I speed past Whitman Road, hitting 100 miles per hour, trying to outrun the flashing lights on both sides of my truck. Is a picture that serious? They can't even see me through the tinted windows. All they're getting is a shot of my truck.

I make a hard right onto an access road, forcing one car off the pavement. Tires screech as they spin off in a cloud of smoke, but the other car stays on my tail. "Who the hell is this?"

Another vehicle pulls up to my right, camera lights flaring as it tries to pass me. *Fuck this.* I floor the shit. With all the work I've done under my hood, I blow right by them, nearing a major intersection.

Damn, do I floor it or deal with whoever's in the car?

The intersection's coming up too damn fast to think. Reaching for my glove compartment, I decide to handle their asses. They don't want this smoke, especially when I'm packing. Plus, heading full speed into a busy intersection doesn't make sense. I start to brake, but nothing happens.

"What the hell?" I stomp on the brakes, pumping the metal, but the truck isn't slowing. One of the cars on my left slows, but the others stays on my ass.

"Shit!"

Ducking into the other lane would risk a head on collision, so I swerve right, sideswiping the car still there. Sparks fly as metal grinds on metal, my foot pumping the fucked up brakes. The intersection gets to me fast, lights coming from every direction. The roar of oncoming cars and the flare of headlights blind me as I barrel ahead, out of control.

"Hell!" I yell.

A crash erupts from behind, slamming my truck with brutal force, spinning violently. The impact throws me toward the passenger seat as a grinding churning noise blares in my ears.

Glass shatters, shards flying everywhere, blinding me, blocking my vision. My feet feel disconnected from the pedals, useless against what's happening. Suddenly, the truck flips, leaving me suspended upside down. Dizzy and disoriented, I struggle to focus, glimpsing the steering wheel as everything blurs.

Crushing pain hits from the back of my head. *What's hitting me?* Something pins my legs in place, keeping me from moving.

Time and space spin out of control. *Where am I? What's happening? Did something hit me?*

Darkness creeps in. My head feels like it's exploding, and I can't stop it. Pain spasms through me, making it impossible to figure out my next move.

Glass and darkness fade in and out of my vision.

Cassidy.

Darker.

No... Miss Blade...Ma...

The darkness is suffocating me. *Are my eyes open?*

Tron?

"Tron!"

CHAPTER 17

PURPLE BUTTERFLY

Cassidy

"THANK YOU, MR. PITTMAN," RAITH WINKS AT ME, AS SHE replies to my dad. "Anytime you have extra tickets for free food and good vibes, count me in. I can always eat, sir."

Free food is definitely the key to my girl's happiness. She lights up at the mere mention of it, and somehow, she hasn't gained a pound. We're five weeks into the semester and she's still rocking that Ciara meets J Lo's body.

My dad smiles. "Of course, dear. You girls take care of each other," he says, pulling her into a hug.

Raith nods, giving my dad an extra-long embrace that reminds me of our earlier conversation. If that hug doesn't give my dad high blood pressure, I don't know what will. She's absolutely owning that dress.

"Take care, Raith, and you girls come by the house sometime. It gets lonely without my baby girl," he says, glancing my way.

"Yes, sir. And thank you again for the evening." Raith heads for our dorm door, motioning for me to pull her sarong around my shoulders. Thank God it's dark and our lights are busted, or I'd have to explain the marks on my chest.

Dad rests an arm around my shoulders, guiding me toward the entrance. I used to get teased daily when he would walk me to the front door of elementary and middle school, but I never cared. Unlike my sisters, who insisted by age six that he park far away, I've always loved his attention.

"Raith is different in a lot of ways," he says thoughtfully. "I wish your mom could have met her. She was always drawn to people who didn't fit society's standards. Those were her kind of folks."

I know what he means. Mom was so liberating. She never judged, saw color or worried about anyone's sexuality. She simply wanted everyone to live in whatever way that brought them bliss. Bliss was one of her favorite words. She was drawn to those who chased their own happiness, regardless of societal norms. Even with her struggles with lupus, she refused to let the disease define her. I, on the other hand, hated the name so much that I stopped saying it. When she gave me my purple butterfly charm for my bracelet, symbolizing hope for lupus, I wanted to yank it off every time I saw it. For me, it was a reminder of the scaly butterfly rash that appeared on her cheeks and bridge of her nose years ago. But for her it was not letting anything make you fear breathing and living in the unknown. She chose to love life every second of the day.

"Where did you go earlier?" Dad asks, his voice interrupting my thoughts. His hands tighten gently on my shoulder, as if coaxing the truth out of me. I guess my vague explanation about stepping out isn't enough.

I hate lying to him, but whatever's going on with Kylo is so new, and it may end up being nothing. I don't want to worry him by admitting I had another panic attack after years without one, either. A half-truth will have to work.

"I went to the Grove for some fresh air," I say softly. "It felt too stuffy in the gala."

"The Grove?" he repeats, eyebrows rising. "What were you doing in the Grove?"

"It was cooler and quieter," I say, struggling to sound believable.

"You know how I dislike crowds." The explanation is weak. There was no real need for me to go to the Grove for fresh air when I could've stepped outside. I just wanted to get away from Kylo. I can already see this conversation going one of two ways. Dad will either lecture me about my safety, which is normally first, or wonder why I didn't wait for him. That's him, always making sure everything is okay.

My mind races so fast I almost miss the silence. He hasn't said a word.

"Dad?" I try again, rubbing his arm. Still no reply. "Dad?"

"Yes, my sweet girl," he replies, not quite meeting my eye. "I remember the Grove. Your mom and I spent time there. Knew it well."

I'm not sure how to respond, so I remain silent and wait for him to elaborate. "It's hard on this campus without feeling her everywhere," he admits, his voice faltering. Gently, I rest my head on his shoulder.

"I know, Dad," I whisper.

"She loved every corner of this place," he sighs, letting the memory linger between us.

"Yes, she did. She dragged us to every football game, basketball game, chorus concert and bowling tournament they had." We share a quick smile at the memory. My sisters and I never wanted to go, but Mom wouldn't hear it. On game days, she'd blast her loud eighties music, forcing us to shut our doors. Every Saturday morning this was her ritual to help A&M win whatever game was scheduled. I don't know if A&M knows, but Mom might've been the real reason for all those championship wins.

"You okay, Dad?" I ask, noticing how rare it is to see him show his emotions. It bothers me to watch him struggle with her loss. This is new.

"Yes," he says, regaining his usual composure. "If you're okay, then I am okay," he squeezes my shoulder tighter, pulling me closer.

I love him so much. To me he can do no wrong.

"I noticed Kylo Blade couldn't keep his eyes off you during

dinner this evening," he says suddenly, shifting subjects. "At one point, I think the poor boy started sweating. Have you met him before?"

And just like that, he's back to his direct questions. I'm not ready for this conversation, so another half-truth will have to do.

"We met a while back on campus… at the gym," I say, as nonchalant as possible.

"And this is the first time you've seen him since the gym?" he probes. He should have been an attorney with the way he digs for the truth.

"I've seen him around campus since then," I admit, trying to stay as close to the truth as possible without revealing too much.

We arrive at my dorm, and a few glance our way, noticing my dad hugging me. I guess we're still attracting attention, even in college.

"You are coming home next weekend, right?" he asks, changing the subject and I welcome it.

"Yes, Dad. I wouldn't miss it. Plus, I might bring Raith home with me if that's okay."

"Of course, I'd love for her to meet your sisters if they're in town. You know, their social calendars are busier than mine," he jokes, pulling me into a tight hug. Other than my mom's arms, this is my favorite place in the world.

"I'll arrange for you two to come home on Friday. Text me the time," he says. "My baby in heaven must be beaming, proud of the beautiful girl we made. You girls all take after her, but you especially," he lifts my chin, kissing my cheek. "Have a good week and be careful. Always be smart, my girl."

He turns and heads off without another word. I notice he seems smaller, shoulders not filling out his suit liked they used to. I make a mental note to get home more often, to look after him. While I've been so lost in my own grief, I sometimes forget his is just as deep…maybe deeper. He hides it well, but between his slip of emotion tonight and his weight loss, he probably needs my daily check ins more than he's letting on.

I head upstairs, stepping into thick humidity that greets me the second I open the door. Our windows fog up enough for Raith's cheerful artwork to shine, even in the dim light. She traces smiley faces on our glass daily, claiming it keeps her creative juices flowing. With no real ventilation in the bathroom, every hot shower turns our room into a makeshift sauna.

Raith walks out the restroom admiring her smiley face gallery. "That shower water was scorching," she says. "I'll have to catch it in the evenings more often. Speaking of hot, give me all the juicy details of the evening, Ice Girl." I watch her lather herself with enough shea butter to handle five miles of ash. According to her she'll never have wrinkles, and I absolutely believe her. A wrinkle wouldn't stand a chance against that much shea butter.

I decide to shower first, hoping it'll buy me time to process tonight's events and figure out how to explain it to Raith. Or maybe I'll get lucky, and she'll fall asleep.

After an extra-long shower, I'm still just as confused by tonight as I was before, and Raith is still wide awake, impatiently waiting for a update. I finally cave under her laser-like stare, burning holes through my skull.

"All right listen. I'm only telling this once," I finally say, breaking my silence.

Raith sits cross-legged on her bed, elbows propped on her thighs, chin resting in her hands as eager as a kid in kindergarten waiting to win a prize for the right answer. "I'm all ears, and I want the dirty details. Don't leave out anything!"

I tell her most of what took place with Kylo, but I leave out a few things, giving her enough juice to hopefully please her curiosity. When I finish, she continues to watch me intently, her excitement palpable.

"Cassidy," she says, suddenly serious.

"Yes, Raith?"

"I know you're not experienced so use protection... a condom," she says, eyes piercing mine with a sobering intensity. "Are you even on the pill?"

"Raith, who says I'll need protection so soon?" My words lack the confidence needed to sound real. "Plus, I know what to do," I say, knowing Google has taught me everything.

"Do you really?" she asks, her gaze slicing through my flimsy excuse, intense as my dad's interrogations.

My bottom lip ends up taking the brunt of my nerves. How can I tell Raith that all my firsts have happened in the past few weeks... my first touch, first kiss, first orgasm... all with him? It sounds pathetic for someone my age.

"Cassidy," she whispers, her voice gentle. I didn't even know she could whisper.

I mirror her softness. "Yes, Raith?" *Why am I whispering?*

"I know he's your first... and that's okay. Use protection and enjoy this story for your grandchildren. But make it a story to tell." She blinks, then wraps her arms around me, hugging me like the big-little sister she is in my heart. "Text me if you're not coming home, roomie."

I rest my head on her shoulder, trying not to slip off her excessive shea butter. "I will. Thank you, sis."

"For what?"

"For not saying everything you could have and being here."

It's nearly eleven o'clock, so I switch off the lights to head downstairs. "Good night," I trail off, noticing Raith's asleep that quick. We were deep in conversation a half second ago. How does she fall into a coma so quickly? It takes me a few minutes to calm down from the day, but not Raith. She can fall asleep in midair, while diving for the bed, out cold before her head even touches the pillow.

I head downstairs, deciding to sit on the steps instead of waiting on the curb for him. From here, I can see when he arrives.

I wish fewer people were out tonight. I really don't want an audience. Checking my Apple Watch I see that it's *11:10*. He's running late. A knot of anxiety forms in my stomach, and self-doubt creeps in. I question my judgment, check my phone and second guess everything. *Did he say eleven or twelve?* I could've sworn he said eleven. He left the party before I did and I saw Sarah walking back inside alone. I'm not sure if she was going for a Marilyn Monroe vibe, but her red lace outfit was more of an insult to the icon than a tribute. Something feels off with her.

Another glance at my watch confirms that it's *11:20*. Still no sign of him. Standing near the circular entrance, I look over to see if his Ford F-150 is in the lot. No headlights. No cars are in the parking area. I gave him my number, but I never got his, so calling is out.

By *11:32*, I'm debating heading back upstairs and returning at midnight. But I hate to wake Raith. What am I thinking? She wouldn't wake up if a plane landed in our room. I take one last look at the entrance. Maybe I'll walk that way just to check.

Before I can step down to head to the parking area, the door suddenly slams open, crashing into the side of the dorm as Raith runs through.

"Raith!" I shout, trying to get her attention as she runs in the opposite direction. She turns, and the look on her face sends a crushing chill through my entire body. Panic and tears are evident and my heart races at the seriousness of her countenance.

"Cassidy!" she screams, her voice trembling with fear stirring nausea within. "Cassidy!"

I fight to remain calm, but her urgency makes it impossible. "Raith? What is it?"

She grabs both my arms, mouth opening and closing without a word, fear and pity etched across her face.

"You're scaring me. What happened?" I demand, my voice shaking, desperately begging for answers.

"It's Kylo," she finally admits. Nausea takes over me, replacing every other feeling with a dull numbness.

"What about Kylo? What is it?" I ask, panic flaring hot and fast. "Raith, Tell me!"

"He's been in a car accident," her words deflate me, like a balloon losing all its air at once. I watch her shoulders slump, her head dropping into her hands as she begins to sob.

I release her, my mind reeling. A *car accident?* Was he on his way here? Is this my fault? My thoughts race at a thousand miles an hour.

"Raith, are you sure?" I whisper.

She raises her tear-streaked face to meet mine, clutching my hands in hers. "Th...the internet says he didn't make it, Cassidy. I just," she takes a shaky breath. "I wanted you to hear it from me first. Brian called..."

Her words spill out in slow motion, but I'm losing focus.

I pull my hands away from Raith, covering my face as I drop to my knees on the cold ground, head bowed. Tremors course through me, a storm raging inside that I can't contain. Distant voices ring in my ears, growing louder by the second. When I finally look up to see Raith and Brian hovering over me, their expressions are etched with deep worry.

"Cassidy are you okay?" Brian asks, gripping my hands tightly. Am I okay? Will I ever be okay again?

Raith cups my shoulders, and I sense bystanders slowing, watching my breakdown. "Cassidy?" she asks softly.

"Yes." The single word takes all my strength. I'm terrified that if I let go of my emotions, I'll collapse into a panic attack.

"Let's get you out of here," Raith murmurs, glancing at the small crowd gathering around us. "We have to get to Baptist hospital. They took him there. Rumors are circulating everywhere. Let's make sure." She wipes her tears, trying to keep it together, waiting for me to move.

I give the slightest nod, pushing myself up off the concrete. *Please let this be a nightmare,* I pray silently. *Please.*

CHAPTER 18

FROM HALSTON TO LITTLE
LEAGUE SOFTBALL PLAYER

Cassidy

WE PULL UP TO THE HOSPITAL, AND MY STOMACH SINKS at the sight of media surrounding the entrance. Barricades are already going up around the ER, crowds already forming across the street. *How did so many people get here so fast?* I hope his family didn't hear about this from social media the way Raith did.

Brian glances at Raith. "There's a back ER entrance," he says. "Let's head that way to avoid the media. She doesn't need that on top of everything else."

We hurry up the stairs to the back ER entrance, the familiar smell of antiseptic slapping me with the reason I hate hospitals. A crowd of at least sixty people gather outside near the waiting area, pacing, talking and some crying glued to their phones. *Are all these people here for him?* Security guards are stationed everywhere, trying to contain the chaos in the waiting room area. Raith takes off her baseball cap and snaps it onto my head, while Brian drapes his jacket on my shoulders. I am instantly transformed into a little league softball player, but my words fail me. I'm so grateful for them.

"Let's go over here." Brian suggests, pointing to a row of vending machines far away from the mob of anxious people. Only a handful stand there, watching the wave of anxious faces in the rest of the room. I never realized his world was this big. I didn't think so many would be waiting for answers about him.

I turn to Raith. "Any more info?"

She shakes her head, scrolling through her phone. *All these people wouldn't be in the waiting room if he was d....* I can't finish the thought. I can't even say the word. The elevator doors to our right dings open drawing my focus away.

A mob of people flood out, surprising everyone except the security guards, who jump into action, directing them back outside. We made it inside just in time.

"What now?" I ask, my anxiety rising. I want...no, I need answers and soon.

"Let's wait it out here," Brian suggests. "No one's noticed us yet." I nod, feeling lost and empty. I need to know what's going on but so do all these people surrounded by security. *Who are they?*

Reporters begin setting up cameras beyond the crowds, eager for any hint of a story. *How are they even allowed in the hospital?* That's one part of this lifestyle I hate. I value my privacy and with my dad being who he is, it's impossible to stay under the radar. My mom tried hard to shield us from the cameras, wanting a normal lifestyle without all the drama of public scrutiny.

One reporter hoists a camera to his shoulder, and another moves in on the waiting room crowd. I hear her shrill voice before I see her, sending needles down my neck. Her high-pitched tone makes me want to grind my teeth to dust. Brian places his hands on my shoulders as I link arms with Raith, silently begging for any update.

The camera lights beam directly on her, highlighting her perfect makeup and flawless hair. *How did she change so quickly?* "My boyfriend was involved in a car accident earlier this evening and suffered major injuries. He…" Sarah chokes, tears streaming as if she's performing for the cameras.

Raith tenses beside me. "Damn, bitch, keep going!" she mutters, under her breath. I grip her arm tighter, knowing she's close to breaking.

"He's alive!" Sarah finally screams through her sobs, announcing the words I was hoping to hear.

I slump against the wall, relief flowing through me. *Did I hear her right?* I have to be sure. "Raith, what did she say?"

Her answer is a hug, full of excitement. "Cassidy! He's alive!" Raith's arms lock around me, and my face slides into the left-over shea butter, leaving my cheeks greasy. But I don't care.

He's okay. He's alive and that's all that matters now.

In that instant, I open my eyes to someone in the crowd watching me, staring at me. *Sarah.* She's watching me like a hawk ready to dive for its prey. She's no longer upset or crying, just glaring, silently willing me to vanish. Then, as if she was catching herself, she's back into her performance mode. "We were talking marriage," she announces, then suddenly faints, landing in bystanders' arms. The cameras capture every second. She was born for this drama, leaving everyone to assume that marriage is next. Nurses rush in, and I lose sight of her behind the crowd.

Unable to handle any more of Sarah's theatrics, I tug Raith's arm. "Let's go."

"Cassidy don't believe this girl! Kylo left her at the gala while we were there. She's lying! You want me to bust up on the scene and set her ass straight?"

I hold Raith tighter, knowing she'll do exactly that. "No, Raith. He's alive. That's all I wanted to hear. Let's go," I walk toward the stairs, hoping she'll follow me.

Back in our dorm, I change clothes and prepare for my bed, feeling

Raith's gaze on me. I'm too drained to handle any questions. She approaches, placing a gentle hand on my shoulder. Maybe she has a sixth sense for mind reading. Instead of pressing me she flips off the lights and climbs into her own bed.

I close my eyes, needing a moment to myself, a pause to quiet my stampeding thoughts galloping like a wild horse fleeing the stable, racing too fast to catch. *Raith would die for real with that one.*

I feel drained but unable to sleep. The clock ticks by painfully, each second stretching too long to the next. When I can't take it any longer, I slip out of bed, dress quietly, and decide nothing will stop me from returning to the hospital. I'll text Raith when I arrive.

Downstairs, I catch the first bus off campus. There are only two passengers, the driver and one other guy near the back. Good. This should be easy. For some reason, taking the bus feels safer than an Uber in the middle of the night, though I probably shouldn't be doing either.

I head again to the rear ER entrance. As I near the hospital, I see a growing memorial sprawled across the lawn. Soccer jerseys, pictures, candles and team paraphernalia cover the grass. *I know he's a soccer player, but the magnitude of his popularity is widespread.* I'm unfamiliar with this part of his life. *Who am I kidding*, I don't know any part of it at all. I stop to admire the candles, stuffed animals, and pictures. There's so much love gathered here for one man.

Reaching the back entrance, I'm relieved no one notices me. The biting scent of disinfectant assaults my nostrils, reminding me again why I hate hospitals. We spent so many nights in the ER with my mom, some right here at this hospital when we couldn't fly to Houston for her care.

The waiting room I saw earlier is empty now, and any media waiting on Sarah to wake have left. A sign points me in the direction of the ICU waiting room…something I hadn't noticed earlier. *How do I get closer?* Not being a family member or knowing anyone in his circle isn't helping. At least I can be somewhat near him even if not in the actual room.

I enter the dimly lit ICU waiting room, where only one person sits in a far corner. A woman, I think, dressed in a brown hat, scarf, and gloves and an oversized tan sweater large enough to be a blanket. Not an inch of skin shows. She doesn't acknowledge me as I take a seat. She simply clutches her purse, no cell phone, no magazine, no TV, simply existing. I recognize that lost, empty stare. It's the gaze of no hope. Part of me wants to offer some sort of comfort, but how do I manage my own feelings at the moment?

A male nurse appears; I assume he's the ICU night shift. He heads over to the woman, asking if she wants to visit. It takes her a moment to lift her hollow gaze before slowly shaking her head. The nurse notices me in the corner and before he can approach, I stand and meet him halfway.

"How can I help you?" he asks, eyeing my little league softball outfit. "Are you here to visit a patient?"

I drop my voice, careful not to disturb the woman. "I'm here to see Kylo Blade. He's a close friend. Can you help me?"

"Ma'am, I can't allow anyone into his room. It's heavily guarded, and only certain family members are on the approved list."

His firmness suggests there's no room for negotiation, and I'm too drained to fight. "Thank you," I murmur. "I'll wait here."

I return to my corner, identical to the others, equipped with end tables matching lamps and a Bible. Pulling my oversized sweatshirt tighter around me, I tuck my legs beneath myself, replaying the last twenty-four hours in my mind. With nothing else to do, I simply wait.

CHAPTER 19

THE PULL

Cassidy

THIS IS MY FOURTH NIGHT IN THE ICU WAITING ROOM. It's the second night the silent woman isn't here. I wonder where she is. She never spoke, never revealed her face...just sat and waited alongside me in her corner. Somehow, I miss her presence. Now it's just me and the four identical lamp shades, their shadows stretching across the walls, making me feel like they're dangerously alive.

Over the past few days, I've met at least seven different nurses. All of them have the same question: "How can I help you?" They're really nice, but no one gives me any feedback. HIPAA policies lock the information away, leaving me stuck. The uncertainty is killing me and social media is running wild with stories, so I try to avoid it.

My phone vibrates, reminding me I forgot to text Raith that I arrived safely. She's been on my case about staying here all night, but there are too many visitors during the day. No one in Kylo's family knows me, so explaining us is hard. Especially with the rumors circulating that he and Sarah were discussing marriage. It's easier being here at night, unnoticed.

After texting Raith back, I pull out my Creative Writing

assignment, "The Principles of Modern Grammar." It's 1:40 a.m. and focusing on homework is tough, but at least it occupies my mind.

I jump at the sound of the door opening. A male nurse steps in, the same one from before. I don't care for him. He always stares, never speaks, like he's trying to figure something out. I turn back to my assignment, hoping ignoring him will make him leave.

By three a.m., I finish my homework just as the door opens again. It's him, again, and I have no idea why he keeps coming in or why he stares so long every time. What is wrong with him?

He approaches me with a cautious glare, and I hold my pencil ready to stab him, if necessary. *Why am I feeling the need to defend myself?*

"I could lose my job for this," he says, his voice curt. "But for some reason the other nurses here seem to like you," he pauses, taking in my oversized sweatshirt, jean jacket and baseball cap. I sense he's not one of those nurses who actually *likes* me. "Follow me."

I set my books aside in the waiting room chair. "Wait…did you say 'follow me'?"

"Yes." His short, irritated response irritates my nerves, but I'm not about to miss an opportunity to see Kylo.

We walk down the corridor in silence. He's tall and slender, his footsteps echoing on the polished floor.

"He's in bad shape," the nurse warns. "So, no loud crying. We don't need any unwanted attention. His family left about an hour ago but will come back soon. Right now, he's alone." We head through double doors into the ICU. The sterile shine of the floors and rhythmic beeping of equipment wraps us in a cold, clinical atmosphere. I force myself not to look into the other patients' rooms, focusing instead on the curve of the floor, baseboards, and electrical outlets. Eventually, we stop outside an unmarked room, guarded by a security officer.

I take a deep breath, the antiseptic smell filling my lungs. *You can do this, Cassidy.*

The guard steps aside, and the nurse opens the door. The sight before me is something I'll never forget. Kylo's upper body is swollen, almost unrecognizable, his once handsome face now bruised and scrapped. Tubes dangle from nearly every part of him, various fluids flowing in and out. A patch of hair is gone from one side of his head, and a bulky neck brace holds him rigid, tubes snaking from a ragged scar. One leg hangs midair in a pulley system attached to the ceiling, his toes look swollen and bloody. Most of his body is wrapped in white gauze, giving him the appearance of a mummy.

I lean against the wall for support, wishing Raith's greasy shoulders were here to hold me up. Just a couple of days ago, we were at the gala together. How could this have happened? I rest my head on the cold wall, silently hoping it won't crumble under the weight of my dread. *Was he on his way to see me? Don't think about that.*

"Are you okay?" the nurse asks, his words edged with an emotion I can't place.

"No, I'm not okay." My hand grips his arm before I can stop myself. "How is he?"

His gaze flicks briefly to my bracelet and I yank my hand away. "I'm sorry," I whisper, swallowing hard.

He exhales, sounding weary. "I shouldn't be telling you this, but his prognosis is dire. He's in a medically induced coma to help with the brain swelling."

"Can I have a moment alone with him?" I ask, voice trembling.

He frowns impatiently. "Yes, but not long."

"Thank you."

My footsteps echo on the sterile floor as I approach the bed, eyes glued to Kylo's battered body. Gently, I weave my fingers into his right hand, careful not to disturb the tubes entwined with every inch of him.

Leaning in, I inhale his faint scent and whisper. "Kylo, if you can hear me, please come back. I'm here, waiting. I'm not going anywhere. Listen to my voice and fight your way back. You're strong, a star soccer player with a kick that can break through any goal-keeper. Squeeze my hand if you hear me."

My shoulders slump as I release a breath I didn't realize I was holding. I place my trembling hands on his chest, feeling the slow, mechanical rise and fall of his breath. "Please squeeze my hand, Kylo," I plead. "Please…"

Nothing.

"Visiting time is over," the nurse says with a short laugh that makes no sense in this room of tragedy. There's nothing funny.

I ignore him, feeling emptiness creeping in as time slips away. I lean in and kiss one small patch of unblemished skin on Kylo's forehead, careful not to disturb his tubes.

Outside his room, I find my way back to the ICU waiting area. My heart feels anchored here. I need more time. I sink into the same corner seat under the faint glow of a single lamp, hardly noticing that the nurse followed me.

"What are you doing?" he demands.

"I'm waiting for the next visit," I say, quietly.

"That was a favor," he says. "No more visits allowed. You're not family and I risked my job letting you in there!"

Something is off with him. My grip tightens on my backpack, ready to use it as a shield if required. "I understand. I'm not asking for more favors. I know daytime visits are off limits for me, but I'll be here every night in this waiting room."

He shoves his hands into the pockets of his too short green jogger scrub pants. "Like I said, I can't risk my job. It's clear you're not family. For all I know you could be some crazed fan. How do you even know him?"

Before I can respond, he continues. "He's so high profile we have extra nurses and security around-the-clock. I really could lose my job over this."

I hoist my backpack onto my shoulders, preparing to leave. "We met recently."

"Oh really," he replies, dripping with sarcasm, "So, what would his girlfriend, soon to be fiancé, say about your recent meeting?"

I lock eyes with him, an unsettling déjà vu stirring my gut. *Have we met before?* I push the feeling aside and step around him, putting distance between us on my way to the restroom.

"Sorry," he says suddenly. "I'm Damon Lucas, ICU RN," he offers, maybe feeling a bit guilty about earlier.

"Damon, I'm Cassidy. Thank you for letting me see him. I'm not trying to jeopardize anyone's job, but I will come to this waiting room every night. That won't change."

"Okay, suit yourself, Miss Cass," he replies, a hint of amusement in his voice.

Miss Cass? What makes him think he can call me that? "Thank you," I say walking past him trying to remain calm since he's my current hall pass to Kylo.

Back at the dorm, I shower quickly, then change into sweats, and grab my running shoes. The early morning air feels unusually crisp, hitting me with the ragweed pollen that sets off my allergies this time of year. I sneeze, anticipating the headache that usually follows. Still, I need to run to clear my mind from what I saw this morning.

The oval track, its 400 meters of orange and white striped synthetic rubber, becomes my sanctuary. My mom used to call it my Zen, but to me it's my "cloudy zone," the one place where I can vanish from my reality. Running here is the only way to escape the relentless images of tubes keeping him alive, the swelling around his cheeks from the tight straps, and the blood dripping from his toe, suspended in midair. It's the only place I can hide from the heaviness of missing my mom every second of the day.

As I run, my steady pace slows to a jog. Tears blur the rising sun into a fiery blur. These are the tears that never salted my cheeks when Raith told me about the accident. Now they hit me like a category five hurricane, leaving me trembling. I lean over gripping my thighs for support, letting the tears wash down the inside lane of the track.

How did I fall for him this fast? I don't even know him. I don't know his family, his friends, his favorite color or food. Nothing.

The only thing I'm sure of is the pull drawing me to that hospital. All I have are his last words "this is different" echoing in my head. Those words are all I have left.

CHAPTER 20

CONTRASTING COMPASSION

Cassidy

T HE NEXT FEW DAYS BRING NO MORE VISITS TO SEE KYLO. Every time the nurses come in, my entire being pleads for permission to see him, but all I get are kind smiles and regretful nods in return.

My nights now consist of dozing in the ICU waiting room, surrounded by drab brown lamp shades that lurk over me while I do my homework. I've grown used to counting on these silent "ghosts" every night, looming in the corners as if ready to say "Boo." I wish I could change their dusty tan color with something brighter, like a yellow in my dorm and bedroom. But thinking of home reminds me of everything I've tried to bury.

My bedroom at home is filled with yellow, white and gold pillows, where I used to smother my daily screams. I spent so many nights pressing my face into those pillows, fearing the next seizure would be Mom's last. For me, seizure was like the C-word for cancer. But it was the S-word, meaning hurt. The first time it happened I was in the ninth grade, One minute we were watching TV, the next her arms spasmed against her chest, her back arching so severely it looked like an invisible force was pulling her waist toward the ceiling. I'd never seen anyone's lips turn blue until that day, drool trickling from her mouth, her wild heartbeat thrashing against my palms as I tried to keep her steady. I didn't realize I was screaming until Dad rushed in. My sisters never witnessed any of that. But I did. More than once.

That's when I stopped sleeping. Four-hour nights became my norm. Track was my escape, but looking back, I wish I'd stopped that, too. I should never have gone to my final meet that day. Maybe if I'd been home, I could have gotten the ambulance there sooner. Maybe I could have told her it was the S-word, that it would be over soon, like I always had. I could have met her bulging, panicked eyes with reassurance, held her hand when she needed it most. Instead, I was out losing a track meet. The last place I wanted to be and the last place I should have been.

The ache in my heart is the sole reminder of the night. The night Dad's expression of loss, made me faint in their doorway. Even thinking about it now sets my pulse racing, and my chest tightening. Neither of them knew I was eavesdropping one night in the hospital. She told Miss Rita that I was so present in her life, I'd be holding her hand the day she transitioned.

But I wasn't there. I wasn't with Mom the day when she might've needed me the most, and that's something I'll *never get over*. Pretending that everything was okay became my norm, even when it wasn't. It wasn't until Miss Rita found me outside my room, gasping for breath, that the panic attacks became too obvious to hide…my "I'm okay" secret finally slipping out.

I force my mind elsewhere because that's what I do. Scanning the room, I half expect to see the silent woman blending into the background with her earthtones. It's actually a relief that she's not here. But several new faces have joined the waiting room of despair over the past few days. I overheard conversations, reveal one especially heartbreaking story: two children in a car accident, each hospitalized in critical condition and their parents in different hospitals.

Only a single neighbor has come to check on them. Earlier in the week, I left stuffed bears for both kids in the waiting room.

"Cassidy?"

I flinch as a familiar voice invades my solitude. *Damon Lucas.* He's the last person I want to deal with right now. The other nurses at least offer a sympathetic smile, even if they give me no real news or visitation. But not him. He's rude and impatient.

"Yes," I answer reluctantly.

"Come with me." He turns to leave, offering no explanation. Snatching my books and backpack, I hurry after him hoping he's offering a hall pass for a visit.

I rush from the waiting room to catch his slim frame walking down the hall.

I trail him power walking down the corridor. "Have you been here every night?" he asks without looking back.

"I told you I would be," I reply, breath catching up with me. "I meant what I said. That's not changing."

He pauses, still not turning around. "The other nurses have noticed you," he says. "They all agreed to allow you to visit when no one else is here at night."

I sigh, squeezing my eyelids shut in an attempt to dam the swell of tears, but they spill down my cheeks anyway, disobeying my brain. *Why am I crying so much?* This connection feels too new for such a breakdown, but reason doesn't help right now.

"We've put you on the registry as his first cousin, Cassidy Pittman," he continues. "As long as no one shows during the night, you should be fine."

"Can I go see him now?" I ask, voice unsteady.

He tilts his head a fraction, biting his bottom lip. "Yes." He hesitates for a moment, and again, I feel that nagging sense that we've met before, that something's off about him. The way he swings from almost polite to nearly yelling in an instant is alarming. Just because he is helping me doesn't make him safe or sane.

"Follow me," he says, interrupting my thoughts again.

As we walk down the hallway, I take in his boney back as I follow him. He's unnaturally thin. It is almost alarming how his clothing swallows him up and the way his bones protrude through his skin. It makes me uncomfortable just being near him. We pass a few nurses, but no one spares us a second glance. Damon moves straight ahead, swiping his badge at the ICU double doors. Two nurses notice us, smiling with quick nods toward Kylo's room.

A different guard stands outside his room, reminding me of the guards that used to station themselves near my mom's hospital door. I never understood the threats Dad feared, but he insisted on security around her door, just like now.

Reaching Kylo's room, I drop my backpack by the door and hurry straight to his bedside.

"Damon," I say softly, needing answers.

"Yes, Cassidy," he replies, voice tinged with agitation…nothing new. I ignore it.

"How is he?"

"He's the same. Still day to day," Damon answers tersely. "His soccer team and agency flew in special doctors, nurses and physical therapists to handle their prized possession. Honestly, I don't see any fight in him."

The phrase *prized possession* makes me cringe. *Does he even care?* His words imply some kind of judgment, like he's jealous or bitter. Maybe he hates his job or is a disgruntled fan. Or maybe he couldn't kick a soccer ball since the ball weighs more than him. *Not nice, Cassidy.* Whatever it is, he should stop. I don't appreciate his tone or his thinking, especially with him being his nurse.

"Can I have a private moment with him?" I ask, determined to stay polite.

"Thirty minutes and that's it," he replies.

Hall pass, I remind myself. He's my current ticket to visit Kylo. So, instead of unleashing the curse words I normally don't say, I keep my cool. "Thank you," I whisper, voice faintly louder than the machines keeping Kylo alive.

"You know," Damon continues, "I think he's playing some-body. Is it you?"

His words make my fists tighten at my sides. He doesn't know me, yet he makes assumptions regarding my relationship with Kylo? This is none of his business. Plus, this feels like more than a jeal-ous fan.

I take a deep breath, pushing down my frustration. "Thanks, but we're fine," I say, keeping my voice even as possible.

He regards me like he sees something I don't. "You seem to be a kind girl, spending all this time here at night. But these guys like him," he gestures toward Kylo, "they've got women in every city. Someone like him has a piece of ass in each country. This man is worldwide. We've got media from twenty different countries camp-ing out, hogging our conference rooms...all a waste," he rambles, pacing and flicking his gaze between Kylo and me as if we're ping pong balls.

Did anyone ask his opinion? Anger bubbles inside, but I hold my tongue. I watch him. He's so caught up in his pacing he seems unaware of my presence with his hands stuffed and lost in his over-size scrubs. *Hall pass.* I manage a firm, simple, "Thank you," then turn my attention back to Kylo.

I grip the bed rail beside Kylo's bed, trying to steady myself, but it only brings back memories from three years ago when my mom was in the hospital. I clung to her bed rail refusing to go to school until she recovered from her seizure. Miss Rita watched over us both, hoping for any sign that might give us permission not to worry.

Damon's footsteps interrupt my thoughts, and I jump when his bony hands clamp onto my shoulders. His fingers tighten around my shoulder blades, leaving me speechless. "If you want to talk, Cassidy, I can be here for you. Whatever you desire. Whatever..."

I look down at my tennis shoes, then back up at Kylo, hoping the hum of his machines calm my rising anger. Maybe I should be afraid, but I'm not. I want his boney fingers off me. *Who gave him permission to place his frail skeleton on me?* If I didn't require him as my hall pass, I'd twist his boney fingers backward until he begged me to stop. But I do need him.

So, I take a deep breath and answer as calmly as I can. "Thank you, Damon." While my words are kind, I hope it also communicates how uncomfortable I am with his touch.

His fingers press between my shoulder blades longer before he finally lets go. "Okay!" Damon exclaims, his voice laced with uncertainty as he backs away. He resumes pacing, his deep dark set eyes darting between me and Kylo. He seems anxious but not for Kylo's sake.

When he leaves, I turn to face Kylo. The swelling around his cheeks has subsided a bit, revealing more of his handsome features, though a sticky purple bruising still darkens the area beneath his bottom lids. Some of the tubes I saw before are gone, and I hope that's a good sign. Even with the dried blood crusted around a few of his scars, I can't help but see a glimmer of hope amid the pain.

On the nightstand, I notice a bottle of lotion, box of Kleenex, and a tube of coconut oil. Recalling what I once read from Dr. Google during one of Mom's hospital stents and how body stimulation is helpful in encouraging patients, I squeeze lotion into my palms, then gently massage Kylo's arms, hands, and feet. It's something I did with my mom, too, convinced she might wake if I just tried hard enough. Some articles claimed coma patients can hear us, that our voices and touch can reach them somehow.

My gaze drifts over Kylo's injuries, a reminder of the struggles I went through with my mom and I whisper a prayer as I did with her. "I pray you can hear me, but even if you can't, I have to get these words out that I've been too afraid of speaking to another soul."

"Kylo, it's me, Cass. I'm so sorry this happened to you," I almost break, but smash my eyes closed and force myself to slow my breathing to stave off the tears. When I open them again, I focus on massaging his arm around the bruises and bandages as I reveal my innermost thoughts.

"I feel so guilty you were on your way to me when this happened. I hope you were," I pause, taking a deep breath to get my thoughts back in order and end the rambling I feel coming on.

"Everyone thinks it's crazy for me to come here every night and wait for hours. And maybe it is....but I can't stop. I need you to come back," I beg, flashes doing the same thing near my mom's bedside flooding my mind. I clutch my chest as the storm of emotions hits hard, realizing I'm in the same place, begging and praying for a miracle. How is this happening again?

I rest my head in my hands, to convince myself not to give into the emotions clawing in my brain. *You're okay. You're always okay.*

I start with his brother and how he helped him play, filling in high school and college years with everything from the internet. I review all his stats, current endorsements, upcoming season projections and community service projects.

I pause to catch my breath from talking to check my watch. *How has time gone by so fast?* Thirty minutes is not long enough.

Exhaling slowly, I let my gaze drop to the white sheets hiding his bow legs from me. "Kylo, please come back. I need you to wake up. Move your hands. Do something to show you're fighting." His hands remain limp and unresponsive. "Please do anything. Blink. Try to blink, please."

"Kylo, we barely shared much, but you told me this was *different*. If you remember me and Brooklyn feeding the ducks a few days ago, wiggle your pinky. Brooklyn calls you Captain K. I'm not sure why, but she does. You have to come back, Captain K. Find your way back. Just… blink your eyes."

I rub my cheeks again, aware my time is running out. The door opens, and I feel Damon standing there.

"Ca…ssi…dy," he drags out my name, making me grind my teeth. Why does he say it that way?

"Yes," I answer, trying to keep my tone steady.

"Visiting time is over."

"Give me a moment to say goodbye," I say.

He yawns louder than the hum of Kylo's machines. "Okay."

Leaning in, I press a soft kiss to Kylo's forehead, inhaling his familiar sandalwood scent. *He still smells so good.*

"I will be back tomorrow night," I whisper, turn to get my backpack and walk past Damon.

More days pass with moderate changes in Kylo's health from what I can see. My new routine is spending nights in the ICU waiting room, surrounded by different strangers and the occasional reappearance of my corner lady. She's not here every night, but when she is, she sits quietly blending in with her tan sweater coat, matching gloves and hat. She never visits anyone. I can only assume she's a woman, her face is always hidden. She seems different and taller today, maybe she's a man.

The nurses allow me two visits each night, at twelve-thirty a.m. and three-thirty a.m. Thirty minutes is all I get. I fill the rest of my nights with homework, leaving by five-thirty so I can get back to campus.

I spend my nights updating him on anything that comes to mind, breaking news, ESPN basketball and baseball scores, conspiracy theories, my track seasons, favorite foods, favorite color, my mom, dad, sisters, Miss Rita and Raith. I've learned more about his generosity and stories keep pouring in. It seems everyone wants to be part of him right now, sharing stories of how he's paid light bills, sponsored soccer fees and provided equipment for kids. He's helped families with sick children and been a silent hero for so many. He's not the same person I met during our cryotherapy session. Most nights my throat is raw from talking too much. Hopefully he can hear me.

I touch his arm between bruises, feeling the softness that was not there days ago. Those deep valleys of muscles that once bulged under his skin are disappearing beneath my touch. His body is changing. I grab my ten-pound weights from my backpack, thinking they will help in rebuilding his muscles one day.

After his workout, I massage his icy, rigid, ashy feet, wondering if he's ever had a pedicure. He could use a weekly appointment and Raith's shea butter routine. "How was that?" I ask, knowing there will be no answer.

He never replies or changes his expression. Massaging his thick eyebrows, my fingers brush against the white bandage above his eyelid and I realize how much I miss his honey hazels. But I ignore my urge to open them and place my weights back into my backpack. My bracelet catches on the sheet, accidentally exposing his thigh.

I've been fighting the temptation for days to see what's under the sheets. *Is this an invasion of privacy?* But now that they're partially drawn back, I figure I might as well look.

Why did I do that? I stare at his long legs stretching the length of the bed and my heart clenches. A catheter hangs loosely between his legs with tape dangling from three tubes snaking across him. Blood and pus ooze from deep, dark lacerations, surrounded by purple and red bruises, some healing scabs crusting over open wounds.

Tears slide down my cheeks and land on his thigh. I reach for the hospital container wipes on the nightstand, letting my tears mix with the cleaning process. Carefully, I remove left-over bits of cotton and the dried blood clinging to his skin, taking care not to disturb any healing. I thank whoever brought the coconut oil and pour some onto a cotton ball, gently rubbing each abrasion.

I step back to admire what I've done. His legs shine like greasy pieces of golden fried chicken and a smile creeps across my face. *I should take a picture.* "One day," *I whisper to myself,* "You will see this picture."

Tucking him back under his clean sheets, I hope the coconut oil will speed up his recovery. The jar sits next to his Vitamin C I brought and I wonder if I should leave them both out for day shift nurses. But maybe it's safer to keep it a secret. *No one should know I'm here.*

Gently, I massage the scar near his eye, recalling how I did the same for Mom. Miss Rita would order special creams for her scalp, and we'd take turns applying them, but strands of her hair would fall away between our fingers. *Don't think about that now.*

My heart stutters as I sense my thirty minutes winding down. I place his hand on my wrist, a new nightly routine. "Here's another story for the night, Kylo," I begin in a hushed, reverent tone, "This one is from a lady in California. She writes:

"Kylo has never met us officially, but I wrote to him years ago. I felt my son and he had similar upbringings. My son lost his older brother two years ago. They were both soccer players. I won't use names for privacy. But when his brother died, so did a part of him. He acted out, and I almost lost him, too. I wrote Kylo our story. Kylo has been in my son's life for the past two years, encouraging him. They've never met in person, but Kylo texts and sometimes calls him weekly for updates. It's tough writing this. My son's devastated right now. Kylo never wanted anyone to know. He valued privacy. But my son ended up getting two full ride D-1 scholarships, partially because of this man."

I stop, unable to read further, my grip tightening on the cold silver bedrail. "Kylo, do you hear me. Follow my voice. This kid misses you and so do I."

Pulling off my Apple Watch, I hold my wrist near his nose. "Follow my scent, Kylo. Smell me. You've told me how you like my fragrance. Wake for me, please."

Nothing changes. No movement, no expression, only the steady rise and fall of his chest from the breathing machine. *If only his panic attack technique could work for him now; I'd try it.* Resting my cheek against his hand on the bed rail, I feel lost drained of hope, unsure if he'll ever wake.

A soft voice startles me. "Miss Cassidy?" Quickly, I pull away from the rail, careful not to snag any of his I V lines. Relief spreads through me as I spot Miss Gwen, the bubbly nurse, instead of Damon.

"Miss Gwen. How are you? No Damon tonight?"

She slips on plastic gloves, moving confidently around Kylo's cramped room. It's almost comical how ready she is to handle Kylo's six-four-frame despite being maybe five feet tall. "Damon hasn't shown for his last seven shifts. His family even called looking for him. We're a bit worried."

I'm not a fan of Damon, but I would hate to hear that something bad might've happened to him.

"How is my man?" Miss Gwen asks checking his vitals, monitors and medication.

She's called him "her man" since the day we met, often joking that if she were thirty years younger without a hip replacement, osteoporosis and gout he would be her man.

"He's okay," I reply, the uncertainty in my voice tells a different story. "He's hanging out enjoying his massage." *At least I hope so.*

Miss Gwen smiles warmly. "He's lucky to have you here. Ever since the media left, so have most visitors. Maybe five people still come… two ladies during the day, then his friends Christian, Bruce and you."

She turns, adjusting his I V drip, then fixes me with the same knowing look Miss Rita always gives when the advice is coming. "How are you, sweetheart?"

My chest tightens and I offer the same old response. "I'm okay."

"Miss Cassidy, you don't have to come every night. We'll take care of him."

I glance back at his blank expression, the urge in me flaring to breathe life into his motionless body. She's right, but I can't stay away, not when seeing him every day feels like my only anchor of hope.

"I understand, Miss Gwen."

She hesitates, looking torn over her next words. "Sweet girl, you need rest. You have a kind spirit, but you have to be careful. That loony's still out there kidnapping girls. You're such a beauty. I hate to see you here all alone most nights. Do you have family near?"

"Yes ma'am, my family is an hour away."

"Please be careful." The echo of my father's frequent warning makes me appreciate her concern all the more.

"I will, Miss Gwen."

"And, honey, please get some rest between classes," she adds. "You can't keep burning the candle at both ends, it'll catch up to you eventually."

"Thank you, Miss Gwen." A warmth spreads through my chest at her words sounding like Miss Rita. She reminds me so much of Miss Rita back home that I feel an urge to hug her, and this time I don't resist.

"Okay, well this visiting session is almost over. I will come out at three-thirty for the next visit," she tilts her head, waiting for my response.

I step forward and wrap my arms around her, the gesture more for me.

"Thank you for understanding and taking care of our man," I release her, offering a quick wink, feeling lighter from her warmth. As I walk away, I still hear her, sharing all of her plans for him once he wakes up.

CHAPTER 21

LOVE EXPLAINED

Cassidy

WALK BACK TO WHAT ESSENTIALLY HAS BEEN MY BEDROOM, the ICU waiting area, when the familiar sound of keys stop me in my tracks. That jingle and swift stride used to echo through the hallways of my elementary school, signaling his presence before I even saw him.

Before I spot him, the woman from the corner, my silent waiting room companion, bumps past me. Her oversized sweater coat drags on the floor, and she says nothing. She's taller than I expected, towering above me as she leaves.

My pulse quickens as I reach the waiting room, ignoring my old roommate half hoping it's him. And there he is standing in the center of the waiting room, worry carved into his tired features. The lines on his forehead warn me this conversation won't go smoothly. Unsure how to start, I manage, "Dad, please let me explain."

He exhales as though he's been holding his breath, then walks forward and hugs me. The floodgates open, and I cry so hard in his arms that my body shakes. My muscles tense with dry heaves threatening to defeat me. I want Kylo to wake. I want my mom here. I want this hospital to disappear.

"Relax baby girl," he murmurs. "Get it all out."

"Dad, I… I didn't want you to worry," I confess, burying my face into his leather jacket, overwhelmed by shame that my secret is out.

He inhales. "Baby girl, I knew something was going on between you two that night. It was obvious at dinner. That boy was a nervous wreck around you. I was just waiting for you to tell me."

He hands me a clean handkerchief he always seems to have. "You're exaggerating," I say, though a part of me hopes he's right.

"Baby girl, how could he not be?" he replies, lifting my chin gently. His eyes hold their normal concern. "Come this way, I've reserved a side room to speak."

I stare at him in disbelief, amazed at his ability to secure a private space. *Who does he know to get a room at this hospital?*

We head to a small closet room furnished with a cot, tiny desk, TV and mini-fridge. Probably an area for night shift doctors. *Why haven't I noticed it before?*

"Who told you I was here?" I ask.

He hesitates, contemplating whether to share his source. "Raith," he admits. "It took some digging, but she finally did."

"I knew she'd say something," I mutter, resting my face in my hands. I wish I was somewhere else. *Maybe, introducing Kylo to Mom. But that dream feels so distant. She's gone and Kylo is…*

Dad interrupts my thoughts. "I showed up to the dorm since you haven't been home. You were home one day during fall break. Your sisters were even worried, which is new for them. I drove up to campus tonight before Miss Rita could. Raith hesitated to speak, but she ultimately told me your whereabouts."

"Dad, I'm okay," I insist, fighting the urge to fidget.

He watches me, worry eroding his usual calm demeanor. Hopefully he's not seeing the weight loss that Raith saw last week. "I can see you are *somewhat* okay," he says. "Have you been here every night?"

The cot beneath me feels harder than concrete, and I shift

uncomfortably, admitting to myself how I've barely managed three hours of sleep most nights. Raith calls my new look "Gothic" and warns it isn't working. My friends keep asking about my weight loss. Balancing school, track and Kylo has been tough, but my desire to be here every night outweighs everything else.

"Yes, I have, Dad." I bow my head, hating to admit this to anyone, especially him.

He reaches for my hands. "Baby girl, that nurturing spirit from your mom has always run deep in you. From her, to me, and now Kylo. I'm not here to tell you what to do, but you must stay safe. How are you handling everything?"

His concerned gaze falls on my braids, revealing the cracks. "My grades are good. I haven't let them slip. Track practice starts in two weeks, but I've been working out and conditioning. I'm okay." I can hear the tremor in my voice that betrays me.

"Raith is worried," he says gently, but he's fishing.

"I know she's worried, but I'm okay," I lie, fingers closing around the charm on my bracelet. I can't possibly explain what I felt for Kylo. It doesn't make sense even to me. How do I tell Dad that someone I barely know has a hold on me so strong I can't walk away?

Trying to draw strength from my bracelet's charm, I remind myself that my *okays* are getting old. I'm tired of hearing them, too, but I don't want him worrying more.

He paces the small floor, his shoes pounding louder than the hospital's background noise. "I'm not going to tell you to stop," he says. "That stubborn streak that you were born with will do what it wants, even if I say no. But you will be safe. This side of town is dangerous, and they haven't caught this crazy ass man kidnapping and killing girls. Why are you coming so late?"

I explain most of it without diving too deep into all the details that haunt me most nights.

"I see," he says, squeezing my hands warning me he has more

to say. "Sarah Sims is all over social media saying all sorts of things about their relationship."

"Dad, he broke up with her the night of the gala. I made him call her in my presence. She's lying. They are over."

He smiles, thumping the top of my hand. "Baby girl, you don't have to explain it all to me. I can see it in your eyes the way you're talking about him. I've known love before and I know that pull when it's there. But, I like that he was introduced to your take no bull shit pretty early," he laughs, easing some of the tension that was present in the waiting room.

I pull back slightly to look at him. "I just...I can't explain it. He told me it was different, and I felt it too, but this is so much. And now, looking at him like this, I don't even know if he'll ever be the same or if he'll ever wake."

His gaze softens, though his eyes brim with concern. "Reagan, love, true love, doesn't make sense most of the time. It catches you when you least expect it. And sometimes, it isn't the perfect picture we think it's supposed to be. But that doesn't make it any less real."

I chew on my bottom lip, my tears slowing but my chest still heavy. "It just feels too soon to be real. I barely know him, and yet it feels like I've known him forever. Does that make me crazy?"

Dad chuckles softly, his forehead wrinkling as he smiles. "It makes you human, sweetheart. Love doesn't follow a timeline or rulebook. Sometimes, it's instant. Sometimes, it sneaks up on you. But, I see how much this matters to you. I just want you to remember to take care of yourself, too."

I nod, his words sinking in, but the heaviness doesn't leave my chest. "Thank you, Dad, for everything."

He nods. "I understand everything you have updated me on. But I wish you would have told me."

"Dad, I'm so sorry. I should have told you. I didn't want you to worry."

He reaches to tuck a loose curl behind my ear. "I will always worry. That's my job. But delaying news makes it worse."

His hands shake a little, making me worry. "I understand." Having to deal with the sick feeling in the pit of my stomach for being so private with Kylo is something extra I don't need.

He hugs me tight. "If you insist on coming at night, arrangements will be made for Mr. Stuart to drive and escort you into the hospital every night. This room will be reserved for you as long as you're here. It will be stocked with all essentials by tomorrow, including a computer for homework. The same driver will take you back to campus every morning. This *is* going to happen." Once he's made a decision without asking for input, that's it. But honestly, the truth is, gratitude fills me for his protective obsession.

I press tightly into his leather-scented cologne, whispering, "Thank you, Dad." Tears flow again, and I sniffle between words. "I don't know where this is going or if he will ever truly wake up. But I felt something with him. Something unfamiliar, yet different. I'm not sure how he feels, but…"

He doesn't let me finish. "Baby girl, love is natural and effortless; it isn't based on time or reason. I fell in love the day I saw your mom on campus. Nothing could keep me away. She didn't make it easy for me and I was no saint, but I loved that woman. I still do and that will never change," he pauses, turning to me. "Let's head back to campus. Kylo is in good hands, and besides, it's late." He rolls up his jacket sleeve to check his watch, letting out a long yawn.

I want to stay longer but dad's patience is not waiting until three-thirty. I'd better go with him.

CHAPTER 22

EVERYTHING ELSE FADES

Cassidy

"RAITH, I HATE THOSE PARTIES," I GROAN, AS SHE PRACTI-cally shoves me in the bathroom.

"You hate them because you haven't been to one with me!" she counters, grinning like a Cheshire cat. "You've been holed up in that hospital, and I love you for being so loyal to your Captain K. But, Track Star, you need to shake it off tonight. One night is all I want. Is that too much?"

She's right and I need a break from the hospital. Kylo's condition seems the same at least based on the number of tubes still attached to him. My family and Raith are getting impatient with my disregard for everyone else but him.

"Cassidy, you're nervous, but he'll be okay for one night. Give yourself a break. One hour. Head to the hospital later if you have to go."

"How do you know I'm nervous?" I ask.

"Butterfly charm," she says, eyes drifting to my wrist.

I hadn't even realized I was gripping it. Not wanting to explain, I reply. "Okay."

"Are you absolutely in?"

"Yes, let's get ready before I change my mind."

"Cool, we're headed to alcohol, loud music and a bunch of horny ass boys and girls."

Why did I agree to this on a Friday night? I would prefer a quiet night here with her.

"That's the itinerary. Get dressed." Raith closes the bathroom door. "Show some skin. That cute fat booty deserves to be seen. We're partying tonight, friend!"

Walking into the frat house reminds me why these parties aren't my thing. Raith dives straight into the center of the living room, where a makeshift dance floor and scattered sofas form a chaotic dance floor. She is the life of every party. Her energy spreads through the crowd beckoning me to join her on the floor.

I watch her dance to Lizzo's "About Damn Time." She's so carefree, so happy, that I feel a little jealous. She points at me, urging me forward as Lizzo sings.

Why am I still standing here debating dancing? *What is wrong with me?* I have not hung out with Raith in forever. Maybe I need this. After a little push from myself, I make my way to the dance floor.

Seven songs later, we're still at it. The DJ is so good that he has me hoping each new track tops the last. I'm dancing so hard, my hair begins to swell in this 90 percent humidity. Crazy doesn't even begin to describe the wild bush forming.

"I needed this!" I scream over the music, ensuring Raith hears me.

"I know, roomie!" she yells, her excitement infectious. She moves her hips to the beat of OneRepublic, skirt threatening to split. My girl can dance. "I knew you needed to get out and shake it off."

As we move, I catch her eyes wandering past me a few times. Is she blushing? "I see someone I need to holla at. You okay for a sec?" she asks.

"Yeah, go ahead. I'm okay," I say, watching as she heads toward a tall, exotic looking girl with waist length braids. She must be a model, influencer or something as she's dominating the room. I watch Raith slip through the glass door with the girl, disappearing into the dark. She hasn't mentioned anyone, but I've been so consumed with my own world.

I glance around taking in the scene. The frat party is alive with people packed in every corner. Red solo cups litter the room, the scent of spilled beer, smoke and sweat mix, forming that college party scent. I'd prefer the antiseptic stench of the hospital right now.

"What's up stranger?" I turn from my people watching to see Walker staring at me as if he's never seen me before. "Been a minute. I never see you anymore," he says.

It's actually a relief to see someone else at the party that I know since Raith left me alone. "Yeah, I've been busy," I say, not wanting to go into detail.

He stares at me far too long, with his Corona hanging loosely from his right hand while his left rests on the wall above me. The stench of too much alcohol blows from his breath as he hovers too close. He's way past his comfort zone and should know better. He leans in, his breath heavy, and says, "How are you so damn beautiful?"

I dip from under his arm, trying to create some space, but he pulls me back. "I've wanted you for a minute. You have to get that." I look away from his childlike serious stare, feeling bad that our friendship is crossing into the awkward zone.

"Walker, I…" Before I finish my words, he yanks my neck, kissing me hard, attempting to force my mouth open. His hands grip my hips, holding me tight making me uncomfortable with his beer bottle lounging on my waist. I don't have any space to move, and I want to get away from the erection he's pushing into me.

I do what I was taught to do. I grab him by the balls and twist hard, making him bend forward, dropping his beer bottle near me. The loud shatter of the glass goes unnoticed with the music thumping, and I hear him gasp. "Stop!" But stopping isn't an option.

His eyes meet mine, pleading as I release my grip off the fabric of his gym shorts. Good thing for me he had those on instead of jeans. "Back up!" I demand not caring if anyone is watching. The darkness hides us anyway so I think our confrontation is lost in the crowd.

"Cassidy," he whispers, his voice shaky and unable to say more.

I release him, watching him clutch the wall for support. I push through the crowd, checking to see if the sliding glass door is open. The door remains closed, reflecting the lively party behind it. I'll catch up with Raith later. I make my way through the crowd, determined not to look back because that's how it works. According to my dad's security team, getting away quickly is the best course of action. That was my first time twisting someone's balls tight enough to cause torsion. Hopefully, it will be my last. What was he thinking? Why did I even come?

I should have stuck with my original plans.

It takes a while for my driver to pick me up from campus, and by the time we arrive at the hospital, just after five in the morning, the sun is already threatening to rise. It's faint glow outlines the horizon, reminding me I'm too late for my usual visit. I should've been here earlier.

Stepping through the hospital's front entrance, no longer using the rear door since my dad hired a driver, I rush in. Initially, he insisted on walking me to the ICU every night, but I convinced him to wait in the car until I told him I was safe.

Not thinking straight, I push straight through the open ICU doors behind a nurse too caught up on her cellphone to notice me. Usually, the nurse's nod me toward Kylo's room but today they look confused, alarmed even. My heart tightens. Something's off. I look toward his room and spot Miss Gwen standing outside, her face mirroring the confusion I feel.

My pulse quickens, fist clenching at my sides. "What's wrong?" I ask, dread creeping into my voice. Miss Gwen's calm shatters, her eyes darting toward the door.

"Hey Cassidy, wait before you go in," she says, blocking my path with her small frame, trying to guide me away.

I slip past Miss Gwen and a security guard, bursting into Kylo's room full of unfamiliar faces, not caring how this "secret" introduction might look. All focus shifts to me, along with the questioning stares. Why are so many people here?

"Cassidy, come with me," Miss Gwen pleads from behind, pushing me out. "Come with me." But I ignore her, my eyes fixed on the scene unfolding before me.

"Are you family?" a doctor demands, his voice sharp and commanding, making it clear I don't belong. My mind races as I take in the scene, glancing from one side of the small hospital room to the other, searching for answers. *What's happening?*

Kylo's bed is elevated, his head raised slightly. A nurse lifts it higher, and I hear the coarse rip of scratchy velcro pulling apart, hanging in the air, sending trembling shivers through me.

Two women standing at his bedside, cry quietly as they witness the nurse move with deliberate slowness, removing straps from the back of his breathing mask. The gravity of the moment crushes me like heavy weights pressing into my chest. "Wait, what are you doing? Why are you removing his… Wait…" my voice trembles, as my words fade.

Miss Gwen wraps her tiny arms around my waist, trapping me within her grip. "Cassidy, you have to come with me," her voice strained.

I yank my arms back, shooting her a look that says she's lost her mind. "I'm not going anywhere," I answer, making sure everyone hears me.

"This woman is not family! Get her out of here! Why the hell are you here anyway? Someone get security!" The voice behind me sets my teeth on edge. Sarah. Did she think she was going to the Met Gala in that silver shoulder-pad jumpsuit showing too much skin? Perfect makeup, glitter in her hair she looks ready for a show, not a hospital room.

Ignoring her dagger-like stare and screeching demands, I push past Miss Gwen and move closer to Kylo's bed. No one's giving me an answer, so I focus on the only person who might, Kylo. For the first time, I see his handsome face without all the equipment. He looks peaceful, as if unaware of the chaos around him.

"Kylo," I call his name again, louder this time. "Kylo! It's time to wake up. It's time!"

"Ma'am are you family?" the doctor asks, impatience and urgency slicing through his words. *Time is running out.*

I ignore them, my world narrowing to the weak beeps of Kylo's heart monitor, each one sounding more spaced out. The steady hum of machines and the ragged breathing of those around me fade to the background.

"Listen to my voice, Kylo!" I plead, voice breaking. "Find your way back. You're strong. You can wake up. Listen to me. Fight!"

"Cassidy," Miss Gwen calls softly, trying again to tug me aside. If she calls me one more time, I might lose it. But I can't think about it now.

"Fight, Kylo!" I scream, desperate as if my words could somehow breathe air into his lungs from the foot of his bed.

"Get her out of here!" Sarah yells again, face twisted in anger. "I want her gone. Why isn't anyone moving?"

I ignore her and everyone else in the cramped room. "Kylo, listen to me," I call, voice shaking. "You want to live. Run like you're on that soccer field! Don't look back! Run, Kylo! Come back to us!"

"Is anyone listening? Get her out!" Sarah screams again, her voice irritating like an itch refusing relief.

"Be quiet!" the doctor's command cuts through the chaos, silencing us all as he checks Kylo's heart monitor, and examines his vitals carefully.

Then, for the first time, he looks at me seriously and nods. "Keep talking. Keep doing what you're doing."

Relief floods me, granting strength I didn't know I had. I slip my hands under the sheets, fingers grazing cold fabric, as I massage his feet as I've done so many times before. "Kylo, I haven't missed a day. I've given you every sports score, every breaking news story, everything that I could find. Please... Fight! Follow my voice, my scent and find your way back! You can do this. Wake for me!"

And just like that... just like in the movies... it happens. His eyelids flutter, then pop open. I freeze, forgetting how to breathe as silence falls thick and heavy. The moment I've prayed for is here.

Gasps fills the room, and his heart rate quickens. The beeping monitor speeds into the sweetest rhythm I've heard in days.

"Kylo, please listen to her..." a voice urges from somewhere. But my focus is only on him. I refuse to miss a second. I grip his cold feet tighter, too hesitant to speak too loudly, watching the white of his sclera fixed on the ceiling tiles. I urge him... to look at me, to hear me.

"Kylo, fight," I whisper, tears gathering, voice trembling. "Keep coming back. You're almost here. Please..."

He's somewhere else, pupils drifting aimlessly. I grip his feet tighter, as if holding him here could keep me from being forced out. Pouring every ounce of energy into massaging his soles, I pray this will give him strength.

"Please Kylo, keep trying," I whisper softly.

He scans the room, taking in faces, until his gaze falls on me. His honey hazels meet mine with an intensity that sends heat through me. Overwhelmed with emotion, I watch him struggle to form words.

"Kylo," I whisper, heart hammering. "It's me, Cassidy. You're safe. Keep fighting."

He blinks slowly, absorbing the scene around him before his focus drifts to the woman at his bedside. His voice cracks as he manages a single word. "Ma."

That one word is the most beautiful sound in the world. It's a word I longed to hear from my own lips, and the moment I'll never have again. His mother falls onto the bed, hugging him tightly, tears streaming down her face. The doctors gather around him, urging us to move. Sarah forces her way to the opposite side of his bed.

I'm still at the foot of the bed, his toes in my hands, unable to move. I feel Miss Gwen's head resting against my arm, her relief matching mine. We're all grateful for this miracle.

As the nurse steps back, Kylo's mother releases him, allowing the doctors to do their checks. Kylo takes in his surroundings, so many anxious eyes on him. He looks weak, his features drawn into his smaller face, but he's here. The sheets lift at either side of him as his arms stir beneath them, proving he can still move. With a look of confusion, he lifts his hands, examining the I V in his arm, raising both hands as if seeing if they are connected to his body. A miracle. He's alive, aware and moving.

"Kylo, it's me," Sarah coos, leaning over the bed rail to hold his hand. She leans in, trying to kiss him. "You scared me, Ky."

I close my eyes, my stomach twisting at the sound of her calling him "Ky." She has a nickname for him?

"Sarah," he whispers. It was raspy and quiet. But his next name is, "Sarah." *Why?* My heart sinks, a heaviness settling in my chest as Miss Gwen's grip around my waist tightens, as if trying to keep me upright. *Why did he have to say her name?*

"Everyone, we need to check him," the doctor announces. Time seems to stretch thin as the medical team swarms Kylo, examining his eyes, checking his temperature, and asking questions. Amazingly, Kylo responds. He's moving and talking. I watch in disbelief as he lifts his arms, as though testing their strength. This is happening.

"My baby is back," the older lady, his mother, I presume... whimpers, while another woman supports her. Kylo shifts his gaze toward the woman with the salt and pepper Hally Berry pixie cut framing her face. "I'm okay," he croaks, his voice raspy and weak. He sounds like he's in pain and like every syllable might cost. *Does he need water?* I want to help, to say something, but I'm frozen...

rooted in place at the foot of the bed, still holding onto his toes beneath the sheets.

He scans the room, taking in each face and manages a small tentative smile. The haze of confusion lifts as he pieces together who's here. "Christian," he says finally, voice filled with hesitancy and relief, as his friend stands nearby, visibly shaken.

"What's up dog? Been a minute," Christian tries to joke, quickly wiping a tear from his eye.

Kylo nods sluggishly, his mind still working to piece together the puzzle of all the faces around him.

Then his honey hazels find me, and for a moment, everything else fades into the background. The doctors, nurses, his mother, Sarah, Christian… all become distant shapes and muffled voices. His gaze drifts down to the crisp white sheets, resting where my hands are holding his feet. I pull away a bit, giving him space in his long, searching stare. I feel hope and fear collide in my chest. Does he remember me? The depth of his confusion is palpable, and I see a thousand questions behind his tired eyes. Doubt prickles along my spine. Will he understand what I've done, how I've fought for him, prayed and pleaded for this moment?

He tries to raise himself up a bit, still weak and trembling. His brow furrows, and he looks at me as if he's confronting a phantom from a half-remembered dream. His lips part.

"Who are you?"

CHAPTER 23

THIS IS MY CRAZY

Cassidy

MY LUNGS COLLAPSE, PUSHING OUT WHAT LITTLE AIR RE-mains. A low moan escapes my lips as my world crumbles into nothing with those words. He doesn't remember me. He doesn't know me. He forgot us. Everyone heard him say it.

I can't bring myself to meet the questioning stares directed my way, each like a flare seeking help that I can't provide.

Sarah's shrill voice cuts through the silence. "Where the hell is security? She's obviously some crazy fan. Get her out!" Her high-pitched complaint pounds more disappointment into my already breaking heart.

I look at Kylo, not saying a word, but inwardly begging him to remember a fragment of our past. His face remains blank, devoid of recognition, eyes shifting as if trying to recall something lost.

At that moment, three security guards squeeze into the remaining space in the overcrowded room, all focus turning to me. "Are you family?" one asks, voice firm. "If not, you must leave immediately."

No answer comes to mind. I'm not family, not a relative, not his girlfriend, not even a pet.

"Excuse me." Miss Gwen wedges herself between me and the guards. "Cassidy, come with me, sweet girl." Her come isn't taking no for an answer and I find myself forced to comply, realizing I'm not needed.

I can't leave, though. A part of me is under those sheets. *Why?* That's how it feels. I grip Miss Gwen's hand for strength, stealing one last glance back at Kylo. Just as I do, Sarah leans down, kissing him on the lips, staring directly at me the entire time. "Sarah," he whispers, leaning into her kiss.

It's over. Defeated, I let Miss Gwen guide me from the room. My chest aches with every step. Out at the nurse's station, I sprint away from the front desk. Raised eyebrows and concerned looks trail after me, but I can't stop. I push through the double doors, past the ICU waiting room, past the stargazer lilies waging a losing battle against the hospital's sterile smell. Finally, I burst out the front entrance.

My driver waits in the car, expecting a text from me, but I ignore that for now. I need air...cold air. I have to leave this place before my lungs seize up again. Remembering my last panic attack only intensifies my pain. He was there to help me then.

Why is this happening? Why am I so upset? How did I get here so fast?

Darting through the front glass doors, I pass people entering the hospital, likely thinking I look crazy. Outside a chill kisses my skin. It's refreshing and shocking. I slow down, palms on my knees, sucking in major air. *Don't close up, lungs.* Not now. I hope no cars pull into the drop-off lane because I'm not moving.

Glancing back at the hospital, I spot a wooden bench tucked away in a grassy corner, something like a memorial. Perfect, I need to sit and catch my breath.

"Breathe...Cass," I tell myself. *In and out.* I stretch out on the wooden bench, wincing as the cold exposed nails press into my back. My hair tangles against the rough wood, but I don't care. I tilt my head, eyes drifting up into a pale blue sky, free of clouds, where a few birds glide under the rising sun. If dad saw me like this, sprawled out in yesterday's clothes, borderline hysterical, he'd definitely want me home. *This is my crazy.*

Thankfully, my airways clear, and there's no sign of a panic attack. I stare back at the hospital windows in disbelief, trying to convince myself what happened inside was real.

Why does he remember Sarah? Why did I let myself fall so fast? How did I get here and what was I thinking?

I need my mom. I need home. This is too much. I shouldn't be feeling anything this fast.

"Excuse me." An older woman stands before me, genuine concern warming her face as she leans in closer. She notices my feet dangling off the edge of the bench, my hair tangled against the rough wood.

Get it together, crazy. "I'm so sorry," I say, sitting up to give her room. Embarrassment floods over me as I run my fingers through my frizz. How did I forget I'm out in public, doing something unexplainable that the media could easily spin into a story, especially with my dad's name attached to it? That's never happened with us and it's his goal to keep it that way.

The lady clears her throat again, still standing beside me. "I'm sorry. I..." I try to explain but don't, instead patting down my hair. I must have looked completely unhinged in that ICU room. Glancing back at the hospital, I see reporters already starting to arrive. News travels fast… Kylo's awake.

"I was in the room with you when Kylo came out of his coma." The woman says. "Do you remember seeing me?"

I let my eyes settle on her, the early sunlight framing her silhouette. I try to recall if I saw her in Kylo's room. Was she one of the older ladies at his bedside? Everything happened so fast. "I'm sorry," I say. "I didn't realize you were there."

"May I sit?" she asks calmly.

"Sure," I say, making room for her on the rough, wooden bench. She settles gracefully, dressed in an ivory suit, legs crossed neatly, hands folded in her lap. Her hair is pulled back into a sleek bun, and a scarf drapes elegantly around her neck. Who is she, and why is she here on my makeshift "crazy bench" with me?

She laces her manicured red fingernails together, as though preparing for prayer, and adjusts her already perfect posture before meeting my gaze. "I am Diane Crosby. Kylo is my nephew. His mom is my sister. How do you know him?"

I'm speechless for a moment, not expecting this. She's Kylo's aunt? Someone from his family is sitting with me on my crazy bench, while I'm still wearing hot leather, my hair a mess and my emotions all over the place. I glance down at my nails then to my bracelet. The purple and gold butterfly charm catches the sunlight and somehow keeps me going. It's my tiny spark of comfort.

The gentle clearing of her throat brings me back to her question.

"I met Kylo a couple of weeks ago," I manage to say, my words barely above a whisper, so soft it nearly blends with the rustling leaves overhead.

"So, you are the young lady who's been coming to the hospital every night for the past few weeks?" Her matter-of-fact words startles me. How does she know?

"You knew?" I ask, surprised.

"Baby, Aunt Diane knows everything," she says with a smile. "You're the reason his scars healed so well with that expensive Vitamin C you used on him."

She piques my interest by mentioning the Vitamin C serum. "You knew about that, too?"

Baby, there's not much that gets past me," she says with a smile. "I recognized that lush, tropical botanical forest scent on his skin weeks ago. My own skincare line I've used for years has this product and this serum is expensive. Whoever was caring for him invested a lot and not just money, but time into his recovery." She pauses, studying me carefully, as if trying to understand how I could afford such products and why I'd use them on Kylo. Then she pats my leg gently. "When you reach my age, you learn to notice the little things."

I hate to admit it, but I already have a soft spot for this lady.

"I've been here with his mom, Juanita, every morning," she continues. "I noticed that someone else was caring for him. So, I asked the nurses if anyone was coming regularly after us. You see, I knew it wasn't Sarah Sims. She hasn't been here since the night of the accident. She only showed up today because Kylo's agent told her the doctors planned to bring him out of his medically induced coma for the second time. That girl doesn't have a caring bone in her body. What is your name, young lady?"

Second time? My spine tingles at the revelation. He's been through so much more than I realized.

I straighten up a bit, suddenly self-conscious, wishing I had a brush or a hat. "I'm Cassidy," I say, hesitating before adding Pittman. "I met Kylo on campus at A&M."

"What class are you?" her eyes narrow, waiting for my answer.

"I'm a freshman," I respond, noticing her doubtful look. It's a look I know all too well from my dad. "I took a three-year gap before starting."

She studies me as if expecting more explanation. "You don't have a jacket or a sweater. Winter's coming sooner this year. Are you cold?" She changes the subject, and I'm grateful. I watch her gaze drift beyond me, nodding thoughtfully, as if gauging the weather.

"I'm okay," I say, suddenly aware of the chill now that she's mentioned it. I left my sweatshirt in my driver's car.

"Take my jacket before you freeze those muscular arms," she insists, removing her Antonio Melani blazer and draping it around my shoulders. Then she digs into her Coach bag and pulls out a matching fan wider than my shoulders. "I'm having a summer breeze, hot flash… whatever you want to call it. But you must be cold."

"Thank you for the jacket," I murmur, appreciative. "Honestly,

I didn't notice how cool it was when I came out." Without looking at Ms. Diane, I ask softly, "How is he?"

"He's okay. He actually got up and walked halfway to the restroom with little assistance after they removed his catheter. The hospital's full of reporters, sports folk and others who haven't been here for weeks. But that's how it goes," she says.

My voice comes out shaky, almost childish. "Does he remember anything?" I need to know. *Pull it together.*

"No, he doesn't remember much about the accident. But the cops showed us videos weeks ago. He was driving toward A&M, five minutes away, when he was t-boned on his side."

I've waited for days to hear this. He was coming to see me. He was heading in my direction. Something was different, he felt something… like I did. Sarah Sims was wrong.

As the realization hits me, I shift abruptly, heart pounding, thoughts spinning. If he was on his way to see me, then somehow I'm a part of this.

I struggle to keep my emotions in check as I look away. "I'm sorry for all of this. He was coming to pick me up that night. I am the reason…" My words falter as I sit, gesturing toward the hospital, where reporters set up cameras for the breaking news of Kylo waking up.

"Hush now," Diane soothes, drawing me into her arms and rocking me gently, as if I were a child. "I know my nephew. He took one look at you and fell in love. This isn't your burden to bear. If anything, you're the reason he fought back from that coma. What I saw was nothing short of a miracle. He followed your voice, your words, your strength until he made it back to us. He doesn't remember you right now, but in time, maybe he will."

She releases my shoulder, then warmly squeezes my hand. "My sister needs me," she says, glancing toward the hospital. "Do you have a ride home?"

"Yes. My driver is here."

She nods, arching her eyebrow again. "Get out of this cold and

off this memorial bench. I don't think this area is intended for sitting," she adds, pointing to a bronze plaque I hadn't noticed before,
clearly stating East Memorial.

Reaching into her bag, she hands me a card. "If you ever want
to reach him, call me. Take care of yourself. Get indoors, and keep
the jacket."

CHAPTER 24

WAKE ME

Kylo

WHO'S MASSAGING ME WITH THOSE STRONG HANDS? HER fingers take their time, slipping between my toes, touching on that spot where cotton from my socks used to hang out as a kid. Damn this feels good. She smells good, too. *Who is this?*

Everything fades away again. *Where did the light go?* Darkness. *Wake me.*

There she is again. *Who is she?* She's talking, saying so many words. I can't understand. Don't leave me behind in this confusion.

Darkness again. It comes, taking me with it. *Why am I so tired? Who's crying? Why? I can't see.*

The lights grow dim, like a storm rolling in with heavy, dark clouds. So black. I've never seen darkness like this before. *Where are my hands?*

Soft, wet lips press against my forehead, my cheek, my ears and my lips. *Don't stop.* She's begging me to come back. Come back where? *Wake me, please.*

The lights dim again, leaving me too weak to fight as the night swallows me.

What is that smell? Perfume? Jasmine, vanilla, lavender? If I could lick that smell, I would. But it fades too quickly, and goes as soon as it appears. *Wake me, girl. I want to follow you.*

Are those hands touching me? Is someone here? I hear someone screaming at me to come back. "Find your way back! Wake up!" she yells. *Who is she?*

She sounds desperate, begging me to follow her voice. *Did she say kick? Kick what? Who are you? I'm waking for you.*

The fog takes over again, rays of light disappearing. Now it's cloudy and calm, huge cotton balls floating in the air. The light hides behind each one.

I hear a voice… her voice. It's deeper than most women's, carrying a sultry edge with a sexiness. There's a hint of the south in her voice, softened by time, but it sounds like she's lived in California. She's screaming loud enough to scatter my cotton clouds of comfort.

Why is she screaming?

"Kylo!" she yells, louder than I've heard my Aunt Diane scream at me or Tron. *What's wrong with her?* "Kylo!"

There it is again. This time, it's desperate. It makes my damn head hurt worse. I need her to *wake me.*

Everything's heavy. My eyelids feel weighed down by bricks, forcing them shut. The screams magnify everything. I push every ounce of strength just to shut her up and pry my eyes open, to make her stop screaming. Finally, I peel my lids apart, as if they're glued together.

Light comes in slowly, starting like a piercing expanding into a bright, wide funnel.

"Where am I?" Everything's blurry. I blink hoping it will help me focus. The ceiling comes in… I think it's a ceiling, white square tiles coming in and out of focus as the room seems to stretch and shift. There's a white arm…no, a device… hanging from the ceiling down the side of my bed. Damn, wires and cords are everywhere.

Wait, these cords are attached to me: in my hands and legs. *Am I lying down?* White sheets cover every inch of me, confirming

I'm in bed. I'm feeling sensations now, sensing everything. No more fog, clouds or darkness blinding me into blackness.

The light above is painfully bright, like staring in the sun. Even my sense of smell is amped. I can see people around my bed and smell them, too. But why are they staring at me as if I'm lying in a casket? Questions race through my mind. Am I in a hospital? The antiseptic smell, faint and medicinal, tells me I am.

"My baby," I recognize that voice. I turn, stretching my neck muscles, which feel as though they might snap. Everything's tight. *Why is moving so hard?* I have a thousand why's but not one answer.

She leans in, gripping my bed rail, until her knuckles whiten. Her trembling shoulders and thin gray hair are all I see, blurred by my watery vision. Is she crying? She never cries. *No, Miss Blade don't do this.*

"Ma." It feels like fifteen seconds to whisper that shaky word from my throat feeling like fucking fire. I grip my legs, trying to handle the pain from talking. I swallow, but hate it as my scratchy throat burns like raw wounds being soaked in alcohol. The burn is so intense I can't force another word out. Where's the water? There's not enough saliva in the world to calm this fire.

Her sniffle takes my attention from my throat. She's crying. I try lifting my trembling fingers toward her, but it's too much effort. I can't see her tears. I grip my legs tighter to distract myself, and a sweet scent draws me to the other side of my bed.

"Sarah." Did I just say her name? Why is she here? Damn, that hurt. My voice is barely a whisper.

Christian and my agent, Bruce, stand behind her, staring at me as if they've seen a ghost. "What up, Chris?" I manage to ask.

I miss whatever Christian is saying because a guy in the white coat starts poking and prodding me, examining every part of me. What happened to me?

Then I feel it, down near my toes. Is someone playing with my feet? It feels like tiny fingers are wedged in between them, massaging my size thirteens. Damn that feels good. I relax into my pillow, lost in the gentle scrape of nails along my heels. I forget to look at who's performing the magic but wonder who would want to play with my feet.

My heavy eyelids lift again, focusing on the white sheet covering my feet. My gaze travels the length of the bed beyond my toes, where I see hips wrapped in a black bodysuit so perfect that it hugs her narrow waist and curves up to her breasts. Suddenly, she jerks away, pulling her hands from my feet. Did I scare her? Who the hell is she?

My mind is entranced. My tired eyes are locked on her, unable to break from the pull she's casting. Damn, her parents must have been making sweet ass love when she was conceived, because "beautiful" isn't enough for what I see.

She pats her frizzy hair, tucking a strand behind her ear, making me wonder if she just left a party. The outfit doesn't seem like her normal style. She's not comfortable in her skintight bodysuit, satisfying my heavy-lidded stare. She's nervous, fidgeting, her parted lips and uncertain eyes hinting at something she wants but can't have.

I try to push myself up from the bed, but my arms are weak and shaky. How can I get closer? I need to be closer. "Who are you?" I ask, hardly able to choke the words out over my raw throat.

She presses her lips together and frowns, as if my words stabbed at an unhealed wound. The hurt shining in her eye's cuts deep. What did I say wrong?

"Security, get her out!" Sarah's screeches stop the moment, making my head pound, as though someone's hammering inside my skull.

I lay back in bed, my attention fixed on the black leather. She stares at me, as if wanting something, but what? Then with a final plea, tears threatening, she turns and leaves. The nurse follows close behind her, hiding that bodysuit satisfying my eyes.

Christian steps closer, looking like he wants to say something, but Sarah leans in, drawing my attention to her low-cut top. Did she unbutton it? *Wait, what was I thinking?* Everything's off. But,

Sarah's getting my attention with what's peaking between her silver shirt. *Is she wearing a bra?*

"Take it easy, Kylo," she whispers, pressing a wet kiss on my cheek. Her lips make me want more, but before I can lean in she pulls away. I almost forget that the room is full of people, all watching me. Too much is happening fast. My mind's racing, jumping from one thought to another, unable to settle.

I stretch my neck back to Miss Blade, seeing Aunt Diane for the first time. *Has she been here this whole time in that cream-colored suit?* "What?" is all I can get out. I want to ask what happened, but even finding the strength for one word feels like hell.

"Baby, you were in a car accident," Miss Blade says softly, as if reading my mind. A *car accident?*

I lift my eyebrows, hoping she understands my silent question: "When did it happen?"

She doesn't get a chance to answer because three serious looking doctors in white coats enter my room, all eyes on me.

"Everyone out," one of them says, voice firm. "We need a complete physical and don't want to overwhelm him."

"I'm not going anywhere. He's my boyfriend," Sarah protests. Even with my lids heavy and half closed, that voice makes my head split. Please, Miss Blade, read my thoughts and get her ass out.

"Everyone out except for my sister." Aunt Diane's Southern accent cuts through the tension like a commandment etched in stone telling everyone what to do. I open my left eye to see if anyone dares to challenge her. As I thought, everyone leaves, without a goodbye.

Most people close to me know not to mess with Aunt Diane. She's that aunt... the one who spanked me and my brother Tron more than Miss Blade ever did, always finishing with an, "I love you."

Sarah clears her throat at Aunt Diane, as if she wants to say something. She's asking to be thrown out of my hospital window by confronting Aunt D. Her ass must be crazy for real.

I'm too tired to watch, but Aunt D's *don't try me* popping across my bed silences my room.

The soft sound of breathing and faint scent of perfume drifts closer, coaxing my heavy lids open. Sarah's silhouette comes into view, her curves evident beneath the delicate, silky fabric of her shirt. No bra. My body reacts down low, and she notices, stepping closer with a teasing smile. "So glad some things haven't changed. I cannot wait until you are out of this bed."

A throat clears off to our left, the sound cracking like thunder. Only Aunt D can clear a throat loud enough to force an entire congregation from church.

As everyone leaves, I struggle to stay awake for Miss Blade. I can't imagine what these past days, weeks, months have been like for her. *How long have I been in this bed?* The worry lines around her lips are deeper now, her eyes red and swollen. She can't lose both her sons. Tron and me? That can't happen.

Whatever this is, I won't let it defeat me. I can't allow her to live alone. I won't let that shit happen as I force my trembling hand to her gray and black hair. *I will beat this, for her.*

"Son," she calls my name, her voice trembling so intensely that my bed seems to shake. The doc's pause their poking, giving her space to cry in a way I've never seen before. I push through the burning in my shoulders, forcing my arms to hug her. I can feel the frailness of her thin shoulder blades poking her black sweater. She's lost weight…too much. She was already small and now this.

One of the shorter doc's watches every movement, transcribing as she cries. This is the cry she never let me witness after Tron died. She was too strong to let it show then. *I hate this.*

Hearing her pain makes me forget my own. "I'm good," I rasp, throat still raw. "I'm not going anywhere." It takes everything I have to say those four words out, but I need her to feel safe. *That's my job.*

"Ouch!" I jerk my leg away as another doctor stabs my foot. *How many are in here?*

"Okay, I guess you felt that," he chuckles, stepping around to my side.

"Go lite," I warn, my voice still scratchy. "Those are money making feet."

He snorts, running a hand through his hair. "Trust me, I know exactly how important they are. I've been on call every day since you got here. The league insisted. We're going to remove the catheter and start physical therapy."

He raises the bed, and I adjust to all the cords connected to me, as my mind goes into a mental world wind.

What happened?

How long?

Soccer?

"Are you up for physical therapy this afternoon?" the doctor asks. "After a brain injury, the body can move forward quickly if we catch the momentum. Let's not miss any of this coming our way." The doc's question with PT makes me anxious as hell to get ready. There's no need to question. *Hell yeah, I'm ready.*

"Yeah, Doc," I answer, pushing aside the questions about soccer and everything else for later. I'm not ready to deal with the truth just yet.

The main doctor steps back, one hand tucked tightly under his chin, a hint of surprise. "Based on my initial assessments, I expect a full recovery. We'll run more tests to be sure," he pauses, giving me a once-over. "I can't believe you're actually sitting up. It's interesting how you came back as you did."

Something about my awakening confuses him. "What's interesting?" I ask.

He glances at Miss Blade, and they exchange a silent understanding. Am I missing something?

"Baby," Miss Blade says, softly. "We'll talk later. For now, I want nothing but to hear you talk, laugh, sit up, walk and even pass gas."

"You sure you missed the gas?" I joke, forcing a grin.

"Yes, baby I missed it all," she sniffs, squeezing my hands so tight it stings. But I don't mind. It feels good to be alive.

The next few days pass quickly. After a week in the hospital, I'm finally home, ready to start rehab and team physical therapy. The media frenzy was crazy when I left, with fans, paparazzi and reporters clamoring for any glimpse of me walking out the hospital. Security teams were on constant watch, and I think the hospital discharged me early to lighten their load. Back home, more reporters tried to gather, but our neighbors grew tired of the chaos, closing off our privacy gates. I'm grateful. I don't need an audience watching every move. It's hard enough trying to figure this out on my own.

My muscles are so weak, it takes time and effort to get through basic workouts. But, after a couple of days I'm making it through simple routines. Nothing too challenging, but I got a start. That game and Miss Blade are the only things pushing me to walk faster, jog longer and lift heavier weights. I won't let this defeat me.

Physically, most things are good, except for my memory. I have a few scars, some lingering weakness from being bedridden, and a hoarse voice. Other than that, my recovery feels like a miracle after that car accident and thirteen days in a medically induced coma. My short-term memory around the accident is still blank… no recollection of the day I woke or the month leading up to it. But recalling recent conversations is improving, thanks to Aunt D's daily questions. Doc says it's normal and may never fully return. If that's the worst, I can live with it. I can walk, run, and talk. Fucking grateful.

Miss Blade hasn't left my side, and Aunt D moved in to help. They're cooking nonstop, making me wonder if we're expecting company with each meal. Losing thirty pounds in the hospital has them convinced I'm too skinny. At this rate, gaining fifty pounds by the end of the month should come easy. After a week, the scale already shows I'm up seven pounds.

"Alright baby boy, here's two pancakes, three boiled eggs and fruit. Drink at least two bottles of water before you go to physical therapy," Aunt D says, placing the plate in front of me. She then snaps my breakfast napkin and sits there, watching. *Damn Aunt D, I'll eat, I promise.*

I start with my eggs, noticing that she and Miss Blade have on matching red and blue flannel pajamas with yellow socks. Maybe one of my vendors sent them as a gift. I always get two of everything for both of them. Not certain what's going on, but they've been coordinating outfits all week. I drown my pancakes in maple syrup, mainly to keep Aunt D from staring at me like a toddler about to toss food on the floor. I realize I've never seen two sisters more opposite. My brother Tron and I looked alike, even if I was the taller by four inches, but Miss Blade and Aunt D are different in everything from height to style.

Miss Blade, my mom, is 5'1 with a round and petite figure. Her style suits her age, in my opinion, and she rarely wears makeup or tries to change her look. I pre-pay for her hair and nail appointments for a year just to make her go. She hates spending money on herself.

Aunt Diane is the total opposite of my Miss Blade. She's maybe 5'8 with a body according to my teammates. She wants all the attention when she walks in a room and the main reason I get two of everything. She never misses a chance to brag about me to anyone willing to listen. She and Uncle Joe have been married for around forty years with three girls, my sisters from another mother.

Most weekends it was the five of us together while Miss Blade worked two, sometimes three jobs. Aunt D didn't want us home. She always thought trouble was near. *She was right.* Her house was the weekend refuge. Most Saturdays was spent helping Uncle Joe with whatever he was fixing, from cars, to lawnmowers, or a busted sink. He'd have us hold a flashlight for hours, barely breathing, for whatever repair he was finishing. They both took care of us with Aunt D always cooking, but it was never enough. The girls were always full. But I'd end up on the sofa at night, stomach growling louder than the hum of the refrigerator. Uncle Joe would sneak in food after everyone was asleep after not getting caught smoking. I can still smell his smoke breath, heaving. "Diane should know one piece of chicken ain't enough for you. You a growing boy. Take these three pieces and go to bed," he'd say, with me devouring that chicken to the bone and sleeping full.

It's crazy how certain memories stick with you. Even after my coma, I still remember how Uncle Joe watched Aunt D at dinner. He'd sit there, cornbread suspended halfway to his mouth, finger-nails stained with engine oil, just staring at her. He was hardly ever home, always working under a hood at his garage, handing over his entire paycheck to Aunt D every Friday and keeping maybe fifteen dollars for himself. He never wanted anything for himself but he was the closest thing we knew to a dad. The man donated the sperm bounced years ago.

It was Uncle Joe coming to the house, bringing new cleats or soccer balls, always making me swear not to tell Miss Blade. He made almost every game we played if he didn't have to work. I could always count on the smoke clouding the air from his cig-arettes near the scoreboard, with his brimmed hat cocked to the side, arms draped over the fence, watching us play.

He didn't understand soccer. We had gone over the offsides rule so many times during dinner that Aunt Diane proudly told him to give up. I felt sorry for him sometimes. Aunt D could be over the top. She wanted to run everything and everyone. I guess after all these years, Uncle Joe learned how to deal with her and move on with life.

Aunt D shops, attends church and goes to every funeral in the county, even if she never met the deceased. My personal shopper buys all of her church outfits, with all the color, bling and match-ing hats. She sends photos every Sunday of herself walking into church and the funeral for the week, claiming that she brings the Lord in with her. According to her, the Lord doesn't show up until she does in her Sunday best. I still haven't figured out who her personal photographer is every Sunday at church.

I stand from the barstool, scraping the left-over pancakes from my plate, aware both women are watching my every move. They're probably waiting for me to pass out so they can catch me before I hit the floor. At six four and still recovering, I'd flatten them both if they tried that. I open my arms and hug them tightly. "What would I do without you two?"

"You'd be thirty pounds lighter, just skin and bones," Aunt D jokes, smiling as I hold them close. "Juanita, I'm going to marinate the chicken."

She heads into the kitchen, nodding at Miss Blade to follow to prepare the next buffet they're cooking. "Okay, I'll be there soon. How are you, baby?" she asks, her usual concern softening her voice.

Before I can get a word in, something that hasn't happened in years does: tears start flowing. What the hell is wrong with me? My emotions, thoughts… everything is all over the place after the accident.

I sink into the sofa, head in my hands, trying to pull it together. Miss Blade's soft voice comes from behind. "Son, just let it all out." But her words don't help.

I glance up, not wanting to see tears in her eyes but knowing they're there. "I saw the video of the accident last night," I say quietly. "It was close. Every report said if the impact shifted even an inch this way or that, that would have been it for me." Blocking out those images is impossible. The bed of the truck ended up halfway across the street, the cabin crumbled like foil. I was cocooned in airbags, and my truck crushed to half its size. The what-ifs and questions keep circling, triggered by that damn video.

She rests her head on my shoulder, sniffles breaking the silence. "Diane and I saw it weeks ago," she says, squeezing my hand. "I believe an angel must have shielded you," she whispers, tears dripping onto my pants.

Angel? Did I hear her right?

She looks away, her gaze locking onto the fireplace where all of our family pictures line the mantel. "Baby, you shouldn't have survived according to those reports. But by grace, and maybe an angel, you're here with me," she sniffs again, wiping her tears.

I'm still uncertain about this "angel," so I ask softly. "Are you talking about Tron?" I avoid meeting her eyes, not wanting to see the pain that comes with his name.

"Yes, I believe Tron helped you during that accident," she takes a deep breath, steadying herself. "They had to cut what was left of your truck in half to get you out. Joe's friend, he was at the scene, said he'd never seen anyone survive a wreck that bad in his fifty years as a firefighter."

I nod slowly. "He was always protecting me. You remember that?"

She straightens, as if remembering something important. "Yes, he was always there for you, Kylo. He's still looking out for us."

Her words ease a part of me I didn't know needed it. "Are you okay?" I ask, feeling uneasy at the sight of her tears. It's hard to see her this way.

She gives me a smile, not one of those fake ones hiding her pain. I know those well. "Baby, I'm better than I've been in years. A part of me stopped living when Tron died. A mother should never have to bury her baby. But I promised God that if he brought you back, I would stop dwelling in self-pity and cherish everything this life has to offer. For the first time in so long, I feel... free. I miss him, but the pain isn't as deep anymore. I can handle it because I know he's still with us. That's the only way you survived," she pauses, squeezing my hands. "He made his way back to us to save you. Are you okay?"

I swallow thickly. "I think so. While I was in that coma, it felt like I wasn't alone, like someone was pushing me to wake. It's strange."

She nods again, smiling as she pats my shoulder. "Baby, you

had a lot of angels watching over you this whole time." She steps away, leaving me feeling like there's something I'm missing.

Rehab, physical therapy, whatever you call it, is hard as hell. It takes every ounce of strength not to give up. The doctors keep telling me my progress is beyond normal and to wait, it'll happen. But every bone, every muscle, every fiber aches as I ease into my Epsom salt bath. No cold plunge today. That shits out, I can't do it.

I'm being hard on myself and I know it, but I need to gain more muscle. I'm too small. I can't lift what I used to, can't run as fast, can't kick the same. My strength isn't there yet. What if it never comes back? What if…

My cell rings, showing Christian's name, pulling my mind from my "what if's."

"What up sick and shut in?" he jokes, laughter echoing.

"Man, nothing much," I say, leaning back in the tub. "Watching King James beat up on the Hawks, getting my Epsom soak on. I'm done with that cold plunge shit. The PT's better find another way."

"Bro, a lil' ice ain't gone kill you, is it?"

Christian's question brings back memories of coaches forcing me into ice. "I'm done with that unnecessary bullshit. It isn't happening no more."

"Funny," Christian says slowly. "I remember you getting in an ice bath with no hesitation."

"Not me, dog. You got me confused." There's no way in hell I got in ice without force. It used to take three coaches and a call to Miss Blade.

He pauses, making me check for a bad connection. "Chris?"

"You don't remember taking a cold plunge on your own?" he asks.

I shift, trying to ease the soreness in my ankle. I probably should have iced. "Nah bro'. Not me. Why?"

"Forget it," he says, brushing it off. "What's up with soccer?"

I wish I could avoid this because my return to soccer feels uncertain. "Coach called yesterday. The team trainer's been here every day monitoring my progress. They're saying two, maybe three weeks and I could be back practicing. It's crazy. I almost straight died, what, a month ago."

Christian pauses again. "Yeah, I know. That shit was crazy. I'm glad you straight, though. I didn't have anyone else to bullshit with those weeks."

Since Tron passed, Christian's been like a brother to me. We're the same age, both from the south and we understand each other. On the field, there's no Kylo without Christian. He's the one that checks me when no one else can. He doesn't hold back or go along with anything. I missed this dude for real.

"I'm coming over tomorrow night for dinner. Aunt Diane invited me. Yeah, Aunt D," Christian jokes.

"Bro, I told you about my folks. She's got about forty years on you," I say, then lower my voice just in case she's outside listening. They're so overprotective. "Aunt D might put something on you that you can't handle. Leave her alone. What time you coming through?"

"Around six o'clock. You straight?"

"Yeah bro, I'm good."

"Alright, bet."

"Later," I reply, hanging up. I lie back into my lukewarm water, my mind drifting to the accident. Everything's still so unclear. I don't even remember the day I woke from the coma. Miss Blade said I came out, did physical therapy that same day, then slept off and on for two days straight. They thought I'd slipped back under, but the doctors said it was just deep rest. By the third day, I guess I'd caught up on all my sleep, because I was awake again.

I hope my memories return, but if not, I'm grateful for what I have. Whatever was lost during that time doesn't matter. It was too short.

My phone rings again. It's Sarah. I'll finish my soak and call her back later.

Sarah...now that's a fine piece of work. Things were off between us, I know that much. But I need some relief, and what's between those thighs of hers would help right now. My doctors keep
telling me to hold off on getting some. But I might explode if I wait
too long. I'll listen this time since they got me this far.

But Sarah isn't making it easy for me, though. She was over
last night with a dress so short I thought it was a shirt. When she
bent over to get my slides, only her perfect ass was showing, and no
thong. I can still see Aunt D peering over her leopard print glasses,
ready to strangle her. *Aunt D hates Sarah.*

I held back this time, only for Aunt D's sake. I'm sure she,
and her reading glasses, were stationed at my window, keeping
watch. But molding Sarah's breasts into her BMW and getting in
between those legs was my only wish. I can still see her with that
shirt dress on the ground, not caring if neighbors were peeping out
the windows or not.

She never demands answers. Sharing me with other women
has always been normal. She does whatever I ask with no questions
and that shit never gets old. Sometimes watching her with other
women is enough. Maybe I'll do that next week at her place with
them on her leopard print ottoman.

Waiting this long isn't happening. Something's got to change.

CHAPTER 25

BOB MARLEY

Cassidy

HEAR THE PAVEMENT, CASSIDY. MAKE IT FEEL LIKE YOU'RE gliding, almost floating. *My steps are too loud. I'm hitting the pavement too hard. Quiet them, lighten them. Pace yourself… Let it flow like music. Forget everything Cassidy. Just focus on your stride. Pace, pace, let it become a rhythm…*

"Track Star!" Raith's scream jolts me out of my trance. She's behind me, panting heavily, as if Jason from Friday the thirteenth is chasing her.

"What's going on?" I ask, slowing my pace.

"Are you kidding? Did you not hear me calling you a dozen times? It's like you're deaf or something… or do you have on AirPods?"

I reach toward my ears, realizing I'm not wearing them. *Did I really not hear her?* "Sorry, Raith," I say, still catching my breath. "I…I was in my zone."

She bends forward, resting her hands on her knees, her breathing rapid and shallow, like she's on the verge of a panic attack. "A zone? Really?" she asks, squinting at me through the bright morning sun. "And would you stop jogging in place? You're about to make me vomit from all that bouncing straight into an asthma attack.

What's wrong with you and why are you sprinting circles around the track? Is somebody chasing you?"

If this was Jeopardy, I'd choose "No Answers for a 100." But this is Raith and she's going to want Zone 500 for all the answers. "I'm just training. Is everything okay?" I say, hoping she'll drop it.

She wipes the sweat off her forehead. "Cassidy, running full-on sprints isn't normal training. Is it?" Her expression is a mixture of confusion and concern.

I didn't realize I was at it that hard. "I'm trying to get my body right to compete with these younger girls. Coming back after three years isn't going to be easy," I admit, bracing myself for more questions since my run is finished for today. I walk to my cooler to grab some water. "Want one?"

"Yeah, before I die," she replies, limping toward the stands. I wonder how far she ran just to catch me.

I hand her a bottle of water with a slow melting long-frozen ice cube inside. She downs over half of it, then swirls the rest around the ice, probably hoping to melt it faster. "Cassidy…"

She doesn't have to finish. I already know what's coming. "Yes, Raith."

"You're worrying me."

"I'm worrying myself, too," I say, rubbing my temples. The headache that's been dogging me for weeks flares back up again. I've tried to forget everything and bury it all beneath miles of running. "I'll be okay," I add.

She arches an eyebrow. "How do you know that?"

Pressing my palm against my forehead, I try to hold off the throb pulsing behind my eyes. "Raith," I finally say, the confession tumbling out, "he doesn't remember me…he only remembers Sarah. He may never remember me. I have to move on."

She gets up from the bleachers and starts pacing the concrete near the track, an unexpected burst of energy lighting up her stance. "Cassidy. Tell him. He needs to hear it from you," she insists, looking as though she's about to scold her trio of mischievous little brothers.

"No, Raith. It's not that simple. How can you recreate feelings for someone you don't even remember?" The uncertainty in my own voice sounds weak. I know, deep down, it's going to take time. This was not a random hookup. At least, not for me.

She levels me with a stare, the kind that makes grown people shrink. "Look, this is a problem. Look at you. When was the last time you got your hair done? The braids are not you. And you've lost so much weight. Maybe it's all this running like you're Usain Bolt, or maybe you're not eating. You don't sleep. I hear you at night crying, which means I don't get any rest, either. Do you know how hard it is to wake me?"

"Raith."

"No Cassidy, I'm not done. I haven't slept in days, which is saying something for me." She points at her eyes. "Look at these bags. Look at these dark circles."

I glance at her face, noticing no bags as she points toward her lashes. I didn't even think it was possible to wake her. "Raith, I know I've been off ever since…everything happened. I just need… I…" My voice gives out, unable to say more.

"Cassidy. We'll do this in baby steps," she says, shaking her head sadly. "Hair and makeup this week."

"What?" None of what she's saying makes sense.

"Hair and makeup. Everyday."

"Why?"

"Because, if you're not going to be honest with him, life has to move on. Dwelling on what might've been will dim your inner light and leave nothing behind. Prime example… this hair," she pulls the end of my braid that hasn't' been untwisted in a week. "You're going to be Bob Marley soon, and you're doing him an injustice. Don't get me wrong. I love me some Bob Marley and I would've given him some if he was still alive, but this isn't you."

I can't help but grin. "Bob Marley, Raith?"

She laughs. "Hey, the legend could've gotten it, no doubt. But for you, the first two weeks are hair and makeup."

"And after that?" I ask, curious.

"Baby steps. I'll figure that out later. And one more thing, disappearing without texting has to stop. We're going to Life 360 with each other. That fool is still taking girls out here."

I chew a ragged hangnail, so grateful for my girl but still so lost. "I can't find me, Raith."

She puts a hand on my arm and squeezes gently. "Then we'll find you together. But first, you might wanna take a shower... maybe a cold plunge to freeze your v-jay because you smell like a gym bag."

I roll my eyes. "I've been running out here an hour."

She doubles over, panting, appearing out of breath already. "What? How do you do that?"

"It calms me. I used to run when Mom was sick. Taking care of her, homework and track was all I had for three straight years until she." My throat closes around the word I still can't say.

Raith exhales, like she's deciding her next. "Okay, topic change. Where's your phone, Cassidy?"

How does she notice everything? "In our room."

"I have one last request," Raith says, "Keep this phone on you at all times. We need a way to contact each other. Whoever's grabbing girls around here is already up to six."

I nod, too worn out to protest. "Sure," I reply. Any resistance I might have had is long gone anyway as her red coils and blonde tips distract me from forming a counter argument. "Raith, how long have you had that hair color?"

She stops, staring at me as though I've lost it. "You're absolutely freaking me out. This hair has been red and blonde for a whole month! Have I been invisible? I mean, do you see me, do you see me now, right now?" she asks, waving her hands in the air.

My gaze settles on my bracelet, tempted to hold it but decide against it. "I think I'm losing it," I mumble. *Has she really been sporting red hair for a month?*

"Look, never mind," she says, sighing. "Plus, my hair will be different by tomorrow. But I do have some ideas for this." She picks up my braid and quickly drops it, as if she suspects lice might be crawling in my roots. "To the salon!" she yells, in that corny copy-cat TikTok voice.

"Today?" I ask, dreading the idea of going to a salon. I'm not in the mood.

"Yes, today. You need a wash, conditioner, shape and maybe some color, before Marley shows up and tells you to turn your light up instead of down low!"

It's nearly an hour to drive to what appears to be a double, or triple wide trailer, hooked to a rundown rust pink pickup truck. The road feels like a dusty safari scene straight from a movie, tall trees towering overhead, the setting sun painting an orange glow across the sky. If Taylor Swift floated by in a flying yellow dress singing "Wildest Dreams," I wouldn't be surprised. I hold my thoughts in, following Raith inside where the concrete floors are streaked with every color of hair dye imaginable. Browns, reds, grays, gold… like someone literally brushed the floor with hair tint. Each station has floor length mirrors and modern furniture, so the place clearly isn't despite the rundown exterior. Even the shaggy circular rug under each workstation adds to the ambiance, with different shades of cut hair spiking through. But what catches my attention the most are the hairstyles walking out the salon. Every bob, pixie, layer, bun and bang have my attention. *Someone knows what they're doing.*

"Cassidy," a deep voice calls from behind us.

I swivel around. "Uh yeah, I'm Cassidy."

Standing there is a woman with a gorgeous burgundy lip liner and the posture of someone who knows they look good. Instead of extending a hand, she draws small circles around her lips with a pointed, wine-red fingernail. Her voice is surprisingly low-pitched, smooth as smoke.

"Hi, beautiful," she says, her gaze lingering on my strands.

"Candle's my name. And you, darling, have some pretty hair or it will be once we tame it." She draws closer and inhales dramatically smelling one of my Bob Marley ponytails, like she's testing a fragrance. *I should have washed it.*

I stand speechless, taking in her flawless hair and outfit... thigh high boots and trench coat hiding something skintight beneath. Every single piece on her looks like it took hours to perfect. Raith steps in to rescue me.

"She needs something tempting," my girl says, arching a brow at Candle. "Sexy, you know?"

Candle studies my hair intently, as though she's preparing to develop a new color treatment formula to transform my strands, then turns back to Raith with a grin. "Mm-hmm, I see what you mean. That should be easy. Sexy is already there. Only one thing missing… tempting. Leave us, Raith and let me do my magic."

I sigh and walk over, already half regretting Raith's suggestion. "Nothing crazy," I warn. "No major cuts."

Candle meets my gaze with a confidence nearly knocking the words from me. "I don't do crazy, baby. I do tempting. By the time I'm done, making it home without someone chasing you might be problematic." She struts off like she's on a fierce runway, nearly daring me to look away.

Three hours later, after enduring every color treatment that also ended up splattered on the salon floor, she finally steps back. "Cassidy, take a look," she says, smacking her gum and running a hand through my hair.

I stretch my arms out from beneath the sweltering black hair cape as she spins my chair around.

Is that me? I was bracing for something outlandish, but these blonde, golden highlights are everything. Each layer hanging flawlessly, my bangs just grazing my eyebrows. The soft sheen looks and feels like silk. I look different.

"Cassey, Cass…you're going to get more than a few eyes on that field in a couple of days," Candle says, smoothing her palms over my fresh layers. "And it won't be because of those killer thighs. It'll be all this hair in the wind."

I open my mouth to answer, but nothing comes out. My mind drifts to only one pair of eyes dripping with honey. Only he could make me sweat by just existing, by reminding me of his touch, his teeth, and taste of his…

"Cassidy," Raith's voice cuts through.

"Yeah?"

She gives me that knowing look. "You're sweating," she points out. "Who or what has your mind?"

I blow a quick gust of air down my shirt, hoping to mask the little beads forming on my temple. Only one person in the world can make me sweat that much from one single thought.

Candle's perfectly arched eyebrows rise, a hint of teasing lighting her eyes. "Raith, come collect Tempting before I give her another reason to perspire."

Before I can say anything, Raith approaches. "Not this one, Candle. Believe me…strictly into the, uh… other department… penile penetration."

Candle laughs, loud and husky. "A pity, Tempting. A damned pity," she gives me a look as if she wants to devour me. *Whew… the lure in here is high.*

Outside, I feel a little lighter as we head to Raith's mom's car. "So, what's the plan for the rest of the day?" I'm not quite ready to hold up in our dorm.

Raith's lips curl into a sneaky grin. "Well, Miss Tempting, I thought we'd head for a mani, pedi and wax for that overgrown forest."

I bite my lower lip, ignoring her sarcastic jab, but also knowing she's not exactly wrong. Personal grooming has been an afterthought lately, especially anything that involves self-inflicting agony like waxing. Nothing makes the sting of a bikini wax better or the thought of being exposed with my legs wide open, appealing.

Raith cocks her head, waiting, eyes gleaming with mischief. "Where to first?" I ask, cautiously, hoping her next word isn't wax. I'll need time to mentally prepare for strips of hot wax ripping the life from me like Miss Rita ripping the tape from Amazon boxes.

"Mani and pedi first," she says.

At least this location is in a strip mall on the nicer side of town, not some dusty road. Just before we enter, I notice a guy across the street leaning against a utility pole. He's dressed head to toe in black, not moving an inch. *Is he staring at us?* I try to look closer, but Raith yanks me inside before I can investigate. *Who was that?* The door swings shut, blocking my line of sight.

We head straight to a row of nail polishes, mostly neutral shades. I spot something called *Essie's Paintbrush It Off.* Guess this is it, since I see no bright colors are here. The entire place smells like cigars, my dad's scent and it tickles my throat. That combined with the fact that we're the only women around makes me suspect this is an all-male-spa.

"Raith?" I whisper.

She folds her arms and cocks her head in that mischievous way. "Yes, Track Star?" she answers, ending an octave higher. *She's definitely up to something.*

I glance around. Two pedicure bowls, three barber areas and not one single woman in the shop except us. "Is this for guys, only?"

Her smug smile broadens. "Nothing is for one gender, Cassidy."

I lower my voice. "I get that, but are you sure we're allowed here?" It feels like we're getting some serious side-eye.

Raith snorts. "Girl, I can go wherever I want, remember I'm Q," she says, running her fingers through my hair, massaging the ends. *Is she looking for split ends?*

Sometimes it's hard to believe our big Q revelation happened just months ago. It feels like years. Crazy how much has happened since I found my first boyfriend, Raith's baby brother, in a Spiderman costume. It makes me question how Thanksgiving break is a week away.

Raith leans in, sniffing my hair like she wants to eat it, the same way she devoured her three thousand calorie lunch. "Mmmm, it smells so good. I'll have Candle find this exact match of color for me. Maybe, I'll go blonde and long for the holidays. We may be twins by next week."

I ignore her because by next week she'll have cycled through five new styles, and at the rate things are going, I won't see any of them anyway.

A brief hush settles as a nail tech gives us the eye, before escorting us to two massive leather pedicure chairs with shiny copper bowls that bubble with blue-tinted water. Everything about this place screams "male athletes," right down to the oversized seats. Raith and I could practically share one with room to spare. Once I sink into the smooth, worn leather, the scent reminding me of my dad's old jacket, I feel unexpectedly cozy. I reach for Raith's zebra print nails, giving her limp hand a small squeeze. *How is she already asleep?* Her head molds into the cushy headrest, as if it was made for her. Typical Raith, she sleeps anywhere.

A plush blanket gets draped over my shoulders by the nail tech, and the last of my tensions melts away. Fine, maybe Raith was on to something. I settle back, letting the therapist knead away at my feet until I forget about my chipped toenail polish. Suddenly, it's easier to sink deeper into the chair, the drone of the water jets lulling me into a blissful relaxation.

This must be how Daniel Kaluuya felt in *Get Out*, I think, letting the chair swallow me whole. Because for a moment, I'm elsewhere...my mind drifts to a dreamlike place: no voids, no stress, no queasy nerves, no ache in my chest. A place where my family's together, tossing popcorn at each other in front of the TV, kernels scattered everywhere. A place with Kylo. Somehow it all comes back to him. Our time together was short, barely five minutes, definitely not enough to learn his last name. But his deep, raspy voice clings to my memory as if it happened yesterday. The sounds coming from his lips are enough to make me explode in this chair. *What is wrong with me, and how is he this close to me?*

I blink out of my daydream, a little disoriented, as the nail tech moves on massaging my calves. Then a flicker of movement shifts me to the flatscreen mounted. It wasn't on when we arrived. My eyes adjust from the blur of my thoughts, and there he is. Honey hazel eyes fill the entire eighty-inch screen, staring straight through me, stealing my breath along as if it were his own.

I haven't seen him since that day in the hospital when he asked, "Who are you?" His words still bother me. And now he's on TV, looking as if an accident never happened.

He's wearing a khaki suede jacket over matching pants and a crisp white shirt. His hair has grown back to its usual curly fade style, no bald spots. His goatee is new, making him sexier than I remember. I hate to admit it, but I can't decide which lacks my attention the most, his eyes or his lips. Everything is working. Between the discreet earring in his left ear, a black onyx bracelet on his wrist and that quiet swagger in his eyes, he looks younger, healthier and more confident than ever. Honestly, if I didn't know about the accident, I wouldn't believe he'd been in one. There's barely a hint of a scar near his eye. I massaged that scar for hours with Vitamin C. How is it making him sexier?

"Good lawd! Looking that damn good should be illegal!" Raith shouts, unable to tear her gaze from the screen, absorbing everything I just saw. I should be embarrassed, but if I didn't get that reaction from her, I would think something was wrong.

She slaps a hand over her mouth, still staring at the TV. "Oh hell, girl. Are you okay?" she asks, sounding too entranced to glance away. "Friend, I think the Almighty was bragging when he made him."

I get it. I can't peel my eyes away either.

Sighing, I shift in my chair to get closer, wishing I could climb into the TV. "There's no escaping him, Raith. He's going to be everywhere soon."

Raith whips the warm towel off her feet. The nail tech barely has enough time to dodge her. "Look, man, can you turn that off?" she asks, her words low and husky, meaning she's not taking "no" for an answer.

"Raith, I'm okay. He's famous so I'll have to deal with this," I point to the big screen. "In a few weeks, he'll be in every commercial, talk show, highlight reel and whatever else he does."

Her mouth tenses, then she settles back into the deep leather seat, waving the nail tech an apologetic okay. We both relax back into our leather chairs and into the screen, taking up more space than it should in this small area. Why they need an eighty-inch in such a small space, I have no idea.

On screen, an ESPN sports host, someone I've seen with my dad, leans forward, interviewing Kylo. Giant plasma screens behind them play endless loops of him slicing through soccer fields.

"Hey man," the commentator says, "Kylo Blade, professional soccer player, major endorsements and now this. A deadly wreck but able to make it back for possible training camp. The question of the day is: how are you?"

Kylo leans into the camera long and hard, as if contemplating his thoughts. "Better than expected. It was slow in the beginning and hard. But I'll be back."

"Some folks are calling it a miracle that you survived the accident, rebounded from a coma with a complete recovery. What do you call it?" The commentator edges forward, on the hunt for a defining sound bite.

Kylo waits a minute, and the entire salon goes silent, listening for his reply. He draws a measured breath, brow creased. "Honestly, my mom said it best. I had some angels, something like a shield protecting me during that crash. My truck was totaled. And I," he pauses, massaging the back of his hand, lost in thought. "I shouldn't be alive, let alone talking to you on TV. But every day I felt a pull, like something calling me from wherever I was. Sounds crazy, I know," he shakes his head. "Hell, hearing me say it sounds crazy."

The commentator looks rattled, too, placing a hand on Kylo's shoulder. "Sounds like you've had quite a journey, man. You good?"

Kylo shifts his gaze to the camera, nodding with ambition flooding his face. "Yeah, man. I'm good. I don't think anybody will ever understand how good I am," he says, leaving us with that wide, stunning, seductive smile. And, just like that, his confidence takes over the camera. How does he do that with such ease? That natural magnetism radiates through the TV like a heatwave pulling us all in.

"So, when will we see you on the field again?"

"Soon, I hope. The docs say maybe game five. There are no major long-term issues other than memory loss. Everything that happened a month prior to the accident, I can't remember any of it. I came back walking almost the same day after the coma. Crazy."

"You're a walking miracle," the commentator tells him, shaking his head in disbelief. "Man, I'm honored to be in your presence. When I tell you, you made the world stop and pray. We were all in it with you. But before we wrap, I have a little surprise for you... and I promise it's all cleared with Mom, Miss Blade, so you can blame her if you hate it."

Kylo sits up, glancing around as if trying to make sense of the situation. He doesn't care for surprises.

The commentator leans back in his chair, smiling. "I know you run a tight ship when it comes to privacy. Monty, come on out."

A tall Hispanic teenager steps forward wearing Kylo's official soccer jersey, his mom close by. He looks about seventeen or eighteen. The second he sees Kylo, he rushes into his arms.

"This is what people need to know about you," the host says to Kylo and the camera. "Kylo Blade has been mentoring this young man…calling him weekly, paying for his soccer fees, checking on his grades since Monty lost his brother. Monty tell us what you came here to say."

Monty slides a red Stanford soccer cap onto his head and hands one to Kylo. "I'm committed to Stanford with a full athletic and academic scholarship," he announces, tears streaking down his cheeks as he and his mom hug Kylo.

Kylo's back is turned, but his broad shoulders shake.

Memories rush in. I remember reading that letter to him in the hospital about a kid who credits Kylo for turning his life around. I glance around the salon; everyone's misty-eyed. Even Raith's looks glassy. The nail tech hands her a tissue.

"Cassidy," Raith murmurs softly. "If you're not in love with him already, you damn sure should be now."

My face falls into my hands. I sense the nail tech glancing my way, curious with unasked questions.

Raith leans in, gripping the armrest on my chair, as if holding on to keep herself from drowning in her pedicure copper bowl. "Listen, Ice Girl or better yet, Angel, you gotta tell him. He's talking about angels and voices in his dreams. That's you. Not Sarah. Not anyone else. You."

She's half shouting, which makes a few bystanders pause mid-polish. "Raith," I hiss. "Stop talking so loud! I'm not telling him anything. There's no point. How do you conjure up feelings someone lost? You can't just rebuild them out of nowhere. And what am I supposed to say? 'Hey, Kylo…remember we almost had sex at the Grove and in your F-150. And by the way, I'm the one that stayed by your bedside for days while you were in a coma."

"Wait a minute, did you say F-150?" Raith jerks upright, her eyes going wide.

"I forgot to tell you that. Never mind. I can't do this, Raith. I can't. You can't just recreate something that's gone. It was," I shake my head, cutting off my own words. "Never mind. I'm finished here. No wax. Let's go."

"Cassidy."

"Yes, Raith?" My voice comes out louder than I intended. Guilt hits me immediately. She's just trying to help.

"Think about it, Angel," she says, her tone softening in an attempt to ease my tension. "Do you know how many people would kill to be somebody's angel? And he just called you one on national *fucking* TV, Cassidy! His exact words were 'Angel'!" she beams, trying to calm me.

"Raith," I say firmly, my gaze locked on hers. "The answer is no. Leave it!"

CHAPTER 26

IT'S ONLY A DREAM

Kylo

"**C**OME HERE, GIRL," I SAY, SPREADING HER LEGS WIDE, TAKing my time pulling her apart so my tongue can savor the taste of her pretty body. This body feels so familiar to me, and yet so foreign. I can't remember who it belongs to, but I know whoever it is, she belongs to me.

"Don't stop, Kylo!" she screams, pushing my head further where she wants me. Her voice drips with seduction completely different from Sarah's irritating screech. This one entices me, almost beyond the point of control, as I hear my name slip from her lips like a prayer.

I glaze over her tip and then between her lips. Not enough for me. I want more of her. "Spread those legs wider," I demand, and she gives me all the access I need, allowing my tongue to explore while I massage her nipples, feeling them harden under my touch.

"My Kylo," she whimpers, her soft sexiness grinding my face, nails digging holes into my shoulders, telling me she's going to flood my mouth. Her ass trembling in my hands makes me go in harder. "Let it all out." She does, but it drives me to the edge, leaving me unable to wait any longer. *Where the hell is my self-control?* I can't hold back. I yank her to the middle of the bed, trying to catch a glimpse of her face, but strands cover her beauty, making it blurry. I feel that familiar tugging sensation…that I should recognize her. That she means more to me than my next breath. Answers are what I need, but my body won't wait any longer. "Damn, I could rip you apart!" I struggle for control, trying not to break her as I plunge into her tight wetness. I let out a groan that mixes with her moans of pleasure, sounding heavenly better than the New York Philharmonic symphony as our bodies mix over and over again.

A familiar rise builds within me, faster than usual, unstoppable. I'm going to finish faster than normal and there's nothing I can do about it. She feels too good, too perfect to hold back. Her body explodes around mine first, triggering my own release. At the same moment, she begins to fade beneath me, leaving only a glimpse of red lipstick. Slipping from my grasp, I try to hold on, but my hands find nothing but the cold emptiness of sheets. "Come back!" I yell, jerking awake at the sound of my own voice echoing through the quiet room. *Alone.*

Damn, my sheets are damp from sweat, and something else. Groaning, I wipe the sweat from my forehead, thankful Miss Blade and Aunt D aren't here. They'd both be hovering and lecturing me on recovery signs. I've been having these dreams ever since I got home, but this is the first time it went this far, only to end with a quick glimpse of red lipstick fading away on those luscious lips.

No time to figure this out. I need to get ready for today. The sheets…I'll deal with them later.

I'm back to training at A&M's stadium with four trainers, but who missed the memo that I was in a coma weeks ago. Every day they ramp it up…harder, longer and faster like they want me on the roster next week. But my body's still struggling. Doctors keep saying it'll take weeks for my strength to rebuild and my muscle memory to return. I can see it: I'm weaker, slower, and uncoordinated. Half my reflexes feel stuck, like signals that can't connect. The trainers gotta see this shit, but they keep pushing as if ignoring the truth. It's frustrating as hell.

I have to keep pushing. I want to, no, I need to…to prove I can get back to the team.

Once today's training ends, I head over to my aunt and uncle's. I've got a little surprise for my man, Uncle Joe.

Pulling into their driveway, my phone's Bluetooth lights up with an incoming call. *It's Sarah.* She's the last person I'm talking to. I send her to voicemail. She's been clinging more than usual lately spinning this "we're in love" narrative for the cameras and how she spent days at the hospital hoping for my return.

Something ain't right and I know it. Last night, her blow job was so good my toes damn near curled. Still no sex. Ain't no need if she keeps doing that. She left mad, begging, almost desperate, wanting more and I didn't care. But she's trying too damn hard. And her irritating voice is not the whisper in my dreams, that sweetness calling my name. The appeal of it spins me out of control and no one has done that before. These dreams are the only things driving me to sleep to experience it. *Fuck, what's up with me?*

I slam the truck door to my brand new Ford F-150, courtesy from Ford of the endorsement offer they begged me to sign after the accident. Hard to say no to two free trucks. That makes six deals, leaving no room for privacy. Coming back from an injury is challenging enough with my normal media attention, but a major car accident and a coma takes it to another level. Still, I'm grateful for the extras until I figure out my game.

My doubts are still circulating as I walk up to Aunt D's and Uncle Joe's house, relieved to see my package is parked on the street. I pause, wondering why Uncle Joe never let me buy them a new place. His answer has been the same since I started making real money: This is my home. My neighbors are my family, so I'm not leaving. Even remodeling was a flat-out "no."

He opens the door slowly, as if every bone in his body aches. He's wearing dark Dickies, a black button-down and steel toe boots big enough to kill somebody. "Son, what're you doing here?" he asks, giving me a once-over, but not stepping aside, yet. "You good?"

His old rigid expression has been the same for as long as I can remember. "Yeah, Uncle Joe, I was on this side of town. You busy?" At seventy-two, if not older, he's still cutting grass and working in his garage, claiming, "If I slow down, I might as well dig my grave."

After a moment, he steps back and motions me inside. "Come on in, son. You hungry?"

Uncle Joe always keeps something stashed away for me. "I'm good. Ate after practice," I answer, looking around not hearing heels clattering. "Where's Aunt D?"

"She's at some church service or maybe a funeral. She went to a funeral last week at eight in the morning. I didn't even know they could bury folks that early. Between the church and the girls, she's always gone," he says, as he sits in his gangster leaning recliner with more cotton showing than leather. I've tried replacing it twice, but he always drags my new chairs into the garage. That chair has to be older than me. But everyone knows not to sit in it.

I lower myself onto the couch, still uneasy. "I had a question about the hospital, but it can wait," I explain, trailing off as silence settles.

"What's on your mind?" Uncle Joe asks, flipping channels until he lands on *In The Heat of The Night*. He has to be the last person still watching it.

"Just got back from practice," I answer.

He mutes the TV halfway. "How's that going?"

"It's… alright," I lie. His steady gaze doesn't waver. He hears the doubt in my voice and doesn't believe me, so I come clean. "Honestly, Uncle Joe, it's hard as hell. My body's not the same."

He falls silent for a while, staring at the TV but not really seeing it. Finally, he sighs. "Son, I know… But you know what was hard? The real hard part was you surviving that car accident and *coming back.* That was a miracle. Nobody knows what's going on in here." He taps his head with his old, thick finger. "Nobody understands that but you."

He's always straight to the point. "My body's… different," I admit, voice faltering slightly.

"Son, you can't expect it to be the same. That toughness you have is as hard as nails. You were born with it. You didn't lose it. You just gotta find it again."

He leans back in his recliner, his head almost hitting the floor. Damn, Uncle Joe has the gangster lean for real in that chair. Now I see why his cup is there, he doesn't have far to reach. "I feel off," I confess, unable to meet his cloudy cataracts that used to scare me as a kid.

He lowers the volume on the TV. "You got to figure out this new you. Get quiet and learn how to understand it and work with it. Trust me son, if you didn't have it, that team wouldn't still be sending them four expensive trainers from Europe. You gotta get quiet and find a way to work with it," he repeats.

"Get quiet and work with it," I repeat. "You're right. I guess I'm…I'm… scared," I admit, feeling the weight of those words lift from my shoulders. My future feels uncertain, a thought that crosses my mind every damn day.

"Son, that's normal. Ain't nothing wrong with being scared. But my question is, what are you gonna do with it? You got a second chance that never should have happened. You gotta take what life gives you and work with it. Truth is, you shouldn't have walked to my door. But you did. You shouldn't even be talking. But here you are. You got what it takes, son," he says, sitting up in his chair and leaning closer to me.

"Man, Uncle Joe. You always know what to say," I admit.

He gives me a hard look. "Not really. I've just been on this earth a bit longer than you," he says, turning his attention back to Chief Gillespie and Virgil Tibbs arguing on the screen. I know every character in his show. Tron and I had no other choice but to watch it with him.

I stand to leave. "Uncle Joe, you got a second to come outside?"

He nods and begins rocking his recliner back and forth, trying to release the lever to bring the head of the chair upright, that's not working. *This I got to see.* I hope he doesn't end up somewhere in the kitchen or in the middle of next week when it pops his ass up. I'm surprised Aunt D hasn't burned the chair to the ground 'cause it isn't vibing with the other furniture. "Boy, what're you up to now? You got a new ride to show me?" he asks, rolling out his chair, leaving it flat. "Hold on, let me get my truck keys. Gotta get some tools to fix my chair when you leave. I bet Diane's been sitting in my chair and broke it."

I laugh and head onto the porch, waiting for him. Aunt D would never risk her Sunday best sitting in that chair. She's no doubt at church right now planning a burial for its funeral.

Once Uncle Joe joins me in the driveway, I point to a brand new, black Ford F-150. "Uncle Joe, you need a new truck. That old one's from the nineties with a bad motor and busted transmission. Aunt D's always complaining about the oil stains in the driveway. This one's from Ford. Didn't cost me a dime and I got two of 'em, one for me and one for you. Good truck …"

He lifts a hand stopping my ramble in its tracks. "Son, hush that nervous talking," he steps closer and runs his worn fingertips along the shiny black hood, his nails still stained with oil from the eighties.

He steps back, eyes serious as can be. "I told myself that if you made it outta that accident, I was gonna live a little more. That wreck weighed hard on all of us. I never had anything new before. I bought new cars for Diane and the girls for as long as I remember. But I've never bought anything for myself. I only wanted those girls to be happy," he bends checking out the tires. "Son, I'm gonna drive this truck until the wheels fall off. Give me those keys," he laughs, letting out that old man inhale grunt that only he can pull off, then stands one vertebrate at a time walking my way. "Come here, boy."

Man, Uncle Joe still has that strong ass grip. I forgot how this felt. The only other hug I remember was at Tron's funeral, when Uncle Joe was my constant over my shoulder back in the day.

"Son, look at me," he steps back, his eyes steady as I fight to hold my shit. "You did not die in that car accident. But you should have. Now that sounds bad and I hate to say it. But I don't know how you made it out alive. Some didn't get that chance. If you want to be afraid of something, be afraid of doing nothing with that second chance. You got your life back; now go steal your future back."

Damn, those words hit hard. *Be more afraid of doing nothing. Steal your future back.* "I got you, Uncle Joe," I say, nodding hard.

I head to my truck watching him drive off in his new ride. That felt good. Nothing feels better than taking care of family and family taking care of you. His advice is worth way more than any new F-150.

I need some space to think on everything he just said, and I know where to go.

I rest my sore ankle on the rusted bench arm, an old, sun faded plank stained with white-brownish bird droppings. My mind replaying Uncle Joe's words on loop. *Be more afraid of doing nothing with this second chance. Steal your future back.*

He's right. I've got to figure out this new version of me, my body and it's new mechanics. I'm missing that old zone where I'd block everything out: crowds, stats, weather and gossip. My body just worked. I never had to wonder if it would show up. It always did. It was just me and the black and white. Me and those hexagons and pentagons all thirty-two coming my way. Me and the soccer ball. I've known that ball better than anything in my life. Better than any subject. It's different and frustrating as hell. Maybe Uncle

Joe is on to something. I need to "get quiet" like he says, and find that mental space again.

Suddenly a kid takes me out of my thoughts.

"Captain K! Captain K!"

I squint against the sun to see a little girl with ponytails flying. She's limping but running full speed in my direction. *I think*. I lean forward, trying to make sure I'm not imagining things. Is she running toward me?

"Captain K! Captain K!" she shouts again, and I turn back, half-expecting to see superhero Captain K flying in from above.

I hope he lands soon because she's not stopping. *Who is she?* "Captain K!" She throws her arms around my lap as I raise my hands in the air, trying not to accidentally grab her. I'm lost. *Who is this kid?*

A second later a woman jogs up, breathless.

"Brooklyn, you've got to slow down!" she says, eyes darting from her daughter to me. "I'm so sorry, Kylo, we're just…she's very excited."

I stand carefully, shifting the girl, Brooklyn, off my lap to give her space. The woman must notice my confusion because she steps in like a shield. "You're probably wondering who we are. I'm Ellen, and this is Brooklyn."

Brooklyn peeks around her mom's legs, looking up at me. "You forgot me?" she asks.

My pulse spikes and I feel like shit. I hate this part having to explain over and over that I don't remember pieces of my life. "I'm… a bit off after the accident," I admit, forcing my fists to unclench. "Short-term memory loss. I can't remember anything from about a month before it happened."

"Totally understandable," Ellen says gently. "We're just glad you're okay now. We've been following the news."

Brooklyn steps forward, hands on her hips, glancing over her red glasses. "You're Captain K, remember? We played tennis and fed ducks. You're bad at tennis but a good soccer player. You said you only get Tuesdays off from real soccer."

I half-laugh, shaking my head. "I'm...sorry I don't remember. Can we start over?"

Brooklyn narrows her eyes. "Sure. We met here on Tuesdays. You said you were training me in tennis...maybe so I wouldn't laugh at your skills."

I glance at Ellen, who just smiles. "She's seven going on seventy," she whispers, shrugging.

"When can we play again?" Brooklyn fires the question at me without hesitation.

Ellen steps in: "Not today, kiddo...remember, we have that church event tonight."

Brooklyn pouts, dragging out her sigh, and I immediately want to fix it. "How about Tuesday at five-thirty?" I offer. "We can do tennis, then feed ducks. I...uh...remember liking ducks?"

Brooklyn's face lights up. "Yes! Tuesday! You'd better bring your a game, Captain K!"

I flash a grin. "All right, little tennis champ. Bring yours, too."

She hugs me tight, and this time I hug her back more confidently than the first weird half-hug. "I'm glad you're okay," she whispers.

"So am I, little Brooklyn," I say, genuinely meaning it. Seeing this kid...someone I hung out with, but can't recall...hits me hard. *What else am I missing?*

"We should go," Ellen says, pulling Brooklyn away gently. Then she glances back at me. "Kylo, so good to see you moving around. Even if you don't remember everything, it's all right. You look great."

I nod, and they walk off, Brooklyn waving. "See you soon, Captain K! Tell Cassey I said hi!"

I open my mouth to call after them..."who's Cassey?" But they're already too far away.

CHAPTER 27

PANCAKES AND HALLMARK

Cassidy

MY BODY IS STILL ON THE HOSPITAL ICU SCHEDULE. No matter when I fall asleep, I awake at one a.m. and stay up until four. Usually, I lay there listening to Raith snore. Each night before bed, I vow not to think about him, his voice, his eyes, or that smile but come one a.m., I'm replaying it all. I need rest, especially with track practice starting soon, even my evening naps are a bust, thanks to late classes and homework.

I've gained back five of the ten pounds I lost. Dad freaked with my weight loss, so now he sends cooked meals by his driver. Raith has to have a GPS on his car as she never misses him pulling on campus with enough food to feed the entire dorm. I wish I could eat more but stress does the opposite for me, I lose my appetite. Lately I have to force myself to even look at food.

Giving up on sleep, I quietly slip out of bed. Raith's smiley face gallery catches my attention. Our dorm window overlooks the entrance of Woodruff Hall, and I see a couple leaning against the railing. The guy pulls her hair back, tips her chin to his lips but pauses, making her wait. She leans in, all of us (including me) waiting. Finally, he kisses her, palms at her neck, drawing her closer…

hungry, devouring. It's with such hunger, it's as though he's starving for her. She clutches the stair rail, small, helpless and fragile in his arms.

Is that how I looked with Kylo?

I wish I could forget him. From everything I've seen on TV and heard around campus, he still doesn't remember anything and Sarah is not letting go. Maybe he's back in love with her. Or never fell out of it. Did I imagine him saying, "This is different?" I have so many questions but no answers.

Starting today, it's time for a change. It's time to move forward… take back control and handle my feelings. No more wearing myself out over someone who may never recall my name.

I'll go home, get away from campus. Dad and my sisters are in Sedona, so I'll have the house to myself for some quiet time to get my head on straight.

I pack fast, then text my driver. My dad still has him on call. I hate calling him so early, but if I took some random taxi or Uber to the house, Dad would have a meltdown. He means well, but sometimes he goes overboard with the security. I remember Mom saying that he was always a step ahead with our security and if someone hurt any of us that one of them would end up in jail. Of course, Dad always agreed it would be him. But Mom would joke how he'd only be able to handle one day of jail and that it should be her because she knew how to handle the streets.

I snuggle in the back seat of the car with my A&M blanket, hoping to catch a little sleep on the hour drive home.

"Stop, stop! Don't take off his mask!"

"Miss Reagan. Miss Reagan." A voice shakes me gently. I open my eyes to sunlight streaming into the backseat. *I'm outside my house?*

"You're home." Mr. Stuart, Dad's driver, looks at me with gen-uine concern.

"I'm sorry," I mutter, trying to clear my drowsiness. "Didn't realize I'd fallen asleep."

He offers me a hand out of the car. The movement of his blazer reveals the unmistakable outline of a gun at his hip, some-thing I've never noticed.

"Let's get you settled inside and out of this cold," he says, kindly but guarded. He shoulders my bag and heads for the side entrance security pad. He's not as old as I thought, maybe in his late forties or early fifties, but he's tall, in shape and ready to use his weapon if necessary.

Before he can key in the code, Miss Rita opens the door. Usually, she's off when the family's out of town.

"My baby girl!" she screams, excitement hitting me straight in my heart.

I collapse in her arms, breathing in the familiar vanilla scent of home. For a moment everything fades.

Then she eases away, holding back the questions that normally end with me answering *okay*. "Come to the kitchen," she urges. "I'll whip you up something. You're too frail," she nods at Mr. Stuart. "Stuart, take her things upstairs and thank you for bringing her home."

I catch Mr. Stuart's expression as Miss Rita walks away. His jaw is tight, like he's irritated. Or something else.

"Thanks, Mr. Stuart, I'll text you tomorrow about a ride back to campus."

He nods curtly taking our garland decorated stairs until his military style boots hit the top....the same step I fell on the day Mom d ...*Don't think...*

Mr. Stuart has been with us for at least ten years and Miss Rita has been here for as long as I can remember. She was the only person close to my mom at her group home growing up. According to my mom, Miss Rita was a cook there for years. Once we moved here, Mom built a home on the property for her so she'd have a permanent home. Her place is maybe a mile away from ours. I can remember me and my sisters riding our bikes down the dirt road path every Friday to spend the night when Mom and Dad were out together. To me, Miss Rita is my grandmother. She doesn't cook much anymore, but she's always here if any of us need her... especially since Mom.

"Baby girl, look at that hair," she says, parking hands on her hips with a smirk. "You'll have the boys going crazy."

"You like it, Miss Rita? It was Raith's idea," I add.

She chuckles. "Mmm-hmm, very sexy. That girl keeps you on your toes. When is she visiting?"

"Christmas break."

"Good. I like that roommate." Miss Rita bustles about, pulling pots and pans from the lower cabinets. I hope she's not making a breakfast buffet. "So what's on your schedule today, baby?"

"Just some studying and hopefully relaxing. I miss my bed," I admit. The twin XL at my dorm will never compare to my bed upstairs with my sheets cold as ice.

She eyes me, her bun flopping, while she fills a pot of water. "Okay, I'll whip up breakfast, and then we'll have ourselves a girl talk."

Miss Rita has to be in her mid-sixties, but she has the energy of someone half her age, especially when it comes to these "girl talks." It's like she senses our needs at different times. Maybe it's an instinct.

I glance over the bar, watching her prepare too much food but nod in agreement. "Sounds good, Miss Rita. Are you still watching *Young & The Restless?*"

She frowns somewhat, whipping her pancake mixture. "Yes. I think I can write for that show. Sometimes it's so predictable but I've never missed an episode. You?"

"I have no time for soaps with school and track. I'm too busy."

"Umm humm." I know exactly what that means…it's her way of figuring out how to start the conversation I want to avoid.

A good half an hour later, I stare down at an empty plate. I devoured a stack of homemade pancakes topped with pecans, bananas, syrup and melting butter dripping down the sides, plus turkey bacon. "How?" I swallow in confusion. "How did I eat all that? How do you make me eat? I haven't had an appetite for weeks, but for some reason, I just ate 5000 calories of pancakes in five minutes."

She pats my cheeks sending a shiver through me. Her hands are always so cold. "Baby girl, there wasn't love in that cafeteria food. You have to come home for that," she says, smiling so big her eyes glow. "Girl talk and Hallmark movies?" she asks.

"Sure."

She hums an approval, placing brownies on a small plate. "Come on into the family room with me. You'll want these, too."

"Brownies this early?"

She tosses me a smile. "Pancakes first, sugar second. Let's go."

At this rate, I might gain ten pounds before bedtime. Honestly, that might be exactly what I need.

After two Hallmark movies, plus brownies and cookies, I notice Miss Rita dozing off. She hardly ever makes it past the third set of commercials. Still having her here helps ease the loneliness without Mom. Home just isn't the same.

Her quiet snores catch my attention, and I notice how little she's changed over the years. She's still wearing her signature bun, her burgundy lipstick, red fingernail polish and the same house dresses Dad jokingly calls her uniform. She stirs, eyelids fluttering open.

"Oh no, I guess I fell asleep, again," she says, sitting upright and yawning, stretching her arms to a wingspan of a first grader. She's so petite. "How was the movie?"

"The first movie was good, and… so was the second one." We both laugh, knowing she never actually saw a movie's end.

She folds her blanket neatly, places it on the ottoman, then fixes me with a look I know too well. This is the moment she asks what's been weighing on her mind since I got home.

"So," she says gently, "how is Kylo Blade?"

I sigh bracing myself. No point wondering how she knows. Dad probably told her everything. "He's back with his girlfriend," I say, trying to keep it casual. "And I'm moving on. It was… quick."

Her gaze drifts from the TV showing the upcoming Christmas movies on Hallmark's lineup to me. "Baby girl, it happened, and I feel it was only the first chapter of that story."

"Why do you say that?" I ask, sinking deeper into the cushion.

She offers a small, understanding smile. "Only love can make you gain or lose weight as fast as you did," she replies, relaxing back in her chair. "I almost hate to say this, but you may never forget your first love. That first love is hard to put into words. It's like liquid silk flowing, it's softness so profound that it awakens every nerve, igniting an intoxicating mix of pleasure and creating one of the most blissful highs imaginable. It makes you so giddy it's almost delusional, almost unreal and something you never want to let go."

I pull a pillow closer, absorbing her words. Her description of love is so open, honest and she used the word bliss. *Mom's favorite.* I understand what she means. It may have been short. But I get it.

She sits up straighter. "Baby girl, some people never experience that depth of love. Others are lucky enough to feel it twice. But it's a feeling everyone should allow themselves to experience at least once," she exhales and stares off at the fireplace, eyes misty with memories.

"Miss Rita?" I ask softly.

She dabs at the corners of her eyes, then musters a careful smile. "I'm sorry, baby. That took me to a place that only my heart breathes. You see, a woman's heart is much like the depths of the ocean, filled with thousands of countless hidden treasures of untold secrets, each one a story only she can unlock and reminisce in alone."

I never realized Miss Rita had anyone special. It was always her with us for as long as I can remember. Her gaze drifts away from our coffered ceiling, as though drawn to some distant memory, before returning to me with curiosity.

"Baby girl," she continues, "I'm not sure what the future holds for you two, but I'm glad you experienced it. I can't say for certain what it was, but don't let timing confuse you. Love's force is so immediate that it can't be measured by seconds. So, when are you going to reach out and let him know you were the one that was at that hospital every night, worrying John to death?"

My shoulders tense at the mention of Dad. "Was he really worried?"

She nods with a knowing smile. "Yes, your father paced these floors every single night, waiting for Mr. Stuart to confirm you'd arrived at the hospital safely."

"I just…I hate when he worries," I admit.

"It's his job, sweet girl. He's your dad," she shrugs, then lowers the TV volume to near silence, a sure sign she wants answers. "So back to my question. When are you going to see Kylo or call him?"

"I can't," I say, trembling just enough to reveal how I really feel. "How can he miss what he doesn't remember?"

Miss Rita tilts her head. "That's a good question and one I can't answer. That book isn't finished until you write the last chapter. If you felt strong enough to be at the hospital every night for days, then you should feel strong enough to tell him what you had and what you did. He holds the decision in how he handles the truth. But he has to realize that girl on TV is a jezebel after his money."

"She's actually from a rich family, probably has more money than him."

She flaps a dismissive hand. "Hmmph. Well, she's not right for him. I saw them on TV the other day and he was not comfortable. I could tell. That boys missing something."

I hug the pillow tight into my chest, trying to push the words at the tip of my tongue away. "I wish Mom was here." My voice trembles with the "here" and I hate it. I hate showing weakness around them.

Miss Rita sighs deeply. "Baby girl, me, too. Not a day goes by that I don't miss her shining through this place. She was the life of this house, making every day worth living for all of us," she leans forward. "What do you think your mom would've done?"

Mom was unstoppable, pushing for what she wanted, never letting up even in her final days. She was a force to reckon with when it came to her desires. Maybe it was her upbringing, lack of material things or her inability to get them. But she pushed us to the limit in everything we did. We used to call her "the pusher" cause that's who she was. Dad has said countless times that she is the main reason for his success.

"What would she do?" Miss Rita asks again.

I laugh a little, thinking of my answer. "She would have told him everything the minute he woke up and slapped the memory right back into his head," I say with a shaky laugh.

We both break out laughing so hard Miss Rita has to rush to the bathroom for a moment, leaving me smiling at just how much I needed this.

CHAPTER 28

EXTENDED HAND

Kylo

WHY DO *I* PUT UP WITH THIS SHIT?
Sarah's on her fifteenth interview of the week getting her makeup reapplied again. Ever since her first movie release, she can't get enough of the attention with me somewhere nearby. If you ask me, she's just a glorified extra…one more face lost in the crowd. I doubt the studio's marketing team planned anything major for her. This constant circus is her doing.

I watch her in the floor length mirror, eyes closed, as the makeup artist layers on more foundation. There's no way in hell, pre-accident, I would've tolerated this. I've got to ask Christian. It pisses me off that I can't remember shit from before the accident.

My own reflection catches my eye, I become aware of my expression in the mirror. I can't stand her ass and it shows. She's still talking, desperate for attention from anyone willing to feed her ego. The longer I'm around her, the more I know it has to end. She must sense my stare because she meets my eyes in the mirror, then deliberately lifts her dress, spreading those strappy heels wide enough for me and anyone else in view to notice she's wearing nothing underneath.

The image annoys me almost as much as it turns me on, and she knows it.

"Pardon me, Kylo Blade."

I turn, meeting the sober eyes of John Pittman, the legendary movie producer behind most of the blockbuster hits I watch. What the hell is he doing here? He couldn't be here for Sarah's flimsy ass movie. It's not worth his time.... or even ten seconds of a cameo.

"Excuse me, Mr. Pittman?" I ask, forcing respect into my voice. "Yes, I'm Kylo Blade." *How in the hell does he know my name?* I'm not in his circle.

I extend a handshake. I've met plenty of random stars and big shots, but they don't mean shit. Pittman, though, is someone I've respected for years. He came from the bottom, like me and I've studied his business moves closely. Sarah's dad has thrown some deals my way, but Pittman's on another level and that's my long-term goal. Not for the money, but what the money can accomplish to help others. We've been in similar circles but never formally introduced.

He eyes my hand, his face unreadable. His silence is telling, and I sense he's not keen on conversation. "Are you here for the movie?" I ask, trying to read his vibe. Lowering my hand, I can tell somethings off. *Something isn't right.*

"No, Kylo I had a meeting upstairs with Sony," he replies, stressing my name like it tastes bitter. "Thought I'd speak with you," his emphasis on *you* tells me something isn't right. Then he grabs my hand, giving it a death grip strong enough to crack a knuckle. "Heard about your accident. How are you?" His eyes are assuming, like I'll lie.

My ego refuses to show pain, so I hold his stare, clenching against the crushing grip. "Glad you did, sir," I keep it short, knowing I would have said more but he isn't giving that vibe for a deeper conversation. There's this intense energy radiating from him, making me question what's up. He looks almost ready to straight beat my ass.

"Excuse me Mr. Pittman. Have we met?"

He releases my hand a fraction, easing off but still glaring. "Kylo," he grits out, as though it pains him to say my name. "We met weeks ago at the gala at North Carolina A&M."

He rubs his chin, anticipating the wrong words to cross my lips. "The gala?" I echo hungry for any clue from that missing time. I haven't spoken with anyone other than Brooklyn and her mom, so the questions are coming.

He relaxes somewhat, but still with his poker face, checking me for the truth. "Yes, the gala. We officially met the same night as your accident."

The night of my accident is a black hole, lost somewhere. "Mr. Pittman, I lost some of my memories. A full month before or so before the crash, plus bits afterward. Are you saying we talked at the gala, that same night?"

"That's correct." Maybe my answers are easing his tension. He seems more relaxed. "We sat at the table for dinner. You met my daughter and according to her," he pierces me with that stare again. "We spent the evening discussing soccer."

He stops there, waiting for me to respond. How the hell did I forget a conversation with John Pittman? "I don't remember any of that. Can you… tell me more?"

His tight lip expression suggests I'm pushing into territory he'd rather keep private. This man exudes power, and yet he seems visibly uncomfortable with sharing anything with me. *Why?*

"You sat beside my daughter. She'd recall better than I would," he says, face still braced, searching me for one false move. "I think she'd remember it all."

Before either of us can continue, I hear those familiar clicks of Sarah's heels. Here she is with that shrill ass voice. "Mr. Pittman? So great to see you! Are you here for my interviews? My movie is incredible! You've probably seen it with it being filmed here. I cannot believe you are actually here!" Who in the hell can get out that many irritating words at that speed?

"Sarah." Pittman acknowledges, giving her a once-over. Even

for him, her chest is hard not to notice. *Damn, they look fuller.* "Yes, I've heard good things about your film. Are you here finishing the first press round?"

She leans into me, fusing to my side. "Yes, I've been on interviews all week, and it's wonderful, Mr. Pittman!" She loops her arm through mine, pressing close enough that I feel her heat. She's making a bold claim for some reason.

He returns a polite nod, though his eyes linger on the way she's laying a claim on me. Maybe he wants her ass.

She gazes my way, her lips parted like she's trying to seduce me on camera. "And this man has been with me every step of the way, not letting me out of his sight," she announces, kissing my cheek far too long for polite company. "He's such a catch."

Her eyes beg me to play along, so I just stand there, arms relaxed, letting her stage her little performance for Pittman.

"Are you staying for the rest of the interview?" *Is she dismissing John Pittman?* This may be his spot. Hell, this entire block may be his.

He remains calm. "No, my dear. I'll be here for a moment longer. The assistant seems to want you now."

Sure enough, a tall blonde is beckoning her to the set. She wraps a hand around my arm, steering me away from Pittman without so much as an apology.

"We'll see you later, Mr. Pittman!" she calls, voice boarding on frantic. No one's naturally this energetic without a narcotic. Talking to Christian has to happen sooner.

But why is she so desperate to get me away from Pittman? "Head to your interview," I tell her firmly. She knows not to push me.

"Kylo, I hate leaving you," she leans in closer, whining. "Please don't be long. We have major plans tonight, remember?"

"Then finish so we can get to it," I reply. The hope of surprise in her eyes tells me she didn't expect that. She won't like the actual plan I have in mind that doesn't include her.

"See ya, Mr. Pittman," she says, flashing a grin big enough to reveal all thirty-two teeth. That smile will vanish soon enough. I watch her strut off, hair dramatically blowing under the lighting rig.

"Give my regards to your parents, Sarah," Pittman adds, casually reminding me of the lineage among the top 1 percent.

As she disappears, he and I both exhale. "Mr. Pittman, apologies," I nod in the direction Sarah just went. "No idea what has gotten into her."

He laughs under his breath. "Well, it seems you have in some form or fashion."

I shake my head, not liking his implication. "It's not what you think. Earlier you mentioned your daughter might remember that evening."

Agitation seeps through his cool exterior again. John Pittman does not strike me as a man easily irritated, but somehow, my presence alone is a problem. "My daughter was at our table along with her," he points toward Sarah. *Sarah was with me that night? Why hasn't she said a damn thing?*

Before I can press further, the interview starts, and Sarah's high ass pitch nonsense takes over the set. How can one voice bother the fuck out of me?

I watch Pittman cross his arms, focusing on her again, his expression unreadable. Sarah drops my name.

"So, where's that lucky Kylo of yours?" the interviewer calls, eyeing me across the room.

She sits up straight, clapping her hands like she's won a damn prize. *What the hell is wrong with her?* "Oh, he's right over there!" She points to me with her long, claw purple nails, summoning me to come her way. She knows I don't do this shit. I picture myself walking out the door embarrassing her ass. But I also hear my PR reps voice warning. *"Keep your brand clean."*

I shoot Pittman an apologetic glance. "Do you have time to wait? I still have questions."

He nods, tapping my shoulder twice with surprisingly calm composure. "Sure, son, take your time."

Reluctantly, I make my way to Sarah. Her manic energy is off the charts. She practically drags me in front of the camera.

"And here he is the man of the hour!" the host says grinning. Sarah hops off her stool, hooking an arm around my waist. "Yes, *my* man. My beautiful man," she grins. *Who says shit like that? That has to sound crazy to even her ass.* Her eyes dart from Pittman back to me. She kisses me, too intent to be authentic. "Oh, honey, we have to tell them! We can't wait any longer!" she raises her voice ensuring the interviewer hears.

Something's the hell off. "Tell them what?" I mutter, stepping away from the camera view.

She scrambles after me and clasps her hands, lifting them overhead as if proudly accepting a Grammy or an Oscar. "Let me do it!" She wheels around to face the cameras, eyes glowing unnaturally. "We're getting married! Kylo popped the question last week and I said yes!"

CHAPTER 29

THE NAME

Cassidy

MY FEET ARE NO JOKE. I CAREFULLY RUB AROUND THE PUS filled blisters and layers of dry dead skin. Why do I torture myself for this sport when I have no intention of pursuing it professionally? But running does relax my nerves, and lately these nerves can use some serious calming.

I hear my dorm door open and close. "Track Star, where are you?" Raith is back sooner than I expected.

"Hey, gimme a minute to wash my hands." I walk out, balancing a small basin brimming with warm water and Epsom salt, then set it at the foot of my bed. Easing my feet in, I brace for the sting. It hurts but nothing I can't handle. These feet have to be race ready, or at least better, for my meet tomorrow.

"Cassidy," Raith calls. I nearly forgot she was here. She peaks down, watching my feet as if they may bite her. A look of total disgust crosses her face, and I wonder if they're worse than normal. "Girl, you will never wear sandals with those things. What the hell? They look tortured!" she gulps, like she's fighting swallowing back nausea.

I glance at my swollen toes, suddenly self-conscious. At least my nail polish is okay. "That's why my twenty pairs of tennis shoes are in my closet. No need for sandals," I brag, giving her my tight-lipped, one eyebrow raised stare. Honestly, who needs sandals anyway? *Sneakers forever.*

She covers her mouth, letting out a fake gagging sound. "If you say so, hammer toes," she plops near me on our bench, nudging my shoulder. "You okay?" she asks, her expression full of concern.

Am I okay? I guess so, at least for now. It's been weeks since I saw Kylo with Thanksgiving and Christmas passing in a blur. My family tried to act okay, but nothing about us felt the same. Will the holidays ever feel normal again? "Yeah, I'm okay," I say, half-lying, hoping her lie detector doesn't pick up any false movements.

Raith rests her head on my shoulder, red and blonde braids spilling across our thighs. I wonder how long that style will last. "I'm just checking on you," she murmurs, looping a braid around one of her hot pink nails. "A lot's happened these past few months, and we're already three weeks into the new year. I'm just making sure you've left behind Bob Marley hair, jungle v-jay growth and killer fingernails."

I smile at the memory of me maybe eight weeks ago, a total mess. "My v-jay is well-maintained…clean, smooth and regularly sugared. It feels as soft as a baby's bottom. I guess it could be part-icicle, though," I tease, curious if she'll laugh.

She narrows her eyes but manages a crooked smirk. "Cassidy, that was almost funny. How's the knee holding up?" she asks. *Was it funny?*

"Better than it was a few months ago. Are you coming to my meet tomorrow?"

She frowns like I've thrown an insult her way. "Of course, I wouldn't miss you out there. You ready?"

I exhale. "Yeah, I think so. I'm a little nervous. It's been a while since my last race. Plus, I'm older than these girls by, like, three years and starting to feel it. Hopefully, I'm good."

Raith gives me a look that screams *girl, you're clueless.* "No way you're out of shape! But, how in the hell are you planning to run on those?" She points at my tortured toes, leaning for another peek. "Are…are they not infected!" she whispers, bending closer, analyzing my feet like they're a science project.

"They're not infected. A wrap and ibuprofen usually helps. Honestly, I've had worse."

She steps back looking at my feet from a distance, as if they might detach from my ankles and attack her. "Look, there's no way they've been worse," she says, swallowing loud enough to be heard outside. "But do me a favor, don't wake me in the AM. I'll roll in a minute before it starts. Seriously, why are these so early?"

I shrug. "No idea, but I'll let the officials know their schedule isn't working for you," I joke, slipping my feet from the basin. I pat them dry and smear on Neosporin and steroid cream, then cover them with loose socks.

Collapsing on my bed, I hear Raith already snoring. My feet hang off the side while memories of Mom flood my thoughts. On nights before my games, she'd come to my room and *sit*. She never said much. Her presence alone filled the silence, easing my doubts and calming my fear of the next day. Sometimes, I'd wake in the morning, and she'd still be there, asleep, curled under my comforter. She had a way of making each of us feel like we were the only child. My twin sisters swear she did the same with them. *Just being* with us, no phone, no outside chatter. She gave us all of her whenever we were together.

Sleep steals my night away at some point, and I'm grateful for the rest. Dawn arrives quickly, golden light cutting through our curtains. When did I doze off? The last thing I remember is Raith's snoring.

I stretch my fingers through the dust motes dancing in the sunlight, thankful I got some shut-eye before today's track meet. It's the first since that fateful one three years ago, my last race before everything changed. Vivid images of nearly crashing into a pickup truck, vomiting in the driveway, falling on the stairs and seeing Mom's final moments rush in, stealing my breath with it. *Stop*. I command. *Not now*.

I tiptoe to our kitchen corner for two cups of lemon water, Miss Rita's tradition. She always claimed it flushes away "bad toxins" and opens my soul to run better. No idea if that was true, but according to Miss Rita, she and lemon water were the reason for my D-1 scholarships. "Cheers, Miss Rita," I whisper, "May your concoction bring me speed, focus, peace and a W today."

A quick shower later, I dress, then slip out for the sports complex. I wish our first meet was away. It would give me a chance to shake off the nerves. I can't seem to loosen up. I feel tight everywhere. I walk slowly to the complex, with some of my teammates jogging ahead of me on the opposite side. I better stick to walking with my hammer toes as Raith calls them. My new motto at this age is walk to the stadium and sprint to the finish line, hopefully.

I click on my AirPods, letting Tupac's tunes guide me. His words help me forget how Dad's in Europe, and my sisters are busy with their own events. Strange how you don't miss something until it's no longer there. It's lonely not having family in the stands. I never realized how Mom's presence settled me until she wasn't there. She'd claim her favorite seat at the bottom left corner of every stadium, hands clasped like she was praying me to victory. Her absence still stings like a fresh burn, bringing me to tears as I listen to my Tupac telling me don't cry and dry your eyes. It would definitely surprise Raith to know Tupac is on my playlist. He's been with me since my first track season, helping me keep my eyes dry around my family.

"Cassidy," one of my teammates glances at me, face pinched. She looks more nervous than I am. "You good, girl?" She whips her hair into a high ponytail with a neon scrunchie, making her look all of twelve years old. I think my knee aches more after witnessing her youth. "Yes, let's do this," I say, hoping my own anxiety isn't showing.

Walking onto the track stirs every kind of doubt. I focus on exhaling slowly, feeling our competitive edge feeding off one another, like a shared universal vibe present in the air today.

Three years away.

Mom's gone.

Family's not here.

Kylo's not here.

I'm older.

My knee's sore.

Per Raith, my hammer toes are bad.

Stop overthinking, Cassidy. I tell myself. You put in the work to be here. *You deserve to be here. You worked for this.*

I suck in five long, deep breaths, blowing out any remaining doubts. I stretch my neck to the right and left and shake my shoulders to get rid of the final jitters. My fingers linger over both my brows, releasing the tension in my face as it flows down my shoulders, neck and off my fingertips, preparing me to get into my stance. I'm careful not to put too much pressure on my right foot, where the worst of my blisters are, as I distribute my weight evenly between my hands, feet and knees. The calm I've been hoping for finally trickles within my spirit, urging my heart to follow along.

I scratch my pinky fingernail over the track surface, making a nail file sound that draws attention of the other runners. I don't care; it gives me that itch and focus to wait for the starting gun. This is the hardest part of the race for me: standing on the blocks convincing my mind that I actually heard the starting gun.

No delays Cassidy. Hear the gun and take control. *Hear the gun. Nothing else matters.*

"Set."

I rise off the blocks, waiting, heart pounding in my throat.

Bang.

The starting gun penetrates through every cell, bone and muscle, forcing the nervous energy from my body as I lift off the block, pushing through the soreness.

More, Cassidy.

My legs rev up, and I feel that momentum carry me. The track lines become a white blur as everything tunnel visions to the finish, my legs propelling me, as if detached from my hips.

This is the high I love: tunnel haze with only the track in front of me. Just me and the rhythm, no worries, no hollow ache in my heart and no sour feeling churning my stomach.

I lean through the finish. Not knowing if I won or not. I love and hate this part of losing my opponents due to the blurry tunnel at the finish line. Slowing down is the worst part as I see the wall padding coming in fast. *Was that enough?* I reach out slamming the soft wall cushion, a slight pain hits from my sore knee. I bend to hold my wet knees, and wipe the sweat from my brows as I stare at the screen. Is that my name at the top with a 7.2 mark? I see the cheering crowds, the sound gradually increasing, as if someone's turning up the volume. It still amazes me how noise fades when I sprint.

I'm so fixated on the time, I barely notice my teammates wrapping me in a sweaty, squealing group hug.

"Thank you," I mumble, bent over, bracing my knees and gulping for air. I'm definitely not a spring chicken anymore, as Miss Rita would say. Jogging off the track after a run like this normally isn't a thing, but that sprint sucked every ounce of me.

Coach rushes over, bouncing in excitement. "Cassidy, you good?"

Straightening, I tug at my track shorts and shake out my throbbing knee. "Yes, just winded," I reply.

She smiles, pride shining in her eyes. "A 7.2 after being out for years? Hell of a run, Cassidy!"

I wipe my forehead, chest still tight from lactic acid. "Thank you, Coach." That is all I can get out. I gave that sprint everything I had and I love it, blisters, sweaty armpits and all.

We head off together, weaving through the small crowd, hesitant to look up. The stands are scattered with families, but she's not here, my seat stealing mom with her Trojan's hat and sweatshirt embossed with *Reagan's mom* on both sides. As happy as I should be, I would give anything to hear her scream my name again.

My pace slows as I approach the small crowds in the stands,

watching the different indoor events. Not many are here, but some-one's screaming so loud that it's echoing. It's a group in the middle. What are they saying?

I peek hesitantly at the calm student section, seeing multiple cell phone cases. *Does anyone watch anything anymore?*

And then I see them in their own section, away from the other small crowds. It's Raith, her parents, brothers, Brian and Louy are halfway up the stands, waving posters and shaking pom poms, cheering my name at the top of their lungs. *Are they dancing?*

My race is long over, but they're still screaming and moving like I just won Olympic gold. Curious eyes around the stadium glance their way, questioning their enthusiasm because no one's even rac-ing at the moment. If I could run straight up the stairs and hug all of them, *I would*. But I've got one more race. Instead, I blow kisses and they catch every last one. They're so loud that even those waiting for their races are distracted, but not me. I'm laser focused. Their energy fuels me. I'm so ready I forget the ache in my knee and the loss in my heart. I love that girl, and I love my cheering section.

The next race seems easier somehow, and we place second in the 400-meter. My fan club is in full turn up mode now. Brian is doing kick stands in between the line dance they all know as Raith's Dad watches them, convinced they've all lost their minds.

For the first time I feel free, and join in on the line dancing with them, blowing more kisses, and waving at my loud, crazy fan club before heading inside the tunnel to change with my team.

Today was such a good day. No… scratch that…today was an amazing day. I won one race and came in second in the other. That felt good. *If I cursed*, I'd say it felt fucking amazing.

I walk toward the tunnel, feeling better than I have in weeks, no in years. *I did it.* This is an accomplishment, and it's my win. I came back, I did it on my own terms and I line danced.

"Kylo!" The sound of his name slams my heart like a mallet. *Did someone say Kylo?*

CHAPTER 30

BABY DOLL FACE

Kylo

"**M**AN, COME IN." CHRISTIAN STEPS INSIDE, BULLSHIT plastered on his face, hiding something behind his back. I don't have time for his games with everything I got going on.

"What up bro?" he asks, still hiding something.

"Ever since Sarah made this engagement shit go viral, my week's been hell. I've been on calls with my agent, attorney and PR rep trying to do damage control. Then Aunt D came at me with her own words of wisdom. Didn't know a good church going woman who claims to know Jesus personally could drop that many curse words," I grunt, feeling my neck muscles tighten with aggravation.

Christian slips off his boots and picks up a pool cue. I've converted Miss Blade's basement into my personal man cave: an open layout space with a living area, small kitchen, bedroom, work out station, pool table, game room and movie corner... everything I need, complete with an entrance leading to an infinity pool and pond.

He chalks the cue, preparing himself for his normal ass

whooping. "Auntie?" he asks, eyebrows connecting into one long unibrow with curiosity. He heard everything I said, but he's stuck…. on her.

"Man, I've told you about my folks," I say, noticing he's itching to say something.

He bites down on a grin. "Just saying. If anything, ever happens to Uncle Joe, Auntie can get it," he breaks the rack not ignoring my warning. What the hell is wrong with his ass?

I ignore him. "Leave Aunt D alone. Anyway, I've been in recovery mode since last week, trying to handle this shit without damaging my image or endorsements. Turns out public perception is everything. And this fucking phone won't quit blowing up."

My phone vibrates again, another text from my PR team, reminding me not to comment on calls or accept interview requests. I hate all this publicity nonsense with the cameras and social media everywhere. It feels like everyone's watching me twenty-four-seven.

Christian sits down his pool cue and places a small, gift-wrapped box on the side table cheesing again. "Figured I'd be the first to get you an engagement present," he braces the stick against his chest as though protecting himself from the ass whooping coming. He's never serious. Everything's a joke with his ass.

Staring at the shiny red and gold wrapping, I feel my blood pressure rise. "Throw that shit in the trash before it ends up down your throat," I warn, zero interest in whatever joke is inside.

He stares at me. "You good, bro?" he asks, resting the cue across his shoulders.

"Nothing's good. The seasons starting, Sarah's pulling her crazy stunts, workouts aren't going the way I want. Everything's off balance," I admit.

"Season's tough, but fiancé troubles? That's a whole other level," he shoots back.

I grab a cushion and throw it at him, hoping to knock his ass out. "She's not my fiancée, we both know it. Once I get this under control, she'll be back out of my life. I don't remember agreeing to anything beyond hooking up."

Christian's playful grin evaporates. "It's unclear what your "hooking up" means. You don't talk much about it, but y'all been together for a while. It doesn't matter how official or unofficial it is. People assume it's real."

He leans against the kitchen island, studying me with rare seriousness. "What'd you do to her to make her propose to you on national TV?"

I massage my goatee. The same questions been bothering me. I was mad as hell when she announced that shit. I left her ass standing there with Pittman watching. That was a week ago and I still don't have answers. I force out a humorless grunt, trying to deflect the tension. "You know she can't get enough of this."

The heaviness in my chest tightens. "Honestly, I woke from that coma with a million questions. Like why was I with her in the first place? She's always been off, but this current crazy is next level."

Christian pops open the fridge, grabbing his usual coconut water. Miss Blade keeps it stocked only for him. "You'd better fix it before she drags me in for a tux fitting," he jokes. "You ready? Coach wants us at A&M's track meet to see this new recruit he's scouting."

We struggle to find parking thanks to the big crowd, ending up with a long walk to A&M's new indoor track. It's a massive upgrade from when I was here.

"Who's coach trying to steal?" I ask, falling into step with Christian.

"A Ugandan kid with killer speed," he explains. "Never played soccer a day in his life, but Coach says you can teach the game, not the speed."

We head inside. I wonder if my donations are going to this building fund. The facility is huge with seating on one side, gates surrounding the track, plenty of standing room, perfect lighting, ventilation, and concession stands. Even the temp control is right and good for running. A few students immediately recognize me and Christian, wanting autographs and pictures. That's the part of fame I can do without, but I'm grateful for their support. I sign and chat, giving them the real me, not the fake one for the cameras.

Soccer was not popular back in the day. It was a sport no one paid much attention to in the States. Most still had no idea who I was until I returned from playing overseas.

But some things never change at A&M. The smell of this place is still as it was the day Miss Blade left me on this campus. I went hard at soccer, spending all my extra at the field. Those weren't the best days, as some say they were for them. I didn't hang out much and missed so many classes they threatened to put me out. I was angry at the world, mean as hell, and got into a lot of trouble, ending up off the team. But Coach Smith saved me. His take no bull style kept me in line. He was a tough ass, and I needed all of it. Listening was not a skill that I possessed back then and still struggle with, according to Miss Blade.

"What's up?" I respond to the eager faces wanting autographs. There's no way in hell I looked this young back in the day at A&M.

"Alright, give that man a break!" Coach barks at the crowd with his thick Southern drawl. He slaps my shoulder, pulling me in for a side hug. "He isn't nobody but a slow striker, anyway," that old joke again. He used to call me slow even though I was top speed on the team.

I grin. "Coach," I say quietly.

"Come here son," he says, grabbing my shoulder with a slight squeeze and tugging me from the crowd. Some things remain the same, coach never had any patience, but still has that firm ass grip. He peers over me. "Heard congratulations are in order."

I freeze. "Coach, it isn't what you think," I answer, out of ear shot waiting for a story.

He stares hard with that no nonsense, no expression I've seen for years. Coach looks like he did the day Miss Blade dropped me off at A&M. He's always had that weary look, with those permanent frown lines and leather tanned skin. "Well, you either proposed or you didn't? Ain't no in between. According to the news you're a fiancé, nothing's fake about that, son," he confirms, as if he's researched the topic for years.

Coach still has that dry sense of humor that makes you question whether to laugh or not. "We'll talk later," I say, watching the kids still wanting more autographs.

He gives me that same cutting ass stare he always had when I was messing up. "Whenever you're ready. But don't bottle it up, son. You come talk if you need me." I nod, moving away before anyone overhears. It took a while in college to peel me open and get to the truth. But he did, and then he made me go to counseling with the person he trusts the most, his wife. She's a certified trauma psychologist. I could be in jail if it wasn't for those two, Miss Blade and Aunt D. "Alright, let's watch the girls over here and then see my boy. Did Christian tell you how fast this kid is on the field? He's gone in a blink of an eye."

"Coach, he couldn't be faster than me," I shrug, with my ego left wounded.

"Faster, you'll see," he nods, then walks away with his worn-down, hurt back knee ache coach walk.

"He can't be faster," I say, as I follow Coach and Christian. At least before the accident, there weren't many faster. I'm still too slow and it bothers the hell out of me. I rest my arm on the fence, blocking out the unnecessary noise, as I wait for the boys to start, watching the girls prepare for their sixty-meter dash.

I narrow my gaze at the girls. There's something sexy about the sculpted physique of a girl who's been dedicated to track for some time. The training transforms them into all muscles from head to toe without hitting the gym hard. Witnessing those muscular quadriceps wide open and waiting, is a sight to see. *Damn.*

"Bro let's go over here. I'm coming with bad intentions today.

Plus, the view's much better." Christian's eyes slide down some of the college track girls that could land him and me in jail. But, he's right the view is better, so I follow him.

The starter gun fires as we watch the girls sixty-meter dash. All of them are nice, but the one pulling from the middle running in lane three has my attention. "Who is that?" She's running like someone's chasing her, with those sexy legs pushing her past the rest. Damn, she's fast and fine as fuck. She bends, giving us all that ass to think of later as she tries to catch her breath. I should feel bad about watching this teenager, but I don't. Hold your head up, curly hair. Let me see you.

She eventually lifts that glorious ass up to speak to her coach. "Damn!" I lean in, getting a closer look at the bronze beauty with her ponytail flopping as she walks away. I can't see all of her, but I see enough to let me know she's different.

"Bro, you alright?" Christian faces me with worry lines stretching across his forehead, the same look I get from Aunt D and Miss Blade.

I move closer, not wanting to miss what's coming my way. "If you move your big ass head, I can get a better view," I nod in her direction. "Did you hear her name? The one with the blonde streaks." Christian squints, looking toward her, seeming unfazed. This is the type of woman that gets a reaction from everyone, but he says nothing.

I can hardly hear the announcer say her name. Crowds are loud. Who's cheering that loud? Did he say Cass Pitt?

I can't pull away, and find myself walking closer. She stops to blow kisses at the crowd in the stand. A small group of maybe ten has signs and pom poms, cheering loud enough to shake the building. *Are they line dancing?* She walks toward the tunnel on the opposite side. Does she have more races? Fuck it, I'll find out.

"Bro, where you going?" Christian yells after me. Damn, I forgot his ass that fast.

"I'm heading over to the tunnel to get a better view. Tell Coach I'll be right back."

His eyebrows form their normal unibrow, demanding more answers. "A better view at what?" he asks, wanting an explanation.

"Did you see that girl who won the sixty-meter? I couldn't hear her name. Crowds were too loud."

Christian hesitates before saying anything. "I saw her. You know her?" He tilts his head, studying me with the patience of a teacher waiting for the right answer.

"Nah man. How would I know her?" Hell, if I knew her, she would not be at this track meet; she'd be somewhere with me. I wonder how old is she? I hope she's not under twenty. That's too young.

Christian stares away, not answering. "What's up?" I ask sensing he wants to say more but can't figure out what to say.

"Ahh, nothing," he reluctantly says, massaging his bare chin to hold his words.

I leave yelling over my shoulder. "Tell Coach I'll be back!"

"Kylo, you good?" I stop. Something's off, his expression tells me and he's asking too much. I'll figure it out later.

"I'm straight," I reply, walking away as he watches me hard. I navigate through the crowd toward the tunnel, muscles tense and sweat building. Damn, where's the entrance? Finally, I reach it feeling confused with my chase, feeling like a damn creeper because I don't do this shit.

As I get there, she walks out. There she is again. Why am I off? She heads to her next run, leaving me craving to get lost in the smell of her thick hair and touch of her full lips. "Beautiful" is an insult, it's too simple, too basic, she's so much more than that and that word doesn't do her justice.

I linger at the edge of the crowd, my gaze drawn to those thighs, igniting something within me to explore what's hidden beneath those tight track shorts. *What the hell is wrong with me?* It's got to be the accident messing with my head, I don't go down, period.

She tilts her head as though stretching her neck, not turning fully but enough for me to wonder if she's glancing my way. *Am I breathing?* The innocence coming off her, along with the softness of those loose strands framing her face hits me hard. I find myself hoping she's at least twenty, because the urge to brush her hair aside is intense. She sinks her teeth into her bottom lip, those small delicate teeth leaving just enough impression to make me want to break straight through the crowd for a closer look. *Damn.*

As she walks away, an air of silence hangs around us, while others nearby brag as if they actually got a chance. This girl is so far out of their league, they shouldn't be allowed to breathe in her presence. She walks away, unaware of the effect she's having on everyone, including me.

She finishes second in the 400-meter dash, standing tall this time instead of bending over to catch her breath as she did earlier. I was hoping she would. She waves to her fan base and blows kisses as their cheers take over, louder than anyone else in the stadium. Is that... Drake playing? They must've spent serious money on their sound system because the bass is hitting hard, vibrating through the stands.

She hits the line dance with her posse, drawing everyone into her spell without missing a beat. Damn, her ass can dance. She's got all of us under her trance. And now, they're screaming her name...Cassidy.

Wait. Cassidy. Everyone's watching her and I'm stuck on that name. Cassidy. I wipe sweat from my forehead not sure why I'm heated. I feel myself getting hot, trying to focus on that name. Cassidy.

I hold my pounding head in my hand as the pain strikes with the force of a hammer. They're screaming the name Cassidy Pitt. Brooklyn told me to say hello to someone named... Cassey. *Wait, do I know her?*

Shit, that's the question that Christian just asked me. They're screaming Cassidy Pitt. *Fuck!* Do they mean Pittman? John Pittman said I'd met his daughter at the gala. I met Pittman's daughter the night of the accident. But why are they saying Pitt instead of Pittman? Are they cutting off her name? Could it be Pittman?

The puzzle pieces slip together too fast. Too much is coming together. Damn, I have to figure this out. I need time to think, but she's walking this way.

Something pulls me closer to the fence. She passes her fan club, surrounded by teammates. They all cluster around her, all in good spirits, and she's at the center of it. She's heated, but there's a different energy about her, like she just conquered something major. The urge to pull her across the fence to get some answers to the questions in my head is crazy.

"Kylo!" Christian screams. I check him eyeing me, his gaze shifting beyond my shoulder. I follow his eyes and lock onto the most intoxicating scene I've ever seen. *Man....* God took his sweet time creating every part of her delicate portrait. Her hair slips out of her loose ponytail, long curly strands cascading around her face, giving her a doll-like sexiness. Her eyes lock onto mine, and at this moment, it's just the two of us... no one else exists. Everything around us, the track, the crowd, the noise fades to black.

For a split second, she meets my stare head on, an unreadable emotion hidden behind those eyes. My chest tightens. Her expression leaves me with the uneasy feeling I've done something wrong. *Did I?* It's a mixture of whoop ass and empathy flooding from her, with the whoop ass winning.

"Good run, Cassidy." Did I hear Christian right? How the fuck does he know her? She doesn't acknowledge him. She slips away, leaving me with a thousand questions. My fingers bite the chain-link fence, stopping me from vaulting over and causing a scene I don't need. The anger hitting me must be obvious because Christian eyes me, then steps back. I don't know why anger is boiling, but talking better happen fast before I get there.

"Man, you know her?" I ask, agitation rising in my own voice, making me question more.

I step closer to him, anxious. He's not answering fast enough.

"Chris! You know her?" I hope he's not been with her. Not her. Anybody but her.

He lifts both hands in surrender. "Yeah, bro' and so do you," he replies, checking me, then grabs my shoulders. He knows my anger and how fast it hits.

Did he say I knew her? How would I know her? I press my temples, hoping to push answers back into my head and slow my pounding headache. "How, Chris?"

"Ky, you met her," he says. He's serious when he starts calling me Ky.

He confirms all of my earlier thoughts racing in my head. I lean toward the fence to catch another look at her, but she's gone. "When did I meet her? Did I meet her around the time of the accident?"

He exhales, a bit of relief washing over him. "Yeah, bro' you did. Before the accident, you hounded my cousin for days for intel on her. We called her "Ice Girl" for a minute. You told me you got in ice with a girl who was pissed as hell. We saw her later at the café."

Damn, I know her. This damn memory thing is irritating as fuck. Not thinking, I vault the barricade leading to the locker rooms. I'm getting answers... today.

CHAPTER 31

GHOST ON MY CENTER BLOCK

Cassidy

DID I HEAR THAT RIGHT?

There's no need to question it as his name cuts through my fan club, silencing everyone cheering down to the student section scrolling and texting. My steps slow, causing my teammate to bump me from behind. She says something, but I don't hear her. Someone just said the name that makes the pit of my stomach too nervous to keep food in my body. That same name that awakened a maturity within me, igniting desires I didn't realize I had and making me feel like a woman with urgent needs. My legs weaken at the mere mention of him, my heartbeat pounding in my ear drums. Please don't let it be him. *Why would he be here?*

"Good run, Cassidy," a voice calls. Without looking up, I recognize that voice. It's Kylo's soccer teammate Christian who I met in the cafeteria. Everything comes to a dead halt as my nerves creep into uncertainty. Christian's next to him….Kylo's right there, not a tube or I V in sight.

My eyes collide into his honey hazel warmth that once made me forget gravity exists. He looks healthy and free from the ICU.

His eyes are wide, full of confusion and wonder, taking me in as if he knows me. *Does he remember?*

I brace a hand on the chain-link fence separating us. He's so close I can reach out and touch him, to smell him. I could trip and fall into his arms. He's an arm's length away. Only the fence separates us in this small tunnel. *Breathe,* my mind urges me to speak, but my lips won't budge. I can't even swallow.

But his closeness raises so many questions. How can this man be this beautiful? How can anyone be so mesmerizing? How?

The dry lump in my throat is about to make me choke and my eyes are refusing to look away. This is not happening. Too much time has passed since I've seen his perfect lips that had me wide open at the Grove. His strong hands lifted me in his truck as if I weighed nothing. But his eyes have me so lost that I'm unable to recognize my surroundings. *Why is this happening?*

I finally break away, forcing my legs to obey my brain and follow my teammates to the locker room, ignoring Christian's greeting.

My steps quicken. That chaos inside me is deafening. He still has that pull without even saying a single word. A mere glance from him is enough to leave me breathless. He still ignites a longing within me without even touching me. Did I ever stop wanting him? Or was it only waiting, deep under my everyday life, ready to detonate the second I saw those eyes again? How am I back into this insanity that quick! *Did I ever leave?*

He's the source of 90 percent of my stress and anxiety. *Why is he here?* Of all places, why is he at a track meet on A&M's campus? With all his endorsements, commercials, Sarah, and his big comeback, he should be anywhere else, not intruding on my place of peace. At least it was peaceful until those honey hazel's cut straight through my soul. I've got to go…leave, get out of here.

I yank on my sweats, leaving my track shorts underneath and hurry off to find Coach. I'll come up with some excuse, like I'm not feeling well, or that my heart is caught somewhere between lanes two and three, waiting for Kylo to claim it. *This is ridiculous.*

I throw my backpack on and slip out the side exit of the locker room, hoping to avoid everybody.

"Where are you going, Lightning?" Great, it's Raith. How did she get here so fast? They have barricades for a reason.

"Track Star you were on fire today, running like someone was literally chasing you. Did you see your score, run, whatever it's called?"

I roll my shoulders, trying to ease the tightness in my neck, but I still can't form the words to answer her.

She cocks her head, hands fanning the air as if trying to gather the syllables I lost the moment I saw his eyes. "What's up? You just tore up the track, but now you're standing here like you've seen a ghost!"

I brush past her, knowing exactly what she'll say and I don't want to hear it. "Heading back to the dorm," I mumble, hoping she'll drop it. I need to leave.

"Wait a minute," she demands. "What happened between you running the sixty like some hybrid of Sha'carri Richardson and Florence Griffith-Joyner then changing clothes so fast?"

She narrows her slits, attempting to stare the truth out of me. "Wait, is there a ghost here?"

I exhale a shaky breath, forcing air from my diaphragm to explain. "I did see the ghost," I pause, then continue. "Kylo is here... with Christian."

Her eyes grow wider than I've ever seen. "Oh, so you're just gonna keep running from your ghost?"

I don't have the energy for this. "I just..." I stutter, trying not to give her a chance to reply as I walk past her. My mind is made up.

She catches my arm, slowing me. "Look, what you need to do is show those thick ass thighs in those tights and make him wake the hell up!" she yells, hands on her hips.

I knew she would be this way. "Raith. I..."

She cuts me off before I can finish. "Look, he forgot you due to an accident. That's the only reason. But you haven't forgotten him based on how twisted you are. His life is going to keep progressing so you have to keep running and learn to exist. You've been through some tough shit, so I know you're stronger than existing." She waves her hands toward me, making me feel weak. "Look, stop that running shit, take those off," she gestures to my baggy sweatpants, "and leave those tight ass track shorts on. You worked hard for that body. Don't hide it."

I stand there, pinned by her stare, reluctant but knowing she's right. "You're right," I say under my breath.

She leans forward, smiling. "What was that?"

I sigh. "I said you're right." I hate letting those words escape my lips, especially with Raith. She'll never let me forget this.

She steps back hitting a dance move that should be banned from the public. "Say it again! For once, Reagan Cassidy Pittman just said I was right. I want the whole world to hear…"

"I'm not repeating it and no need to use my government name. I like Cassidy," I hug her long enough to melt into her shoulder shea butter. "Thank you for my fan club."

She steps back and shrugs. "Roomie, I was trying to get an entire marching band to show up and play for you in the stands, but B couldn't work it out with the tubas in an indoor facility."

"You're insane, Raith." I narrow my eyes at her, searching for any signs she's joking. But she doesn't reply. "Wait, are you serious? And another question, was that Drake playing during your line dance?"

She grins hits another dance move like she's still in the stands. "Hell yeah! We were about to rock Beyoncé up there, but I brought "Over," by Drake instead. Maybe next time."

I lean in for another hug. "My current fan club is enough for me. Your brothers made my day. Can we go see them?" I sigh, smiling, feeling happiness as we head toward her cheering family.

A few minutes later, after shared hugs, Raith pulls me aside, telling her family to call her when they make it home. I didn't realize that someone calling for me in the stands was needed. She did that for me and here I go again threatening tears. *No more tears.* "Look." Raith says, noticing my watery eyes. "I don't know what's with those, but if I'm waking up early, I'm going all the way out. You killed it today and should be damn proud of yourself. Now pull your shit together and let's go find that ghost."

I nod and let her steer me toward the tunnel entrance. Why did I listen to her? I could be sprawled on my dorm bed with my nose in a good book. But here I am, scuffing down a dim, curved hallway, shoulders hunched, dreading the next set of footsteps, hoping they're anyone's but Kylo's.

He doesn't remember me. Or if he does, it's overshadowed by Sarah and all the noise about his comeback. People say he might return sooner than expected because of his progress. Pathetic as it sounds, I've kept up with his soccer updates online. It's the only way I can chase away the nightmares in my dreams at night, where I include myself in his world. *So weird…*

"Raith," a familiar voice calls. It's Christian. Even though we've met once, his baritone is impossible to miss. Just hearing it replays every memory of Kylo I'm trying to erase.

"What's up?" Raith replies, slowing so he can catch up. I realize my arm is latched around her biceps, my face nearly buried in her shoulder. Good Lord. I must look like a lost kid.

Raith slows, her pace matching mine. Her eyes flick to me, sharp and unblinking, almost daring. "Look, you got this, and I'm glad you took off those track pants. Now pull your head the fuck up, show those thick ass thighs, and tell him," Raith encourages, her voice distant as my heart pounds with the possibilities waiting around the corner.

I lift my gaze to the rows of cinder blocks, counting them, one, two, three, four, five, six… until I'm staring straight at him.

He stands, still and deliberate behind Christian. The faint smell of cologne mixes with the concrete air as he leans casually against the cinder blocks, with that face that's never been absent from my nights. He stares at me, as if I'm the ghost that he was for me after my race. Everything stills, those honey beauties dragging me like a slow burn, never hiding their interest. My stomach knots. He's not even trying to be subtle, and neither am I, caught in the moment, paralyzed by the sheer intensity of it.

His broad shoulders stretch the fabric of his fitted shirt, muscles taut and my gaze can't help but dip lower, following the cut of his body until I'm stuck on the way his distressed holey jeans hang low on his hips. That teasing vee. The way his body moves that moment is too familiar, too close to my dreams.

He scratches his head, his gaze drifting to my chest, where his honey hazels linger, bold and unashamed. There's no attempt to hide his interest and neither of us moves. It's as if we're both stuck in this moment, paralyzed, unable to break the spell.

"Damn, this is some intense shit. I feel the heat radiating off both of you!" Raith shouts from the side, her voice cutting through the tunnel like a siren.

The spell is broken leaving me unsteady. I rub the sweat from my forehead, trying to calm myself, but that quick, I'm missing the scar from the accident near his eye. The Vitamin C I applied twice a night must have done its job, fading his scar partially. But somehow, it's the perfect addition to his face.

How can a scar make him sexier?

"Raith," Christian calls out, his voice rising above the passing crowd. "What's up? Been a minute!"

She walks toward him, her style drawing his attention. "Yeah, it has been, Beautiful One. What's up with you?" Raith's voice is full of flirtation, reminding me that she's still looking for someone to help pay her way through college.

He steps back, checking her out, lingering on her bright pink hair. "You tell me," he replies, voice heavy with interest.

"I told you," she says, words forming to embarrass me. "You don't want none of this. I got that stuff that make you go crazy. Consider yourself warned, Christian."

Others notice and comment as they walk through the tunnel.

Why is she never aware of her surroundings? She makes every situation crazy with her inability to remain sane, and this one is at the top of her list. Christian bends over laughing and starts twerking on her as if they're both listening to the same song telepathically.

I'm so caught up in Raith that I don't sense Kylo getting closer, his presence radiating in the air like heat. But my body did as it heats up hotter on its own from him invading my space. Some things remain the same.

He reaches out, extending his hand. *Is this for a handshake?* "Kylo Blade."

"Dude, is that all you got! You have got to come stronger than that!" Raith screams from across the tunnel, leaning casually against the center block wall, arms folded and one leg bent.

Why is this happening?

Kylo looks at her, confusion building, with me wanting to melt into the floor. "Do I know you?" he asks, shifting his gaze between her and me.

"Hell yeah, you know me and damn sure as hell know her," Raith points in my direction.

Interesting. I've dreamed of this moment for weeks. It was more roses and kisses, but this is a mixture of awkward and insane, quickly turning into crazy. This is not my fairytale dream.

He turns to me, ignoring Raith, his expression a mix of confusion and curiosity. "How do I know you?" he asks, and those words, those exact words, are everything I wanted to hear. The words I wanted to hear when he peeled his eyes from the ceiling at that hospital. The words I wanted to hear when I urged him to remember and the words I wanted to hear since he awakened. Just easily, and without a worry, doubt or question slipped from his lips.

Before I can speak, I back away to the wall of the tunnel, avoiding any closeness from him. But his honey hazels are so intense they follow me, as if I might disappear. "Kylo, we met a month prior to the car accident," I sigh, hating to say the words I should have said weeks ago.

He leans against the wall, steadying himself, his hands pressing into the concrete for support. Tiny beads of sweat glisten on his forehead, and I can't look away from them. He wipes it with the back of his hand, grateful that I'm not the only one feeling the heat.

"Are you okay?" I ask, the words slipping out before I can think. My hand reaches toward his arm, almost instinctively. *Why did I do that?* It felt so natural, it surprises me.

"I'm good," he replies, his gaze dipping to where my hand rests on his arm. His fingers gently remove mine, but instead of pulling away, he intertwines our fingers. We stay this way for a while, soaking in the simple touch of our hands. "With the accident, I lost a month of memory. I don't remember anything from thirty to forty days before it happened," he speaks slowly, his words weighted, each one carefully chosen.

His eyes search mine, almost like he's seeing me for the first time. The expression mirrors the one he had in the ice bath, and I realize his honey hazels are drunk with the same desire I felt when he was between my legs in his truck. It's raw and unfiltered. "I don't have a clear understanding of what happened," he admits, his voice thick with longing. "But I owe you an apology for forgetting someone like... you."

His words pull me closer to him, an invisible force not letting go. I can feel him taking me in again, his eyes tracing my body with a slow, deliberate heat as he moves from my chest, south to the v between my thighs. His lips seem to beg for a taste of the aroma I hope he gets familiar with again. His stare is unapologetic, like he can't help himself, completely unconcerned with what he's doing. It's bold and unashamed.

"Did we?" he asks, his voice hoarse, the question both a challenge and a plea. He bites his bottom lip, his honeys burning a hole straight through my track shorts to an area already wet and not from running.

"No," I answer quickly. "We did not, and I would appreciate it if you would bring your focus back to my eye level," I say, surprising myself that I can get those words out.

He lifts his gaze, uncertainty creeping in, but no embarrassment showing. "I'm sorry," he starts, trailing off as if unsure how to continue. "I'm not usually like this with..."

His words falter, but then he looks at me again. "You're just intoxicating as hell. I felt the pull watching you run, and I didn't even remember I knew you. I walked from the other side of the stadium to find you after your last race."

He looks away, maybe uncomfortable, but his words continue to spill anyway. "Me telling you this isn't normal, so I know something happened between us."

Relief pours, as if he finally admitted something too much to keep inside. "I need to understand because this... this feels different," he leans in closer, but I can't seem to focus on anything except his words: "this feels different," he said that the night of his accident at the Grove. Those are the words I've clung to for months, hoping this was real.

His attention shifts over my shoulder, and I follow to see Vice President Reed of A&M approaching. Kylo releases my hand, and *I miss it already.*

"Kylo, good to see you. How are you?" VP Reed inquires, pulling Kylo into a bro' hug.

"I'm well, sir. Better than I was a couple of months ago," Kylo replies, with his normal cool and effortless charm.

I watch their interaction, Kylo's natural aura winning over VP Reed easily. Some people have an innate ability to attract others, regardless of status or background. Kylo is one of those people. His natural charisma is magnetic.

"I'm glad everything's okay after the car accident," VP Reed says. "I can't believe it happened the night of the gala. I'd just seen you. We were all praying that you'd pull through." His gaze flickers between us, assessing, and I can feel Kylo's eyes shift back to me, lingering in that familiar way. It's the same way he looked at me

earlier, absorbing me, taking in every detail, his expression revealing a satisfaction that sends shivers to the tips of my nails. *Is this
really happening?* I'm afraid to let myself believe it.

VP Reed turns to me. "My apologies. Cassidy, how are you?
You were as fast as a lightning bolt today." I chance looking at Kylo
only to see him smiling. *What's funny?*

VP Reed continues. "Congratulations on the win," he says,
patting me on the shoulder careful not to get too close like his bro'
hug with Kylo.

"Thank you, it feels good to be back out there again," I reply,
though my words feel hollow.

VP looks back at Kylo. "This young lady is going to take us
to the Olympics."

Kylo straightens abruptly, slipping back into his familiar
charm. "Yes. No doubt." His baritone deepens, and a sense of shyness creeps over me as I realize something. I'm still that lost girl on
my dorm steps, waiting and hoping for him to pick me up.

"Well, it's good seeing you both," VP Reed says, his attention
shifting as he prepares to leave. "I have another function to attend,
but before I forget, I received your engagement invitation yesterday.
I think my wife followed up with the contact on file, your planner.
Take care, Kylo, so you can get back out there."

VP Reed walks off, and my heart sinks to the soles of his polished black shoes beneath the hem of his gray suit pants, leaving
a hollow ache in my chest. *Did he say engagement party?* Is Kylo
marrying Sarah?

Kylo turns to face me, his expression shifting, struggling to
hold the explosion brewing within himself. But at this moment I
don't care. "Are you engaged?" I choke out the question, unaware
of my volume but obviously too loud seeing Raith and Christian
glance our way.

He appears frustrated, hesitant, unsure what to say, so I repeat myself. "Are you getting married?" My question drips with irritation, and I feel all eyes on us.

He lowers his head, rubbing his forehead as if the words he wants to say are stuck, trapped somewhere in him. He doesn't answer, and I can feel the distance growing, thick and uncomfortable between us.

"Never mind," I mutter, shaking my head. "Don't answer. It's none of my business. It was good seeing you again, but I have to meet my coach," I grip my backpack tightly, looking for a way out, my escape route.

I move past him, but his fingers graze mine, and that familiar spark surges again. I stop, my body rebelling against my mind as my escape plan crumbles. It takes everything in me not to turn back.

"Wait Cassey," he calls softly, and the use of my name catches me off guard. He's the only one who's ever said it like that, along with Brooklyn. "Things are not what they seem. I need time to explain."

I freeze, hoping for any hint that he remembers anything. But nothing changes. His expression is still unreadable. "Let go," I demand, pulling away, the frustration growing inside me.

He releases my hand, stepping closer. My heart races as he closes the distance, narrowing the gap between us. "I have questions about us. Don't go," he pleads, his tone holds hints of anger.

I release the breath I've been holding since running out the hospital months ago and give myself a chance to take him in…the curves, scars and sexiness of his face. This might be my last chance to be this close to him. Without thinking, I move toward him, rising on my toes, my nails digging into his neck as my lips find his. I wait until he opens up for me, fully exploring the wetness of our kiss. His arms wrap around my hips and then the center of my back, claiming me as his own. It's a repeat performance of the Grove and in his truck, our kiss deepening with a desire I can't put into words. We're lost in our world, not caring that we're both in public eye, tasting this last moment between us.

I pull away, breathless, my hands resting on his arms to steady myself. I try to avoid his gaze, but I can't escape the feeling of him.

"It was nothing, Kylo," I say, the words coming out more broken than I want. "Congratulations on the engagement."

I turn away quickly, feeling a tear forming but I make it stop. *No tears.* Engagement?

As I walk away, I hear him call after me. "Brooklyn said hello, Cassey." Of course he would say that now.

No turning back.

Never again.

CHAPTER 32

MY FAVORITE STRAWBERRY PIE

Kylo

SIT IN MY TRUCK OUTSIDE MY HOUSE AFTER THE A&M MEET, asking myself, "What the hell just happened?"

I know that girl. How do I not remember her? I need answers. She left mad so quick, with Raith chasing after her, that I couldn't stop her. And once people started recognizing me, security had to step in to get us out. I got to find her to understand that kiss, it wasn't just a kiss. It had me so caught up I felt off when she left.

We had something. I know it because she isn't the type to kiss that way in public. I've been with the type. She could barely lift her head when she saw me, but she was comfortable enough to touch me. That kiss was damn telling. But it felt like a goodbye. Like she's not planning to see me again.

What did I expect after that mess with Sarah. I gotta fix this shit? Those heart-shaped gapped lips need me and I need more.

Where does she like to go?

Is she really Pittman's daughter?

What is her thong size?

Damn.

I got questions and I need answers.

I jump out of the truck and head inside, stretching my ankle as I go. It still bothers me, especially now that practice is getting more intense. Aunt D's car is in the driveway. I hope she's not here to cuss me out in five different languages. I'm not feeling that today and hungry as hell. Hopefully she and Miss Blade have food ready.

I open the door smelling something cooking. Good, I need food to get my mind off those thighs and soft ass lips. *Shit.* "Aunt D. What's up? Where's Miss Blade?"

She faces me with two pans and a knife in her hands, looking ready to battle. "Juanita is on her way; I beat her to the house. She's probably out there driving like she's chauffeuring Miss Daisy in the backseat."

Aunt D always got jokes but who is Miss Daisy? "What are you making?" I ask, seeing red juice all over the counter. *I hope that comes up.*

She prances over, her apron matching her other evening getup. Aunt D changes clothes, purses, shoes and wigs twice a day. She'll have short hair in the morning and by lunch, it's five inches longer and a different color. "I'm making your favorite strawberry pie. I told you I'd make it, and I had some time today."

I walk around the kitchen island and wrap my arm around her narrow shoulders. My ladies are so little. Cassidy's small too but *not everywhere*. She's got a grown woman body with those soft breasts pressing against my chest hinting that she's at least a D cup. They were so full in her track suit with that pretty color that I had to hold back from taking a peak. *Damn.* And those shorts? Everyone around was looking at her ass. I need that body covered up, because that body is *too* tight for anyone else to witness but me. My hand slipped down her track jacket to investigate what was hidden and it was what I thought. I couldn't keep my hands off her softness, but her hard nipples pressing against my chest told me everything I need to know.

Aunt D walks away bringing my attention back to her. "I love strawberry pie," I say, leaving out the part that Miss Blade's strawberry pie is better. No need to go there with the negative. Plus, Aunt D's nice right now and not how she was a couple of days ago after the wedding announcement. I sneak a couple of strawberries only to have my hand swatted away. "Those are million-dollar hands you're hitting."

She winks at me as she slides the pie into the oven. "No son, you have million-dollar feet. The hands? They're free rein."

I sit at our island, resting my ankle on the barstool, my gaze fixed on the Carrara white marble countertop, lost in thought. *What happened between us?*

"Kylo, are you okay?" Aunt D's voice pulls me from my thoughts. What did I do to make her think something's wrong? Damn, did I stop breathing and not realize it? I try to ignore them when they do this, but it happens every damn day. One slow movement or sudden jerk, and they swarm me like bees wanting nectar for their honey.

"I'm good," I answer, but I'm lying. "I met someone today." Why the hell did I say that? Dealing with Christian on the way back was enough with all his questions.

"Met someone today?" she asks, eyeing me over her green reading glasses, the pair of the hour. She has a hundred pairs of tiger print, yellow, black and white reading glasses waiting for her to remember where she left them.

Her raised eyebrow over her frames tells me she wants details. "I met her before the accident," I admit. "Around the time I lost some memory. It drives me crazy that I can't remember what happened."

"Who is this mystery lady, handsome?" Aunt D leans over the counter, resting her wandering hand on my shoulder. She and Miss Blade touch a different spot on me daily doing their own physical examination. They're either going to drive me crazy or find my next illness before my docs do.

She walks away, tapping the counter with her fingers as she sets the oven timer. I should have kept this private. "She attends A&M and runs track. Her name is Cassey. Cassidy Pittman and she's…"

Aunt D leans in again, dish towel in her hands not moving. "She's what?"

"She's beautiful." The words come out more softly than I intended. This is new territory for me. I've never talked about a woman around Aunt D or Miss Blade.

"Did you talk to her long?" she asks, pushing her reading glasses higher on her nose as she returns to slicing strawberries, not taking her attention off me.

Why in the hell am I having this conversation? "Not long, Aunt D," I say, shaking my head. "I think we had something. I couldn't get enough details before VP Reed mentioned the engagement and then she left."

Aunt D nods, axing the strawberries determined to kill them. Man, I feel sorry for that fruit; they're getting what I felt last week when she heard the news. "Well, handsome, what did you expect? You are getting married, right?" she asks, mad, her head tilting. Her neck will need a heating pad in the AM from that tilt.

"Aunt D, you know marriage is not happening with Sarah. I'm not marrying her. But I have to handle this right. My PR Agent has me waiting until we can get ahead of the story, but Sarah's already mailing save-the-dates. The VP of A&M told me today. I haven't spoken to her in a week, and she's setting dates. Dealing with her ass is about to push me to drinking. I'm trying not to catch a case." Damn, I cursed.

"Sorry, Aunt D."

She frowns, her lips curled at the corners. "I got mine in the mail today. Your sister opened the envelope and freaked out. I can't say that I was pleased, either."

Her eyes narrow. "You've got to fix this soon, Kylo. Before *I* find a way to end it myself. I mean it!"

"I know, Aunt D. What's Miss Blade saying?"

"Well, not much. She's afraid to say anything because she's not sure how you feel," Aunt D replies, her voice calm but pointed.

"She gotta know this isn't happening. I'm not marrying that girl."

"She may think it," Aunt D says, "but she's not ready to say it out loud until you call it off. You've been with her so long, she's probably wondering if her family's got something on you, keeping you from leaving. You've got to get control and end this soon."

Aunt D drops the strawberries into the side bowl, gripping the knife with a look that says she's ready to get in someone's ass. I better get this under control before she handles it for real.

I stand, stretching my arms and neck, trying to shake the tension. "I have to handle this carefully. Times are different now. You can't break up with people without consequences. Social media sees to that. Bad stories hurt reputations, and reputations lose endorsement deals. Things are going too well to mess up what I've got going on. I landed four major endorsements after the car accident. That's some serious money."

"Kylo, no amount of money is worth you living in lies," she says, firmly. "You've done well over the years. How much more do you need?"

She doesn't know about my soccer issues, but she's right about one thing. My money's good. I've done well with investments. I could stop playing tomorrow and live comfortably, me and the next few generations of my family.

"How long until the pie's ready, Aunt D?" I ask, hoping she'll let me change the subject.

"Thirty more minutes." She narrows her eyes. "So, tell me about this girl."

That was too easy. I'd better take advantage of the subject change while it lasts. "Not much to tell," I say, standing and heading toward the stairs. I don't feel like talking about Cassidy, especially not with Aunt D. Why did I bring it up in the first place?

"Hmph," she says, planting her hands firmly on her hips.

Something ain't right. "Aunt D, what's up?"

"One thing about you, handsome. You've always had beautiful women. Even in high school before all of this soccer stuff. But I never heard you speak a word about any of them. You've been with Sarah off and on for years without a single compliment. I may not agree with everything about her, but she is a beauty. Describe this Cassidy girl for me."

How do you explain something that's beyond words or at least beyond my vocabulary? "She's your complexion and maybe your height with long curly hair," I catch myself before mentioning the dip in her chin that makes me crave to lick her there, or how the softness but possessiveness of her hand on mine seemed to dissolve my anger. I hold back on describing the sweet scent that hung even after her race or the way the gap between her legs showed me her innocence, making me want her in ways I didn't expect.

Ten minutes with her, and she left me feeling all of that. *Damn.* "According to Christian we had a past before the accident. He doesn't know much but he did say I got into an ice bath with her."

Aunt D's confused expression has me holding back a laugh. I know what's coming before she opens her mouth. "Wait a minute, you willingly took a cold plunge, Kylo?"

"That's crazy, right? She must have something on me, for real," I answer.

She bends to pick up the towel from the floor, laughing. "Son, I remember Juanita threatening to have Joe watch you get in those baths. The coaches couldn't make you do it. So, how'd this girl convince you to do that?"

"I can't remember. I wish I could," I reply, rubbing my ankle absentmindedly. "Could use a soak today."

"So, this young lady has you all tied up in knots, I see," Aunt D says, adjusting her glasses, not letting the subject go.

She got too many questions. "What's up with all the questions?"

She sets the knife down, sits next to me and pats my hand

gently. "Well, let's just say a girl was at the hospital when you came out of the coma, and I have a feeling it may be the same girl."

Her words hit me hard. I yank my hand away as if she'd stabbed me with the strawberry knife, shock spreading across her face. "What?" I ask, waiting for her to answer but battling in the middle to stay calm.

"Yes," she says steady. "There was a young lady at the hospital. She was there when you came out of the coma."

I grind my teeth trying to hold the frustration boiling inside me. "Why didn't you say something earlier?" Aunt D raises her eyebrows at me. Maybe my tone is off, but answers aren't coming fast enough. "Sorry, but I need to know everything," I apologize, knowing she and Miss Blade still have a way of keeping me in check.

"Well," she starts, "I spoke with Juanita and we decided not to say anything until the time was right."

The right time? The right time should've been when I came out of that coma. The right time should've been when I came home. Weeks ago. "Aunt D, is this the right time?" I ask, unable to hold on. I know this part of me, and so does most of my family. It's been months, and this girl was a part of my life *ten*, she was at the hospital, *nine*, how did we meet? *Eight*, she made me get in ice, *seven*, control it Kylo, *six, five, four.* Not even realizing it, I find myself in the family room and not in the kitchen. *How the fuck did I get here?*

Taking a deep breath, I walk back into the kitchen. Aunt D is there waiting, her expression gentle and understanding, making me feel guilty for what just happened. I've had anger issues since I was kid, everyone knows, but it seems better. At least *I hope so.*

"Sorry again, Aunt D," I say quietly. "It's hard not remembering everything, and this girl, woman, whoever she is… was a part of my life," I trail off, unable to find the words.

She lets out a soft sigh, her shoulders drooping slightly. "Kylo, something happened with you and that girl," she says slowly, her voice full of emotion. "Because she's the reason, and I mean the *only* reason you're standing here in front of me."

She removes her green reading glasses and sets them aside, motioning me to sit next to her on the sofa. She's trying to keep me calm, noticing I'm battling not to go straight hot. "Please explain, Aunt D," I say, urgency taking over my voice.

Once I'm seated, she takes a deep breath, holding my hand in that firm church grip the way she used to when I was a kid. "Well," she begins. "As we've told you, the doctors met with us concerning trying again with your medically induced coma. We didn't know what to expect and your mom couldn't make that decision alone. It was too much."

Her voice cracks slightly, but she pushes forward. "They started reducing the medication, and we waited. Once the nurses removed all the meds and oxygen, we listened as your heartbeat slowed, praying hard for a miracle."

She squeezes my hand tighter, and I feel the weight of her words. "Kylo, we thought we were going to lose more than you that day. This was our second attempt at bringing you back. I thought I was going to lose my sister, too. She was barely holding on. To lose one son is devastating, but to lose both her babies? Unthinkable."

Her voice trembles. "We watched as they unplugged the machines. I held Juanita with everything I had while your heart rate slowed. It was too much for Joe and the girls to witness."

Aunt D wipes the tears from her cheeks. I hate to see her cry, she and Miss Blade don't do that. As much as our small family has suffered over the years they don't cry. I hug her, as she rests her second wig of the day on my chest.

"It was bad, Kylo," she says softly, her voice trembling. "But your mom needed me and I wasn't leaving her side."

She pulls back, her eyes heavy with memories. "Kylo, out of nowhere, this girl comes into the room, screaming for you to wake up. She looked so wild I thought she was crazy. The nurse tried to hold her back, but she got past her. Then they called security, but she wasn't letting you go."

She pauses, and I wait, hanging onto every word. "It was as

though God was pouring strength into this girl, giving her what you needed to wake up. She grabbed your feet under that cover before security could make her leave and brought you back."

Aunt Diane stops, and I want to squeeze it out of her, but I remind myself to hold back. "Kylo," she whispers, her voice thick with emotion, "it was like she was breathing life into you. She spoke to you, her words filling your lungs with air, pushing your spirit back into your body. It was powerful. It was…in my opinion…love."

Her words hit me in a place none have done. I swallow hard, my chest tightening. "But when you finally opened your eyes and looked at all of us," she continues, "there was one person you didn't remember."

My hands tremble as I reach out, wiping her tears. "What was her name?" I ask, my voice barely a whisper.

Her uncertainty meets mine, filled with the same worry Miss Blade often has when she looks at me. "Baby, her name was Cassidy."

CHAPTER 33

WHO'S IRRELEVANT?

Cassidy

WHY DIDN'T SHE TELL ME SHE KNEW? RAITH KNEW ABOUT the engagement, but instead of saying anything, she let me walk into dreams, hopes and butterflies, all while wearing my A&M track shorts that felt like they were cutting me in half. Maybe I would've known earlier, but I was so tired of seeing him on social media, news and every working TV that I gave myself a disconnect week. Raith's only excuse? "He needed to see you because there's no way in hell you were ever going to say anything."

As much as I hate to admit it, she's right. She usually is.

But... *marriage?* How is he going to marry her? How did that happen? He broke up with her that night. He said they were together because of their agents.

Stop.

I'm not going back to the truck, not asking myself for the one thousandth fifth time. *Why did I let him do that to me?* That's over. No more. I'm done.

When I asked him about the engagement, he didn't deny it. He didn't say he wasn't getting married. He... said nothing. But I gave him a chance, right? I *did* give him a chance.

Here I go again. No more questions. There's nothing to figure out. Nothing. It happened. It's done. He's getting married and whatever this was, is over.

I need to move on. That's what I'll do. But, *how?* I don't want anyone else, especially after that awkward encounter with Walker's balls at that last party. It's funny how he avoids me now, both of us pretending the other doesn't exist. He forgot our non-crossing line. He had to know it was there. Maybe it was the alcohol.

My mind drifts back to the question of the moment: *marriage?* They were done the night of the accident. I know it. I still remember the phone conversation, her scream… like my dentist's drill grinding into my last cavity. Honestly, I question his judgment in women. Something is not right with her.

Wait. Now I'm judging her. That's not right.

I'll get my hair done. It's been weeks since my last highlights and cut. It's all about me today. He's moving on and so will I. No more self-pity.

Since its last minute, I'll catch an Uber instead of calling my driver. Plus, Mr. Stewart sitting in the salon with me watching Candle make one false move with my color treatment is not what I want today.

The salon buzzes with the comfortable chaos of a mixture of scissors clipping, running water, random music and hum of customers laughing and chatting. Exactly what I need today: downtime and people watching.

I find my corner with its tiny end table, reminding me of my spot at the hospital, with better decor. The modern design here would put those drab hospital monotones to shame.

My mind wanders to the tall, thin woman I'd seen in the hospital. *What made me think of her now?* She didn't even look back when she bumped into me in the hallway. People can be so rude for no reason.

I settle in, flipping through a *Good Housekeeping* magazine, trying not to appear too obvious as I soak in the scene around me. Maybe I'll add a pedi while I'm here. My hammer toes probably need some TLC after my last track meet. I laugh to myself, remembering Raith's horrified expression the first time she saw them.

Strange how I met both Kylo and Raith on the same day. I know everything about Raith. But Kylo? What do I honestly know about him?

I know his lips, his breath, his touch and the way they make me feel. But the rest? It's only what I've read. His rise to fame with soccer, his brother's death, his charity work...those are the stories that flood Google. Not one bad thing, story or mishap has ever come to light. He's private, sharing what he wants, and always on his own terms. Even his soccer interviews are brief, straight to the point, with a quick "yes," direct "no" and nothing else.

I hate to admit it, but I fell hard for the little things. How he opened the door for me at the tennis match. How he drove his truck with his hat turned backward. How he asked me questions about what I was reading. How he took care of Brooklyn and Monty as if it were second nature.

Beyond that I know nothing.

I don't know his favorite color, his likes, his dislikes or even what he eats. But here I am tangled up in feelings I can't shake. Miss Rita was right that something was pulling me to that hospital nightly.

And that something isn't letting go.

I glance away from my Good Housekeeping article to see the local news report: the same man is still kidnapping women. Ten victims now. What makes people sink to such evil? I know mental health is real but to physically harm so many? That's another level. One of the victims was from campus, so the school has gone into lockdown mode. My dad's been breathing down my neck about hiring around-the-clock security, but I told him to calm down. I'll be careful. I know some of the girls watching thought it could never happen to them. *But it can.*

It took no time for my hair today as I checked my reflection in the mirror. There's something about changing hair color that makes you feel brand new…kinda like what eyelash extensions do. I was born with long lashes, so I don't wear them daily. When I do, I think *how'd I ever live without these?* Same with my streaks. I'll keep them until summer. They give me a confidence boost.

I smile recalling Miss Rita's words. "You'll drive the boys crazy." *She's so funny.*

Suddenly, a high-pitched, all-too-familiar voice drags my attention from my reflection to the salon entrance. She's talking nonstop, demanding attention from anything and anyone…yes, even the ladybug creeping up the mirror. My shoulders tense under my black cape, as her shrill assaults my ears. She scans the room like a runway model, strutting in with a forced confidence. A giggle builds in my chest, hard to suppress. What type of performance is this and where can I get whatever drug she's on? She approaches my chair, head tilted as though trying to place how we might know each other. Her sharp heels click-clack steadily to a stop behind me, her gaze skimming down my strands to the edge of the cape. Then with a well-practiced flair, she rests a hand on her hip in a way only someone born into practiced privilege can manage.

"Cassidy, is it?" Sarah Sims asks, biting her bottom lip in a forced gesture of seduction.

Caught off guard, I swivel around, barely believing she knows my name. "Yes," I respond, taking in her too tight tank top, green jeans and heels. *Has she gained weight? Does she ever dress down?*

She inhales softly, tipping her upper lip toward her nose, as if taking a whiff. "I'm sure you've heard the news about my upcoming nuptials to Kylo," she says, her voice dripping with contrived humility. "I'm testing out salons to decide which lucky one gets the honor of styling my hair for the day." She folds her arms across her chest, gazing around the salon, as if expecting an applause. *Really?*

"Oh, you do comprehend that he proposed, right, Cassidy?" she prods, locking eyes with me as though testing how far she can push me.

I lower my head so the assistant can remove my hair cape. My eyes catch on the flash of her ankle bracelet glinting under the salon light…two letters: K and B. The sight of those dangling initials triggers a strange tightness deep within me. "Congratulations," I force myself to say, determined not to fixate on "K + B" or her deliberate use of the word "comprehend."

Her cold, narrowed gaze meets mine before she responds. "Thank you, Cassidy. I have to meet with the shop owner, so have a good day," she turns away, lifting her hand just enough to flaunt a large pear-cut diamond ring that gleams under the overhead lamps.

My heart slows at the thought: *he must've bought her that ring.* Why, though? I know why logically, but it doesn't make sense in my chest. She's halfway out the door when she pauses, calls my name again. I'm so lost in thought, I almost miss it.

"Cassidy," she repeats, stepping closer, practically throwing out a hip in the process. She yanks her hair back, nearly breaking her neck in half like she's in some audition. *This is comical.* She leans in, voice dropping so only I can hear. "Make yourself scarce, bitch, and leave me and my man alone. You're irrelevant." She says it just loud enough for everyone to catch her nastiness.

The words seek in with agonizing slowness, heating my skin from the inside out. Did she call me a bitch? *Yeah, she did.*

It takes a second for it to register, but when it does, a calm, focused anger roots me to the spot. "Irrelevant?" I say loudly, same volume she used. "Are you sure *I'm* irrelevant?""

Her eyes widen, flicking with uncertainty. "Explain something for me, Sarah," I say, stepping forward. She inches back into her speechless pose. "I was at that hospital every night. Was that irrelevant? Those honey hazel eyes of his practically burned a hole through my track shorts a few days ago. Is that irrelevant?" She blinks in confusion. "And his jammed right finger that won't straighten. You do comprehend that question, right?" I don't give her time to respond. "For the record, it was all over me a week ago."

Her face morphs from pink to burgundy, possibly a shade not found on any color chart. "Maybe you should ask yourself who's really irrelevant?"

I didn't think it was possible to shut up that irritating voice of hers. But I do. "Do not ever call me a bitch again," I demand, drawing out the word "again" so everyone within earshot catches it. Even Candle peeks out from the washroom, eyes wide.

Without waiting for Sarah's stammered comeback, I walk off, the stunned faces of her friends trailing me. I hate that word, it's too casual for me. Maybe that wasn't the full truth, but she requires something to think about. Plus it felt good turning her purple with my words.

I head out, knowing the park is my next stop to calm my mind. I wish Brooklyn's chatter could be my distraction, but it's too late for tennis.

An Uber drops me near the main entrance. No people here, thanks to the cooler temps, just me, a couple of lovebirds and some honking geese that have left a trail of green cotton poop everywhere. I won't stay long, not with the sun going down and a kidnapper on the loose.

I trudge up to the dead, grassy incline to the closest bench under three bare crape myrtles, branches stripped of leaves like skeletal arms. The ground is dusted with brittle leaves and bird droppings. The sight is downright haunted. But I sit on the rusted wooden bench, ignoring its flaws for my people watching. Some days, the geese scare me more than anything. They're fierce about blocking the path for anyone who dares approach before their young cross. At least they care about their babies, which is more than I can say for some.

The winter chill shifts into the edge of spring, pollen season lurking around the corner with vengeance, making everyone sick with allergies. I tilt my head back, letting my hair fall behind the bench. I didn't get much sleep last night, haven't had more than a handful of hours since I heard about the wedding. My eyes close, and the late-day sun warms my forehead. But my mind drifts to Kylo. Always does.

He said this was different at my track meet. I believed him, hoped it was real. But here he is, set to marry Sarah? That doesn't make sense. He never actually said he *wouldn't* marry her, though. But everything Sarah does screams *look at me, I'm a bride-to-be.* And I'm stuck wanting to rewind those hospital nights, when at least I got to see him.

What would Mom do right now? She always had an answer. Whether I liked it or not, she'd be right.

As always, there's only one final stop in my thoughts: him. He's the one who invades my dreams nightly, taking me to far-off exotic places. *Why Sarah, though?* All that fakeness. She's everything I'm not.

How can I want him this badly, this fast? It's a heat that won't quit. The way his hands snaked around my hips, sneaking beneath my track jacket in search of bare skin, told me everything he wanted. Especially when his lips claimed mine so deeply, not caring who was watching. I'm sure he's usually private, but right then, he didn't care. It took all my strength to pull away and slip out of there.

"Kylo, Kylo!"

A voice echoes in my head. Am I dreaming someone's shouting his name?

My eyes yank open to complete darkness. My fingers dig into the bench beneath me, trying to figure out where I am. I'm lying down on a rough, wooden bench, the sky beyond black. "Did I fall asleep?" The question is barely a whisper. I haul myself upright, stiff and disoriented. My hands vanish in the darkness and I cover my mouth, noticing the faint glimmer of moonlight cutting through the swaying branches overhead. The scene feels like a horror movie and I'm the last character left.

I force a deep breath and remind myself that I'm in a park, probably alone. The fear creeping over my spine suggests otherwise. My instincts scream, eyes might be watching from the surrounding trees. I glance back quickly, the thought of someone lurking in the woods sending my heart into overdrive. I waste no time imagining the monster in my mind appearing from the corner as I bolt into a full sprint to the entrance, desperate to reach the safety of streetlights.

"Siri, get me an Uber," I pant, fumbling with my phone as I run.

What was I thinking, drifting off on a park bench this late?

My dad, Raith, Miss Rita, every single one of them would kill me if they found out. Not to mention, a kidnapper's been targeting women around here. Slowing my pace is not an option as I hear my tennis shoes on the sidewalk pavement and my heartbeat in sync. I reach the sidewalk near the traffic light, where my Uber left me earlier, in record speed, breaking all past track records.

Then…impact. My body slams into something solid. It feels like a brick wall landing me hard on my tailbone. Pain spears up my spine.

"Sorry. I didn't see you!" a man's voice rasps nearby. Still dizzy from the collision, I see his outstretched hand.

But I don't focus on the man obstructing my view of the traffic light. With a few cars passing, the darkness cloaks him… and anything else. I want to be anywhere but trapped here with a stranger. Groaning from the ache in my knee, I scramble to my feet and hurry off. Apologies don't rank high on my priority list right now. The sooner I get to my rideshare the better.

"You okay?" His voice, a bass note scraping the chilly air, follows me.

I hustle onto the corner, shoving away the stinging pain in my leg, checking my Apple Watch. One minute until my Uber arrives. I risk a glance over my shoulder to see him stepping closer. A few more feet and I'll be under the street lamp's glow. Then I can see his face…if I really want to.

I straighten. Let him see I'm not some easy target. Even in the dim haze, his black hoodie is up, black pants, black shoes, no socks with pale ankles peeking out. He's tall and slim. Headlights from an approaching SUV illuminate the pole in front of me, slanting shadows across his face. I catch only the shape of his jaw, half hidden by the hoodie.

"Stunning," he murmurs, voice full of something that twists my guts.

Nope, not the time to be polite. I pivot, darting past the traffic light into the intersection. The SUV driver spots me, slows, eyes darting from me to the hooded figure. It's my rideshare, black SUV, hazard lights blinking.

"You call for the Uber?" he asks, rolling down his window.

"Yes," I manage, voice steady but determined.

The hoodie-lurker stands back, half-lost in the shadows. The driver studies me, then shoots him a wary glance. He doesn't need more explanation. He unlocks the door.

I climb in and slam it shut, twist around, heart rattling in my chest.

The Uber driver locks all the doors, and I watch the stranger standing outside, his hand resting on the pole, head bowed, exhaling vapor. As we pass, the streetlight sheds no light on the motionless stranger. What in the hell is wrong with him? I snap my seatbelt into place, seeking more protection… not from a car accident, but from the guy outside the truck. I take one last glance over my hunched shoulders and praying hands peeking behind the headrest to see through the back tinted SUV window. He's standing in the center of the street, arms straight at his side without his hoodie. I feel as though he's aware that he's hidden. At least that's what the CSI, SWAT shows that Miss Rita watches at home are telling me. I swear, I will never go to the park alone again. What was I thinking, anyway? Why did I even do that?

"Miss, you good?" The Uber driver's voice breaks through my dark thoughts flooding my brain. His eyes brimming with concern, meet mine in the rearview mirror.

"Yes," I reply, forcing a weak smile. "Just get me to my dorm, please."

We turn right, heading toward campus, streetlights whipping by in a blur. I risk one last glance over my shoulder, catching a glimpse of him standing there in the middle of the street, arms rigidly at his sides, an ominous silhouette against the night. A chill trembles my core, and I can't shake the feeling that he's after me.

By the time the Uber drops me at the circular driveway, all parking spots are taken. I jump out before the car fully stops, sprinting inside the building like I'm on the track again, flinging myself into the elevator and punching my floor number. *Never again.*

The moment I reach my room, I lock the door, kick off my shoes, slide into bed, and hide under the comforter as if the smoking hoodie followed me. I wish Raith was here, but she's never around.

My head is pounding, trying and failing to piece together what happened. One second he wasn't there, and the next he appeared from the darkness. My paranoia skyrockets, convinced he's lurking somewhere outside.

I need a distraction. Where's the remote? Easing the comforter from my face, I shuffle across the room, checking the closet and behind the shower curtain in the bathroom just in case. My breathing grows ragged, but no one is there. I'm being ridiculous.

I climb back under the blankets, only for the TV to show "Breaking News" in glaring red letters. It's always "Breaking News." Exhausted, I pull my bulletproof, throat protecting, kidnapping retardant comforter over my face hoping Raith shows up soon. Maybe she's with that girl from the party. She's tight-lipped about it, which means she must really like her. I just hope whoever this girl is doesn't break my girl's heart.

I grab my phone buried somewhere in the sheets and text her.

Where are you?

I set my phone aside, watching the screen dim and eventually go dark. My imagination runs off again, maybe Raith's missing or she's been kidnapped. *Calm down, Cassidy. She's probably just out.*

Maybe a shower will clear my head.

Once I'm done, I dare to peek through the curtains again. No person in a gray jumpsuit or a smoke breathing black hoodie stands out there ready to chop me up. Just Raith's silly smiley faces drawn in the condensation on the glass staring at me.

I slip into bed again, spraying Dr. Teal's lavender mist cocooning myself in my covers. Maybe I'll dream of Kylo tonight, the only fantasies that manage to chase my nightmares for a few blissful minutes. Actually, it's not calm or bliss. It's more of a thigh clenching, teeth grinding, lip biting release that hangs in my mind, haunting me every hour of the night and fueling my insomnia. So, where will you meet me this evening, Kylo? Will we go to our second home in Cabo San Lucas or maybe back to his truck.

Why am I thinking of another woman's man? *Sad.* I have got to get a life and fast.

Just as I'm drifting off, my dorm door slams open, startling me so hard I nearly slide off the bed.

"Give me the remote. Hurry!" Raith shouts, voice high with panic. She snatches it flicking past channels. She lands on the local news, taking a seat at the end of my bed.

"Raith?" I rub my eyes. "What's going on?"

She's breathing like she sprinted a marathon. "I texted you back. You didn't respond. You asleep?" Glancing at my phone fighting for its life between my mattress and the wall, I see she texted at 11:36, and yeah, I was actually asleep.

*Her message said **watch the news.**

"What am I supposed to be seeing?" I ask again.

She mutes the infomercial. "He killed another girl, Cassidy," her words tremble. "They found her maybe an hour ago." She looks ready to vomit or cry, maybe both.

My entire body tenses. "What do you mean, Raith? Who was

she? Where?" I inch closer, the comforter sliding to the floor. If I have to shake it out of her as I did the night of Kylo's car accident, I will.

Her gaze shifts to the half open curtain, as though expecting a killer to climb through. "Somewhere near the park you go to… the one where you meet Brooklyn. He…" she presses a shaking hand over her mouth. "He did more than kill her, Cass. They said it was," she can't finish.

A chill crawls up my spine. "Raith, just tell me."

She clutches the pillow beside her, knuckles pointed. "He cut her…like, on her lower abdomen and…pulled out," she stops abruptly, tears gathering at the corners of her eyes. "Cassidy. I'm so scared."

I stare at the TV, anchor mouthing words we can't hear since Raith muted it. But I don't need to hear it. My blood runs cold. That's the same park I've used for a quite escape, the place Brooklyn calls Captain K's spot and the one I just left.

"It happened there?" I whisper horrified.

CHAPTER 34

WORLDWIDE

Kylo

Ever since Aunt D told me Cassidy was the one at the hospital, everything started falling into place. She's the same girl in my dreams, the one with the faint red lipstick urging me to come back. Back then I never saw her face, just that whisper pulling me from the blackness.

But after seeing her at that track meet, the face is there, along with my questionable bed sheets most mornings. No denying the attraction is there. I felt it the second I spotted her in that tunnel. One glimpse of those toned legs rounding that white curve was it for me. Her curls escaping her ponytail, her face angled low made me want to reach out to tilt her pointed chin.

I'd never had the urge to just slip a hand under someone's chin, tilt her head up, and look them in the eyes. But I almost did. When she finally lifted her gaze, everything faded, like a movie scene on mute, and all I saw was her.

Her expression was a mix of doubt and confusion. I saw her hands trembling on her track bag. And that gap between those lean thighs…man. I was straight disrespectful in my thoughts, but I couldn't help it. Sweat broke out on my skin just staring, but my mind was stuck in that soft space and the way her breath came slow and measured. The urge to tear those shorts off, pull those legs around my shoulders and taste every drop from her was mad crazy.

That's new territory for me. I don't go down on women. Not with Sarah, and the one time in high school barely counts. But I have a strong urge to get between those thighs with Cassidy and spend some time. If I ever knew her that way before, I sure don't remember. But I want to know.

I need water. Hell, I need a drink, a smoke, anything to settle the noise in my head. This is supposed to be my first game, but my mind's not on the field. In the past, it was me and the black and white ball. No distractions, no doubts. Now, I'm wrestling a weaker body, slower reflexes, and delayed processing. Yes, my doctors say a delay is normal, that it'll ease up, but I'm feeling the pressure. The coaches and trainers seem upbeat, but I know they see my struggles. They talk a good game, but their sidelong glances confirm what I already suspect: I'm not the same.

Despite weeks of brutal PT, heavier weights and daily training, they activated me last week. Today, I'm officially set to play. A part of me wishes for a delay because I'm not sure I'm ready. But I also know the owners won't wait around on their highest paid athlete. I can't pretend I'm not *scared*.

Sitting on this stiff hotel ottoman, I rub my ankle, the main left-over pain from the crash, while staring out at the city. A drizzle came through earlier but never lasted, leaving only a few stray drops on the window. I half hoped it'd keep raining all day. Instead, the sun's coming out, like the weather mocking me.

My uncle's words ring in my ears. He told me I needed to figure out this new me and get quiet enough to manage it. But it's hard to focus with all this wedding bullshit around me. At least twenty people have congratulated me on "my wedding" date. Who the hell sets a date without the groom? My PR Agent claims we should stall one more week before we blow this shit on Sarah's fake engagement. I ain't stalling forever, and I sure won't drag Cassidy into this shit. Not yet.

She will be mine, and nothing will fuck that up. But one thing I know, Pittman keeps his life private, and that's how I want it for her.

I drop my phone onto the table, restless from Aunt D's latest text about Sarah. That girls doing the exact opposite of keeping things private. I've ignored every one of her five hundred calls. Last night, her father tried cornering me about prenuptial agreements. Sarah's an only child set to inherit millions. Good ole Pops wants to make sure his money stays locked in the family for generations. Sarah mentioned that he even has private schools picked out for the grandkids. He's got their whole future preplanned.

That's not for me. I'm not here to fit in his world. I'm here to build my own. No one is dictating how I care for my family. Plus, having children with Sarah was never going to happen. She's too self-absorbed. She's not nurturing. I need someone who'll be all in for raising kids alongside me. Sure we'd have plenty of help because I'm the type to get jealous. Even with kids, I'd still need my woman every night, in whatever way I want her. I know that about myself. I find myself wondering if Cassidy thinks about having kids. *Where the hell did that come from?*

My phone vibrates again. Miss Blade. I'll call her back later. But her calling is another reminder of what I really want in a partner. She stopped her world for Tron and I and made us decent. I don't think she's ever touched a doorknob, carried a grocery bag or pulled out a chair when we were near. Those things came routine and without complaint because we understood her sacrifice. Growing up, we never saw her date or even take a night off to herself. She always told us to listen to, compliment and protect your own family.

After Tron died she shouldered all that grief alone. It was her in the stands, sitting away from everyone else in her gray work uniform, black steel toe boots, the faint scent of metal clinging to her from the plant. She worked on a production line, assembling car transmissions and always carried the scent of metal. It wasn't bad, but it had a noticeable, industrial aroma.

She never complained about the extra hours at work or the bills going unpaid. Nor did she ever say one negative word about our sperm donor, even though he never spent a day with us.

I rub some Icy Hot into my ankle, remembering Aunt D's story of how she helped handle my medical decisions when I was in that coma. Thinking about her dealing with all that uncertainty by herself kills me. Lately, I've been around more often and she's asking questions by way of Aunt D who tells me everything.

Aunt D told me she worries I'm getting depressed, because I'm holed up at the house most days only leaving for practice or PT. She's wrong. I'm not depressed. So much shit is happening between my body, my memory, Sarah's marriage stunt, Cassidy, I'm bouncing from one thought to the next, but it's Cassidy and soccer dominating my mind.

Hefting my workout bag over my shoulder, I slide on my Bose headphones for some hype music and leave the hotel room.

I follow the long corridor toward the bus, spotting Christian up ahead. Part of me wants to slow down and avoid him. Instead, I pull off my headphones and catch up.

He turns around, that unibrow already forming the question. "Yo, you good?" he asks. We haven't talked much in the last few days, so I know he's got questions, no doubt.

I shrug. "Yeah dog, just burning off nervous energy. Ready to get my shots back." I *hope that happens* because truth is, my nerves are gripping me harder than any defender.

For the past few days, I've done my best to avoid the noise of social media and TV. Everyone seems to have an opinion on how I'll perform in the first game. I don't need there noise. All I need is my circle and my focus. Tonight, we're up against Toronto FC. It should be a solid match, but doubts still creep in.

Rubbing my temples, I try to clear my head, block out my

stiff body, the game pressure, Miss Blade's worries, and Cassidy. No point removing Sarah; she was never there to begin with. I laugh to myself, wondering why she's still after me. She's around for reasons that make no sense, especially after the accident.

I'm so lost in thought that I don't notice I've stopped walking until I see Christian up ahead, arms spread in a silent question. "You coming?"

"Yeah, man, I'm coming," I say.

Nothing compares to the adrenaline walking through a stadium tunnel, the fans on their feet, the energy in the air, my teammates bouncing off each other with pre-game hype. That fire puts you on top of the world where nobody can touch you. The beat of the cleats hitting the concrete, trash talking and the vibes from everyone is a hype that's hard to describe.

And then I hear it. "Kyloooo!" My name echoes across the stadium, easily fifty thousand strong howling "o" in unison. It hits different now than it did before the wreck. Some of my teammates check me, with that juice ready for battle. But the stares are telling me something else. They're waiting on something. *Is it me?*

I try to lock in, recalling how it felt before. A push from them won't help. Usually my bite for the game is solid, but the aftermath of the accident lingers, making me doubt. I slow as we near the mouth of the tunnel, images of the coma, rehab and what could have been, losing everything, hitting me at once. The team jogs out, but I hang back, feet refusing to budge.

Christian and a few others linger near me. The rest are already charging on the field. "Kylo, you good?" Christian asks, worried. "Sixty thousand deep calling your name, bro'. They want you."

I stretch my neck side to side, trying not to lose my shit. "I'm fine," I manage to grunt.

"Yeah, I know you're good. You've always been good. Now you're back. Let's fucking show'em," he says, hand on my shoulder and waiting, the roles reversed from our old days.

I appreciate his hype, but I hope his ass is right. "Shit just hitting me at once," I admit.

"As it should," he says. "Let's show 'em who's still made of that nasty dog shit and get this W." He takes off tugging me along. Outside, he waves to the crowd, pointing toward me as we enter the stadium. This dude has had my back since day one and still does.

The red and yellow shirts in our almost sold-out stadium make me grind my teeth. The hollow of everyone screaming my name got me so off that planting one cleat in front of the next takes effort. The thought that they're cheering for me hits different. Some of these people were on their knees praying. They've never met the real me, only the soccer player they follow. People don't truly know who you are but still treat you as if you're a hero. I'm no hero.

I look past the thousands in the stands to see my team and the opposing team standing in the center circle, pointing me toward the center mark. This is ultimate respect from both clubs, and the last thing I want is attention. Holding the bridge of my nose is the only thing keeping me together. I jog to the center of the field and stare at thousands of fans waving flags. The red and yellow dominate today, but the Toronto fans are equally hyped, with the noise level off the charts. This right here is enough to break anyone. Uncle Joe was right. I'm walking, talking and back on this field, in front of thousands when reports said it might not happen. This is my shot, that second chance Uncle Joe was talking about last week.

I search the area where Miss Blade and Aunt D are seated. I can always count on those two, they cheer louder than anyone else. Even though she's in the stands, Aunt D's voice carries over thousands as she blows kisses my way. She loves my games. I see Miss Blade pointing at me on the screen and then to the sky. This woman always knows what to do. That's her way of telling me that she and my brother are right here with me. Right here.

Okay, I got this. It's just winning the car for the summer from Tron. "Let's go!"

I head through the tunnel, avoiding all the hell, and into the locker room. I got to get the fuck out of here. They're going to crucify the hell out of my ass. That was the worst game of my career, no, my life. I can hear reporters already clogging up the far end of the tunnel, with their phones, cameras and questions.

"Kylo! What happened out there?"

"Are you going to be back for the next game?"

"You seemed off your stride... still recovering from your accident."

"Kylo... over here."

The relentless heat of their damn questions makes my head hurt. Too much is coming at me too fast and holding on isn't happening. I don't even have words to explain what the hell happened on the field.

I see my agent, Bruce, shouldering his way through my teammates and the reporters. He's already taking in the situation. "Yo man, I got a back exit to avoid all the press," he says. "Your mom and Aunt Diane were waiting for you by the front, but they swarmed them. The PR team will escort them another way. They'll meet you at the house later. Get changed, I'm getting you out."

He knows not to let me handle a row of reporters right now. "Thanks man," is all I manage to say. Nothing's left. I couldn't find my zone on that field. My circle, my territory where it's me and the ball was nowhere. Those are my spots, my territory. I own them. Or *at least I did*. Today, I couldn't find shit. I couldn't dribble the ball well enough to qualify for my high school soccer team. What in the hell is going on? Before coach could bench me, I shot him the look that nothing was left. The L was hard enough, but the looks from my teammates weighing on my shoulders was too much. Being on the sidelines not battling to get that W is new for me.

I take a quick shower, throwing on fresh clothes, ignoring how the scalding water and cheap shampoo can't scrub away this heavy sense of failure. No interviews, not today. Fuck that. I can't pretend to be okay when I'm not. No talking today.

"Kylo." Damn, that voice came quick. I turn to see my coach with that stiff face, shedding no light. Even the team hates being around bad omens because they all dipped. A stiff piece of paper slaps lightly into his palm again and again, telegraphing more bad news before he speaks.

I grit my teeth, forcing calm. "Talk, Coach."

He sighs and hands me the paper. "We're placing you on injured reserve for a few weeks," he says, pausing, like I have something to say. I don't, so I grab my bag and walk out. "Kylo, you'll be ready once we return," he calls after me.

I don't want self-pity nor do I care for fucking false hope. One damn game and that's what he got for me. Fuck him. I don't have any words for his ass. It was one bad game and they're benching me. I've been the face of this franchise, bringing crowds bigger than they've ever had.

The locker door slams behind me. Immediately I find myself nose-to-nose with Bruce again. "I've got you an exit, no media. We out," he says. "We'll do the spin tomorrow. Let's just get out clean."

He's earning every dime I pay him. A swirl of adrenaline, shame and relief slips through me, adrenaline because I hate running from my problems, shame from tonight's disaster and relief because I just want to disappear for a minute to catch my breath.

Bruce turns to Christian, saying, "I have a driver pulling up on the side for Kylo. Can you take his truck home, and maybe we can fool the press this evening?"

Bruce is firing off directions with unmatched precision. But hell, he's paid generously to handle shit like this.

I pull my hoodie over my head to hide the eyes and follow

Bruce along the long narrow gray corridor, ignoring the shouts behind me. Tonight I need silence, not a microphone of my name being called, gossiped, tweeted, emailed, texted, TikTok to the grave. I never cared before, but this feels different up against doubts.

I follow Bruce down the dimly lit janitor tunnel that opens onto a back exit. A black SUV idles there, headlights flashing. This had to be arranged in advance, like a presidential-level escape. I hand Bruce my keys so Christian can drive my truck home, then slip into the SUV, keeping my hoodie pulled as my thoughts race.

Bruce has known me for years. He understands when space is my next, but this feels more preplanned than usual. Did he have doubts?

We pull away, heading opposite the traffic. Maybe they alerted everyone to clear game day congestion just for me. My phone buzzes with a text from Bruce.

> **Tell the driver where you want to go. I'll handle the logistics.**

There's no need to be around anyone right now. I need a low-key spot to decompress. I text Bruce to find me something private.

Thirty minutes later, we're in Raleigh, pulling into a restaurant adjoining a hotel. The driver hands me a key with 2213 etched on it. Damn, this was preplanned.

He parks in the loading zone, hazards on, gesturing me to follow him. We stroll through the restaurant kitchen, pans clanging, steam rising, a mix of seafood aromas filling the air, past cooks and waiters who don't even look up. Not a single waiter, chef or cleaner spares me a glance. It's almost too smooth, like they were coached. Works for me. Being unnoticed is what I want.

We step into a private elevator shaft at the back. Everything about it screams luxury, polished steel, plush carpeting. My gut tells me this won't be cheap. We jet up to the twenty-second floor.

The elevator doors open straight into a penthouse. *Damn,* The foyer alone expands my basement. Floor to ceiling windows reveal a panoramic skyline view. Definitely a step above even the nicer places I've stayed.

"Sir?" I turn to see the driver/security/food guy and I guess packer with a small travel bag. *Is that for me?*

He's all business with his solemn glare and unblinking stare. "Bruce sent your favorites to the restaurant. Food will be here in thirty. They'll leave it at the foyer, no disturbance. The bar's stocked with top shelf liquor, mixers in the fridge, water, electrolytes. Also," he hands me a black business card, "if you're looking for company tonight, call. The bag has clothes and all your personal items."

No judgment. He's done this before. Bruce reps some of the best in the league. He's always ready for anything. I might actually take him up on the offer of company tonight. Maybe two women this evening to blow off some steam and everything else.

He taps the business card on the table. "Call if you need anything." Then he disappears back into the elevator, leaving me in silence.

The penthouse exudes a sleek, modern vibe. Exactly what I like, clean lines, high-end finishes and white. *My color.* Probably around two thousand square feet. A smaller living room flows into a master suite positioned at the center of an expansive living space, more windows, and more insane views. I grab the remote off a marble side table and test the mechanized drapes, watching them glide shut.

Next, I check the black leather overnight bag. It's filled with what I would've packed myself, not generic stuff, but my brand of deodorant, my face wash, all of it. I change into a t-shirt and night pants, collapsing onto the king-size bed. It's only six p.m. Too early for sleep.

My phone lights up, a barrage of texts from Miss Blade, Christian, Aunt D, my cousins, Coach Smith, PR staff, Sarah, Sarah's dad, handful of random women and Uncle Joe.

Uncle Joe? Who in the hell helped Uncle Joe text me? Probably got Aunt D or one of the girls to help him. Despite my pissed off mood, the thought of Unc messing with a smartphone brings a grin. It took me two days to show him how to work his Bluetooth. *Man, that's some funny shit.*

I text Miss Blade, so she won't worry, letting her know I'm alright because she's already called me four times. One thing I refuse to do is leave her in the dark. Last week, we talked about Sarah… Aunt D told me how concerned she was…so Miss Blade knows why I'm not rushing to update everyone on this bullshit wedding. Stressing over Sarah's ass is the last thing Miss Blade needs. I watch and wait for the three dots on my screen to stop blinking, knowing *she's trying to figure out what to say without saying too much.* I should go home, but don't have the energy to handle all the questions. I need some downtime to replay everything, over and over, until I understand what happened and what didn't.

I text everyone that I'm good…except Sarah…then press the side button on my phone and swipe right, shutting off all calls. I'm done talking to the world tonight. Miss Blade said she's praying for me and will wait to hear from me whenever I'm ready.

Damn, even my bed is right with four flat pillows. I pile all four on top of each other to create a Sleep Number vibe and lean back, massaging my neck to calm the tension.

I wasn't ready today. I, along with the sports commentators, had doubts for weeks about my first game back, and I should've listened. My coordination felt so off that one of the reporters commented on it as I walked through the tunnel. If he noticed, everyone must've too. It's like my brain and body are out of sync, both moving in slow motion, refusing to follow simple damn commands. It's fucking with my head, making me doubt everything.

Did the team feel sorry for me, letting me come back just to fail publicly. The trainers had to see I wasn't right. Even in practice, it felt like everyone was holding back around me, being cautious, giving me space I don't need. I could feel how they challenged me, like they never wanted to go full force. I pushed it aside but it was real.

Flipping the black card in my hand, I remember the nights I'd use it for a quick hookup, but not tonight. I'm in no mood. Only one person is on my mind, Cassey. Does she watch soccer? Did she see my shitty performance? Would she even care?

There's a huge flatscreen flush-mounted on the wall, but I can't bring myself to turn it on. I already know the opinions, the doubts, the garbage. No point feeding that fire. I've always believed in my own ability, even when everyone else doubted if a kid from the hood could play on this level. At the end of the day, it's me putting in the work, not the one screaming at the screen, unable to run a lap. But I'm not sure if I can pull it off again. Can I recover from a near fatal accident and return to top form?

That TV is too big to deal with all the opinions, doubters and naysayers, so I open my laptop on the nightstand instead. This place has a remote control for the lights, music and alarm…all prime, top notch. I'll ask Bruce about the price points, maybe it's for sale. I never wanted a place of my own, but now I'm thinking differently. Damn. I don't even know if that girl wants me like that, but here I am, thinking about real estate. *What the hell?*

I type two letters in Google and see "Kylo Blade" trending again. *Come at me.*

"Bad day for Kylo Blade."

"Blade left, team traveling without him."

"Blade back, what come back?"

"Is this the end of Blade's career?"

"Kylo's return was weak."

I slam the laptop before I read more. I'm not sure if I cracked the screen or not, and I don't fucking care. I'm getting there quick and counting to calm isn't helping. I grip the comforter, trying to stay grounded, fighting the urge to break everything in here. My chest is heaving, my pulse raging.

This is the version of me that my family hates. The one I can't control.

Fuck soccer.

CHAPTER 35

WHERE IT STARTED

Cassidy

"**W**HERE ARE YOU GOING?" RAITH DEMANDS, BLOCKING our dorm door so I can't leave.

My first thought is why she is holding me hostage, but I bite back any sarcastic comment. She's been on this kidnapping story for days, warning me not to go anywhere alone. It's exhausting, and I don't feel like another lecture. I didn't even tell her I was at the park. Didn't tell anyone, not even Dad. Part of me wants to keep it from him, already knowing what will happen.

"I'm going for a run, What's up?" The forced casualness of my "what's up" is not erasing the worried frown lines around her lips.

Raith's eyes narrow. "Oh, hell no. You're not leaving without a GPS tracker on you. And where's your phone?"

I roll my eyes. "You realize I usually run by myself, right?"

Her arms sweep out as though addressing a huge audience. "And you realize somebody was murdered at that park, right? You're not bulletproof, Cassidy."

I do realize that. I also know I've taken more risks lately than I ever did in high school. I would have never taken a bus in the middle of the night to a hospital or fallen asleep at a park. I used to be too cautious, planning for every outcome. Somewhere, maybe with Mom's death or my new college freedom, that careful version of me left.

"Does campus security even carry weapons? All they ever do is eat and sleep. If you have to go to the track, then we go together."

"What?" I can't help but laugh. "You can't even jog to the cafeteria for food without complaining."

But she's putting on her tennis shoes, and I regret her intrusion. With security stepped up on campus and her repeated warnings, maybe I should be grateful she's coming but right now I want to lose myself in the steady rhythm of my stride.

"Come on," I say, "but keep up. I'm not slowing or waiting on you."

"Track Star, don't wait. I got this," she brags, knowing she wouldn't have this if Jason from Friday the thirteenth was chasing her.

After a good half-hour on the track, I feel that familiar pace creeping in where my thoughts drift away, free of racing heartbeats and always stressing. If only this calm could stay, but it never does. I slow for Raith on my fifth lap. Her t-shirt is soaked through enough to win a frat party wet t-shirt contest and her labored breathing reminds me of an overexcited dog, tongue hanging out.

"You good?" I ask, trying to keep a straight face.

She clutches her chest, gasping between breaths. "I'm over here fighting for my life! Fighting to live, Cassidy! But you're still running. What in the hell is wrong with you?"

Sweat pours from her temples like a faucet. I place my hands on my hips, desperately trying to hold back laughter. "Did you not get that runner's high?"

"Hell no!" she straightens, eyes wide. "My body don't do runner's high. It might handle another kind of high." She holds two fingers to her lips, faking a blunt inhale. Then exhaling dramatically, she points to my gym pack. "You wouldn't happen to have an albuterol pump in there, would you? I can't get enough air in my lungs."

I ignore her, handing her a bottle of cold water. She sucks the water and air, leaving only the ice cube. Glad it was water; otherwise she'd be drunk.

I glance at my phone when it starts buzzing nonstop. Nothing good ever comes from this many notifications. My hands tremble so badly I can barely type my password. Scrolling through the messages, I see at least fifteen texts plus some missed calls.

"What is it, Cassidy?" Raith asks. Even after almost dying from our run, she never misses a beat.

I curl my neck toward the phone, hunched over the screen. "Hold on," I whisper.

Raith leans, trying to peek. "What the hell's going on?" she mutters, grabbing her phone. "What the fuck?" Her reaction tells me she's seeing the same madness. "That bitch. That fucking bitch!" she fumes, her adrenaline surging with me wondering where this newfound energy came from.

I read the messages again, struggling to believe them. Why would anyone do this, and how did it escalate so fast? My dad is going to be furious. As if on cue, the next caller ID is him. He knows. I ignore the call, letting it go to voicemail. My privacy, my family...

"Cassidy!" Raith's voice cuts in. I can't bring myself to respond as I kneel, my head spinning. Did Sarah Sims really go on social media, calling me Kylo's stalker? Claiming I'm the reason for every problem in his life? None of this should even matter to the public, so why do they care?

A beep signals a new post of video. I force my finger to hit play. It's a clip of me and Kylo kissing at A&M after my track meet, cut short so it doesn't show him pulling me closer. *Who filmed this and how did she get it?*

Another headline: *Sarah Sims set to file additional legal measures, alleging a restraining order is in place.* A restraining order? She's delusional.

Raith's eyes dart from her phone to me. "Cassidy. We have to move, now." She jerks her head up at the screech of tires outside. A black truck roars into the Harris Complex lot, going way faster than it should.

"No idea who that is but I've got a bad feeling they're here for you," she warns.

The paparazzi? *That can't be happening.* My mom spent years keeping them away from us. I can't deal with this. "Come on Cassidy!" Raith shouts. We sprint for the building where my world turned upside down the day a man named Kylo Blade walked into my ice bath and asked me to move closer.

I almost run to the building, hoping he'll magically appear inside, taking everything else away, including this mess. No idea why I'm still fooling myself. I still want him.

"Track Star, don't run," Raith hisses, grabbing my arm to slow down. "You'll draw attention."

She's right. The campus is busy, sprinting away would cause a bigger scene. We slip inside the sports complex, heart pounding. Some glance up as we pass, eyes lingering a second too long. My anxiety spikes. Maybe I'm imagining it, but it feels like a whisper follows. One girl looks up, then quickly back at her phone, like she's confirming if I'm *that* Cassidy. I've always hated this aspect of my life. Growing up with Dad's fame meant Mom constantly worked to shield me from it. She did her best. Now with my name trending, all that protection feels undone.

I pause near the doorway, the whisper hitting me like crashing waves, each syllable relentless demanding to be heard. I hate it. Now I get why Mom always steered clear of Dad's spotlight? She was forever with us, rarely by his side at those glitzy events. She stayed hidden shielding us from the life that came with being John Pittman's children. Only now do I realize how rarely they were photographed together and how she seemed okay letting him handle that world alone.

"Follow me." Raith grips my arm and tugs me down the hall, leading me straight to the room where it all began. *How am I back here, again?* The same stale, nasty stench assaults me, the one I tried to scrub away months ago. I stand there, biting my bottom lip, staring at the old tin tub that's caused me nothing but pain, loss, more pain, confusion, more pain, embarrassment and more pain.

With a hard kick, I send the ice bucket flying, water flooding the grimy black grout on the floor. Stray towels, cups, bands, equipment, balls, medical supplies, anything within reach sails across the room. I want it all to feel how I do. Every ounce of it.

Collapsing to the floor, I'm so drained I can hardly think. There's nothing left inside me. I'm tired of all of it. Wiping my tears, I feel the rough fabric of my sleeve against my damp cheeks, the weight of everything crushing down on my lungs. My breathing goes ragged. That's when Raith's voice cuts through the chaos bouncing in the background, her energy a contrast to the turmoil within me.

"Hit that shit! Rip it the fuck up! Break all of it!" she shouts, almost like she's preparing for jumping jacks without the jack. She's in a Mike Tyson fighting stance, bouncing around the dilapidated room on her toes as if she's in a boxing ring.

"Raith! What...what are you doing?" I ask, trying to anchor myself as a smile creeps in on my frown.

"Fighting with you while you hit that meltdown, roomie!" she hollers. The image of her punching the air, braids swinging, pushes me into helpless laughter. Raith's insanity paired with mine is exactly what this room was missing.

I yank my hair free, re-knotting it into a high ponytail, hoping it keeps the sweat soaked strands sticking off my forehead. "I'm gonna get that... bitch," I mutter, shocked that I said the word aloud. I hate that word.

Raith plops down beside me on the dusty linoleum. "What is it?" she asks gently.

I shrug and she nudges my shoulder. "I knew that 'take no bull' girl was still in there. You just needed a push. Go on tear this shitty place apart if you want to. Hell, I'll even help. C'mon!" She waves me to stand, still bouncing on her toes, envisioning some epic UFC showdown in her head.

Scanning the wrecked space, broken glass, tossed equipment, shredded towels I can't believe I did all that so fast. "I'll have to pay for this," I groan, resting my sweaty head against the wall.

"Look, we'll figure that out later. It's not like anyone can tell a difference with all the mold and fungus." Raith's tone is dismissive but oddly comforting.

My gaze wanders to the window, half sealed with battered plastic. I cringe at the thought of anyone witnessing my tantrum. That's the last thing I need, more drama.

My phone vibrates in my pocket, a grim reminder that Dad's likely already concocting a master plan to make this all go away. I haven't given him any trouble in three years and this first-year of college has been unrelenting.

I lean into Raith's shoulder, catching the mixture of sweat and shea butter on her skin. My fight with the room has me too drained to do much else. "What were you doing back there?" I ask, curious to understand who she was fighting with earlier.

She turns to me, eyes reflecting that something serious happened. "Friend, mental illness is real. You have to find a way to let out the anger and hurt before it destroys you. When I saw you tearing up everything," she picks up a piece of shredded magazine and fans us both, "I knew you were trying to get it out. And yeah, I got carried away fighting with you. I was excited for you. Some people give up and allow all of that to rob them of their happiness, their wellbeing and eventually their life. But you started fighting."

Tears spill down those high cheekbones, which people pay good money for, making mine come freely with no regret. "Cassidy,

I know this feeling," she whispers, dropping her face deep into her chest. *My Raith.* "When I saw you fighting, I started wrecking them with you… for your mom, for this pain you're trying to ignore, this extra petty shit and for you. I knew you were going to be okay. I just didn't know it until now," she says, waving her hand around the room, which now requires a major cleanup. "So, you know I can get a little carried away."

I'm speechless, absorbing everything she's sharing, even though she's downplaying it with a smile. I tug on one of her long extensions hanging between us. "Yes, you can get carried away, but that's what I love about you, Miss Marching Band Line Dancer." We both laugh lightly. "Didn't know you had that type of wisdom in you, girl."

She shrugs, letting my compliment slide. "Yeah. It doesn't come out often. You know you'll have to stay low until things blow over."

She doesn't want to dwell on our wisdom topic, so I drop it. "I might head home later today," I say, realizing those five missed calls from my dad means an evacuation of my dorm is already in motion.

Raith leans back and massages her neck, then looks at me. "You know there's always an extra sleeping bag at our place. My mom is headed to pick me up today. They're heading out of town, and the boy's want me home. So, I'm taking care of the crew. Spiderman would love to see you."

I manage a grin. "I'd rather hang with you and my little first grade boyfriend than go home and be on lockdown. Once I go in that door, I probably won't see daylight again."

"True," she says, laughing. "But we gotta get you out of here first," she retrieves her phone while I gather the debris. Hopefully, no cameras caught my meltdown. I really don't need vandalism charges. "I'll call B and tell him to meet us out back."

A few minutes later, I yank my hoodie over my head and cinch the drawstrings tight as B pulls around to the side door.

Russell Street is crowded with students, or maybe I'm imagining everyone's watching. Either way I need to leave.

We hop into B's car, and he drives us back to the dorm into our entrance, and one thing takes over the magnolia's lining. There's three black SUV's parked out front. No question whose they are, either the president of the United States is here with his detail or my dad's security arrived earlier. Probably the latter.

"Damn," Raith murmurs leaning toward the window. "They got here fast. You good?"

I wrap my arms around her, holding on perhaps for the last time in a while. "I'm okay, I guess," I say. She returns a quick squeeze before letting go.

"You sure?" she presses.

"I'll survive," I lie, swallowing the lump in my throat. Between my dorm drama, all this pressure and no clue how to handle it, escaping might be best, but I hate leaving Raith, B and Louy behind. "Thanks, B," I say, shooting him a grateful look as I slide out.

He smiles. "Anytime. Text me once you're back on campus."

"Sure."

With my backpack slung tight around my shoulders, I cross the paved walkway to my dad's black-tinted SUV, gripping the silver door handle. I really don't want to open this car door. But before he can reach for it himself, I pull the handle, sliding into the captain chair separating us. He's already on one phone barking orders about "killing the goddamn story immediately" while gripping another phone in his other hand, ready to throw it out the windshield.

I rest a hand gently on his shoulder, shaking my head for him to hold back. Sure, Sarah's a pain, but destroying her future? That feels like too much, even if I wanted her out of the picture fifteen minutes ago. He ignores me, signals the driver to start moving, then glances in the rearview.

"Wait, my stuff is still upstairs!"

"I'll have someone pack your belongings," he says firmly,

depositing both phones into the console's cup holder. "We're going home. How are you?"

He sounds scary calm. My father can switch from volcanic rage to cool control in seconds. "I'm okay," I lie. Those words have become an automatic answer every time something goes wrong.

He studies my hand in his, all while mentally orchestrating what might be World War IV against Sarah. "Have you spoken with Kylo since everything went live?"

I wasn't expecting that question but I should have. "No," I admit. "Haven't talked to him in a while." I'm not even sure what else to say.

His gaze shifts to the passing cars on the highway as he absently rubs his chin. "He'd better handle this situation, or I will." That level measure usually means he's already drafting battle plans in his head. His demeanor feels almost unnatural, but that's how he is. The more serious things get, the calmer he becomes. *His reaction should be studied by psychologists.*

"Dad," I murmur. "It'll blow over soon."

He spins on me so fast my stomach clenches. "Maybe, but not if it's left to fester. He played his match a few days ago. Did you see it?"

I didn't realize he was cleared to play. "No. Didn't know he was back on the field."

My father's jaw tightens. "It was bad. People are saying he'll be cut or might just quit on his own."

Quitting? That doesn't sound like him. Then again, what do I even know these days? "Didn't hear that," I say, trying to keep any emotion out of my voice.

"Reagan."

Startled, I lift my eyes. "Sorry, Dad. It's hard to believe he played if he's still recovering."

He exhales and taps his phone like it's a stress ball. "We'll get you home. There's extra security at the house. Your sisters are off traveling, and I'm about to cancel my trip to stay with you."

"Dad… no. You don't need to do that. I'm used to the media crap…"

He slams the console with his palm, rattling both phones. I jump at the clang. "Not like this, baby girl!" he yells. "Your mother tried her hardest to keep you three out of the spotlight and for good reason. People twist stories until you're unrecognizable. Don't underestimate that."

I watch him sink back into the unnerving calm and decide it's best not to argue. "I know," I whisper. "Really, I'll just hang with Miss Rita. You don't have to cancel your trip."

He opens his mouth, exhales and picks up the phone. "I want you home for a few days until this settles. The university is cooperating. No classes in person, my people will send you assignments. If anything must be proctored, it'll be under my conditions."

His efficiency, while impressive, is suffocating. My mom always warned me to not stand in his way when he's decided on our safety. We pass through the gates and see an unmarked car parked outside. Probably the press. A short conversation with security later, then they guide the truck toward the house. I cannot imagine what awaits us at the house.

Dad looks so imposing, even taller and bigger than the night of the gala from the truck. Even though it's too much, I love this man. Maybe, I should tell him what happened at the park incident, it's been nagging me.

At last, we park and I spot Miss Rita standing by the door, arms folded. Before I can get out, she's opening my door, pulling me into a hug, her sweet vanilla scent hitting me. "Come here, my baby girl," she says, wrapping her arms around me once again. Even though the media does not faze me, I don't want to be the target of everyone's scrutiny.

"Baby girl you okay?" her eyes widen, silently hoping I'll say "yes." That anxious motherly look has never changed in all these years.

"I'll be fine," I say, letting her warmth steady my nerves.

She studies my face another moment, then nods. "Good, be-cause you know how I get. Let's get you settled, and I'll cook some-thing to feed your soul. I have a new pancake recipe, plus we can talk. Yes?"

"Pancakes?" I ask, a hint of a smile breaking through.

"Yes. Nothing a good pancake can't fix," she says, pressing a light kiss on my cheek.

CHAPTER 36

WHAT THE F?

Kylo

THREE DAYS HAVE PASSED. NO CALLS, SOCIAL MEDIA, NO texts, nothing. I'm starting to smell my own funk, which means hiding away in silence forever is not an option. I glance around the bedroom, noticing how clean it is. Have I been *sleeping that hard that I miss the cleaning staff?*

I sit on the side of the bed to stretch my sore ankle, summoning enough energy to shower.

The bathroom lights blind me, but the rainfall shower makes up for it. I take my time, appreciating the warm water as I delay checking back into the chaos and noise of hell.

Eventually I emerge and search for my phone charger. The thing's been off for days. I haven't spoken to anyone since the game, and I know everyone's waiting.

I pull on a pair of sweats and order room service. Enough is enough. I better face this shit. My phone vibrates on the nightstand, threatening to vibrate itself onto the floor.

Damn, who the hell texted me this much? I swipe through the messages, trying to read them all. "Wait, What the…"

Every text is an article, one after the other, not only about me, but Cassidy. I rub my temples, a headache forming, realizing being away this long was a mistake. Damn.

"Siri, call Christian!" I bark at the phone, hoping Siri doesn't fuck up because her ass can't seem to understand shit. Damn, what is the hour, day and date? Christian could be halfway across the world in another country.

"Bro, you good?" he answers on the first ring, like he's been standing by for days.

"I'm straight," I begin, but he cuts me off, not letting me finish. I hate being cut off.

"You sure? You ghosted us for three days and nothing. You can't go off the grid for that long. Everyone's worried, team, family and coaches. What's up with your ass?"

I cut him off; I have one thing on my mind. Cassidy. "Do you have Raith's number?"

He hesitates, then sighs. "You heard what's happening. They got her name out there bad. People dragging her through the mud like she's guilty of murder."

Fuck, hearing him say that makes my blood boil. I pick up the closest thing to me, *the remote*, and hurl it across the room, wishing it could hit Sarah's ass in the fucking forehead. "Get in contact with Raith. I need to find Cassidy…now. No more fucking waiting!" My own voice bounces off the walls, loud enough that the restaurant staff downstairs might hear.

"Calm your ass down man," he fires back. "You can't just ignore everything else, like your soccer career. Wanna fill me in on that?"

"I don't give a damn about that right now! Get me the damn number!"

I hang up, chest heaving. Next call: Bruce, my agent. He answers on the first ring breathing hard. *What the hell is he doing?* "Ky, glad you're calling. We need to talk ASAP. The team can't reach…"

"Not now, Bruce. I need a driver. Get someone here now!" I say, ignoring his heavy breathing.

"Kylo, Kylo we do have to make decisions, though," he insists. "We can't keep putting this off."

I still don't get why he thinks calling my name twice is going to make a difference. "Get the driver and the PR reps on the phone. This shit with Sarah ends today. No more fucking waiting. Fuck the endorsements. Get the driver, Bruce!"

Christian calls again before Bruce can protest, so I switch over. "Tell me you got Raith?" I say.

"Yeah, but it wasn't easy. Cassidy's at her family's place. She had to leave campus because of the media shitstorm. Raith didn't want to give me the address, but she said if you were smart you'd Google the shit. You really about to drive over there?"

"Damn straight," I mutter, yanking clothes into the duffel bag. "Nobody's stopping me."

"Alright but get your shit together. She's got major security after all the threats. Word is her dad pulled her out of school."

This is all so fucked up. And all on me. Wishing I'd done something sooner; I zip up my bag. A knock at the door cuts through the guilt and the thought from running to her damn house. When I open it, the same driver from before is standing there in black attire.

"Chris, gotta go. Text me the address," I say, adrenaline coursing through me.

I follow the driver downstairs through the restaurant, with a different staff working, still avoiding eye contact. The driver loads my bag into the sleek black SUV.

"Did Bruce give you the address?" I ask, sliding into the backseat.

"Yes, Sir," he replies, fastening his seatbelt.

"What's the traffic projection?"

He checks the GPS. "Light traffic, maybe an hour. Sit back and relax. I'll get you there faster." I slump into the backseat of the SUV trying not to let the tension eat me alive. Maybe he senses my mood because he flips on his hazards and speeds off.

"All right," I choke out, sinking into my seat and fishing for my phone out of my jacket to Google "Reagan Pittman." Damn, the entire page is giving her straight hell courtesy of Sarah's loud ass mouth. There's even a video from her track meet. *Damn her ass is fine.* Watching that kiss has me wanting more, and I'm sure the 1.2 million viewers who watched it feel the same. Me and this girl had history, but I can't remember any of it.

All the headlines are lies, with this bogus marriage, talk of a restraining order and rumors about Cassidy being the cause for my game. Another reason I hate social media. Anyone can say anything without consequences. But why the hell is Sarah pushing this so far? Her ass is fucking crazy for real.

I've let too much time pass with Sarah holding the narrative. I've got to get to Cassidy… Reagan Pittman, apparently and find out what happened between us. We're talking today and nothing, including John Pittman will stop that. He was angry as hell the last time he saw me and he had every right to be but I'm getting answers today.

The phone vibrates on my thigh. Sarah. Seeing her name is enough to make me crack the phone in half. I block her and text my PR rep.

> Get me a new number today. Turn this shit off and update my family ONLY with my new number.

Bruce calls, but I send it to voicemail. One problem at a time. Right now, Cassidy has my attention as I scroll through more comments.

"She's a bitch!"

"Home wrecker!"

"Sarah did the right thing!"

"Money can't get you everything, boo!"

My fists clamp around the phone, my index finger brushing the power button. No more. I need space, fast. This backseat is too cramped and frustration is gnawing.

"Sir?" the driver asks, eyes meeting mine in the rearview. The man radiates seriousness, like he could take out five guys unarmed if needed.

"Pull over," I say.

He veers onto a wide, empty shoulder off the highway, stepping out before I can reach the handle. Tugging my hoodie over my head, I step into a swirl of dust, pebbles crunching under my Jordan's. For a minute, I concentrate on that sound, gravel shifting, wind sweeping, distant train blowing its horn.

I force a few deep breaths, the wide open land reminding me of a desert except for the towering skinny pine trees, overgrown grass and wildlife. Whoever owns this land put it to no use. It stretches for miles with no houses or stores in sight. *This would be a good place to f…*

I stop myself from finishing, already recognizing my calm with that thought. I get back in the SUV. The driver follows suit, pulling back onto the road so aggressively it spits an orange dust storm behind us.

"Mr. Blade, we're approaching in two minutes," he says, meeting my eyes in the mirror.

I nod, relieved I got out before my anger boiled over.

I stare out the window, hoping the scenery will keep me grounded until we arrive. A towering black wrought iron fence looms ahead, stretching for miles in both directions. It's height screams an unspoken warning: *Stay the fuck out.* The closer we get, the more the landscape shifts to manicured shrubs, tall pines and fewer wild patches. I notice three cars across the street, and five men outside, cameras at the ready. Damn, they're serious.

We slow as we approach a guard shack on the left. I adjust my seat back, hoping no one can see me…yet.

"Pull in," I tell my driver.

Two security guards built like Dwayne Johnson step forward, guns visible. The sight of them makes me angrier. Is this for her because of me?

My driver lets down his window.

"Sir, this is private property," one guard warns, voice tight, black t-shirt tucked into cargo pants. He shifts his hand toward his gun and points back toward the street. He's not opening the gate.

"I have Mr. Blade in the back," the driver says calmly, nodding toward the dark rear windows. "He's here to see Miss Cassidy Pittman."

One guard heads into the stucco guardhouse, leaving the other watching us, hand never straying from his weapon. While we wait, I notice the area. The guard shack could be a small house or apartment based on the size sitting between four lanes. He has lanes entering and two lanes exiting with the brightest white street lines I've ever seen. *Do they paint them daily?* The thick, black, wrought iron gate guarding the entrance to the compound seems to stretch all the way to the treetops because I sure as hell can't see the top of it. If the guard shack looks this big, the house has to be crazy ass rich. He probably has enough firepower in there to take out the entire local police department. Even the shrubbery looks like my barber got a hold to them with his scissor cut.

Inside the shack, I catch a glimpse of the guard on the phone, nodding and shaking his head. Damn, I hope it's not Pittman. This is taking too long, and my anger is creeping to my plan B that will land me in jail. Finally, after what feels like thirty minutes, but is probably close to five, he emerges, opens the gate, and motions his partner aside.

"The two lanes become one. Stay on the main lane to the house," he says, stepping away, but eyeing me through the tinted glass as though I might jump out and start something. *Calm down, I haven't tried anything... yet.*

The gate swings open in seconds, faster than I expected for something that big. My driver raises the window and eases along a winding drive flanked by pines and a carpet of pine straw. Then it changes into dogwoods, their spiral branches giving way to the most massive mansion I've ever seen. It's an almost blinding white structure with a Moroccan feel. A huge circular driveway sweeps around a multi-tiered fountain. There are enough windows on the front to be a hotel. *Damn.* The guard shack has nothing on this. This is so far out of my league. I've been following and studying John Pittman for years but never even thought to Google his home. Even the style of this is too much for the state of North Carolina.

We roll to a stop near the front, the mansion's exterior reflecting in the car window. My nerves hit. This is a level of wealth that says *you can come in, but you'd better watch your step.* The driver kills the engine, and I force my lungs to move while he opens my door.

I step out, eyes zoning in to the security detail posted at each corner of the house. They're on high alert, ready to kill a squirrel if it gets too close. All focus shifts to me as I make my way to the entrance. "Don't go anywhere," I say to my driver, just in case this goes sideways.

The front door seems a mile away, flanked by two flights of stairs split by gleaming white concrete, leading up to three massive, oval-shaped windows and a heavy wrought iron door. It's so big a semi-truck would struggle to pass through it. Not a speck of dirt in sight. Everything is immaculate. Before I can search for a doorbell, the massive door swings open.

A petite woman in a floral print dress, hem below her knees, steps outside. White tennis shoes and a gray apron complete her getup. Her arms fold across her stomach, and she stands firm, blocking the entrance to the at least twenty-foot-high doorway. By the raised brow on her face, I sense she's the captain of this ship.

"Mr. Blade, I presume," she says, voice carrying no warmth. "How can I help you?"

I choose my words carefully, suspecting she's the final gatekeeper. If Pittman were around, he'd have greeted me personally or stationed a guard to do it. That's how it works. "I'd like to see Cassidy," I say.

"Oh, I know," she says curtly, not budging or changing her fixed facial expression.

Not certain of my next move at this point because no amount

of charm is moving this lil' lady. "Is she available? I'd like to speak to her," I force a small grin, one that has gotten me what I wanted in the past, but not with her.

"She's not available to you," she fires back, her words calm but firm.

I take a slow breath trying to keep my composure. *Count.* "Why not, ma'am?"

She lifts her chin, stepping outside the threshold, forcing me away from the door. "Did you see the front gate? The security detail? The news, social media…any of it?" Her cool demeanor cracks, eyes burning as she stares me down. "They've been plastering the story everywhere. She's even gotten death threats. That's why these men are standing guard."

"I just saw that three hours ago," I answer. But that was the wrong thing to say based on how she's staring at me, as though she's ready to slap the shit out of me.

She sets her jaw. "A few hours ago?" I can tell she doesn't believe me. "This has been all over every news outlet, every social media feed, and talk radio station for days now," she gestures at the guards by the garage. "They're here day and night. So, no, Mr. Blade. You cannot see Cassidy." Her words rip through me.

I jam my hands in my pockets and back up. "I only need five minutes."

"Five minutes or fifty the answer is no. Do you know that girl came to the hospital every night for weeks with you? She would get there at midnight and spend the night with you every night!" she screams again, pointing at me on every "you," making me madder with her short finger coming my way. "You see she was not on the visitors list. She took care of you and made sure you were not alone. She would leave every day at five a.m. to head back to school on a dangerous bus that we knew nothing about. She did that every night! Now this!"

Everything hits me at once, leaving me with no calm and ripe to hurt something. "It was Cassidy with me every night?" I demand, stumbling closer to the round lady, desperation clawing at my chest. My head pounds, and I hear someone pop a car door open behind me. "That was Cassidy with me every night? Are you saying it was her?" My voice cracks with urgency. She takes a bold step forward, meeting my challenge as if she believes she can take me.

"Yes, Mr. Blade, it was her," she says, leaning in with an odd, satisfied gleam in her eye, like she's getting ready to tell a joke. "Surely, you didn't think it was Sarah Sims, did you?"

The mere mention of that name scorches through me, igniting a fire in my chest I can't put out. No more hiding. *Nothing's left.* I turn and jump several steps running toward that got damn entrance with all the fucking media Sarah help to create.

I run past the security guard at full speed, up the curves of the one lane. *This shit stops today.* My vision hazes with sweat dripping in my eyes, but I push forward until I see that damn metal gate. The gate with all the stories, the fake bullshit and Sarah having control. No clue how far I've run, but the guard shack appears fast. I'm too focused to care.

I barely notice I'm straight sprinting until screeching tires somewhere nearby brings back the four lanes in front of me. That fucking gate is close now. No idea how long the driveway is but my adrenaline is on fleek 'cause I reached the shack fast. *Is that a horn blaring?*

Guards rush out of the shack, gripping their holsters. Time bends in and out of slow motion as I veer around them heading straight for the nosy reporters. They're about to learn the truth as I rip their wrong asses apart for every lie. I shove my hands through the narrow space between the iron bars and shake the gate with everything I've got, rattling violently, with all my strength, ready to snatch it open. Now they see me...cameras turned, and I'm done being silent.

My wide-legged stance shoots pressure into my ankle, but I ignore the stab of pain. I wave both arms motioning them to come over, forcing them straight into a muddy ditch to reach me. They'll do anything for a story and I'm about to give them one.

"You motherfuckers! Here I am! Come get it!" I yell, voice hoarse from the run and pent-up anger. "You stay the fuck away from Cassidy Pittman!" I roar, locking eyes with the nearest camera lens. "She is the reason I'm alive!"

Adrenaline throbs through my veins, fueling me as I keep going. "She was my girl before the accident!" My voice cracks in raw desperation. "And she's the only reason I'm still breathing!"

I gulp more air, struggling to push out more words. "Sarah and I? We're fucking done! Cassidy was with me every SINGLE night at the hospital, but I didn't remember her! She's the only reason I survived!" My chest seizes, starved of oxygen, but I refuse to stop. "Sarah Sims is not my fiancé. She lied about all of it. She lied! Leave Cassidy Pittman alone…leave her the fuck alone! She's my angel!"

Hands clamp from around my neck from behind, shoving my shoulders down, choking off my words. "Get the fuck off!" I yell, twisting away and swinging at the pair of guards crushing me at the gate. One guard ducks, but another yanks me backward before I can do more damage.

Everything collides into chaos… screams, screeching tires, people yelling in frantic spurts. I'm thrown hard from behind, hitting the pavement cheek first. Concrete scrapes my skin, sending a blaze of pain through my face.

"Damn!" The pain tears through my head, cracked gray and white asphalt full of pebbles bite into my skin as I fight to breathe. A heavy rough boot lands dead on my spine, forcing me face-down.

"Keep his ass down. We're on high alert!" one of the guards shouts, twisting my arms behind me. I feel the bite of zip ties or something sharp digging into my wrists. "We were already suspicious of him at the gate!" another yells. Is he talking about me? Suspicious of me? *Am I slipping?*

My head pounds so hard I can't think. Vision hazy, I catch sight of an SUV that's come to a stop nearby. One of the guards step away to answer his phone, shouting into it. I only make out fragments. "Yeah, he's making a scene! Pittman said handle it. No, ma'am. Did Pittman confirm?"

His voice bounces in my skull, each word sending a fresh stab of pain.

He stomps out of the shack, black combat boots nearly clipping my head. "Get him back in the truck!" he orders. "Take him to the house!"

Rough hands yank me upright, slice the binding off my wrists, then haul me back to the truck. One of them shoves me into the passenger seat so violently my shoulder slams into the center console. "Watch it! No need for that," growls a voice behind me. It's my driver I think but it's hard processing.

My vision fades in and out as we speed away from the gate. I try to straighten myself but I can't fight the dizziness. Time stretches and collapses. Before I know it, we're pulling up to the estate, the high arches of the front entrance coming into view.

I don't feel right. I need to get out and walk. I need…. Damn, there she is…Cassidy. Standing in the doorway, wearing a short green dress, her hair catching the wind. She freezes, eyes locked on the tinted SUV. I freeze, too, the only movement in me is the rise and fall of my chest. *Does she know it's me behind the glass?*

I force my head up, desperate to push open the door despite every ache in my body. If it takes me crawling up all one hundred of those damn steps, I'll do it. My fingers fumble for the handle, but then I see her rush down the stairs. *Come to me, girl.*

She stops outside the truck, her gaze piercing through my fucking soul. Damn, this woman takes all my thoughts. Just seeing her calms me. How do I want her? I don't even remember her. But I know one thing. She'll be mine. I'll make her want us.

Get in, I silently urge her to open the door.

And like that, the handle clicks open. She slips inside with a grace so natural it should be in an etiquette video. Her legs twist toward me as her tiny hand rests on the center console. She looks back at the open door, waiting for my driver to close it. She's never had to close a door before. Her delicate sweet scent drifts into my space, instantly soothing the storm in my chest. I want to lean in and figure out where that scent is coming from. Is it her hair, her natural scent or what's leaking between those legs? She's fucking pulling me from sitting here.

I must look completely off because her eyes latch onto me full of worry. She leans in closer, and I manage to ask, "What's wrong?"

My voice sounds strained even to my own ears. I promise if someone hurts her, I may end up in prison. Nobody's ever bothering her while I'm around. And if I hear one more story of reporters telling lies, I'll personally tear them apart. The cops are still circling the accident full of theories. Maybe the media's partly to blame for this shit.

And then I feel her. Her touch interrupts my thoughts. She slides her soft hands under my chin, tipping my head toward her. Her minty breath floods my senses, and I ease into her hold without a second thought. Why is it so easy to fall into her like this? She reaches for a tissue from the center console and starts dabbing at my cheek.

"You're hurt. What happened out there?" she asks, pressing the tissue near my right eye. Her parted lips release cool sweetness that makes me want to lean in until there's no air left between us. Damn, she asked me something, but I can't remember what, not with her touching my face like this.

"I," I stammer and forget how to speak. But I need her hands to remain where they are and somewhere else down low. It's messing with my head...already turned on and losing the tight leash I keep under control. Shifting in my seat, I try to hide the rush of heat rushing through me. If she keeps going like this, I might lose it right here, in the back seat.

Why am I acting like a clumsy teenager? *Pull your shit together, Kylo. You're a grown ass man.*

She leans in closer, eyes scanning me from head to toe. "Are you in pain? Do you remember what happened a few minutes ago?" she asks, her voice holds a gentleness, but there's a worry simmering beneath it. "You were in a medically induced coma not too long ago…this could be serious. You're bleeding."

"I…don't know." My voice sounds weak, almost childish. *Get your shit together, Kylo.*

Her expression changes from anxiety to anger, brows knitting tight. "Is your head hurting? Did you black out? How much do you remember?"

She checks my cheek again and wipes away more blood. *Don't stop.*

"I'm good," I manage.

"No, you're not." She tosses the tissue in the trash and yanks the passenger door open, her eyes fierce. "You're coming inside." She gets out before I can form a response.

I watch her circle the front of the truck, her posture screaming authority as she waves at my driver and guards, all of them suddenly on high alert. Hell, I don't care as long as I can come inside with her.

She opens my door and gestures at the guards. "Help him out. He's hurt. You really didn't notice the blood?"

I slip out of the truck, forcing my legs to be steady. Each step wobbles, but she's on my left and my driver grips my right, both bracing me. She might be only a buck fifteen, but she's holding her own.

Everything feels off as we approach the first set of stairs that look like they belong on some state capitol building. *Damn, when did these steps get so tall?* My fingers grip my temples, hoping to force the dizziness away. The light narrows, everything blurring my edges. My legs go weak and the concrete shifts beneath my feet.

Damn. Am I…am I about to pass out?

Her alarmed voice cuts through the haze. "Kylo!"

CHAPTER 37

DARKNESS AGAIN

Cassidy

N OT AGAIN. THIS CAN'T BE HAPPENING AGAIN, HIM PASSING out after weeks in the hospital last year. Security and his driver struggle to lower his heavy frame onto the sofa. I scramble to yank away the extra pillows just as they plant him face-first into the cushions. He takes up the entire length of our tan sofa, his large Jordan's hanging off the edge, arms spread wide and unmoving.

I hesitate to touch his jammed finger, wondering how long it's been bent at that angle. If he had gone to the ER, they could have splinted it. I remember wearing one for weeks after a fall during one of my track meets.

It was one of the things I noticed about him when he dipped into my ice months ago, his finger. But the first thing? His chest... then those honey hazel eyes.

That feels like years ago.

Now, he's here, unconscious, and I'm not even sure why. Miss Rita told me there was trouble at the gate. I told her to let him in, that I'd handle Dad later. I need answers, but why now?

I dig my nails into Kylo's scalp, hoping to wake him. Nothing.

Without realizing it, I slide under him so I can rest his face on my thighs. His breathing is slow and even against my skin, reminding me of the nights in the hospital.

"Miss Rita, call our on-call doctor right now!" I shout over my shoulder. She rushes off, leaving three security guards and his driver, all of them tense, as if ready for a fight. I'm not sure what went down outside, but nobody looks happy.

I catch the youngest guard's eye. "Sir, could you get me a cold compress? Miss Rita knows where everything is in the kitchen," I say.

He doesn't move at first. Did I pick the wrong person? Finally, he steps forward, and something in his stance changes. "Anything else, Miss Cassidy?"

"That's all. Please hurry."

He nods and walks away. The other two guards pace. The driver is on his phone. Whoever he's talking to is loud with anger, enough for me to hear the shouting from here.

Kylo jerks suddenly, and I grab his shoulders, instincts kicking in, like how I'd cradle Brooklyn near the pond. Why am I still so protective of this big man? Even unconscious, he's large, his head almost burying itself in my thighs. That small L shaped scar from the accident peeks out.

"Cassidy," I hear Miss Rita's soft voice. She's holding out a cold compress with shaky hands. She might not like him, nobody in my family really does after all that's happened, but she isn't heartless.

I press the cold compress against his cheek, praying for some response. Nothing. It's like he's in a heavy sleep. This is not happening again. I clench my teeth, refusing to accept it. "Miss Rita, I can't do this twice."

She glances at me, sorrow etched on her face. I see Kylo's driver dial another number. It's been maybe three minutes since we got him inside, but it feels like longer. Without thinking, I scream.

"Kylo! Wake up!" My voice hits a higher pitch than normal,

but I'm not standing by if there's a chance he needs help. I press the compress harder against his temple, squeezing his hand. "Kylo!"

"Cassidy, maybe you should wait until the doctor arrives," Miss Rita suggests softly, though I can hear the worry in her voice.

I refuse to just sit back. "He's not responding!" Tension thickens the air. Even his driver's anxious as he speaks into the phone, pacing behind the sofa.

"Kylo, we're not doing this again. Wake up! Wake the hell up!" I shout. My voice echoes through the house, so loud staff in the next room probably freeze at the sound.

But it works, because at last his honey hazels peel open. He blinks several times, his impossibly long lashes, one's women pay good money for, fan across his cheeks. Slowly, he shifts, still resting on my thighs, gaze drifting as he tries to figure out where he is.

My next breath stalls in my throat, waiting to see if he remembers passing out or anything.

"Cassidy," he whispers, and the air trapped in my lungs collapses, my dress tightening across my chest in response. The soft way he says my name fills me with both hope and dread.

"Yes, Kylo," I manage, my voice low.

He slips his hand from mine and presses his fingers in slow circles between his eyebrows, lids squeezed shut. Maybe he's trying to rub away the pain I hope isn't there. "Did you wake me, again, twice?" he asks, eyes serious and unwavering.

I'm glad he remembers blacking out as a smile crosses my face. *Gently*, I answer, "Yes, I did. You were out for maybe three or five minutes this time."

His hands drop, and I study his face for signs of discomfort. But he reveals nothing. "My family doctor is on his way to check you," I continue in a rush, feeling questions coming. "Can I get you anything? Do you know where you are? Are you hurting?" My anxiety flares, words spilling out in one breath, and I realize I don't know where to rest my hands, which were on his shoulders seconds ago.

A side smile edges his mouth, amused by my flood of questions.

"I'm sitting on some warm, soft thighs," he says, then reaches up to lightly pinch my chin, guiding my face so I have to look at him. He leans deeper into my lap and inhales as if he's in pain or just drinking me in. Then he exhales a warm rush of air under my dress. It sends a quiver straight between my legs. I can't believe he's doing this. Why did I say that? *Yes*, I can believe it. This is the same person who got into my ice bath. If he hadn't passed out, he'd be on the floor getting comfortable on the carpet.

"Nothing's changed. You're still the same," I begin but then notice everyone leaving the living room. For a second, I wonder if they overheard us.

"Cassidy, I'll show the doctor in when he arrives," Miss Rita says softly from the doorway, as though she's witnessed enough. She doesn't even look annoyed like she did ten minutes ago.

"Thank you," I reply, grateful but also embarrassed. A part of me wonders how Mom would have handled this, because I certainly have no clue.

Miss Rita halts at the threshold and glances over her shoulder. "You need anything, baby girl?" The words baby girl should make me cringe. Shouldn't she be angry like before?

"No, Miss Rita, I'm fine," I say, trying not to sound embarrassed.

"Yes, you are," Kylo adds, twisting away from me to look at her. "Thank you, Miss Rita, for telling me the truth."

She fixes him a measured look, leaving me hoping she didn't hear his answer. She simply nods and says, "You did well out there. Now I know," her voice is calm and oddly affectionate.

I blink, confused. "Know what, Miss Rita?"

She eyes the two of us, a slow smile working across her lips. "I know you two will make ugly babies," she declares.

My jaw drops. "What? Ugly babies? I'm not pregnant, Miss Rita!"

She tuts. "I know, baby girl. Too much pretty in one couple makes an ugly baby," she mumbles, gathering up her apron as she heads off, leaving me to stare after her in disbelief.

I can't help but laugh. "I'm sorry," I tell Kylo. "She's never been one for filters, and she says every year past sixty lets her add a little more spice to the commentary. And she's doing just that."

He gently props himself upright on the couch, shifting away just enough to put space between us, the air thick with unspoken words. So much that needs to be said, but I don't know where to begin. Eventually he breaks the silence.

"Cassidy, are you okay?" he asks, genuine worry lining his voice.

Am I okay? The past few days have been a nightmare. Despite Dad's best efforts, we haven't killed the media frenzy. The random death threats caught me completely off guard. People who know nothing about me have threatened my life just because Sarah posted a ridiculous story. It's insane.

He notices my tension and slides closer, fists tightening over his knees. "I see it's been rough," he says. "Tell me."

I swallow, pressing the heel of my hand against my temples. "It's not just the rumors," I admit. "It's worse watching my family deal with the chaos. My dad sent my sisters away for a while, some-where safe, and they're under heavy security. Thankfully, they're loving the around-the-clock food catering and fancy accommoda-tions," I force a weak laugh. "But, I hate being the reason people I love are in danger."

Kylo's jaw sets, hands curling. "I'm so sorry. Has anyone hurt you?" he asks, his gaze shifting to the family photos crowding the mantel. A thick vein runs down the side of his neck, pulsing like it's ready to burst. He's barely holding it together.

I grip my hands in my lap, resisting the urge to rub his shoul-ders or trace that prominent vein with my fingertips. It's too soon for me to touch him. "No one's come near this house, not with the round-the-clock security Dad has set up. He even stopped helicop-ters from flying over when he caught an ariel shot of our home on social media. No idea how he did that. But the story it's still trend-ing. I just want it over. I miss my family, Raith and school and," I stop short, swallowing the word *you*. Too soon, too raw.

He starts pacing the living room, voice reduced to a mutter, counting something under his breath. "The story is done," he grinds out, then raises his voice. "It ends today," *Is he counting?*

"If you say so," I whisper, registering the anger still coursing beneath his words.

"Pull out your phone and Google me," he demands, whirling around to face me. "I bet these motherfuckers already posted it."

I stare at him. "Already posted what?"

His jaw clenches. "Just do it. Google us. My name, yours. See what pops up."

Curiosity and unease mix in my stomach as I unlock my phone and start typing. Before I can finish spelling Cassidy, the screen fills with search suggestions. Cassidy Pittman and Kylo Blade, video after video. My gut twists. I tap the first link.

There he is captured on camera, storming toward a gated area, hurling curses at the paparazzi. The look in his eyes is frantic, a desperation I've never witnessed, even in the hospital. The footage zooms in on our security guards wrestling him to the ground, slamming him onto the pavement so hard it leaves a nasty gash.

"They didn't need to tackle you that hard," I murmur.

He shrugs, eyes still on the screen. "They did. They were protecting you...even if it was from me."

My gaze flicks from the phone to him, finding his stare heated and restless. My heart thrums uncomfortably as I reach for calm. "In that video, you called me your angel. You said it there...and on TV. Kylo, do you...remember anything about us? And is there a marriage," I force myself to stop, anxiousness heating me.

He shakes his head slowly. "I wish I did remember," he admits, voice rough. "All I know is what people have told me. That you stayed at my bedside for days. Then I saw you at the track meet. It was like a magnet. Couldn't walk away. I've never had that feeling before." He takes my hand gently, doesn't lace our fingers but tugs at my nail tips like he's testing what's real. "And no, there was never any marriage. That was a lie."

He cuts himself off, anger burning through his eyes. Silence stretches between us, charged with too many questions and not enough words. Finally, he shakes his head, giving me the answer before he speaks.

His voice lowers in frustration, "Maybe one day it'll come back. I know you've been on my mind ever since I found out all you did for me in the hospital. It feels like there was something between us then, and I feel it now," he glances lower at my body before meeting my eyes again, "I'd never marry that..."

He stops short, maybe not wanting to waste his breath. Whatever the reason, it's enough for me not to hold back. I lean in, eyes sliding shut, silently begging him to meet me halfway. He does and my breath shudders the moment his lips brush mine. He kisses me so passionately that it should be a crime for anything to feel this good. I open like a thirsty flower in full bloom as his tongue sweeps inside getting familiar again with my taste. He's slow and hesitant, but I want more and not gentle. I lean in closer, holding his neck and sucking his wet lips into mine. He reads my urgency and our soft passion turns to a force, caving us closer. Our intensity leaves us both breathless and wanting more. He pulls away, leaving our foreheads remaining together.

"Damn, girl," he mutters, voice thick with need. "See what I mean? That right there isn't normal. It's different."

I inhale a shaky breath as he pulls back a fraction, our foreheads still touching. I whisper, "Kylo, we should wait for the doctor."

He exhales against my skin, voice taut with desire. "Beautiful, I'm coming right back for those thighs. Watch..."

"Why do you say things like that? That part of you hasn't changed."

He smiles and settles back against the sofa, arms stretched wide, practically spanning the cushions. His wingspan covers the entire back of the sofa. With a slight nudge, he draws me closer. I let him, relaxing into his warmth.

"Those thighs have been on my mind since that track meet,"

he murmurs. "I lost all memories we had, but I know something was there. I need to know everything. Tell me." His calloused fingers ghost up my leg slow and warm.

I squirm away slightly. "I will. But not with your hands on my leg. I can't think straight."

His narrow mouth curves into a mischievous smile. "Touching you is all I've been thinking about, but...I need answers." He slides me onto his lap as though I weigh nothing. My hands hover awkwardly, unsure where to land...his face, his shoulders?

"After the doctor checks you out," I say, keeping my arms close.

"What if I'm not willing to wait?" he asks, his hand gathering my hair, baring my neck with his warm moist breath against my skin. Before I can say a word or figure out what to do next, he's licking my ticklish spot near my collarbone. I bite my lip, and lean away for his wet tongue cleaning me. No longer able to fight it, I straddle him on the sofa, arms sliding around his neck no longer caring.

"Yes," he groans, biting my neck as if I'm a piece of ripe fruit, eager to savor my juicy sweetness. I lean in closer, giving him everything he desires. I'm so glad this part has not changed with us. This explosive attraction that takes my thoughts and pretty much everything in me away. I need him...

What was that? A throat clearing from somewhere behind us. Ohh...no. My stomach drops. I jerk away from Kylo, eyes darting to see our longtime family doctor of twenty-one years standing near the doorway, stethoscope and medicine bag in hand. Embarrassment doesn't begin to cover it. He's known me my entire life, but never seen me like this.

My first instinct is to move off Kylo's lap, but he tightens his hold around my waist, not bothered at all by the third set of eyes in the room. Finally, he angles a glance at the doctor. "Doc, I presume?" he says, flashing a half smile before looking back at me. "Can you come back... later? My hands are full."

My mouth drops open. "Kylo, why would you say that?" I ask, attempting again to wiggle free from his hold.

"I'll always say what I feel around you." His seriousness pulls me back as he leans forward to kiss me again, then lifts me off his lap placing me on the sofa, with an effortless ease. The raw strength of that simple motion stokes my hunger for him even more.

Get it together, I remind myself, but my body's not listening.

Turning away from me, Kylo faces the doctor, an older friend of Dad's, Dr. Garett. "He's all yours," I say, realizing the guys need privacy for an examination, so I start to stand.

"Don't go," Kylo murmurs. The deep, raspy plea draws me back, protective and unwavering, like a helicopter Mom ready to beat the monsters away. I sit back down, making sure there's not an inch of space between us.

Dr. Garrett checks Kylo's vitals, shining a light in his eyes and probing carefully around his ribs and head injury. "From my basic exam, you look stable. Change that bandage a couple of times of day and follow up with your team doctor. Let them know about this episode, the fall and any additional pain. Otherwise, you should be good."

Kylo stands towering over Dr. Garrett's short round frame to shake his hand.

"Thank you for coming out, Doc. Let my driver out front know how to contact you for payment."

Dr. Garrett waves a hand. "No problem. It's not every day I get to check on a pro soccer player. Get yourself back on that field soon. You defied the odds once; you can do it again."

"Appreciate it." Kylo walks him to the entrance, then reaches back for me. I slip my fingers into his as he pulls me closer to watch Dr. Garrett leave out the foyer. Silence creeps as we're both left alone in the living room again. I snuggle my head into the dip of his back, loving how tall he is and how small he makes me feel.

"What happened with us?"

"How was your game?" We speak at the exact same moment.

He pulls me closer to the fireplace and I can't help but notice he's the only person whose head has ever come close to tipping the mantel. "We'll speak about the game, later," he says, impatience and something else in his voice. "Tell me about us. All of it," he says, bringing my index finger across his chest to his lips for a long wet suck. The feel of his tongue, swirling around my finger sends heat through me, and I find myself molding against him again, craving more.

Clearing my throat, I remind myself to stay focused. "I'd like to take you someplace quieter. Somewhere we can talk without distractions. Up for a short hike?"

Kylo slowly withdraws my finger from his mouth, resting it on his chest. "Privacy can be dangerous, Miss Pittman," he warns, his raspy voice low and serious.

I slide my arms around his waist, and meet his gaze with a steadiness I don't quite feel. "I'm not afraid. Are you, Kylo?"

CHAPTER 38

HIDE AWAY OASIS

Kylo

TRAIL BEHIND HER, FOLLOWING HER THIGHS THROUGH A half-mile hike, battling a damn headache and the distracting curve of her hamstrings. I need her mouth again, those trembling lips, but if I give in, I won't stop. Especially on a day like this. The weather is perfect, not humid and not too hot. Just right for...

I remind myself to take it slow with that thought. I can't mess this up. This is new and different. I hate to admit it, but I don't know what I'm doing yet.

The loud branch crack under her boots gets my attention. My gaze shifts from her thighs to the trail ahead, back to her legs, climbing higher with each step. Why in the hell did she leave that dress on? If it rides up any closer to the tip of her ass, I might yank it off.

We finally reach a flat area filled with towering trees and wildflowers, overgrown vines stretching so high they almost cover the top of the trees. Is that an outdoor structure? It looks like a tent or camping setup, hiding in the woods almost camouflaged, like it's meant to be missed.

"What is this?" I ask, glad for the distraction from her thighs. *What does John Pittman have out here?*

She turns to me, placing her soft hand in mine like we've done this before. *Have we?* "My mom died three years ago from lupus," she says quietly, her voice carrying the weight of grief. "She loved being outside and surrounded by nature. So, Dad had this built for her."

Her eyes glisten with sadness, stopping me dead in my tracks. I know that pain. I hate that she has to feel it too.

I gently hold her hand, still wrapping my mind around the fact that she's John Pittman's daughter, mourning the loss of her mother. Losing Tron was hard enough, I can't even imagine losing Miss Blade.

She pulls me forward, leading me to a tunnel like entrance draped with vines and flowers, hiding a curtain door. "No shoes allowed. Place them here," she says, pointing to a wicker basket filled with other shoes.

We walk up a slight incline into a space that leaves me in awe. Tan curtains cascade from the ceiling, pooling on the ground like soft waves of fabric. In the center of the room stands a striking bare tree, its grayish brown branches stretching toward the ceiling, disappearing through the top of the structure. The floor is a sea of pillows, maybe a hundred, scattered in soft shades of tan, pink and blue covering every inch of space. Drapes envelop the room from ceiling to floor, giving the vibe of a luxurious circus tent.

She walks to the side of the room and flicks two switches. The curtains slowly roll down, revealing the surrounding trees, plants and the setting sun. Warm golden lights fill the space, creating a soft glow around us.

I squint, trying to figure out if a screen is separating us from the outside, but it's so sheer it's almost invisible. The tent and tree inside give the illusion that we're on an island of pillows, surrounded by exotic plants, the whisper of leaves and distant chirping of birds.

The sound of water draws my attention. A nearby waterfall cascades from a cliff, its soft hiss blending with the serenity of this place. This is fucking crazy, a hidden oasis in the middle of nowhere.

Money can seriously buy you anything.

I shift back to her as she walks toward me, her innocence shining through despite the weight of the memories this place holds for her.

"My mom spent hours out here. Sometimes entire nights, especially toward the end of her illness. This place has air and heat with visible and hidden waterfalls. Everything is man-made, just the way she wanted it. She called it her tree of hope," her voice trembles as tears gather in her eyes, locked on the tree at the center of the room. "Dad always wanted her safe. He didn't want anyone spying on her, especially in her final days."

She kneels on one of the pillows, extending her hand to me. I hesitate, then sit beside her, feeling out of my element. She seems at ease, more comfortable with me than I am with her.

"The structure is camouflaged from the outside," she continues, her fingers holding the butterfly charm on her bracelet. "It was her outdoor island, a place for her clouds, stars, and sounds of the wild. This was her sanctuary."

Her voice falters, and she trails off, tears streaming down her high cheekbones. The sight grips me. *Don't cry.* Please don't cry. I can't do that. Without thinking, I pull her into my arms, cradling her like I could shield her from the pain. Her familiar scent fills my senses, igniting something deep inside.

"I miss her so much," she whispers, trembling in my embrace. "After three years, I thought the pain would lesson, but it still feels the same."

"I'm sorry," is all I can manage, holding her tighter, surprised by my instinct to protect her, as her tears soak my shirt.

She pulls back, sitting up to wipe her face. *How does she even cry pretty?*

"When you came into my life, I had just started college at A&M," she begins her voice soft. "I took three years off after my mom died. I stayed home to take care of Dad and my sisters. I lost three D-1 track scholarships, but I didn't care. Everyone tried to convince me to go to school, especially Dad. He thought time away from home would help, but I wasn't ready to leave. I spent every hour here with them." Her gaze meets mine, searching for something, hope in her eyes. "That's when I met Brooklyn."

"Brooklyn?" I frown, shaking my head. "I don't remember... But when I saw her at the park, she told me to tell you hello. I didn't know she was talking about you." *Damn this short-term memory loss.*

Her smile returns, small but genuine, and she leans in to kiss my cheek. *I'd kill for that smile and those lips on me.* Where in the hell did that come from?

"Alright Captain K," she says playfully. "I'll tell you everything."

"I'm listening, beautiful."

She settles back into the pillows, her hand resting on mine. "Well, we met at A&M in an ice bath..."

I listen to every word, from the ice bath, to meeting Brooklyn, the truck, the gala, the Grove, the accident, the hospital, my recovery, the A&M track meet, Sarah and now this moment. How in the hell did I forget all of this?

Tension tightens in my chest with the urge to burn off some steam. I stand, pacing across the cushions unable to stomp like I want to. We could've been together this whole time. *Fuck.*

I glance back at her, realizing she's been through a shit load in the past few months, and this new story is making it worse. *I'm the reason for everything bad in her life.* Her face shows worry in her delicate features and that's on me. *Damn.*

"What is it?" she asks softly, her tiny hand resting on my cheek.

Don't lose your shit, Kylo. She hasn't seen this side of me, and it's too soon to let her meet it. "You've been through too much because of me," I say, my voice low. "and this memory loss. Too much time passed. You were in that hospital with me every night. You were the one to wake me, and I.... forgot you."

I remove her hands, needing space to think, but immediately regret it when I see the turmoil creeping on her pretty face and the uncertainty what to do with them.

"I'm sorry," I say, my voice thick with guilt. I reach down, smoothing the faint worry line near her left eye. "I don't want you worrying about anything, not this media shit, not me, none of it."

Her lips tremble, slightly parted, waiting. *No more waiting*, girl.

I pull gently at the loose curl near her neck, tangling my fingers into her ponytail. "Take this down."

A hint of lavender takes over as she lifts her arms to untie her hair. Loose curls fall into a mess accenting her narrow eyes begging for something. I hope she wants the same thing I do because waiting is not happening. I rest my hands in her silky strands bringing her closer, brushing her heart shaped lips that should be a sin to have. I kiss her softly, as though she's the water my body needs to survive. How can anything feel this good, this right? *Open for me, girl.* Let me in those wet soft trembling lips. We're thinking alike as she holds my neck and wraps her legs around my waist, pulling her closer. *Perfect fit.* She molds into me as if she was meant to be there.

"Umm," a soft moan escapes her as I explore every part of her mouth, wanting her sweet taste. I carry her toward the tree of hope, my grip firm on her soft curves, as her hands cling to my neck as if I may run away. *She's fucking perfect.*

I pull away from her, hating to do it. "Beautiful, reach for the branches on the tree. I'll lift you. Place your legs wide open on my shoulders." That damn tree with the branches. That shit is perfect. *Pittman is a creative genius.*

Her confusion lasts for maybe a moment before she complies without hesitation. I lift her around her thighs to both branches. "Hold on tight, beautiful. I promise I won't let you fall." That's a new word for me… promise. "Place both legs on my shoulders and spread them wide."

She does it with little effort, showing off her upper body strength with her biceps popping. I love her dress and all the access it provides.

What is she doing? Her focused eyes lock onto mine, drilling into me with an intensity I can't escape. "Hold me, Kylo." I do as she says, watching her grip the branch with one arm, she uses the other to pull her dress up and over her head, leaving her in nothing but a lacy green bra. *She's not as shy as I thought.*

Letting go of the branch, she unsnaps the clip of her bra with a slow, deliberate motion, exposing the most tempting, natural curves I've ever seen. Nothing about her is fake, she's all real.

She bites the strap of her bra playfully before letting it fall to the pillows beneath her, leaving me completely captivated.

The green lace swings to the pillows, landing between my feet as she raises both arms to grip the branch above. She bites her bottom lip, and for a moment, is that…*shyness?* She glances away, avoiding me, as though she's hiding some secret beauty.

She has no reason to be shy with me. I want her completely at ease, without a hint of doubt. "Look at me," I say, gently pulling her narrow chin until her eyes meet mine.

My fingers trail slowly up her flat stomach, the heat of her skin drawing me in. They find their way to her soft nipple, teasing it until it peaks into a hardened golden pebble beneath my touch. The fire building inside me is impossible to ignore, every part of me needing her. *Why did I put her up there?*

Her head falls back between her arms, exposing the delicate veins beneath her skin as her grip tightens on the branch above. The intoxicating scent of her arousal surrounds me, consuming me like an addictive drug. How can anyone be this sexy?

"Please don't stop, Kylo," she whispers, her legs spreading wider over my shoulders, her voice trembling with need.

Damn, I want her, but this got to be right. This is different. *Slow down.*

I pull away from her smooth skin, resting my head between her thighs. *Slow down. Do it right,* I tell myself. But then her nails dig into my scalp, pushing me closer, her legs pulling me into her warmth.

"Why are you stopping?" she asks, breathlessly. Her eyes sparkling with a mix of desire and trust. She seems so comfortable with me here, but this is new territory. I don't do this. I don't go down on women. *Have I done this with her before?*

Those nude nails in my hair aren't helping. My thoughts run crazy as I turn away, trying to slow my brain before I do more. "Anyone out here?" I ask, my voice low, almost a growl, fighting the urge not to bite the strings of her thong.

She pulls my head back, her serious eyes meeting my confusion. "Please stop talking," she says firmly. "Everyone is out of town except Miss Rita, and she doesn't even know how to get here. No one does, not even security."

Her gaze drops to my hand resting on her thigh. She smiles, her confidence growing. "Put your hand back where it was."

Her hair falls between her cleavage, her shyness fades. My fingers slip between the delicate lace of her green thong, gently tugging at the wet string. "Nobody needs to see this," I choke out, surprised by the anger building within me. *How the hell is her clit this pretty?*

"Why are you talking so much?" she asks, impatience coloring her voice as a furrow forms between her brows, the worry line near her left eye deepening.

I lose the fight within myself, my fingers slipping into the wetness beneath her thong. Her skin and sight of her make me ache to lick her tip. "Damn, how are you like this?"

She lowers her head, her arm moving to cover her breasts, and shyness returns. It stops me in my tracks. *She said we've done things in our past, but what things?* She's not fully comfortable with me yet, and it makes me pause, needing her to relax.

"Don't do that," I say softly. "You're beautiful inside and out."

Her smile is small at first, then it reaches her eyes, making them crinkle slightly at the corners. The way they almost close in pleasure makes my chest tighten. *Damn.*

"You said that at the Grove," she murmurs, her voice dipping with emotion.

"What else did I say at the Grove?" I ask, curiosity growing, but not enough to stop my fingers from teasing her wet string.

The breeze catches her hair, swirling it around us, mingling with the scent of her arousal. It's intoxicating and before I can think, I bite the thin fabric of her thong. The delicate lace gives way under my teeth, tearing it into shreds of green string.

"Kylo, what are you doing?" she asks breathlessly, her hands gripping the branch above for balance.

Sexy isn't the word for her. I need another word because she's beyond that.

I inhale the remnants of the torn green fabric, her scent wrapping around me like a drug. *Damn, I'm losing control.* "These are going home with me," I say, my voice thick as I shove the lace in my pocket.

She grips the branch with both hands, her legs wider on my shoulders, her confidence testing my restraint. My control is slipping fast and *I'm about to fuck this up*.

She's naked on my shoulders, the setting sun casting a golden light around her, highlighting every curve. The sound of the nearby waterfall drips nearby adding to my drunken state.

Her stomach rises and falls with each shallow breath, her breasts catching the dust in the sunbeams, her peaks making my mouth water. "You said you wanted to eat me until my juices flowed down your face… at the Grove," she whispers, arching her back just enough for my lips to graze her slit.

Fuck. My breath stops at that thought. "Have I done that to you?" I ask, my voice barely steady.

She buries her head into her neck, her curls falling over her expression. "Yes, Kylo," she murmurs, her voice muffled but clear enough to knock the air from my lungs. "You did this to me… in your truck."

Damn. This girl has something over me for real. First the cold plunge, now this? Those are two things I don't do.

"What do you want me to do?" I ask, my voice low, the pull between her legs becoming unbearable. Her scent is making me weak. A taste is all I need.

"Please," she breathes, the desperation in her voice making me hard as hell.

"Please what, girl?" I growl, my restraint fading. I need to hear her say it, to unleash the desire that's burning between us.

She exhales slowly, gripping my head again and pulling me closer. "Please, make me flow down those lips again," she says, her newfound confidence taking over her shyness, igniting a fire that I may never extinguish.

"Come here."

She opens wider, giving me full access to her beautiful slit. But something else is bothering me. "Cassidy…"

She lowers her head, inhaling deeply, her eyes locking onto mine. *Is she angry?* Damn, she's mad. This is new. No one gets mad with me, especially not women. I don't give them that kind of time.

A stray strand of hair lands between the rise of her chest, drawing my attention to a delicate half heart-shaped birthmark. *Damn.*

"I want more," I say, tracing the birthmark with my fingertip. "I need you for me. Nobody else's. Just mine." My voice drops, softer but more certain. "I know this is fast, but I don't wait. If I want something, I get it. Life taught me young that nothing's promised. I want you in my life. My girl. My girlfriend…"

The word slips out, surprising even me. *Girlfriend?* That's a first. *What does that even mean for someone like me?*

Her breath quickens, her chest rising and falling unevenly. I lift my gaze, meeting the moisture in her eyes. *Don't cry. Please…*

"Say something," I urge, softly, almost pleading.

"Yes, Kylo," she whispers, her voice trembling. "I'm your girl. My heart chose you months ago. I was just… waiting for you to wake and remember me."

A single tear slips down her cheek, landing on my hand like a drop of fire. Her words sink into me deeper than I expected. She said heart.

"I'm sorry," she says, wiping her tears. *Is she apologizing for crying?*

"No one gets to have you but me. You're mine," I grit out, my voice sounding more possessive than I intended. Maybe even crazy. But, I need her to understand that she's mine, and no one else gets between these legs but me.

"Okay, Captain K," she sniffs, as a smile breaks through. "Now, please stop talking and.."

I cut her off, sealing my lips against her soft flesh. My tongue licks her center slowly, deliberately, savoring every inch. She grinds my face, guiding me, telling me what she needs. My hands trail up her body, teasing her nipples back into stiff peaks.

"Kylo!" she screams, her voice echoing through the golden glow of the setting sun.

"You're too loud, girl. Can anyone hear us?" I murmur, half-teasing.

Maybe she thinks I'm pulling away, because her thighs clamp my face with the intensity of a soccer goalie catching my best shot.

"I have dreamed of this every night for months," she confesses, her voice breathless but strong. "The sun is setting and this is private land. No one will hear us, and honestly, I don't care if they do. I want you! Give me what I want," she demands, leaving me wondering if she's spoken to me that way before. Listening to anyone is new for me. Did I listen to her before the accident?

Her words stir something in me. I'll shut her pretty ass up.

I part her gently, exposing her delicate pink warmth and lean in to taste her. Her soft ass gives me the perfect leverage to get lost in her wet slit, savoring the sweetness that coats my lips and tongue.

My hands slide up the dip of her back, finding their way to her breasts again, twisting her nipples just enough to make her gasp. Her legs tighten around my shoulders, forcing me deeper, spreading her wider as I drown in the sweetness dripping down my mouth.

She grips the branch above with both hands, her hips grinding against me with a rhythm that feels almost choreographed, controlled but primal, like a dancer on a pole, giving herself over to the moment.

She's so damn wet, her body pulsing under my tongue as I explore every part of her.

Damn, I hope she hasn't done this before. Her hair falls past her waist, catching the glow of the burnt orange and pink hues of the setting sun. She leans back slightly, exposing the delicate curve of her neck. She's so damn sexy, I feel like I'm about to break something. This right here is on another level.

I love being outside, but being out here with her is different. It has me on a high with a rawness running through me. I want to devour her, eat every inch of her.

"You smell so damn good, girl. I want this every day," I admit, surprised by the truth in my words. That's new for me, wanting something every day, someone every day.

"You can have it every day, whatever you want. Please don't stop," she whispers, her voice blending with the splashing waterfall, as I suck her soft innocence.

Her scent is new, her taste pure and untouched. *I hope.* I hate to admit it, but if she'd been worn over by someone else, it might be a problem. The thought of her with someone else stirs something deadly in me, making me want to bite and to mark her as mine.

My teeth graze scissor her clit not too hard, but enough to make her understand this is serious. She's mine. I lose myself in her sweetness, in the addictive taste of her, vowing never to let go, to never hurt her.

Her body reacts in waves, trembling with currents that ripple through her, hitting from every direction.

"Please don't stop… don't stop. I," she cries out, her voice cracking as I hold her hips in place, her legs falling wider on my shoulders. Her moans echo through the clearing, the birds and wildlife witnessing our connection, our unrestrained wildness.

There it is. I taste her. *Fuck, she's sweet…* addictive, like candy. I could lose myself in her, climb inside and never want to leave.

"Give me all of you. You taste so damn good," I whisper against her, my tongue exploring her depths, savoring every drop of her sweet nectar.

"Kylo," she moans, her grip tightening, pulling me closer. The grip of her hold and the rough bark of the tree scraping my knee make me stop.

"Am I bruising you?" I ask. I forgot her back was in the center of a splitting branch.

"Kylo, what is wrong with you? Nothing is bruising me! There is no one out here and I don't care if I scream!" she shoots, pulling my head back between her legs with a fierceness that makes me pause.

Maybe something is wrong with me. I've never stopped to ask anyone anything before. But this... this is different.

"Let go of the tree," I say, trying to read the defiance already arching in her eyebrows. I can tell she's about to refuse.

"Why?"

Did she really just ask why?

"Cassidy, let go of the tree," I repeat, firmer this time. I don't usually have to repeat myself, hell, most women already know what's coming. But she's not getting it, not yet.

"Kylo, I'm okay. Trust me, I would tell you if you were hurting me," she says again, impatience matching mine. But I don't back down.

"Let go of the branch before I pull you off," I say, my voice firm. She exhales, her shoulders deflating, shaking her head from side to side.

"There is nothing wrong with me," she claims but let's go of the branch, anyway.

I'll be the judge of that.

Her legs stay wrapped around my shoulders as I carry her to the pillows. I take my time, laying her naked body onto the soft pink and blue cushions. The remnants of her pleasure smear my chest like a second layer of skin, as I lay her down.

"Now what?" she asks, stretching her body against the neutral pillows, her nipples disappearing into the plush fabric. *Damn.*

"Flip over, girl, let me see."

"Really, Kylo?" she teases, but she does as I ask, flipping onto her stomach and giving me her hourglass figure to admire. Her skin blends into the pillows, flawless and perfect, as if it was meant to be there. Not a single scar, dimple or imperfection is on her.

This shit is unreal. I can't even spot a hangnail or scar on this woman. She is a work of art, perfect, and that ass waiting for me. How can anyone be this beautiful? It's a rare thing to witness a body that meets a face, perfectly matched to the intelligence and kindness managing it all. She's all of it: fine, beautiful, smart and kind.

"Thank you!" I breathe, the words escaping me without thought.

As she glances around the tent, her hair falls over her eyes as she crosses her legs hiding her innocence. "Who are you thanking?"

I didn't even realize I said it out loud. *Damn.* "A higher being. Come here," I say, pulling her closer as she flips back over to face me. My lips crash into hers. *I need her.*

"Kylo. You still have on clothes. Can I see you?" she asks, pulling back before I can. *She stopped our kiss before I did.* The uncertainty in her eyes pulls at something deep in me, and I notice how she leans back on her hands, her golden nipples tightening as cool air brushes her skin.

She lowers her head slightly, her arms crossing over her chest. Her discomfort is clear and makes me want to slow down, to take my time with her. But she asked to see me, and a request like that isn't going unanswered.

I take my time, removing my shirt, watching her closely for any sign she wants me to stop. Nothing. I slide off my boxers, exposing myself. Her eyes widen, the shyness fading as she takes me in, like she's never seen this before or anyone else.

"You're so bi…" her words trail off before she finishes and I smile inwardly. It's okay. Nothing, I haven't heard before.

"Come here," she says, her voice soft but insistent. I hesitate, not wanting to rush her. I want this etched in my memory forever, as she's already displaying signs.

Approaching me on all fours, her movements are fluid and deliberate; her body both alluring and powerful, like a tiger stalking its prey. She stops to kneel in front of me, her hair falling to the center of her back, framing her body like a masterpiece.

Her gaze meets mine, intense and unwavering. "What are you doing?" I ask.

She runs her tongue over her top teeth, as if checking them, her eyes locked on me with a mix of curiosity and intent as she inches closer. "Can I…I want to," she starts, but trails off, her gaze drifting to my midsection, unmistakably focused on what she wants.

"I would love to," she whispers, her voice unsteady but bold.

"Umm," is all I manage to say, caught off guard by her shift. She's gone from shy to a freak in seconds. This isn't something I'm used to turning away, but this is new territory for the both of us.

She hesitates briefly before reaching out, trembling slightly as they massage me, tentative at first but growing in confidence.

"Fuck!" I say, the fire igniting under her touch burning hotter than I expected. The sensation leaves me speechless, stripped of thought. I allow her to explore; hoping she'll grow to love this. *Did I say love?*

My attention shifts to her hair, draping around her shoulders like silk as she continues her slow strokes, leaving me brick rock. The intimacy of it feels different, raw and new. Her inexperience shows, but it only makes the moment more intense.

She leans back, running her hands through her hair, her nipples threatening to touch my leg as she stares at me, waiting for my next move or permission. Hell, I don't have an answer. Her trembling fingers lift me into her soft, wet lips, moving up and down my length with a tenderness that sends shockwaves through me.

"Fuck," I exhale, the onslaught of emotions hitting me all at once, enough to make my knees weak. *What the hell is this?* Damn, she's doing this right. No, she's doing this fucking perfect, better than right.

She pushes me. "What are you doing?" I ask, feeling her guide me as I step backward.

"I want you back against the tree, with your legs wide open for me," she says, her voice confident and sultry.

I smile at her balls. I just told her the same thing. She's doing this just right, her wet lips working me in ways I didn't expect. "Aww, girl…I can't do this in your mouth." That's some different shit for sho'. I've allowed hundreds of lips to swallow without a thought.

"I don't care what you want. I know what I want," she says, leaning in surprising me as she opens her mouth wide, taking me in deeper than I thought possible. Does she have a gag reflex? Her mouth is slippery, wet and soft, her suction tight. The determination with her stroke has me wide open, no defenses left. *What the hell is she doing to me?*

I'm not going to last long and that shit isn't normal. Her touch alone got me all fucked up.

"God damn, girl make me remember us," I hiss as her tongue circles me with precision, like a pro. I'm stranded, completely powerless to hold back. My hands move to stop her, knowing where this is headed, but she grabs me tighter, leaning her head back, taking me deeper and leaving me with no resistance.

"Damn, girl…" My body takes over, pumping in and out of her mouth, ignoring every warning my brain sends to slow down. I had hoped she was a virgin, but the way she's doing this has me questioning everything.

Then her soft hands rub against my hardness, adding pressure as her grip tightens, her tongue swirling around me, her determination evident.

"Kylo," she murmurs between breaths, her voice thick with desire.

I can't hold back any longer. "I'm going to," I start to warn, but before I can finish, the heat building inside me explodes. "Ohhhhh!" I jerk in her, unable to stand as sweat pours from me. That has never happened that fast before. She sucks me dry, not missing a drop.

"Shit… damn, girl. That was good as hell," I say, voice shaky.

I finger one of her golden beads between my fingers realizing something. I'm out of breath, breathing hard, feeling as though I've just run a marathon as I press her into the pillows.

I sink my teeth deep into her soft flesh, biting her, unable to stop the build in me. She meets my strength pressing me hard to her chest with her legs wrapping around me with her dampness mixing with mine.

She grinds against me, her movements so hard that the slippery suction of her wetness drowns out all background noise.

I pull back, breathless. "Cassidy, I want you. I want all of you."

She inches lower, positioning herself between my legs telling me what she wants. "I need you more, Kylo. I know we just got back together, but I can't wait. Please... make love to me."

My fingers tangle in her thick hair as I exhale deeply, pressing my forehead against her, already regretting what I have to say. We've gone too far. Holding her tightly, I force myself to focus, praying for the right words. "I can't disrespect Pittman in his home."

She stiffens in my grasp, disappointment, embarrassment and maybe shock cross her face. Then something shifts, her innocence replaced by determination. She's not giving in. She pulls away, as I back up, trying to create space.

"I can't do this out here," I say, my voice firm but strained. "I've already done enough. Pittman would have my ass if he knew I was out here doing this with you on his property."

Her dad is the only man alive who could stop me from getting into her. But I respect him. I always have. I can't start this off wrong.

"So, you're afraid of my dad?" she asks, teasing me in a way that makes me ache to bite her full lips.

Before I can respond, she moves, pulling away just enough to catch my attention.

She positions herself, legs wide open, her eyes locked on mine with a challenge I can't ignore. *What is she doing?* Her index finger trails slowly between her lips, down the curve of her neck, gliding between her breasts, and stopping at the enticing pull between her thighs.

Her manicured fingers get lost in between her legs, the glistening moisture catching my eye as she spreads herself wider.

That's enough to drive me damn crazy.

"I'm doing this," she whispers, her voice soft yet firm as she massages her breast and trails her fingers down to her wetness. My fists tighten at my sides, trying to keep myself in check.

"Kylo," she breathes, her voice drawing me in as she turns and bends over on all fours, exposing nothing but her perfect, beautiful ass all while continuing her slow massage.

"Damn, girl. I told you why I can't," I answer, not convincing myself and finding it hard to resist. *Fuck.* I crawl toward her getting ready to do something that I've never done.

"This is your fault, Cassidy," I grunt, still not understanding how my control is gone.

"I don't care, Kylo. Do whatever you want," she says, her voice lighting a fire inside me. I didn't need her permission after her little show, but hearing her say "do whatever you want" makes it that much easier to lose myself in her.

I spread her thighs wider, leaning in to bite her ass. Fuck, I want all of her. There's no turning back plus her ass is too tempting. I pull her closer, spreading her muscular legs apart, biting down harder this time, punishing her for even tempting me.

She looks back over her shoulder, her curls cascading onto the floor. "Do it again," she says.

Did she just say what I think she said?

"What did you say?" I ask, needing to be sure.

"You heard me. It felt good. Do it again." Even when she's bad there's an innocence with her that confuses the hell out of me.

"You're a bad girl, Cassidy?" I ask, curious about the way she's balancing this freakish confidence and lingering shyness.

"Only your bad girl," she says, biting her bottom lip, telling me who she belongs to.

"Damn right," I growl, reaching under her to spread her thighs, opening her up for me. I lick where I've never gone before and she doesn't flinch. Instead, she spreads her legs wider, pushing herself closer to where she wants me. Her grinding grows harder, her intensity showing me her desires.

I suck on her like she's the air for my next inhale, wrapping my arms tightly around her waist and sliding my fingers into her slick wetness. Damn she's so slippery, I feel like I can cum, again.

"Faster... Don't stop. Kylo, this is too much. I...I'm going to explode again," she cries, her voice trembling with need.

With that, I spread her legs further apart, my fingers working her wetness while my tongue sucks her sensitive spot. I massage her until she's so drenched she's slipping and sliding against my fingers, her body out of control. *I've never had anyone this wet.*

"Kylo, keep," she gasps, trembling out of control again. Her cream flows between my fingers, her body tightening and holding my hand hostage.

She collapses onto the pillows, her breaths coming fast and hard, still gripping my hand.

"You're going to kill me," she says, turning her gaze back on me, her eyes filled with awe, like I'm her superhero. *Yeah, I'm your Superman,* didn't Brooklyn tell you?

She peels her damp hair away from her forehead, sweat glistening along her skin catching the soft light. She squints at me, like she's trying to focus. "We haven't even had sex," she breathes, resting her tiny hands over her plush lips trying to catch her breath. "That was everything..."

The awe in her voice, wonder in her eyes, got my ego hitting a thousand. *Am I staring at her the same way?* She's beautiful, fine as hell and smart. She's a triple threat. And she doesn't even know it.

Most women with the big three are bad in bed. Not her. She might just be a straight freak and that's exactly what I want.

"Cassidy?"

"Yes? I love how my name rolls off your lips," she replies exhaling slowly, snuggling into my chest. She spreads her legs wide enough to pull my hand in between them, her possessiveness with her innocence are going to take some getting used to.

I pull her in closer, trying to focus on something other than what's already soft and wet. *Focus.*

"That was a first for me," I admit. "I've never done that with anyone. Never had a desire. But when I saw you I couldn't stop. Did that bother you?" I ask, realizing this is another first. When have I ever cared if I bothered or offended anyone?

She turns in my arms, keeping her sexy thighs open for my wandering fingers, then places her finger on my lips. "I have something to tell you," she whispers. "During our time together, there was something that I didn't tell you."

Fuck.

She shifts in my arms, tucking her face away, her body stiffening slightly. *What is it?* "Stop with the shyness," I say, then pull her narrow chin back to me, losing my battle with her wait.

Her fingers drift to her forehead, massaging the space between her brows as uncertainty bounces. She cocks her head to the side, expression shifting as if seeing me for the first time. "I'm trying not to let these honey hazel eyes distract me," her voice is low and hesitant. "But they always do. Who else has these in your family?"

The tension crawling up my spine is all too real. *This question. Damn* I usually avoid talking about my eyes, but something tells me she needs to know.

"My brother," I say, my voice quiet but steady. "We're the only two with the... honey hazels."

She stiffens, resting her hand on my cheek like she already knows what happened. "Sorry for asking," she murmurs.

"Why?" I finally ask, hesitating. Normally, I avoid everything about him.

"Because it bothers you," she says softly. "And if it bothers you, it bothers me."

Damn, her answer hits hard, telling me we had something

deeper, more serious months ago. I hate this memory loss. I need to remember all of her.

"You have something to tell me?" I ask, impatience creeping in as I struggle to hold on.

She hesitates, her fingers brushing her lips before she speaks. "This is all new for me. You were my first touch, my first kiss, my first hickey, my first…" her voice drops to a whisper, her eyes traveling downward as the shyness creeps back. "I am a virgin. So, whatever you do to me will be my first."

This girl is a gift. She's special. I suspected she was inexperienced, but not to this extent. Her first kiss? How? I pull her back into my arms, her thick full hair cushioning my chest like a pillow. She spoons into me, her bare skin making me harder than I was earlier.

"How? You're fucking perfect," I ask, needing to understand.

She clears her throat before she speaks. "When my mom got sick, my life stopped. I only wanted to help her. I didn't hang out, or anything like that. My dad hated me missing those rites of passage, as he calls them. But honestly, I wouldn't have changed a thing. I only wanted to be with her and my family," she pauses, with her emotions so raw I can feel her battling to hold back tears.

She sits up suddenly, maybe to push the thoughts away *and I instantly miss her closeness.* Damn. "Kylo, I only want you. And now that we have another chance, I don't want to let it go. What we had was so short months ago that I questioned every day if it was real. The only thing you left me with the night of the accident were your words. 'This is different.' That's all I had to hold onto. I gave up so many times, but Raith told me every day to tell you. And then, when VP Reed told me about your engagement, I really tried to let you go and forget. But I couldn't. These honey hazels kept making their way back to me. And now that I know the truth, I want us. I want what we started months ago."

Her words shock the hell out of me. *Damn.* "What did we have months ago and how long have my eyes been honey hazels?"

Her lashes sweep down as she closes her eyes, biting into her full bottom lip. "It was new, and warm, almost safe. Short in time but," her eyes open. "Special. We were just starting our first chapter. We didn't know much about each other, but I felt it. It was something different. *You* felt it, too."

She rests her trembling hands on my chest, nodding under my chin.

"Kylo, I agreed to be your girl earlier because I want to try. I know you don't remember, but I want to find out what we had. Your words, stayed with me. Maybe it'll grow. Maybe you'll remember. But I want our start, honey hazel."

Her eyes drop to her fingers tracing absent patterns across my chest, her anticipation clear. Damn, she's more mature than most women I've met, and she's only in her early twenties. "The worst part about this," I say, my voice low, "is not remembering you. You went through hell without me and that won't happen again. You're mine, and I'm yours. We'll figure this out because it is different. That's why we're not doing this out here."

She searches my face, her side smile creeping in, leaving me fighting not to bite her bottom lip.

So, you're still afraid of my dad?" she asks, her grin widening.

"Hell yeah," I reply, trying to lighten the mood, but the seriousness settles back in. "He can stop planes and helicopters from flying over his property. Put your clothes on. We're heading back."

She struts away, unbothered in her birthday suit, making it hard to focus. "Are you sure, Kylo?" she calls over her shoulder.

As we make our way back along the path, her words replay in my head, the weight of everything she's told me settling in my chest. She spent nights at the hospital, praying and taking care of me while I had no memory of her. She took the bus alone every night, at that time of night.

She should've never been on a bus that late. What did Pittman think of that?

We near a familiar clearing, the thinning trees signaling we're close to the house. The sound of footsteps snapping thin branches fills the air. Suddenly, she stops and I collide into her back. Before I can steady myself, she presses her ass into me, her hands finding my neck, squeezing, tightly. Instinctively, my hands move to her waist, then to her nipples. *Damn, I can't get enough of them.*

"The house is just over the hill," she says, her voice sultry as she glances back, "and the surveillance cameras are there, too. Are you sure there's nothing that I can do to change your mind?" Her hands guide mine between her legs, where she's already wet.

I pull back, knowing what she's doing. As I step back, I trip over a bare limb. Damn, this girl doesn't take no for an answer. *This is different.*

She turns to face me, her gaze burning into my sweatpants. "Are you certain we can't have a moment before we go up?" she asks, her hands slipping inside my waistband, disappearing from view.

How in the hell does her bare touch turn me on so fast? She's a quick learner, and I know we're going to be good together. I take her bottom lip between mine, sucking her tongue into my mouth as her hand strokes me with the skills of a straight pro, leaving me confused until my brain finally decides to work.

I pull away, gripping her arms gently but firmly to her sides. "I told you no."

She shakes her narrow shoulders free, her determination crazy. "Kylo, you can if you want to," she whispers, leaning into me, her soft breasts pressing against my chest. *Why is she making this so damn hard?*

Ignoring the angel on my shoulder telling me to stop, I twist her around, letting the devil win. She reaches back into my sweatpants again, as her muscular thighs spread, her bare ass pressing against me since the green lacy thong is shredded and in my pocket for later.

How the hell is this girl dripping again? Nothing but wetness. The slippery moisture running down her thighs is unreal. The evening breeze catches her dress, lifting it just enough to expose that toxic body, leaving me powerless. She holds the adjacent tree with one hand while stroking me with the other. She's so soft and slippery that the moment I touch her I fucking lose myself.

"Harder and faster, Kylo!" she cries, her voice filled with urgency. "Don't stop...please don't stop!" Her wetness floods my hand.

I run my index through her slit, caressing her clit, unable to grip that waterfall she has. She's gripping me so tight that exploding again is coming too fast.

"Damn!" I mutter, trying to catch my breath. How the hell is this happening so fast? I move to pull my pants down, needing to spread my legs to let it flow, but she kneels, taking me in her soft, warm lips again sucking me off.

"Shit!" My entire body tremors as I shoot inside her warm suction. "Damn, girl! You got me out here bad!" I cum harder with a force leaving me weak in my knees clinging to the tree for support.

Her curious eyes look upward, framed by long lashes revealing a mix of innocence and bad girl. She gazes at me, licking the corner of her lips as she swallows, her shyness returning as she wipes her mouth with her nude nails.

"I love the way your sweetness tastes flowing down me," she says, her voice soft but deliberate. "I'll tell you exactly how I want it when we make love."

I laugh to myself, confused as hell. *Who is this bipolar, shy, sex freak?*

"Let's go, beautiful," I say, shaking my head. "Before I break your back off against this damn tree."

CHAPTER 39

FINALLY...

Cassidy

LYING ON MY BED, REMINISCING OVER THE PAST FEW DAYS has me feeling dizzy, woozy and carefree. Raith would die if she heard that description, but I can't help it. *What is this feeling?*

Every thought of him from Tuesday puts a smile on my face and dampens my thong. Never did I think I'd be this open with anyone. Sex has never been on my radar or something that I'd even thought about until recently. Like Tuesday... three days ago recently.

Lately, I've been waking most nights, hyper aware of his hands, his mouth, his voice. The memories are so vivid they make me ache, just remembering how he touches me, how I bite my bottom lip until it hurts. Sometimes I wake on the verge of an orgasm, my body on fire from wanting him so bad.

I would have had sex with him right there against that tree if he'd wanted to. *What has gotten into me, or maybe, what hasn't.*

The most amazing thing was the oral sex. I had no idea what I was doing, but the way he reacted to my touch, *to me*, made my confidence skyrocket. The taste of him, the way his body heated made me feel powerful especially when he asked me to make him remember. I tried to suck the memory right back into his head. *That right there. Something has to be wrong with me.*

I know he's been with plenty of women more experienced, but I think I shocked him. I know I shocked myself. The embarrassment of it, everything I was doing, made me shy. But his tongue made me forget. I can do this with him every day. *What is wrong with me?*

Dad still isn't letting me out of his sight or back on campus until the media fuss cools. Kylo's blowup at the fence helped push most of the reporters to other stories, but it sparked new rumors about us being a couple.

After a few long conversations with Dad, he finally agreed Kylo could visit. He uses the side entrance daily to avoid the cameras. He's been here every afternoon this week, and it's been so easy, so natural with him. We've spent a little time hiking, watching movies and learning more about each other. Even our bodies snap perfectly into our own jigsaw puzzle when we're snuggling on the sofa.

I check my Apple Watch. Kylo should be here in fifteen minutes. The memory of waiting like this months ago makes the back of my neck tense. I stretch it to ease the lingering tension from that night, and hope that never happens again.

Time to get ready. I force myself out of bed, my mind already thinking what to do with my hair. Days ago, this was never a thought. A ponytail and tennis shoes were my norm during the week. But lately, I've been changing it up and wearing makeup and trying different hairstyles. I never paid attention to my looks before or did the extra, but Kylo drives me to embrace my sensual side.

The way he notices me, as if it's the first time he's ever seen me, has me planning to give him something new every day. The awe in those honey hazels makes me feel…find the word, Cassidy.

Getting more alone time with him has been hard because he's refusing to go any further. Maybe it's morals or maybe something else holding him back. If I can get him outside, maybe he'll do more. Because I need more of him in me… literally.

Miss Rita clears her throat by the doorway, making me jump.

"Lost in dreamland again, I see," she says, folding her arms across her floral house dress.

Where I've been all week, lost in his kisses, his fingers. If I said that out loud, Miss Rita might have a stroke. "Oh…nowhere," I mumble. "I'm just…ready to get back to school, I guess. It's my first-year back, and I've already missed three track meets. I need to hit the field. Plus, I miss Raith."

Her eyes narrow, reading my face. "I get that. But John doesn't play with your safety. Never has, never will," she says, leaving no room for argument.

A silent sigh lingers in my chest. "I know, but the story is dead. The reporters haven't been around the gates for days. Even social media is better. They've moved on to bigger stories by now."

"Ahhh…social media," Miss Rita says with a chuckle. "The thing that makes folks feel good about themselves from a thumbs up." She places a tray of cinnamon rolls in the oven, her laughter light and teasing. I'd bet anything she's baking them for Kylo.

"It's called a *like*," I correct her, trying not to laugh. "No one my age even uses Facebook anymore."

"Baby girl, things are bad if a 'thumb' makes you feel good about yourself. No internet should have that type of power over you young folk."

"I rarely pay attention to it, Miss Rita. It's too addictive."

The doorbell chimes, and my heart skips a beat. How does this feeling have me lost in a crazy haze where everything else fades away? *This is definitely different.*

Our security heads to the door, escorting Kylo into the kitchen. The outside breeze carries the intoxicating scent of his cologne ahead of him. He smells incredible. *What is it?* My body heats instantly, and he hasn't stepped foot in the kitchen yet.

How does he affect me like this?

"Miss Rita, what's that smell?" he asks, walking straight to the kitchen, past me without a touch. Over the past few days, I've learned that food always comes first for him before anything or anyone else.

WAKE ME   339

It's surreal how quickly he feels at home here. Everyone gravitates toward him, like paper clips drawn on a magnet. Even Miss Rita and the staff love him, but not Dad. They're cordial but not overly friendly.

I watch as his long, muscular legs flex with every step, showing off his natural confidence. Are some people just born with confidence, or is it something you learn? He's not arrogant, just comfortable in his own skin.

Hopefully, soon he'll meet the rest of the crew. They're never home. Always traveling together. Right now, they're in Europe for the week, competing in a dance competition. From the outside looking in, they seem inseparable, needing each other more since Mom passed. Sometimes it leaves me feeling like an outsider, like I'm not a part of their unbreakable twin bond.

His rough hands slide under the lace of my top, massaging my bare shoulders. Even though his fingers are as coarse as sandpaper, the skin-to-skin contact takes me to another level. "Hey Beautiful," he whispers, his raspy baritone wrapping around me like a warm blanket. Then he leans in, kissing my forehead. Even his scent makes me tighten my thighs. *What cologne is that?* He smells so good.

"Hey," I reply, my voice soft as my shyness creeps back in. My multiple personalities kick in confusing me, from my shy introvert to this oversexualized vixen dictating how she wants it. Is this normal?

Something has awakened in me that I didn't even realize was dormant. Thinking back to the tent makes me almost embarrassed. Who was that girl, legs wide open, trying to get him closer? What was I doing?

"Whew..." The word escapes before I realize it as he leans in closer.

"Am I the reason for the whew?" he whispers, his lips grazing my ear as Miss Rita stirs something on the stove, pretending not to notice.

I exhale, biting my lip, feeling the pressure build. "Yes, that was for you."

He looks amused, his gaze unable to stop drilling into my heart. "You ready to go?" he asks, cocking his head to the side.

"Yes!" That was too much excitement. *Calm down, Cassidy.*

"Good, beautiful." He takes my index finger, pulling me toward him as I slide off the barstool, helplessly following. "Let's go."

"Alright you two, no trouble, now. It's your first day out the gates," Miss Rita warns, her words of caution nothing new.

He releases my finger and circles the island with a teasing grin. "Miss Rita, does it look like I can be trouble?" he asks, spreading his arms wide.

"Yes, you look like some handsome, big trouble," she replies. "Be careful with my baby girl, you hear me, macho man?" She attempts to punch him in the chest, I think, but it lands somewhere around his stomach. Miss Rita is so short.

"Yes, ma'am. Nothing will ever happen to her while she's with me," Kylo says, his voice steady, glancing at me with a sly look that makes my stomach flip. *Will he do this already?*

"Alright you two," Miss Rita says, handing Kylo a container of cinnamon rolls.

Once inside his new Ford F-150 truck, he leans back, motioning for me to come closer. He reclines it even farther, creating more space. *How far back will this thing go?*

I straddle his hard thighs, exactly where I want to be. Before I can fully adjust, his lips are on mine, kissing with a need that's impossible to describe. His hands grip my ribcage firmly, his thumbs rising higher and higher until they gently ease my dress down.

I return his kiss with equal intensity, savoring every second, not wanting to miss a moment. My hands slide into his neck, massaging deeply as my nails dig into his skin, anchoring me to him. My body's desire overpowers me, leaving no room for hesitation, no space to slow down.

His thumbs pull my nipples from my lacy bra, making me grind against him harder for the friction to cum. His rough, calloused hands unhook my bra with practiced ease.

He holds me tightly around my waist, as if I'm planning to escape.

"Damn, I've missed these pretty beads, girl," he murmurs, his tongue brushing over me, taking his time with each one savoring every second. I lean back against the steering wheel, overtaken by the heat and urgency of his mouth. He's milking on me like he's nursing.

"I just wanted to see you naked," he whispers against my skin. "But once I start... I can't stop." He pulls my ponytail back, exposing my neck and sinks his teeth into me with at bite that's possessive and raw. My alter ego kicks in, wanting him to bite harder.

"Harder, Kylo," I grit out, my voice strained but careful not to scream too loud in case security is nearby.

He sucks into me puncturing my skin for blood, as though he's trying to take more than I can give. I arch against him, surrendering, offering more, everything he wants. His teeth graze my breasts, biting down like I'm the last drip of ice cream melting off the side of the cone in his truck months ago.

My body moves on auto pilot, grinding against his hard midsection.

"Slow down girl," he says, pulling back, holding my hips in place and snapping my bra in one motion.

He leans his forehead against my chin, taking slow, deep breaths. "You got me out here in this driveway, wide open. Damn," he grunts, shaking his head like he's battling to stop.

His hands tighten around my waist as he tries to lift me back in my seat, but I cling to him, pulling his head back to meet my lips. "Open, baby. I need to taste you," I whisper, caressing the side of his face, sucking his tongue into my mouth with an intensity that matches his.

Without warning, he stops. Effortlessly, he moves me, placing me in my seat like I weigh nothing. *He's so strong.* At a hundred and twenty pounds, he handles me as if I'm featherlight.

He removes the windshield shade, cranks up the air conditioner, and leans into the steering wheel, his chest rising and falling heavily.

"Girl, I have to stop before I mess up and have sex with you on Pittman's property," he says, snapping his seatbelt into place.

He could have done that a week ago. *What is wrong with me?* I need to change the subject. "How much do you weigh?" I ask, desperate for a distraction as I watch him maneuver his truck down our winding driveway. I love watching him handle his truck.

"This is two twenty of solid muscle," he replies, hitting his chest and flexing his arm into an L shape. "There's no fat on here, lovely."

He's an entire human larger than me. Raith would definitely laugh at that description. But with a hundred pounds on me, it's true. "Where are we going?" I ask, curious. He hadn't been willing to share our destination earlier.

I hope it's somewhere just for the two of us. I don't want to share him, especially on our first official day as a couple. *A couple.* That's so new for me. *I have a boyfriend.* My heart felt like it was going to explode when he asked in the tent, but he wouldn't know because my thoughts were on one thing, his hands, lips and tongue.

I didn't think he'd want this so quickly. I've had more time to fall for him, to get to know him, than he's had with me. *Are we rushing this?*

"I thought we'd go meet some people," he says, his voice uncertain as if testing the idea. "It's about an hour drive from here. Is that alright?"

His honey hazels linger on me, waiting for my answer. I want to be wherever he is. I don't care, as long as it's with me. But I don't say that. Instead, I reply with, "Sure."

Why is the shyness creeping back? There's something about him that makes me want to melt inside of myself sometimes, to retreat. But then there are moments when I want to suck him dry, to have him completely, leaving nothing behind. *What is wrong with me?*

I shift in my seat, unbuckling my seatbelt to get comfortable, positioning myself toward him.

His eyes widen in surprise as he watches me lean my head against my window and spread my legs wide on his seat. "Put on your seat belt," he says through clenched teeth. His gaze chasing between my thighs and the road. "I'm not taking any chances with you. Make it click, Cassidy."

There's something in the way he says my name that makes me want to obey. *But not completely.* I slowly adjust my seatbelt, other plans forming in my mind for our hour-long drive.

I prop my legs apart again, savoring the way his cautious glances hang between my legs before returning to the road. He sits up with his left arm straight on the steering wheel, shifting to the slower lane as he decreases our speed. His free hand wanders down… down…exactly where I want it. Where I *need* it.

"Girl, what are you doing?" he asks, his fingers brushing against my bare skin. He notices, no thong.

I wish I could explain it myself. I often don't know why I do half the things I do with him. It's like something takes over my thoughts, my body, everything in me needing release. *Am I going crazy?* Instead of sharing that, I say, "Let's play a little Q & A."

His smile fades into something more dazed. "You think you can handle Q & A while I do this?" he asks, his fingers working their magic, tickling my dampness. *Whew he's doing this so right.*

"What's the first question, Cassidy?" he murmurs.

How did I forget the Q & A? How am I supposed to form questions when all I want to do is scream. His finger slips out, leaving me lifting my hips to beg for more until I see what he's doing.

His fingers disappear into his mouth, his lips wrapping around them like he's savoring a popsicle on a hot summer day. A *cold popsicle, Cassidy? Really?* But that's exactly how it looks, slow, deliberate, not missing a single drop.

I shouldn't be surprised by anything he does, but somehow, I always am. Maybe that's why he affects me so much.

He faces the road, his focus steady even as his hand find its way to my wetness again, massaging until the unmistakable sound fills the truck. *How am I this wet?*

I lift to give him better access, forcing myself to remember a question. "What's your favorite color?" I ask, voice shaking.

"White," he says, without hesitation.

"Why?" I whisper, gripping the seat to control the sensations building inside me.

"It's pure, clean, untouched," he murmurs, his voice deep and steady. "What's your color, beautiful?"

I can barely keep my eyes open. "Yellow," I reply.

"Why?" he asks, his fingers don't let up.

I struggle to focus. "Why beautiful?" he repeats, his fingers making me wetter.

"It makes me hopeful for," I gasp, forcing the words out, "happiness."

"Do I make you happy?" he grunts, his fingers finding my breaking point. The cold air from the AC hits against my legs as his fingers send me climbing higher, closer to the edge. It's like scaling a mountain, only to tumble over the peak in freefall. My body shakes out of control, the release leaving me weightless floating in midair before gently settling back onto his truck seat.

"Yes," I manage to say through shuddering breaths. "You make me happy. So happy."

My breathing slows, and he continues to massage me gently. I open my eyes, adjust myself in his seat feeling off. Guilt and shame hit me hard. *Why did I do that? What is wrong with me?*

I reach into my bag for wipes and my thong, my mind racing. *Is it normal to act this way? Do most women feel like this?* Maybe I should call Raith. This is all so new to me.

"What is it?" he asks, full of concern. "Did I hurt you?"

That's a strange question. I don't think he's even capable of hurting me, not physically.

"No..."

"Then what is it?" He leans closer, his scent of cologne taking my senses, clouding my thoughts. I want to pull him closer, undo his jeans straddle on his... Cassidy, *stop and get it together.*

I place my left hand near the side of my face, avoiding his honey hazels drilling into me. "I think somethings wrong with me," I admit, quietly. "I can't stop myself when I'm with you."

My shyness shows her ugly color again, making me glance out my passenger window, hoping for a distraction. But there's nothing, just trees for miles, their branches coated with yellow pollen, waiting to turn green.

He takes my hand into his, rough calluses grinding me. "Soon, beautiful," he says. "This isn't easy for me. Hell, I want you more than anything. But I want us to have more time. This is more than sex for me. I want you... I want us... I want this to last. Plus, I have a special place where I want to take you for your first time."

He tightens his grip on my hand and lifts it to his lips, pressing a soft kiss to my knuckles.

"What does *soon* mean? I don't know if I can wait long. It better get here quick before I take what I want!" And here she is again, my alter ego kicking in telling him exactly what I want. *He has to think I'm crazy. I'm starting to think so myself.*

"Is that right? You think you can just take it?" The surprise in his voice and the drawl catches my attention, making me glance his way.

"I think I can be persuasive enough when I have to be," I reply, voice steady despite the chaos in my chest.

His grip on the steering wheel tightens as if it's the only thing keeping him away from reaching me. "Yes, you can be," he says, his voice thick with restraint. "I love your little feisty ass."

Wait a minute... did he say *love?*

After an hour's drive, we enter a gated community. It's a newer neighborhood, with young trees barely able to stand upright without their wire supports. The homes are immaculate but vary in design, each sitting on what looks like three acres of land.

My nerves suddenly begin to creep in as I glance around,

wondering if this is the home he shares with his mom. He'd mentioned this place once, but I didn't think it would be our first stop. *I'm not ready to meet her.* I feel like I need more time with him, *more alone time.* He's met most of my family except my sisters and… Mom.

I wonder what she would think of him. What would she think of us? Would she be okay with this?

"Why are you so quiet?" His question brings me out of my thoughts, making me jump slightly. *Calm down*, Cassidy.

"Are we meeting your mom?" I ask, half hoping we're not, wishing for somewhere private. I'm okay with meeting his family eventually, but I want to make a good impression.

We pull into the driveway of a well-manicured home in the center of a cul-de-sac, surrounded by pink crepe myrtles. The tan stucco home has a wraparound porch with rocking chairs, planters and hanging flower baskets overflowing with ferns. It's a blend of rustic charm and modern elegance, reminding me of Miss Rita's home on our property. *I love it.*

"Yes, we are," he replies, shifting the truck into park. But there's hesitation in his voice. "I told you, I want you in my life so that means being around my folks. The other ones I love," he pauses as if surprised by his own words. *Did he just say it again?*

I want to climb into his lap, but I push the thought away, reminding myself that it would be a *bad idea.* "Okay," I say quietly. "I just… don't want to disappoint them."

He looks at me the way he did at the Grove when he told me everything about me was beautiful. How do I remember all his expressions so well?

"My family's cool," he reassures me. "Plus, Aunt Diane is here. You've met her … right?"

The memory of the hospital flashes back, sitting on my so-called "crazy bench" with her telling me this probably wasn't where I should be. *Great*, she might already think I'm unhinged.

"Yes, we met," I answer, remembering the jacket she left behind.

I'd better get it out of the house before Miss Rita steals it. She fell in love with it the moment I showed it to her.

He gets out of his truck and motions me his way. Holding his hand, I step to his side, checking my makeup and hair in his side mirror before straightening my dress. "How do I look?"

His lips curl into a grin, his honey hazels glinting with amusement. "Beautiful enough to eat," he says, his voice deep and steady. "From the day you got in my ice, to the track field, to when I woke up on those sexy legs of yours. You should never have to ask."

His words "beautiful enough to eat" hits in an area already missing him. Why did he say that? "It was my ice bath not yours, Kylo. I was in there first, and you barged in with your big feet and asked me to get closer. I think someone told you our story wrong."

He smiles, resting his hand on his chin, as though holding back a laugh. "And did you obey?" he asks, his left eyebrow arching, waiting for my response.

"Of course not. I left you alone and in the dark," I reply, crossing my arms.

His eyes narrow, studying me like he can't imagine that ever happening.

"You're sure you left? Christian told me about the ice. What were you wearing?"

"A two-piece bikini," I say with a slight smile, remembering Raith's teasing when I told her about it.

"That's the reason I got in that ice. Girl, you might've solved a fifteen-year problem for my coaches. You sure you didn't get comfortable?" his bottom lip catches between his teeth as he waits for my response.

My heart skips at the familiar words. *Get comfortable*. He said those exact words months ago.

"I'm sure you think I'm easy, based on my recent escapades. But no, I left you in the dark because you were rude."

"Nothing about you is easy, Cassidy. Believe that," he says, pulling me behind him toward the stone sidewalk. I try not to stare at his bow legs, making me walk faster to keep up. How does he make Nike sweats look so good? I stare away hoping the brownish tan sidewalk matching the color of the house takes my attention. I count each stone careful not to stand in the grout. *Why am I counting?*

Before we reach the porch, the front door swings open. His Aunt Diane stands in the entrance wearing a cream cashmere sweatsuit, motioning Kylo to step aside.

"I knew we would meet again," she says warmly, pulling me into a comforting hug. Her embrace is strong and enveloping, her spicy-sweet Victor & Rolf Flowerbomb perfume surrounds me.

The scent hits me hard, stirring something deep in my chest. *Mom.* It was her favorite. I don't think I've ever noticed it on anyone else until now.

Kylo clears his throat, breaking the moment. "That's a long hug," he jokes, a teasing smile tugging the corners of his lips.

As Aunt Diane releases me, I glimpse between the two of them, my eyes misty with embarrassment but *no tears*. "I'm sorry," I say, hastily as both she and Kylo watch me. I need to explain. "That hug reminded me of my mom. I'm so sorry." Why am I always so emotional? Pull it together, Cassidy. You *don't want his family thinking you're some kind of weak mental case.*

"Oh, sweet girl. You have a lot of those coming," a soft voice echoes from the foyer. I don't need an introduction, it's obvious she's Kylo's mom. They share the same face minus his honey hazels.

"I am this guy's mom, Juanita," she says, pointing at Kylo's chest before pulling me in for another hug. *I could get used to this.*

I can barely get a whisper out, but I try anyway. "It's such a pleasure to meet you."

"We've been looking forward to seeing you for weeks," she says, pulling back to hold me at arm's length. She's short, with a round frame and short pixie cut that fits her perfectly.

"Miss Blade, come on," Kylo says. Is that embarrassment coming from him?

Miss Blade shakes her head, smiling at him. "Well, we have.

Come in, young lady. The pictures Kylo showed us don't do you any justice. You are simply breathtaking."

"Thank you," I respond, hoping my earlier breakdown didn't make anyone uncomfortable.

"I told you, Juanita," Aunt Diane interjects, crossing her arms with a knowing smile. "When I saw her at the hospital, I knew Kylo took one look at her and fell in love."

"You two do realize I'm still in the room, right?" Kylo asks, his voice full of fake irritation.

"Of course you're here. You take up the entire room. Come here, son."

I watch both women embrace him, and he kisses them on top of their heads, towering over them. *I love this for him.*

He excuses himself, heading to the kitchen. "What y'all got cooking? I'm hungry."

Aunt Diane follows him, shaking her head. "Well, that's nothing new. This boy eats like every meal is his last. Help me set the table," she says over her shoulder.

I can't help but smile, wondering how he's hungry after eating four cinnamon rolls on the way here. He said sweets were his thing months ago and I guess that hasn't changed.

Miss Juanita motions for me to follow her into a beautifully decorated sitting room. The bay windows are framed by an outside garden and the room is filled with African artwork, carved masks, sculptures and textiles. Each piece is alive with geometric patterns and animals, especially elephants, as the focus.

"Have you traveled to Africa? All of this is so beautiful?" I ask, my eyes lingering on a carved wooden lion standing in the corner.

She looks around the room as if seeing it through my eyes for the first time. "No, sweet girl, I've never traveled to Africa, and at my age, maybe never will. But it's a place that lives close to my heart," she says, adjusting her body toward me and reaching for my hand. "Thank you for bringing my son back to me."

Her words catch me off guard, leaving me speechless. I open my mouth, but no words come, so I nod and wait.

"What I watched at that hospital was a young woman pouring all her strength into bringing my son back. What you did was more than a miracle. It was a yearning to get him to come back, not only to us but to you," she pauses, her gaze softening. "Do you love my son?"

Her question hangs in the air, lost in between the tribal masks decorating her walls to the carved lions, standing guard in the room. I feel a sense of relief when her kind eyes shift away, giving me space to gather my thoughts.

I don't know what to say. It still surprises me how I was at the hospital every night, taking the bus. That has to be a scream for love, right? But how? My dad always said there's no timeline when it comes to love, and I think he's right.

Every time I think of him in that hospital, a piece of my heart aches. Every night I spent without him felt like a struggle, and the thought of him not being mine takes my breath away. Even now, I feel the urge to look back and make sure he's okay and breathing with his smart mouth ready to say something crazy.

This whole thing is short, fast and doesn't make sense, but deep down, I know I can't be without him. I want the Kylo who cared for Monty, Brooklyn and so many others with genuine kindness. The Kylo that makes my body burn like a broken thermostat.

"Yes...I think I do love him. Still confused at how fast it happened, but I really do," I whisper, admitting this to the last person I thought I would...his mom.

She nods, her face softening. "I understand, sweet girl. Kylo may not yet. You see, it takes men a little longer to navigate matters of the heart. But I saw *your* heart in that hospital room and I thank you from the bottom of mine for what you did that day."

She hugs me with the grace of a mom who understands my emptiness, her hand gently patting my shoulder as I snuggle into her embrace. It feels like the comfort I've missed for years. Kylo's mom is truly special.

She releases me but holds onto my hands, her warmth feeling me. "That was a bit much to share but you're the first girl, well girlfriend that Kylo has brought home," her words catch me off guard.

"You all's time together was short," she continues, her voice kind but firm, "Kylo shared that with me. But there's something about you that's bringing my son back to himself. I haven't seen him smile or look at ease as he did a few minutes ago at the door in years. He's faked so much over time, trying to make me think he's alright. But in my soul, I've known he wasn't. When he walked in here with you today, I saw my little boy's real smile from the tenth grade. I haven't seen it since," she pauses, looking at the bookshelf before settling back on me.

"You're the reason for that, and I never want it to disappear. You both deserve to love without fear of loss or the weight of time."

She rises, her movements slow and deliberate, resting her hand on her lower back. "Come over here, please. Can I show you someone?"

I follow her to a white bookshelf built into the wall. Her trembling fingers reach for a large picture in a gold frame. "These are my babies. Did Kylo mention to you that he had a brother?"

I look at the photograph of two boys, their clothes tight and worn. Kylo, though inches taller, hugs his older brother, leaving no space between them. His carefree smile is so different from the man I met months ago, who rarely let his teeth show. Even during his interview, his smiles seemed for the cameras, not for himself.

I trace my fingers over the little boy's smile, wishing I could bring back even a fraction of that happiness for him. "Yes, he mentioned it earlier in the week," I say softly. We'd talked briefly about Tron, but Kylo never dwelled on it and I didn't push. I didn't think he was ready.

She places the picture back on the shelf as though it's her most cherished trophy, her hand resting on her heart. "He died in a car accident years ago," she says, her voice trembling slightly. She sniffs, managing a small smile as she looks at the gold frame.

I read about Tron while Kylo was in the hospital, but I never brought it up during our late-night talks between twelve and four a.m. I didn't want to risk him choosing to follow the light to be with his brother instead of coming back to me.

"I'm so sorry," I say, lightly touching her narrow shoulder. My eyes catch the sparkle of the gold frame again as the load of her loss fills the room.

"A mother should never have to lose a child, and a child should never have to lose a mother. None of this should ever happen," she says, her loss radiating in the silence between us. I know this feeling all too well and hate to live it daily. *Why does death have to happen?*

Her shoulders slump as she exhales deeply, the sound igniting that pit of nausea that comes with thinking of loss. "The pain is so deep and constant that some days, it's hard to make it," she admits, her eyes glazing over with unshed tears.

"I know," I whisper, nodding. *No tears.*

She places a comforting hand on my shoulder, her grip firm yet gentle, as though trying to squeeze strength into the both of us. "I'm so sorry about your mom, sweet girl. Whenever you have a moment like you did at the door, do not ever apologize or hesitate. I'm your shoulder now, and these hugs are just for you."

Footsteps approach from behind, and soon an arm rests on my shoulder. His scent surrounds me, warm and protective, as he hugs us both. She and I relax into his chest. He's big enough to fit Aunt Diane in a group hug too, if she wanted to join.

"You two okay?" he asks, softly.

His mom stares at him, then back at me, as though seeing this moment for the first time. "Yes, my love. I was showing Cassidy.... Tron."

His body stiffens instantly, his muscles hardening as the tension ripples through him. I don't loosen my grip on his back, afraid he might shatter if I let go.

"I miss him," he mumbles, barely able to get the words out, each one full of pain.

I see his mom hold her breath, trying to stay strong for him. "I know you do, baby," she says, gently, her voice trembling but steady. "I'm so glad to finally hear you say it," her arms tighten around us both, a tremor passing through her as if she's releasing years of buried sorrow. "He's still watching over us. That never stopped, son."

She releases us, and I already miss her presence. "Okay, you two. I'm going to help your Aunt Diane with the food, then maybe we'll watch a movie after dinner," she says, smiling as she hugs me again. *I needed this.*

Kylo loops his arms around me, his palms resting on my stomach. My eyes catch the glimmer of the gold frame again, and though I hesitate, I can't stop myself from asking. "You okay?"

His chest feels so tight against my back. I almost hold my breath, waiting for his exhale.

"It won't go away. I miss that dude every second of the day," he says, his voice strained, not overwhelmed with visible emotion, but carrying a tension so rigid it feels like it might break him.

It makes me ache to take his pain away, to loosen the weight of this on him. I turn to face him, rising onto my tiptoes bringing him closer. "Then, never let him go away, Kylo. Keep him with you. He lives here," I say, placing my hand over his heart. "He lives here when you need him, when it hurts, when you're afraid and when you feel alone. Never let his memory go or that gold frame. He always lives with you. That's where my mom lives."

My voice trembles, but I keep my gaze steady.

He leans in closer, his fingertips brushing the center of my back. "You're so good. That makes me one damn lucky man with your pretty ass."

I was hoping he'd say more about his brother, but he's not ready. I won't push him.

"Oh, so my 'ass' is pretty?" I tease.

Awe crosses his face, his expression screaming, *Are you for real?* "Every part of you is pretty."

"Well, we better go before I show you again how pretty it is," I reply, tempted to run my tongue in the center of his right dimple. Instead, I opt for a kiss.

"You're a bad girl," he whispers into my ear, the heat of his breath making me hotter.

"Correction, *your* bad girl," I rephrase, grinning.

"Damn right," he kisses my forehead, lingering long enough for my body to heat even more. Whew this man truly makes my clothes want to fall off. Those were Raith's words. *I miss her.*

These two women together could open a restaurant. That meal was absolutely amazing. *Who makes Greek chicken, roasted potatoes, green beans and red velvet swirl cake for lunch during the weekday?* Between these two and Miss Rita, I could gain ten pounds in a week. "Thank you both for an early dinner. It was beyond good," I say, hoping my compliment does it justice.

"Well, you didn't eat enough," Kylo's mom replies, her voice soft but full of concern. "Are you sure I can't make you more?"

Normally, more dessert is a big *no* but that moist red velvet that melted in my mouth earlier? *Hard to resist.* "Would you mind if I had another slice of cake?" I ask, knowing I should probably stop while ahead.

"I told you, Miss Blade, she has a sweet tooth like you," Kylo says, with a grin, making me wonder what else he tells her.

"I don't eat that many sweets, Kylo," I add, narrowing my eyes at him. *What is he talking about? Do I?*

"I don't see you turning down anything sweet," he replies, massaging his goatee with mischief brewing in his eyes.

Ohhh …. I get what he's talking about, and it's not food. *I'm going to kill him.*

He leans in as he walks past me, his voice low and teasing, "I love how your sweetness flows down my body."

"Kylo!" I squeal, hitting him on the shoulder twice. *I can't believe him*, but I should.

"I'm just saying," he jokes, heading around the counter to wash his hands and slice the cake. Both women watch him closely, their eyes following every move like he's never cut a slice of cake before.

Kylo places the knife in the sink, and grabs a napkin and hands me the plate with an expression telling me he's not done as he murmurs, "Save room for later."

I almost choke on my icing.

"Okay, you two, we'll have mint tea in the sunroom. Come this way," Miss Blade says, looping her arm through mine and escorting me. Normally, this level of comfort with someone would take time, but with Kylo's mom, it's been so easy.

I nibble on the cake, noticing the uneasy silence in the room and the soft clink of my fork on the plate. Both Aunt Diane and Miss Blade keep glancing at Kylo, their lingering worry visible, as though there's something unspoken weighing on them. *What is it?*

"Miss Blade, not today. I told you, I'm not talking today," Kylo says, standing and walking out of the room, leaving me lost with what's happening and even more confused why he's calling his mom Miss Blade.

"Kylo, we have to talk!" she yells after him, her determination making me jump. He doesn't look back. *What am I missing?*

I look between the three of them, realizing I'm out of the loop.

"Kylo, we have to talk about soccer!" Aunt Diane screams, her hands thrown wide before she clasps them together as if praying for divine intervention.

"No, we don't!" Kylo yells from the hall, frustration in every word.

"Son, it was one bad game. There's no need to throw it all away because of that!" Aunt Diane's pleading sets off questions. *Throw it all away? What's going on with soccer?*

Wait a minute… He is playing soccer, right? "Excuse me, what's going on?" I ask, hoping it's nothing serious.

Aunt Diane sighs, meeting my eyes. "Oh, you don't know. He hasn't been to practice in days. No contact with his agent or the team. His agent has been trying to reach him for over a week now. He even came by yesterday, but Kylo refused to talk or even see him."

My stomach drops as I turn toward the hallway, piecing it together. Why hasn't he been returning calls? And then it hits me. He's been with me every day this past week. *Am I the reason?*

"How bad was the last game?" I ask, hesitantly, guilt twisting in my chest.

"It was bad!" Kylo's voice suddenly cuts through as he reenters the room. I didn't even hear him come back. He stares at the three of us, his jaw tight and eyes blazing. He shakes his head before storming out again.

Is he counting?

I glance between Aunt Diane and Miss Blade, feeling just as startled as their expressions suggest. "Why is he doing this?"

They take turns explaining everything about his body, not responding during training, lapses in memory and judgment and the worst game of his career marking his supposed comeback.

"We don't want him to throw away his chances and give up," Aunt Diane says softly, placing a consoling hand on Miss Blade's back. "He's come so far. It's heartbreaking to watch him shut everyone out like this."

Miss Blade leans forward, resting her arms on her thighs, covering her mouth with her fingers. Their bond reminds me of Raith and my crew back home. The sisterhood, the way they hold each other up when the world feels too heavy.

I sink back into my chair, trying to slow my brain. *Focus.*

"What do you mean give up? Do you all think he's serious about not playing anymore?"

Miss Blade nods, expression grim. "Yes, in so many words that's his plan. At least that's what it seems like. He hasn't returned any of Bruce's calls."

"Bruce is his agent, right?"

Miss Blade answers. "Yes, he's been with him since he started playing professionally."

I let her words sink in. My dad mentioned his game was bad, but I've been floating in la la land, lost in Kylo and ignoring everything else. We talked some about it, but he always has a way of steering the conversation away from the uncomfortable. *I've got to get better control of that.*

"Where is he?" I ask.

"He's either in the trophy room or downstairs in his place," Aunt Diane replies.

I walk to the hallway, finding him seated in what appears to be a sports room filled with memorabilia from soccer and football games. *Did he play football, too?* He must have won every soccer award possible because the room is covered with pictures, certificates, and news articles of him. There are a few photos scattered here and there: his mom, brother and three girls who I assume are Aunt Diane's daughters. But most of the space is dedicated to Kylo's awards.

I laugh softly at the picture on the table where he's towering over his entire family. *He's so big.* I love how Miss Blade saved it all. My mom did the same thing for us.

As I step into the room, Kylo notices me. His eyes lock on mine, unblinking. I let the moment linger, the clicking of my heels echoing in the quiet space. *I'll wait.* The tension stretches between us as he slowly walks toward me, his gaze never leaving mine. *Is he trying to read me?*

His fingers brush my hair from my face, gently tilting my chin upward. His kiss is soft, almost pleading for forgiveness. *Be strong Cassidy.*

I pull away, feeling shock in the air that makes him visibly uncomfortable. He's not going to distract me this time. He steps back, uncertainty crossing his face. "I have to apologize to Miss Blade and Aunt D," he says, turning toward the door.

"So, you're going to give up. Just like that?" My words are louder than I intended, but I don't regret it.

He freezes, his back to me, hesitant to turn around. "I've made my decision. No more talking."

Did he really just say that? "We're talking, Kylo. Now," I say firmly, refusing to back down.

He exhales heavily, his eyes narrowing as he finally faces me. "This has nothing to do with you, Cassidy."

"What?" I ask, disbelief laced in my voice. "Did you not say a week ago I was your girlfriend?"

"Cassidy," he starts, but I cut him off.

"Did you not say it?" I repeat, making sure he understands the question.

"I did," he admits through clenched teeth.

"Then this concerns me. What concerns you, concerns me. That's how this works."

Confusion invades his usually normal cool face. "You have to understand. I tried. My body's not the same. I lost control of myself. I'm not coordinated. It's like being trapped in a nightmare, fighting, screaming to get out, but your body refuses to respond. And my head," he taps to his temple, his voice breaking slightly. "My head's fucked up. My processing is off."

"You're right," I say, steady. "Your body isn't the same, and you can't expect it to be. You were in a major car crash that led to an induced coma."

He relaxes slightly, as though we're finally agreeing. "That's what I've been trying to tell everyone. I knew you'd understand," he says, gauging my reaction as he steps closer.

I hold my ground, creating distance between us. "But what I also understand is that you fought to get back. Back to me. Back to your mom. Back to your family and the sport you love. You woke up with a determination to live. That day, your look said it all: *I'm not going back to that place.* You even told me you get everything that you want. You don't give up easily."

His expression softens, surprise widening his eyes as I continue. "It's still in you. You're afraid of failure and that's okay. We are all afraid. I was terrified before my first track meet, after three years, but I did it. That's normal. That fear is normal. But before you give up completely, I want you to think of someone."

"Think of who?" he asks, his voice heavy with sadness and uncertainty, stirring a deep desire within me to hold him close. Comforting him would be so easy, but I stand my ground.

I point to the photo on the table. "Think of him. What would Tron tell you to do right now?"

Kylo exhales deeply, his shoulders sinking as he walks back into the room sitting on the green ottoman. "That stubborn ass would be breathing down my neck at practice, making me run until I passed out," he says, his voice cracking as he lowers his head into his hands.

"At the end of the day. Do it for him and for yourself. No one else," I say softly.

"And if I fail?" His question makes my heart ache.

I move closer, finally allowing myself to sit on his lap. I cup his face, lifting it to meet my eyes. *Bad idea…look away.*

"The hardest thing in life is deciding whether to walk away or try again," I say, my voice gently but firm. "I don't think you can live without trying. All you've ever known is soccer."

I pause, choosing my next words carefully. "You have another chance to live and another chance to try. Can you honestly live your life without giving it one more shot, Kylo?"

CHAPTER 40

THE REAL ME

Kylo

I T TAKES SOME SERIOUS DISCUSSIONS TO GET ME BACK ON THE field. According to my agent, Bruce, he had to sell his left kidney, kiss some ass and make a couple of promises to convince everyone I was serious about my future with soccer. They gave me three weeks to train and qualify for active status for the thirty-man squad and I damn did it.

Training was the most intense I've ever experienced. Running three miles twice a day to build my endurance, squats, step ups, push-ups, and four hours of nothing but soccer drills has been my last few weeks.

I haven't seen *my girlfriend* in a week only because of her. We visited the hospital earlier to take food to the staff that helped me, but other than that, not even a date. If it wasn't for soccer, I'd be on campus every night, licking that beautiful sculpture of hers.

It's crazy I've held off this long without sex. That's been harder than this soccer come back. Thoughts of her open, sexy thighs and that wetness glistening, takes my dreams, even my daydreams. Maybe it's the whole *virgin thing* that's got me off, or maybe… I love this girl. Is that what this is?

Today is the day before my game. This came fast, too fast. Days have been speeding by, and for a sec, I thought about delaying my comeback. But dealing with Bruce, Miss Blade, Aunt D and especially Cassidy would be hell. She knows how to dig her nails in when she wants something.

I wish she was here right now, but she wants me to rest before the game. That stubborn side of hers is something new for me. I'm not used to anyone telling me no or even having a strong opinion. But she got me straight about soccer real quick. Thinking back, she was right. Giving up after one bad game didn't make sense.

If this game ends up anything like my first one, that conversation with Cassidy will take a different turn, and she'll have to understand along with everyone else.

I head to the back entrance of the hotel to avoid the media. I need space to get my head right and slow my thoughts. Cassidy's been sending me morning yoga and meditation videos to help with my mental processing. The shit may be working.

At first, I didn't even watch them. But by the third day, she got so mad she didn't call until I had an update on the videos. *Her feistiness is real.*

Getting quiet with my mind and adjusting to this *new* body has taken me to another level of focus. Figuring out how to move differently, how to adjust for the slowness, has been harder than I thought. Meditating three times a day to find my new normal is more exhausting than the physical workouts.

This mental comeback has been torture, with doubts weighing heavy. I've never had to fight so hard to escape this frozen, slow motion feeling. I know I'm not one hundred percent yet. I need more time. But the game is tomorrow. I'm better than three weeks ago, for sho, and the team is taking another chance.

I lay on the hotel bed, thinking about every possible outcome for the game. I know that field and ball better than anyone. I just need to find my rhythm again, like Uncle Joe said.

I set my alarm and notice a text from Cassidy.

> **If you win tomorrow, I plan to allow some extremely naughty things to take place.**

I text back. **Elaborate.**

> **You'll have two wins tomorrow: your game and me. Until then, no distractions.**

Damn. Just thinking about her body is a distraction. She has a way of taking my mind off the obvious, my game.

You gave me something to play hard for, I text back.

> **Get some rest. See you tomorrow.**

> **Yes, ma'am, beautiful,** I text.

I place my phone on the nightstand and attempt to relax. I've got to drown out all thoughts of failure, doubts and relax. This is my game, the one I own. I know that leather ball inside and out, down to all thirty-two polygons. No math teacher taught me that, only me.

My body has to relax for tomorrow. It will be tough. No dreams or insomnia. Sleep is what…

Maybe someone heard me because the next thing I hear is my alarm buzzing. Nine hours of sleep. Hell yeah, I'm good.

I move faster than usual, doing my three S's in record speed while blocking the noise. All outside doubts, worries and fear from the last game have to stay buried. That shit's over.

A familiar knock, three knocks, then one more, grabs my attention.

I throw the rest of my stuff in my Telfar duffle and open the door. Christian barges in his energy filling every corner of my room.

"Why are you here so early?" I ask, checking my watch to make sure I'm not late. It's 7:15.

"I figured your scary ass needed a pep talk," Christian says, sparing no words as usual. His unibrow quirks, adding to this relentless charm, or annoyance, depending on the moment.

The self-doubt tries to claw its way back where I buried it. *Bury it deeper*, I demand with every cell in my body. I sling my bag across my shoulder to follow Christian out. "Man, I'm good," I reply, keeping it cool.

"Bro, I know you're straight. You killed it at practice. You just gotta trust it, that's all," he says, following me down the hallway toward the bus.

Christian knows how important this game is for me but is keeping it cool and steady. Not just Christian, but my entire family hovers, quietly watching over me from a distance. They're careful not to get too close, but are there in case I fall off my bike without training wheels.

Outside the hotel, crowds are already gathered, shouting and calling for autographs. Hearing them scream my name feels… different this time. The energy is infectious, a buzz crawls under my skin and makes me want to be the guy they're cheering for. The guy they expect to win.

It's not just attention, it's motivation. *I need more of it.*

It also makes me question something deeper. *How was I before the coma?* During my first game back, the team had that same halo effect as my family… waiting, watching for a reaction, for something. *Was I different back then?* I need to know.

"Christian," I say, slowing my pace. "What was I like before the accident?"

"What?" He stops, eyes zeroing in on my head. *Damn, I'm not bleeding*, I want to say but hold back. "You good, bro?"

"Yeah," I reply. "But what was I like? With you all?"

He pauses in deep thought rubbing his chin. "Humph." After a sec, he finally answers. "Bro, you were the energy, the glue. You brought the excitement and the *I don't give a damn* attitude every day. Every practice, every game you treated like it was your last. You drove us hard to practice and play on your level. Damn near impossible to understand."

He shakes his head, a smile tugging at his lips. "You didn't take any bull from anybody. Quick to get in our asses if we were slacking. You had this adrenaline, this fight that never stopped. Sidelines? Hell, you hammered us harder than the coaches did. You never got tired, never got discouraged. You were a straight fucking vibe… the rhythm for the team."

Damn. I feel the difference now. I can tell how everyone, except for Cassidy, watches and waits. They're waiting for the old me to show up. Someone I used to be. I've been feeling this nagging sense of expectation for weeks, like something's building inside, ready to break free.

Enough of this bullshit.

I don't know who I was before all of this, but I know this: This game will be played as though it's my last breath with no second chances.

"Hell yeah," I mutter under my breath.

"What bro?" Christian stares, likely trying to understand why I'm talking to myself and how to protect me from me. *Damn.*

"Nothing," I reply, still replaying his description of who I was. *Man, the entire team must be watching me closely and waiting to see if I'll react the same way I used to.* My past set the bar, and now they're holding their breath, waiting for someone else to show up.

As we head to the tunnel, I realize for the first time I never said thank you. This dude's been by my side through all of this. "Man, thank you for everything. I should've said it a long time ago."

"You didn't have to say anything. That's what we do. We're family."

"Humph, I know, Chris, but still I'm grown enough to know how to say it. It took too long to get here."

He pauses, walking back toward me in the tunnel. "Get out there and kill it. That's all the thanks I need. Kill that shit today, alright!"

We pound fists as we've done for years. "No doubt," I say, following him deeper into the tunnel.

As we step into the entrance, the crowd's energy and stadium smells ignite something deep inside me. The nerves I carried all week dissolve. My mind is clear. Right now, it's just me and the ball. That's all I need.

I'm here to prove something, not to anyone else but myself. *I'm the baddest to ever do this.* The self-doubt? It's buried six feet under, and that shit ain't coming back.

I sprint onto the field, waving my arms to pump up the crowd. I want them to feed off my energy and know I'm back. But as I take in the roaring cheers, it hits me: these people were praying for my recovery.

I bow to each corner of the stadium, pressing my hands together in gratitude. *They need to know they're part of this moment, too.* The roar grows louder, sending chills across my skin and putting me in the most grateful place I've ever been.

The team stays by my side, feeding off the crowd and my energy. Christian, *my hype man*, is losing it for real. *Damn, I love that dude.*

I find the area to my right where Miss Blade normally sits. The jumbotron catches me checking the stands, and soon my family is on the big screen for everyone to see. Aunt D sits with her church outfit on at the game, Miss Blade's hands clasped in prayer, and my girl, has one hand fisted against her lips and the other pressed over her heart.

A single tear escapes her eye, and the camera catches her wiping it away. *She knows my struggle better than anyone.*

And that's when I get it. *I love this woman.*

Her hair whips around in the breeze, strands tangling as her eyes stay locked on me. *Damn, she's beautiful.* I've thought that a thousand times this month, but every time feels like the first. I'm a lucky ass man. And to think this woman came to that hospital every night just for me.

She blows a kiss and I catch it midair. *Damn, am I blushing?* No doubt she has that effect on me.

The camera zooms in on her again, and she gets as many cheers as I do. I don't think she even realizes it because her eyes are still on me. Aunt D nudges her, pointing at the jumbotron. Her smile fades as her normal shyness takes over, she covers her lips, leaning into Miss Blade's hug and hides her face.

The camera pans back to me, and I blow a kiss. I want the world to know, she's mine and nobody else's.

I turn back to the field. I know what's next. I know what I have to do. *Tron, this game is mine.*

"Bro, Dog, shit your ass is back!" Christian's excitement is so real that he has me moving away from him jumping everywhere.

"Everyone move back! My boy's walking through!" Christian says, clearing a path to keep the crowds behind the tape along with security.

"Damn, proud of you, bro! That was all the thanks I need. Your ass is back on another level!"

For real, I don't know how I ended up back here so fast. The game was a blur. The only option was to show up with the doubts buried. I had to dominate the field, trust this new body and not be afraid of what it could or couldn't give back. I pushed harder than

I thought possible, and it was hard as hell. The crowds are a welcome distraction, giving me an excuse to walk slower.

But I *did* kill it. I found my rhythm, my circle...the zone I hadn't felt in months. I didn't even notice the game was over until the clock hit zero. It was just me and that black and white ball. No outside fears. No noise. Goal after goal. I don't even know how many I shot. But there were more goals than misses. That zone was *real*, and I loved every damn minute.

"Dog you good?" Christian asks, turning to look at me, probably wondering why I'm dragging. *Tired as hell.*

"Yeah! More than good, man."

"Then hurry your ass up. They're out here waiting on you. I'll go ahead and get my five seconds in before you take over the spotlight," he says, referring to our post-match press conference. I avoided the last one, so this will be my first time back at the podium in months.

"Bro, you *killed* it! That shot from center field? That's some out of this world shit!" Christian yells, his long arms waving like he's directing traffic. "You're back on another level! What in the hell got into you during those three weeks of training?"

What didn't get into me is the question. Cassidy. But I got plans for her today.

"Thanks, man. But you better get out there before they skip your ass. Warm them up for me!"

Christian shakes his head, pointing at me before heading toward the press room. That dude is my hype man for real.

I shower and change quick. Cassidy and I are leaving together after the interview, and I've got the evening planned for us. No dorm tonight, she's staying with me. I've already made arrangements to avoid the media, including separate cars and a few detours. We may not be private anymore, but whereabouts can be.

The press room is packed with reporters, commentators, and fans as I walk to the stage. I'd forgotten what comes with a major win, but this is insane. There has to be hundreds crammed in here for this one game.

This win is on another level for me but the amount of press in here is crazy. I silenced the doubters and haters from my last game, but I know they're still itching to have their say.

"Kylo, Kylo, Kylo… over here."

I take a seat with my manager, the excitement fading. This is the crowd, the same one that tweeted, emailed and analyzed every second of my last game. I don't have much love for them, but Bruce told me to act cordial. His exact words were, "*Act like you have enough fucking sense to keep those damn endorsements.*"

"Kylo you were in a zone out there today. Everyone could feel it, could see it. How does it feel being back?" the first reporter asks. *Not bad.*

Fake it, Kylo. Give them the TV smile. Sell it, get those endorsements and get this shit done. "It felt good. Real good man," I reply smoothly.

"Totally different from the last game. What changed?" another reporter asks. He's the one that interviewed me right after the coma, the guy who worked with Miss Blade to fly Monty to the show.

"Well," I say, leaning into the mic, "let's just say I had a couple of guardian angels watching my back today plus I found my zone. That made all the difference in the world."

"Guardian angels? Tell us about them," he presses, his grin wide as he pulls his twists back.

I scan the crowd, looking beyond the cameras and lights until Aunt D catches my attention in her hot pink suit. She's not waving in the crowd, but she's impossible to miss. Who wears a hot pink suit to a soccer game? She points to the other side of the room.

And there she is. Cassidy. *Why is she in the back?*

She's the reason for all of this. How can she be that gorgeous? Our eyes lock, and for a moment, everyone else fades away. She makes me feel like *the man.*

Damn, the admiration in her gaze sends me to another level. *Yeah, Superman will show you his powers this evening.*

How can two people have this kind of connection? If this is love, I may not survive. I get what it is, but this is new. Hell, she has my ass up here straight floating.

"Kylo, tell us about these angels," the reporter asks again.

I pause, choosing my words carefully. "This is going to sound crazy," I begin. "Growing up, my brother was my guardian. He beat up more people than I care to admit back in the day. I should've died in that truck accident. It's a straight miracle that I survived. He's the only reason I got out of that truck alive. Some sort of way he saved me, man. He's still taking care of me."

I glance at Miss Blade, nodding. "And then a special person stayed with me, talked to me, took care of my wounds and made sure to wake me."

Out the corner of my eye, I see Cassidy's shyness. She tucks her head so deep into her neck, hiding her face from me. Her humility, her humbleness, it makes me love her even more. *This is love. I love this girl and I'll tell her tonight.*

"Do you want to expound on that special person?" the reporter asks.

Most already know Cassidy after my gate performance at the house, but I don't want the extra media attention on her. The car accident still has unanswered questions and ongoing investigations.

"Not today, man. I already said too much," I reply, giving them the fake Kylo smile they want, swagger charm for the camera, playing the game I know too well. At the end of the day, business runs the game and I plan to exploit every advantage that comes my way. But I hate this shit.

They ask my manager a few questions and start to wrap up our segment. I see Bruce motioning me after my interview block is done. I turn back, trying to direct Cassidy to follow me so we can jet. Hopefully, we can get to our destination without me getting in that body too fast. Holding back with her has been torture.

I try to catch her attention through the reporters and cameras, but my security team surrounds me, blocking my view of her. I stop in my tracks, my eyes locking on some guy standing behind her.

He's staring mesmerized to the point of being motionless. *Who the fuck is that?*

I push past my detail, moving in the opposite direction to get to her. Whoever that mother fucker is looks crazy.

"This way Kylo. Move! We need to get you out of here," one of my security team says, sounding urgent.

Why? They pull me toward the other side of the room. *Is there a security threat?* This isn't making sense. Fuck them, I'm going to Cassidy.

I push through my detail, trying not to draw more attention. But I need to get to her, something feels *wrong.*

"Kylo!" they call my name, their voices alarmed. Bruce catches up, his face tight. "You're causing too much commotion, and we have a security breach. What the fuck are you doing?"

"Bruce, I don't give a damn about a breach. I have to get to Cassidy. Something isn't right."

Maybe he sees the worry, because for once he doesn't question me.

He pulls out his cell, speaking quickly. "Get to the back with Cassidy, now. You can make it through the crowd faster from your side."

I see the other security detail moving faster on the opposite end of the room, cutting through the chaos. The rest of the team sticks close, refusing to leave without me. I'm on their heels, pushing through the flashes of cameras and voices shouting my name with the towering presence of college basketball players in the crowd.

Who the hell invites a college basketball team to a soccer press conference?

Who the fuck is that standing behind her?

My chest tightens, burning as I shove through my detail to get to her.

"Cassidy!" I shout, but my voice is lost in the sea of commotion. *Damn.*

I stop myself from picking people out of my way to get to that mother fucker in that black ass hoodie. The other detail makes it to the back before I do, but when I arrive, she's not there.

"Dammit, where the hell is she?" I growl, pacing the back of the press room, wiping my mouth as anxiety gnaws at me. Cameras flash, capturing my reaction and my detail searching.

My phone buzzes in my pocket, and I exhale, relief flooding me. I answer without even checking the screen.

"Cassidy, where are you?"

There's silence on the other end, then a streak of laughter.

"Honey..."

The piercing, whiny sound of her voice cuts through me like burning flames, making me hit a thousand. My grip tightens on the phone, and for a second, I almost crush it.

How the fuck does Sarah have my number? And why the hell is she calling?

"Fuck!" I growl, the word tearing out of me as I slam the phone down.

CHAPTER 41

LITTLE BUTTERFLY

Cassidy

T HE ATTENTION KYLO GIVES ME FROM THE PODIUM, SUR-
rounded by reporters, cameras and diehard fans, makes
me burn for his rough, callous hands. My heart pounds so
loudly I wonder if anyone can hear it.

His handsome presence dominates the room, every word
hanging in the air as everyone lingers on his next move. Being a
part of his world, and all the attention it brings has me mesmerized not just by his popularity, but his natural swagger to handle
it. I see why everyone wants to be a part of whatever he's offering.

He's so at ease with all the cameras, the questions and the
fans. It's like he was born for this. Not me. I'd rather be hidden under a rock or tucked in a corner with a book than in the
spotlight.

Trying to blend into the crowd, I stayed back after returning
from the restroom. The standing room works for me, no cameras,
no prying eyes and definitely no jumbotron.

I hesitate before peeking at him seated at the table with his
manager. I can tell he's searching the crowd for me. When our
eyes lock, it feels magnetic, as if everyone else disappears, leaving

only me and his honey hazels. The reporter has to call his name twice to pull him back.

I look at my hands, nervously twisting my fingers, hoping no one notices. His words "special person and guardian angel" echo in my mind. The jumbotron earlier was more than enough attention. I'm tempted to hide in the nosebleeds at his next game.

A nudge at my side brings me back to the buzz of the room, filled with excitement from Kylo's win. "Pardon me," I mumble, without glancing at the person beside me.

Then I feel it, a hot breath escapes down my neck, making me shutter.

"Follow me, do not make a scene, or the blinking red dot pointed on Blade's shoulder will be more than just that. Move..." a voice whispers, the words sending ice through my veins.

Am I hearing things. I try to turn, but his hand grips my waist, holding me in place.

"Turn your seductive ass, or I will shoot him with millions watching. You want that, my little butterfly?"

Who is this, and why is he calling me butterfly?

"Please don't," I plead, trying to move, but his grasp tightens, keeping me rooted.

"You heard me, Cassidy. Move," he hisses, his voice low and menacing.

This can't be happening. There are too many people in this room for him to try anything, but we are in the very back with all attention on Kylo. I'm not leaving. I glance at Kylo, hoping he'll see me, but the man's hand digs into my navel, pulling me backward.

"Your choice, Cassidy," he says, his words venomous. His fingers scrape hard metal against my bare stomach as he lifts my shirt slightly. "Do you want to see his head explode on national TV?"

My breath catches when I see the red dot flicker on Kylo's forehead. *Oh god, he's serious.* Am I the only one that notices this?

Think, Cassidy. I reach for my wrist, but he grabs it, twisting my arm behind my back.

"Follow me. Now. Or I shoot," he growls.

I pull free, but his sweaty hands squeeze tighter, trapping me. My breathing spirals out of control as panic takes over. *Calm down, Cassidy.* Focus. I open my mouth to scream, but a stabbing pain in my side nearly buckles my knees.

What was that? Did he pinch me? My legs weaken, and I want to scream, but nothing comes out.

His gloved hands cover my mouth and nose, suffocating me. Wait… *How am I already away from the press room? How is this happening?* My legs feel like they're moving, but I don't remember walking. My vision blurs, and dizziness takes over.

"Stop!" I try to yell, but no one notices and no one looks my way. Do they not hear me? I elbow him hard in the ribs, but his only response is a low hiss.

"Bitch!" he mutters, low enough for no one to turn our way. Another sharp sting in my side sends pain shooting through me. My limbs collapse under me as fear consumes me. *What is happening?*

"Help…" The word feels distant, barely audible. Did I even say it? *Say it louder.*

"Help!" I scream…or did I? Everything is so foggy and I'm so weak that keeping my eyelids open is a struggle. *Think, Cassidy.* Hit him again. I aim at his side once more, but it's not hard enough to slow him.

Another sting. This one burns, sending a wave of heat through me. "She's okay. My girlfriend had too much to drink today supporting her biggest fan, Kylo Blade. Excuse us," he says and no one stops to help or check on me.

His frail arms lift me, cradling me against his chest. My mind screams for my eyelids to open, but my body won't respond. My vision fades, leaving me with the memory of his crooked smile and sour stench of his breath. He has me…

It's sticky and damp, and the heat is unbearable. My clothes cling to my skin like a suffocating layer. *Why am I so hot?*

A tickle in my scratchy throat turns into a violent cough, each hack tearing through my chest. Tears spill down my cheeks, cooling my burning skin. Bending over would help, but I can't move my arms. They're tied tightly to my sides, leaving no room to move.

My coughing eases, but the dryness persists, leaving me even thirstier. My face droops close to my chest as intense dizziness hits, my stomach twisting like a spinning carnival ride I can't escape. Please stop. I need this to end before I vomit. I hate vomiting...

Did I blank out?

Water drips from somewhere behind me, each drop echoing louder and louder, resonating with the intensity of a bass drum at every splash. Each hit vibrates my brain, and I pray someone turns down the volume. My head feels heavy, and lifting it takes all my strength. The pounding is relentless, and I hold my breath, trying to avoid the rancid moldy stench in the air.

What is that smell and why is everything so amplified in my head? I hold my breath to slow the rush of nerves hitting me all at once to focus on seeing. My eyelids strain open, my eyebrows nearly touching my hairline as I fight to lift them. It feels as though glue has been smeared on my lashes, keeping them sealed shut.

Are they open? A creeping shiver vibrates through every cell making me shake through my bones as the black takes my breath. I've never felt darkness, this smothering and isolating. There's not a pinpoint of light anywhere in this black darkness.

I open wider darting from side to side to convince my brain that they're actually open. *Are they open?* I can't tell. The dark is something supernatural robbing me of my senses. I can't feel my feet, my hands or my arms at this point.

I've got to get loose and get out of here. I strain to move any part of me willing to listen, but everything is bound tight with something coarse tearing into my side. I refuse to give up. I try to rock what feels like a wooden chair from side to side, hoping to break it against the floor. But, in my current state, I can barely manage to move.

"Butterfly, how are you?" His words slice through the dark air leaving me afraid to breathe and fighting my rising panic. I pull my shoulders tight, trying to keep his touch away from my trembling insides as dread claws up my throat. *Where is he?*

The darkness blinds me, and I can only anticipate feeling him come closer. *How is this happening?* How did I let myself get in this situation? I sit still, squeezing my insides with my teeth clattering echoing off the walls. My nerves are so rigid and tense that they paralyze me down to the soles of my shoes.

A lantern gradually illuminates the room, dimly casting large finger shadows in the corners. I stare hard, battling blurry vision and sleepiness, until hand shadows take over the wall. *What is that?* Different shapes emerge: a rabbit, a goat, and then something else.

"Beautiful butterfly." The voice from behind makes me jump. The butterfly starts small and then grows larger and larger until it fills the entire room. My chair rattles beneath me, the clanking sound of its legs on the floor echoing against the silence. It's the only noise besides his slow, deliberate breathing, getting closer and closer.

My mind races, flooded by the what if's. *Is he getting ready to slice my throat? Is he planning to… rape me?* Nothing stops my thoughts from images in my head continuing to create every possible bad outcome.

I'm no longer sleepy. Maybe the drug is wearing off because I'm becoming more aware of everything around me. Movement is possible again.

The fire from the lantern casts a low glow, just enough to see my surroundings. It's some kind of basement, the walls the color of dried mud. Trickling water drips from somewhere above, maybe the ceiling or tunnel. *Is this place flooding?*

The ground is uneven and cracked, resembling hardened mud with scattered dirt and holes forming most of the flooring. Then I see it...a sight I'll never unsee.

In the center of the room stands a cell. Chains hang from the door handle and random ropes are tied to the gray metal bars. Inside is nothing but a filthy, white bucket in the corner. The sight of it brings the vomit clawing at my throat earlier up with me forcing it back down. *I will not vomit.*

Behind the cell is a king-sized bed, its disheveled sheets barely covering a thin, stained mattress. The dark red stains... dried blood. *How many were here before me?*

A desk and a chair sit next to the bed's metal frame, more chains draped over them. Something else catches my eye...a long, brownish sweater with matching pants hanging loosely over the back of a wooden chair. The monotone colors send a chill through my bones, a fear so visceral it grips my very soul.

He was there all those days and nights watching and waiting for me at the hospital.

Tears stream down my face, triggered by the depths of fear that awaken every sense in me. I can taste the sourness of the mattresses' metallic stench. I can hear the clang of a cell door slamming shut, trapping someone with no hope. I can smell the rotten decay of death that clings to this place, locking in fear.

"You figure it out, my little butterfly?"

His question carries a melodic tone, the word "butterfly" lingering on a high note as he slowly pulls off his black hoodie.

I gasp, as I take him in. Deep-set, red eyes bulge from his pale boney face. Stringy blond hair mattes the length of his sweaty skin. His sharp, boney shoulder blades cut through his shirt like knives, ready to cut through. He looks like a meth addict, hollow, broken and terrifying.

"Stop looking at me that way. I'm not crazy, you know," he says. Definitely signaling he's beyond comprehension.

I stay quiet, not daring to speak or even breathe too loudly, my gaze stuck on the ground. *Think, Cassidy. Think.*

"No harm will come to you beautiful but-ter-fly," he sings, dragging the word out like he's savoring it. Each syllable slices the air cutting my brain mentally in half leaving me half shaken and half on edge to fight.

How am I here and not at the press conference with Kylo? The thought of not seeing him, my family, Raith makes me sick to my stomach.

His feet scrape against the rough floor, jerking my attention to him as I track his every movement. My body is so tense that every sound traps me, holding me captive like a prisoner in my own mind.

He places a tray of food on the table behind his monotone clothes. I can't see what's on it because the long sweater draped over the chair blocks my view. But what it doesn't hide is the light casting shadows off the walls, amplifying the horrors of the room.

The dirty sheets are all over the place as if a struggle had taken place, drawing my eyes back to the blood stains on the mattress. My stomach churns, and the metallic taste in my mouth intensifies as I stare.

He approaches slowly, his footsteps pounding against the uneven floor. My heartbeat syncs with each step, dragging the moment into slow motion. His gaze drifts down my body stopping at my bare feet. *Where are my shoes?*

"Open butterfly," he says, softly. My heartbeat lags, afraid to seek another beat as he places an olive in my mouth. His finger lingers against my bottom lip, rubbing it, smearing the red lipstick Kylo asked me to wear to the game.

Not certain if I should chew, but instinct takes over, my body desperate and starving for nutrients. I bite into the olive hesitantly, its salty juice flooding my mouth and triggering a unexpected cough, possibly from dehydration. Something has sucked all the moisture from my throat, leaving it raw and burning, waiting for flames to escape.

"Water?" he asks, his words halting everything.

I hate how each word whiplashes me, holding me captive. My eyes follow him as he moves to the table, watching him strain to open a bottle of water. His lips press firmly against the cap as he twists it off, placing it on the table. "Drink beautiful," he says, holding the bottle to my lips.

I should question this but I don't. Instead I let the water soothe the fire in my throat. It's the best water I've ever tasted.

I don't even realize my eyes are closed, lost in relief, until I feel his scrawny fingers running through my hair. He pulls out my hair tie in one motion, letting it fall against the back of the chair. I'm no longer thirsty, my dread mounting as his rough fingers force my neck back.

"You need more water. Don't be afraid. I'm not going to harm you. That's not my intention," he says, forcing my neck back with his rough fingers. "I've watched you for months, waiting for my chance to take a peek."

He places the bottle on the floor, his eyes lingering on my chest. My next breath is lost somewhere between panic and no hope.

He pulls my top slightly open, his long skinny finger slipping inside and brushing against the skin between my breasts. *Don't move. Don't react.* I keep my eyes open, willing him to stop.

His finger moves up and down slowly, his eyes fluttering shut as if savoring every second. *Eyes open.* "The pleasure I'm getting from a simple touch is enough to drive me insane. Do you even realize the effect you have on me? On everyone? You're like hydrocodone, oxy, morphine, codeine and fentanyl wrapped into one dangerously powerful drug."

I cringe, trying to pull back, hoping it will make him stop. "Stop," I demand my first word to him without hesitation.

"Oh, and she speaks," he smirks, pulling his hand but not before peeling my bra aside. His breathing quickens as mine slows to a halt.

"You're beautiful everywhere, how I imagined you," he heaves, his frustration spilling into his voice. *Is he angry?* He steps back, smooths down his hair, and jams both hands into his pockets. "Our time has come, and I am more than ready, my butterfly."

He paces, his voice lowering as his eyes narrow with a mix of anger and longing. "I still remember you from our first encounter at the fair. You walked past me, a scent so sweet that it's never left my nostrils to this day. I couldn't get enough of you, watching you, even eating everything at the fair. But then one of your friends noticed me."

His gaze fixes on me, waiting for confirmation. But I stay silent.

"Do you know how desperate I had become to get you? I kidnapped you from a news conference. I couldn't wait any longer. I watched you at that hospital night after night. Cassidy. I was there even when I wasn't and you never noticed! And then your dad had to interfere and ruin everything. I had plans for you a long time ago. Every night, I watched you sleep in the waiting area for him, taking care of him like he was your whole world!"

His screams make me jump. "I wanted you! I watched you jog with that girl almost every day at the stadium. It was like you were running from someone or something. I watched and waited so I could make my move. And then *he* came back. His ass was supposed to die or marry Sarah. But no, he had to come back and try to take what was destined for me. Well, that's not going to happen. You're mine now, beautiful butterfly."

He leans in closer, his breath hot and rancid as his tongue licks my neck, sliding up to my cheek. The smell makes me gag, dry heaves traveling up my chest, escaping into a loud gasp forcing him to pull back. He looks at me with disgust, but something else appears in his hollow eyes. *Disappointment?*

He begins pacing, his skeletal frame moving awkwardly as he faces toward the bed. *Is he hiding from me?* Did he really think I would welcome any part of his disgusting touch? He's insane, and

I need to play this carefully. But first, I've got to ignore the lingering halitosis on my skin from his spit making my stomach churn.

I glance up slightly, my eyes following his approaching legs with a tray of food in his hands.

"Eat my beauty," he says, setting the tray on my lap. "Because next, I'm going to bathe you to… wash Kylo's touch away forever."

His skeletal thighs straddle my legs, his sunken, hollow eyes staring directly into mine. His frailty only amplifies his menace. His pointy bones press into me, and for a moment, I wonder if he'll slice me open with a sudden move. His gaunt, gray appearance scares me.

He picks up an apple slice from the tray and attempts to separate my lips. I clench them shut, refusing to give him what he wants. My body shakes uncontrollably, as if I'm in 10-degree weather, my nerves barely holding it together. His frustration grows, as he narrows his eyes, pulling the apple back. Lines etch deeper into his forehead.

"You don't have to eat. But I will. I will dine later this evening," he sneers, his eyes dropping to my jeans zipper.

My resolve ends as tears spill down my cheeks. *I don't want his hands on me. I don't want him near me.*

I try to slow my mind, but the room begins to distort, objects growing larger, then smaller. My vision blurs. Am I hallucinating?

He smiles, his blood shot eyes widening. *The olive.* He put something in it.

His hands grip my shoulder, using it to steady himself as he stands. Is he hurt?

I can barely think as fog grips me again, and the heavy door slams shut behind him, suctioning me into a hollow echo in my head. I feel trapped in a dungeon with the heavy six-inch solid wood door and metal latches sealing the frame, the pressure making me wish my ears could pop.

I need to figure this out. Am I repeating myself? My thoughts spiral, confusion clouding my own mind as everything slows to a crawl. The room spins like a merry-go-round, and for a brief moment, I wish I were back at the zoo with my mom. Her shampoo scent blowing in the breeze, the safety of her presence, feeling like a lifetime ago.

If the spinning stops, maybe the confusion will fade.

I try to move my hands, but the coarse rope binding them digs into my wrists, sawing into my cuticles. *They must be bleeding.*

I bend forward, the raw sting of the rope cutting into my waist as my chest rests against my thighs. If I can stand, I might be able to break the chair or hit him hard enough to knock him out.

My trembling fingers jab into my ribs, my focus narrowing as something catches my eye, a faint glimmer of hope. It is the most important object in the room.

The thin gold and silver bracelet on my wrist sparkles faintly, its six small diamonds catching the dim light on my wrist. It awakens me, as if Red Bull is coursing through my veins.

Why didn't I think of this earlier?

Dad's jeweler designed matching bangles for all of us, each one engraved with our family crest. The six diamonds represent all of us, including Miss Rita.

Adrenaline surges through me like a shot of caffeine. Sweat drips along my brow as I swallow saliva, desperate to wet my dry throat. I need more water, but the bracelet resting between the course, tannish rope on my wrists is my sole focus.

My elbow trembles as I push with everything I have to bring my hand closer. The rope is too tight, biting into my skin, but the smell of his breath on me is a constant reminder that time is not on my side.

I lean toward my hand, ignoring the saw slicing into my stomach. *One chance. That's all I have.*

Every fiber of my weak body strains as I twist my back to the breaking point. My tongue stretches, tasting the fibers of the rope, it's rough texture scratching my dry mouth triggering another violent cough. I don't care if I cough a lung out, I want stop until I reach it. I bite into the twisted, prickly rope, pulling it away from my raw wrists, not caring how dirty it tastes.

And there it is, my gold and purple butterfly charm of hope, sparkling with the only shred of possibility in this nightmare.

I sink my teeth into the bracelet, saliva pooling and dripping my chin, tickling my neck. If I can get it in between my teeth, maybe I can maneuver it. The sweat loosens the rope, giving me just enough space to angle closer. I clamp down on the bracelet like a dog refusing to let go of a bone, inching it farther back into my mouth.

The bracelet scrapes the inside of my lip, and the metallic taste of blood fills my mouth. I suppress the scream that begs to be released, knowing any sound could be bad.

Where is it? I ask myself as gallons of saliva drain my wrist, soaking the rope making it harder to find the button. I nudge the bracelet with my nose, desperate to locate the slight rise of the clasp. My jaw almost dislocates as I stretch wider, ignoring the pain.

The rope cuts deeper into my waist, dampening my shirt with blood or sweat. I don't care what it is. *I will hit this button.*

My tongue slips under the clasp, brushing against the slight rise, and I feel it…a faint vibration.

I freeze, holding my breath. Was that real? Or is my mind playing tricks on me?

I pray. *Please, let it be active.* If my dad or Kylo doesn't get here soon… No, stop thinking like that. Focus.

The memories of the chains, the cage, the hospital clothes, the bloodstained mattress, all of it crashes over me, suffocating me with the heaviness of a ton of bricks. Weighing on me heavily enough to choke me, I realize how much danger surrounds me. Shivers travel from my toes to my hands, making every part of me twitch as I try to block it out. But it's too much.

Then I see it.

My breath, lost in fear, collapses into my chest as the blinking white dot reflects off the stringy tan rope. It's working.

The bracelet that I argued with my dad for years about wearing is working. The bracelet that I told him would ruin my high school days is shining. The bracelet that I almost left at home because I was with Kylo is blinking. The bracelet with the purple butterfly charm that I hated because it represents lupus, something I promised my mom that I would never take off, is glowing.

My thoughts of the bracelet are shattered by the heavy thud booted footsteps echoing in the distance, eerily reminiscent of our security team back home. Slowly, I push myself upright, fighting through the strain as my back stiffens, a painful reminder of my mom's inflamed arthritis. *She never complained.* Just thinking about her makes the walls around me feel higher, thicker, and more suffocating, growing into a terrifying crater that leaves me feeling more fractured. My bottom lip quivers, trembling as if I was back in our tin tub back on campus. *Our tin tub.*

The door creaks open, and a cold draft wraps around my bare ankles. My focus stays fixed on the ground, not daring to look up as his strong Old Spice cologne fills the room. Is he trying to cover up unwashed funk?

"Beautiful Cassidy, look what I have for you," he says, stopping at the table near the bed. *I keep my gaze fixed on the ground.*

His footsteps hurry toward me, and his bony fingers grip my chin, forcing me to look up. He's wearing different clothes now, a loose black t-shirt that swallows his thin frame, slack jeans that look two sizes too big.

"Yes, butterfly. No dress, no bra, no lingerie. This empty box is the surprise for me. An outfit of *nothing*," he snorts, his voice rising like he's a circus announcer.

His words sink into me like a dagger, twisting deeper with every syllable. That word panics every cell in my body, to the deaths of my soul, leaving me with one option: Tears. I can't even wipe them away as they streak my face.

His long fingers wipe my tears from under my eyes, his touch slow and deliberate. "Yes butterfly, you were meant for me. My prize! I will not kill you. We will live a long, happy life together. I'll have you every day."

His fairy tale fantasy only deepens my panic. My voice does me no favors, or maybe I've reached the point where death feels close, and everything begins to unravel.

I can hear sobbing in the background, and it's me. The weep is raw and vulnerable, echoing my emotions as they spill over. I can't control the whimpers, and my stomach convulses, but my mind is racing. *Am I having an outer body experience?*

"You see, beautiful Cassidy, you are the reason for so much. I was with you at the park. I could smell you sleeping, illuminated by the moonlight casting shadows off your silhouette. I protected you that night. I didn't want anything to happen to you while you slept, your butterfly resting on that delicate wrist."

He walks behind me, one slow deliberate bootstep sending chills through every hair on my body. He lowers himself onto my lap, straddling my thighs, and yanking at the ropes binding my hands.

"You're hurting me!" I yell, my voice harsher than I intended.

His eyebrows lift in surprise, a slight smile forming on his face, amused. Even though tears still stream down my face, something deep inside rises within me to fight back, and she just stepped forward to introduce herself to him. Yeah, this is insane... now I'm referring to myself in third person, but at this point, I'll take it.

His expression changes as he snatches my hair, yanking it back so hard that if I had clip-ins they'd be on the muddy floor. His mouth crashes onto mine with a force that signals one thing: he's ready to take what he wants.

If he's going to go through with it, I won't make it easy without a fight. I sink into his dry, fishy lip, biting down with the strength of an alligator devouring its capture. Blood fills my mouth, the metallic tang mixing with saliva dripping down my chin. I don't care anymore. He'll have to beat me to death before I let that happen.

A sudden force knocks the air out of me, making me release

his lip. My lungs collapse as they struggle to inhale. Blood streams down his mouth, and he pounds my back over and over again, each blow making me feel like I'm seconds away from passing out.

"You bitch!" he screams, jumping to his feet and wiping the blood from his mouth. He stares at me, disbelief etched into his face like he's never seen his own blood before.

I see his hand move back, and I brace for it. His slap cracks across my face, sending pain shooting from my cheek to a tooth in desperate need of a filling. My arms are still bound, but they feel slightly looser.

He charges at me, grabbing my wrists and toppling the chair, sending me crashing to the muddy floor. My knees scrape against the dirt, the burn adding to the aches radiating through me.

"I was trying to be nice, butterfly. No more!" He shouts, yanking my wrists upward as I lie tangled in the chair. His next move feels excruciatingly slow as I look up, only to meet cold eyes. He stares between me and the blinking white light of hope. Everything begins to move in slow motion as his focus lands solely on my bracelet. The purple and gold butterfly captures both of our attention.

"What is this!" he yells, his voice no longer a fairy tale land at the circus but deep, mean, dry and scary. We both glare at the bright light hitting my purple butterfly growing stronger blinding the room with its magnitude of importance tied to my escape. He yanks my wrist so hard that it feels like my arm might be torn from its socket. *Did he dislocate my shoulder?* The pain is unbearable, leaving me numb to his relentless tugging as he tries to unclasp my bracelet.

"Please stop," I beg. I can't take it anymore. Everything hurts from the breath from my lungs, to the bleeding skin on my knees to the stinging in my cheeks to my jawbone and my shoulder hanging limp. *Don't slip away.* I push myself.

"What is this!" his screams grow louder, anxious for answers. "What is it!" he demands, repeating himself, as he drops me to the ground in my chair. I land on the only part of me not screaming in pain, my hip.

He storms over to the table, his boney frame searching for something. *What is he doing?*

Nothing prepares me for what he reveals when he turns to face me. A long, shiny broad knife is nestled in the curl of his white knuckles. My heart sinks as I see blood dripping from the razor-sharp pointy edge, leaving stains on the mattress. He holds the black handle and runs his skinny fingers along the silver blade, eyes wide and psychotic, locked onto me.

This is it, and everything in me feels it. My entire body convulses in fear, worse than any panic attack. He holds my arms aloft, the shimmer of his blade sending tremors throughout my limbs for what's about to happen. He cuts the rope off and sets the knife down, but his grip around my wrist is so tight that I can't move. I catch a glimpse of him watching my white light of hope as he focuses on my bracelet, trying to unclasp it.

It falls to the ground with a clatter, and my heart sinks with it. He picks it up and throws it near the wall, where the gold and silver shatters into pieces. The butterfly charm floats in a shallow puddle of water pooling in the corner, dimming as it drifts away with my faith.

He saws away the ropes binding my legs, but I feel no desire to move. My gaze stays locked on my butterfly disappearing into the murky water.

"Get up! We're leaving!" he shouts, growing more frantic and psychotic, telling me he's beyond his breaking point. I push weakly on my left arm, trying to stand. His slap sends me crashing back to the floor.

"What is that bracelet?" he roars, his voice vibrating off the walls, shaking everything in this dungeon. He's no longer at the circus, he's somewhere else entirely.

"Nothing," I whisper, spitting out a clump of blood onto the dirt. I will never tell him what it is. Never.

His arm swings back, and his fist connects with my eye, sending pain shooting through the back of my head. My vision fades as I slip in and out of consciousness.

"Get up! No one is taking you from me! No one!" His scream pierces the air, shaking me awake, though my body feels like it's shutting down.

He bends down, roughly pulling me to my feet. "Move!" he demands, but I don't do anything. I can't even stand, let alone walk and I have no intention of trying. Plus, I don't feel like moving. So, I'm not.

He slings me over his shoulder, his knees buckling under my weight. Grabbing the edge of the table for balance, he steadies himself before moving again. It's going to be almost impossible for him to carry me. We probably weigh the same. His boney hand travels up my legs, resting between them.

"This'll all be mine," he mutters, darkly.

The pain is so overwhelming that his touch doesn't even register. Keeping my eyes open is my only focus.

We head toward the entrance, and he pulls the door open without bothering to lock it. The sound of water sloshing against my dangling limbs mixes with droplets hitting my face. The tunnel we enter is flooded, darker than the room we left but my eyes swelling makes it impossible to see.

My mind finally catches up. We're outside. I'm outside.

Do something. *Scream, Cassidy. Scream.*

"Please," I whisper, but it's barely audible. It's not enough. I dig past the pain, past his crushing grip on my legs, and push through the fog of the drug still sapping my strength. Then I let out a scream unlike anything I've ever done before.

It's deafening. I force every ounce of air from my battered lungs, my voice rising through injuries, carrying a desperate need, longing to see home again. For a moment, I question if the high-pitched screams bouncing off the tunnel walls are coming from me.

My cries echo everywhere.

Louder. Did I imagine that, or did someone say louder? I don't waste a second questioning, searching through the darkness or feeling the water hit my face. I inhale as deeply as I can while hanging upside down and release another scream. Louder this time. The shriek roars, bouncing off the walls, as my lapse of perception leaves me dazed with confusion. *That is me screaming, right?* I'm not sure, but I can't stop myself.

Louder. Who's saying this?

"Shut up, you bitch!" he growls, tightening his grip on my thighs as water soaks my clothes.

Fight.

Maybe my inner delusion is guiding me, but it feels as though someone is whispering in my ears, urging me to fight, to survive and to escape. Uncertain where the fight comes from, I clench my fist and go to work on his back. I slam into his back with everything I have, over and over, with enough force, hoping to break his spine in half. My nails dig into his thin shirt, clawing at his skin, trying to cause him the same pain he's caused me.

Gripping his waist, I bite into his side. *"I'm living."* The words escape, loud and defiant. I can't tell exactly where my hits are landing, but I keep kicking, biting and hitting with every ounce of strength I have left.

Suddenly, he throws me down onto the wet concrete. Pain shoots through my body as I land on my shoulder. Stinging pains shoot from my arm making my hand go numb. But something else gets my attention.

Is that light? Yes! Streams of light are coming in through the small holes in the tunnel. Resting against the wall, I try to catch my breath, my eyes drawn to a glint of metal on the ground. *Is that a gun?*

"Shooting you was not my plan, Cassidy," he says, his voice dripping with death. "But, I will. Shut the hell up or I'll take your clothes off, fuck you with this gun to your head, and shoot you at the same time. Do you understand?"

His breath reeks, and I can feel it against my skin. The cold barrel of the gun presses against my legs as his voice grows darker.

"Be still," he commands.

I freeze, my heart racing as a faint shimmer catches my eye. Is that a syringe?

"What is that?" I ask, my voice trembling. I don't expect an answer, he won't give me one. But I see him prepping a needle.

Don't think. Act.

Death is too close. I hold my breath and keep quiet enough to push through my exhaustion, leaning toward him. I basically collapse on him, and to my surprise, he falls with me. We both crash against the tunnel wall, splashing everywhere. He groans, his grip loosening.

I'm out of his grasp.

I don't think I move.

I slam my elbow into his groin, again and again until he doubles over in pain. "You bitch!" he screams, his voice echoing off the walls.

I don't wait. I do what I do best.

I push myself up, ignoring the searing pain in my legs and force them to move. My feet slap against the water, weighing me down as I stumble forward, every step heavier than the last. *Run, Cassidy. Run.*

"Come back here!" he roars, his anger consuming the tunnel.

I push harder, the water splashing violently with each step. "Cassi… dy!" his screams grow louder, the deep rage in his voice trembling the walls.

A loud bang explodes in the tunnel, shaking everything. *Was that a gunshot?*

I don't need to look back to see the sparks lighting the entire tunnel. Bullets ricochet off the muddy walls, scattering like fiery flares in every direction.

"Come back!" he shouts, his voice echoing, the splashing water behind me growing louder. *How is he catching up to me that fast?*

Move, Cassidy. Move.

Another gunshot fires, the roaring sound ringing in my ears. Then…

Out of nowhere I feel it… a burning, stabbing sensation rippling through my body, igniting my shoulder in flames. Agonizing pain radiates outward, slowing me to a crawl.

I summon every ounce of strength in my legs, forcing them to push toward the light beaming at the end of the tunnel. *Legs, please. Just hold me up* a little longer. *Get me to the light.*

Confusion engulfs me, turning everything blurry. My vision swims, my breath ragged. Exhaustion weighs me down, my body too tired to keep going.

I have no more screams left, no energy to move and no strength to fight. Every ounce of hope feels stripped away. My legs fold beneath me, sending me crashing into the icy water. It splashes around me, chilling my bones to the marrow.

I drop to my knees, crawling forward one agonizing inch at a time. Each movement heavier than the last, I drag myself forward, inch by inch, like a toddler determined to master a commando crawl.

As I struggle, hands grab me.

Darkness rushes in, swallowing me whole. The black void stretches endlessly, a swirling, suffocating pit of nothing.

He has me.

**DON'T MISS TWICE: SAVE ME
COMING SOON!
CHECK MY WEBSITE FOR UPDATES**

WAKE ME
READING GROUP GUIDE

DISCUSSION QUESTIONS

1. When the book opens, Cassidy is rushing home. What were your initial thoughts about what was happening? How did it make you feel?

2. We meet Raith early in the novel. Cassidy immediately recognizes Raith's clothes and appearance. In your opinion, was Cassidy's questioning appropriate so soon? How would you have handled the situation?

3. What are your thoughts on why Kylo calls his mom 'Miss Blade'?

4. Captain K is the name Brooklyn gives Kylo. Do you think there's deeper meaning behind it? What meaning would you attach to the nickname?

5. Several supporting characters weave through Wake Me. Who was your favorite supporting character and why?

6. What brings Cassidy comfort throughout the novel? Is there something in your own life that brings you the same comfort and peace?

7. Both Cassidy and Kylo have experienced significant loss. They each struggle to cope in their own ways. If you could give advice to either Cassidy or Kylo on managing the stress of grief, what would it be?

8. After reading the novel, what do you believe the purple and gold butterfly on the cover symbolizes?

9. The pull between Cassidy and Kylo feels intense and fast. Were there moments you questioned whether enough time had passed for such a strong connection? Why or why not?

10. In one emotional scene, Miss Rita asks Cassidy, "What do you think your mom would've done?" referring to how her mom would have handled Kylo's memory loss. If you were in Cassidy's situation, how would you have responded? What advice would you give someone facing something similar?

11. One important character, Cassidy's mom, never appears in an actual scene but is deeply felt throughout the novel. What is one of Cassidy's mom's personality traits that you admire or appreciate?

12. Cassidy's love for Kylo is young, fresh, unfamiliar and over-whelming. Miss Rita suggests that if you're lucky, you might experience a love like this twice in a lifetime. Have you ever felt a connection like theirs? What are your thoughts on that idea?

13. After the accident and the induced coma, Kylo struggles with his body's connection and rhythm. Cassidy recommends med-itation; Uncle Joe advises getting quiet to rediscover yourself. What would you recommend for healing and rediscovery?

14. Was there anything about Cassidy and Kylo that surprised you as their story unfolded?

15. There's a danger lurking throughout the novel. Who do you think it is?

ACKNOWLEDGEMENTS

I apologize in advance because this is going to be long.

The phrase **"Thank You"** almost feels too small for the amount of gratitude I have in my heart for everyone who helped me on this journey. So instead of just saying it, I'm going to show you what you did and how you made me feel during this process.

Okay, here goes...

♥ **Mom:** My pusher, my auto-repeat motivator, my toughest critic. The reason this book exists. Your brutal (borderline roasting) critiques made me rewrite this almost four times. And guess what? You were right.

♥ **Sister:** You're a woman of few words. I am a woman of way too many. I know my annual birthday Facebook novels drive you crazy, but for six years, you've proofread them anyway without blocking me. MVP status.

♥ **Editor (Joseph Editorial):** You taught me so much. You're more than an editor, you're a woman of God, a teacher, a friend, and the GOAT of editing.

♥ **Beta Readers:**

♦ **Niece:** You pushed me past my limits when I wanted to stay surface level.

♦ **BFF:** You were the first to say, "Publish this book." I will never forget that moment. *I remember exactly where I was when you said it... Starbucks drive-through line.*

♦ **BFF:** You admitted you hadn't read an entire book in a while, but you couldn't put mine down. That means everything.

♦ **Auntie:** You gave me my first review in five unforgettable words: "This book made me moist." ☺

♥ **My Son:** Your explanations of the game were priceless even if I'm still confused about the offsides rule. *Oh well.*

♥ **My Baby Boy (Son):** The baddest when it comes to TikTok content. You keep my social media from being tragic.

♥ **My Daughter:** My forever plug for what her generation is reading, loving and living.

♥ **My Man of Twenty-Four Years:** Your website expertise, branding genius, and patience with my late-night writing marathons are everything.

♥ **Butterfly Warriors:** Thank you for sharing your stories, your strength, and your unwavering ability to find beauty in the storm. You are the reason this story has deeper wings.

♥ To every single reader who purchased this book, messaged me, emailed me, or tagged me on social media. You're the real ones.

The hardest part of this journey was opening myself up and letting people witness my art. You welcomed me with open arms.

I am forever grateful.

Forever in awe of your reviews.

Forever appreciative of your kindness.

And yes, I have to say the words:

Thank you.

From the bottom of my heart.♥

More to come soon, until then....

Just Love,
Trice

ABOUT THE AUTHOR

Trice McIntyre is a rising voice in contemporary romance, known for stories that wrap you up in passion, humor, heartbreak, and all the beautiful chaos in between. Her characters don't just fall in love, they stumble, leap, and crash into it, peeling back every messy, breathtaking layer until they find their happily ever after.

A proud graduate of South Carolina State University in Orangeburg, South Carolina, Trice earned her Bachelor's degree in Electrical Engineering Technology, because who says you can't love both circuit boards and epic love stories? Her obsession with romance started early, sparked by a forgotten Harlequin novel she found tucked away at her grandmother's house. (Was she too young to be reading it at ten? Definitely. Did it ignite a lifelong passion? Absolutely.)

When she's not juggling wife, mom, daughter, sister, friend, Godi, and work you'll find her escaping into the world of writing, where imagination has no limits and peace feels just a page away. Through every story, Trice pours the best parts of herself onto the page, blending real-life causes and emotions into the heart of her novels, always with a promise to support the very causes that inspired them.

CONNECT WITH TRICE:

WEBSITE: tricemcintyre.com

INSTAGRAM: Author_TriceMcIntyre

FACEBOOK: TriceMcintyre, Author

TIKTOK: @TriceMcIntyreAuthor

www.ingramcontent.com/pod-product-compliance
Lightning Source LLC
Chambersburg PA
CBHW020013120726
47903CB00004B/1263